*Sometimes love
is just waiting to be found...*

PINO

"PERHAPS I SHOULD RETREAT BACK DOWN TO THE BEACH AND LEAVE THE TWO OF YOU ALONE."

"No!" she cried. "No, I think you should stay right where you are and . . . and I think you should kiss me."

The dark eyes widened. . . . "I beg your pardon?"

"Will you please kiss me, sir! And will you please do so with all good haste before Lord Barrimore realizes that *we* have seen *him.*"

He gave a little shrug and bowed forward, obliging her with a brief meeting of the lips.

Anna glanced surreptitiously along the path. Barrimore had emerged from the trees. It seemed as though his pace had slowed . . . but he was still coming their way.

In a blaze of frustration, Anna reached up and twisted her hands into the loose folds of Emory's shirt. "Was that your best effort, sir?"

His eyes darkened to the color of chocolate even as his arms slid deliberately around her waist to pull her forward against his body.

"My best effort, then," he mused. "As you command."

He bent his head to hers and Anna made a soft, stifled sound in her throat. His body was hard, his arms like iron, and he was crushing her against him, almost lifting her off the ground. . . .

PRAISE FOR MARSHA CANHAM'S PREVIOUS NOVELS

PALE MOON RIDER

"CAPTIVATING . . . Lush and sensually explicit . . . Canham has written a grand adventure full of heroic men and dastardly villains, and with a beautiful heroine who has spirit and determination, and even saves the hero on more than one occasion."
—*Booklist*

"This gripping tale kept me up well into the morning. Tyrone will steal hearts and haunt dreams. Renee is enchanting and full of fire. Don't miss this new arrival by Marsha Canham."—*Affaire de Coeur*

"SPLENDID!"—*Bell, Book and Candle*

"Ms. Canham has written many wonderful books. . . . this tale of a damsel in distress and an unlikely, reluctant hero further showcases her ability at storytelling."—*Old Book Barn Gazette*

"Entertaining plot twists . . . enlivened by sharply drawn characters and plenty of sex."
—*Publishers Weekly*

"A JEWEL OF A TALE . . . [a] glorious tale of romance, adventure, and intrigue. Ms. Canham's lush, descriptive style brings Georgian England glittering to life and there are plenty of deftly woven plot twists to keep readers turning pages long into the night. *Pale Moon Rider* is a story you won't want to miss!"—AOL's Romance Fiction Forum

Dell Books by Marsha Canham

Swept Away

Away

MARSHA CANHAM

A Dell Book

Published by
Dell Publishing
a division of
Random House, Inc.
1540 Broadway
New York, New York 10036

ISBN: 0-440-23521-9

Printed in the United States of America

Published simultaneously in Canada

November 1999

10   9   8   7   6   5   4   3   2   1

OPM

A long overdue thanks to my first editor, Maggie Smallwood,
who took a chance on an unknown,
and to Malle Vallik, who found the manuscript in a
mountainous slush pile
and told Maggie they might have a good thing there.
I value both continuing friendships dearly.

Prologue

*T*HE MAN WHO had nearly succeeded in bringing the world to its knees sneezed and wiped his hand on his coat. It was cold in front of the open window, the wind brisk off the sea, laden with the dampness of a week's worth of raging storms. Something even more ominous lurked out there in the darkness and mist. The riding lights of the British warship *Bellerophon* could just be seen, if one knew where to look, hovering at the mouth of the estuary like a predator crouched in the shadows waiting for its prey to appear.

Napoleon Bonaparte knew where to look. He had been tracking the movements of the warship since she had first been sighted taking up her position in the blockade nearly three hours ago. There was anger in his expression and not a little disdain as he thought of his own navy, never fully recovered after its crushing defeat at Trafalgar some years before.

For a man whose reputation had already assumed legendary proportions, Bonaparte was small in stature, his figure squat, his paunch an ignoble swell over the tight-fitting white kenseymere breeches. His hair was fine as silk, reddish in color, his eyes gray and brooding and capable of instilling fear in all who met him. At the moment, dread of becoming the target of one of those piercing glances commanded respect in the half dozen men who stood tense and silent in the room behind him.

"Excellency, it is beginning to rain. You should come away from the window, else you take a chill."

"Do you know the English news sheets refer to me as 'that Corsican Ogre,' " he said, dismissing such petty concerns. "They accuse me of treason and urge the Bourbon puppet to demand my execution. Me," he said with a shake of his head. "*Me*, the man who saved France from drowning in her own blood and made of her one of the most powerful countries in the world. Now they call for my execution and would make it a public spectacle."

He clasped his hands behind his back, visibly reining in his temper before he turned and addressed the solemn gathering of officers. "Who do you suppose would dare wield the blade? Louis Capet? He only dares to enter Paris behind the heavy guns of the allied armies. Weak, pompous, cowardly fool. Like his father before him, he can barely execute a bowel movement without assistance."

"Louis would never dare issue such an order, Excellency," said the former grand marshal of the French army, Henri-Gratien Bertrand. "He does not have the stomach for it. A cut finger and he pukes his guts on the floor."

Bonaparte nodded smugly. "Then his brother, perhaps? Now there is a stout fellow, by any measure, with guts enough to unleash a private army of assassins on me. He must feel he is bound to succeed one of these days, must he not, Cipi?"

Franceschi Cipriani pursed his thin lips in an effort to contain a smile. There had been at least thirty failed attempts on Bonaparte's life over the past decade alone, all of them made at the instigation of the persistent Comte D'Artois. The last devil-for-hire had tossed a bomb at the Emperor's state carriage as it passed by and had blown the vehicle twenty feet in the air, horses and all. Unfortunately for the erstwhile assassin, the blast had also taken off his legs, but he had lived long enough to be informed that the carriage had been empty, and Napoleon fifty miles away at the time.

Of all the dour-faced men crowded around the door, Cipriani was the only one who could afford to smile. He was neither a soldier nor a courtier. He was dressed in gentleman's clothing now, but at the blink of an eye could appear in stinking rags with several days' growth of beard concealing his lean, pointed jaw. A master spy and deadly assassin in his own right, it was Franceschi Cipriani who had discovered that the allies had been planning to remove Napoleon from Elba to an even more remote location, and it was Cipriani who had made arrangements for his Emperor to escape the island and make his triumphant return to France.

For one hundred days Napoleon had marched boldly across France at the head of an army loyal to the core, eager for revenge. Following the debacle at Waterloo four weeks ago—a battle that could have, *should* have been won—he had been forced to ride by night down deserted streets and across windswept fields to the small port town of Rochefort, and from there to seek refuge on the tiny island of Aix, in a grim stone cottage overlooking the mouth of the bay. With the armies of four countries fast on his heels, he had nowhere left to run, nothing but his anger and contempt to hide behind.

Some of that contempt was directed now at another member of the stone-faced group.

"You have remained remarkably quiet, my bold sea-hawk. Have you nothing to say?"

The man stood half in the shadows, one broad shoulder leaned against the wall. He was dressed in the elegant clothes of a gentleman, wearing a fine woolen jacket with high molded lapels, an embroidered silk waistcoat worth a year's soldiering wages, and a muslin cravat so white and precisely pleated he might have recently come from an evening at the opera. He was easily the tallest man present, a full hand's width above Cipriani, which made him tower a head and half a shoulder above the stocky Bonaparte. His features were in shadow, but his smile was as white as his stock as he responded to the Emperor's question.

"What would you have me say, Excellency? The Prussian army is a day behind you, the Swedes have the roads to the north blocked, the Spanish guard the south. They would want nothing better than to have you try to fight your way through, thereby removing the need for any puppet king to sign an order for your execution."

"Montholon and De Las Cases"—Napoleon paused and tipped his head briefly toward the two men standing beside Bertrand—"are convincing in their arguments that I should make for America. The colonials were our allies during their own war with England and would not be hasty to comply with any demands to surrender me."

"I agree it would be a wise choice, Excellency, but you would have to get there first." The tall man's eyes briefly reflected a glitter of candlelight. They were an intense, dark brown, almost as black as the thick waves of hair that curled over his collar. "The *Bellerophon* is a seventy-four-gun ship-of-the-line, manned by the same fighting crew who created havoc at Trafalgar. Onshore, there are guards on every dock, soldiers in every village, patrols watching every mile of coastline. You could try dressing yourself in rags and hiding away in the bilge of some local fishing vessel, but I warrant even the poorest excuse for a boat is being thoroughly searched. Would you really want to be discovered buried under a pile of fish heads? I shudder to think what the wags who write the news sheets would dub you then."

The errant curl that fell over Napoleon's high forehead seemed suddenly darker against the whiteness of his skin as he blanched, offering proof that he had already imagined the ignominy and did not need to hear it put into words. "I have, until recently, worn the Imperial Crown of France, gentlemen. I have no intentions of replacing it with a fisherman's cap, now or ever."

"But sire," one of his minor officers protested, "you cannot simply abide here and do nothing. The British foreign office has spies everywhere. By morning your presence in Aix will be the best-known secret in Europe."

"I am counting on it," Napoleon said quietly. "And by morning, it will not matter. Lord Westford will no longer need his legions of spies to inform him of my whereabouts, for he will know precisely where I am at all times. Be assured," he added, "there are plans under way to remedy the unfortunate situation we find ourselves in at the moment, but until they can be put into effect, I must once again appear to be the docile, defeated lamb quaking at the thought of slaughter. General Montholon, you will kindly send word to the brave compatriot who stands willing to run the blockade that his services will not be required. Colonel Bertrand, you have dispatched the missive to the captain of the *Bellerophon* advising him that I am prepared to surrender my sword into his hands?"

"It was delivered an hour ago."

"It is fitting that tomorrow should be the fourteenth of July," Napoleon continued. "The very day the Bastille fell to the citizens of France and thus set us on our glorious path to honor. And it will be honor, gentlemen—fine English honor that saves us now, for I will convince this British captain that I come to him in peace to kneel at the mercy of the English people. Like Themistocles, the Greek general who was forced into political exile after he defeated the Persians, I seek asylum from my enemies and put myself under the protection of the laws which govern England's own Prince Regent."

"Do you really think they will believe you?" the Englishman asked.

"Why would they not? I have been fighting battles and waging wars in one form or another for thirty-five of my forty-six years. I doubt Wellington, with whom I share the same year of birth, has been at it half that length of time, yet he has already declared his desire to live quietly and anonymously in some small village in the English countryside. Whether he does or not remains to be seen, but he seems determined to put forth the *illusion* of docility, does he not?"

"Is that what you are doing? Putting forth an illusion?"

It was not Bonaparte but Cipriani whose lips flattened

in a slow, malevolent grin. "Surely you do not expect us to tell you all of our secrets, Captain? If we did, they would be poorly kept secrets indeed, would they not?"

Bertrand led the other officers in shifting back several less than subtle paces. It was no secret whatsoever that Cipriani did not trust the English mercenary, despite having hired him and his ship to effect the Emperor's escape from Elba. Nor was it a surprise to anyone that the Englishman returned the feelings of distrust and animosity tenfold. What astonished them was that both men were still alive. They could only surmise it was the hand of one man who kept them from slashing each other's throats in the dead of night, and he raised it now with a sigh of exasperation.

"This is neither the time nor place to see who can piss the farthest," Bonaparte said. "In fact all of you may leave me now. I need time alone to compose an appropriately contrite letter to the British captain. Cipi—did you manage to find anything resembling a palatable wine on this god-forsaken islet?"

"Will a bottle of your favorite Vin de Constance do?"

Bonaparte dismissed the others with an impatient flick of his wrist. When they were gone, he extended his arm to take the heavy green bottle Cipriani had produced.

"You have never failed me, have you, my lifelong friend?" he mused, lapsing comfortably into the Corsican dialect they often shared when they were alone.

"And I never will," Cipriani promised. "Let me kill him now. Tonight. We have no further use for him."

"Ah, but perhaps we do. I am told the English have increased the reward for his capture. They want him brought to trial almost as much as they want me. How much of our plans do you suspect he knows?"

"We have been careful to speak of it only amongst ourselves. In the letter your brother wrote, he did not mention any specific details, though I thought he was somewhat imprudent in mentioning certain people by name. It could—"

Cipriani stopped. He was staring at the top of the table. "The letter. Did you move it, Excellency?"

The former Emperor of France turned and scanned the sheafs of documents, maps, and dispatches that covered the wooden surface. "No. It must be there somewhere."

Cipriani started sifting through the sheafs of paper, scattering some carelessly on the floor, but his search proved futile. "It is gone." He stopped again and looked up. "He was standing by the door when we all came in, but when I called your valet to fetch your surtout"—his eyes flicked back to the side of the table—"he was standing here. He could have taken it. He *must* have taken it."

"Oh, come now, Cipi. In a roomful of my most trusted officers?"

Cipriani's cold, hard gaze leveled on his master. "I warrant he could pluck the eyes out of a snake and leave the serpent none the wiser."

"Then you had best kill him," Bonaparte agreed, his fist tightening around the neck of the bottle. By sheer dint of will he refrained from smashing it down and shattering the glass into a thousand pieces. "Kill him and get that letter back, for there can be no room for error now, Cipi. Not this close to our ultimate triumph!"

Chapter 1

SHE THOUGHT HE was dead. There was nothing to indicate any life in the half-naked body that was being gently nudged to and fro in the shallow water of the tidal pool. The cuts and scrapes that marred the broad slabs of muscle across his back and shoulders were a bloodless raw pink; the skin itself was yellowed as old tallow. He was dressed only in thin linen underdrawers which ended at the knee and were secured about the waist with a slackened drawstring. He might as well have been completely naked, however, for the linen had been rendered nearly transparent by the water, and though her eyes did not linger overlong, she could plainly see the sculpted curves of his buttocks, the shallow dimples in the small of his back.

Just as a chilling shudder of revulsion scraped along her spine, the surf swirled forward, clattering across the sand and shingle to surround the still form. The blue-gray lips opened with the fresh incursion of saltwater and it was there, in the expelled rush, she saw the silvery foam of bubbles.

Annaleah Fairchilde gasped and jumped quickly back. Her gaze darted around the jumbled rocks on either side of the still body as if she half expected to see a dozen more corpses scattered among the boulders, but the beach was deserted as always. A treacherous fog had blanketed the coastline through the night; the last of it was just burning off in the early morning sun, but she had not heard any alarms to signify a ship blown off course, nor any church bells tolling to call out the villagers.

Yet the body must have come off a ship. Torbay had become an important seaport during the two decades of hostilities with France, and the entrance lay just to the east beyond the jutting promontory of Berry Head. Between the three villages that comprised the harbor of Torbay—Brixham, Paignton, and Torquay—there were always vessels in these waters and, periodically, stories of a body washing ashore that had not been properly stitched into a weighted shroud.

But this one was alive.

She looked down again. Thick, wet strands of dark hair lay across his face, obscuring most of his features from view. His eyes were closed, the long black lashes spiked against his cheeks. His upper torso was broad and well-defined with muscle, his thighs lean and hard as those belonging to the men she had seen climbing nimbly up the tall masts of sailing ships. The one hand that lay palm up in the sand was square, the pads of the fingers white with calluses; the other was clenched in a fist, the arm folded under his head. It was this meager bit of leverage that had probably saved him from drowning.

If it had saved him.

Annaleah glanced over her shoulder, the panic rising in her chest again. The cove was small and isolated, the beach less than a half mile in length and curved around water that was too shallow for anchorage, too turbulent beyond the breakers for fishermen to set their nets. The inlet itself was ringed by steep limestone cliffs, the cracks and crags populated by colonies of screaming gulls, most of which were in the air now, circling in white flashes above as if they too were waiting to see if this tempting morsel of fleshy driftwood would live or die.

Widdicombe House sat at the top of the cliffs, accessed by a steep path that had been worn into the face of the rock by a few thousand years of high winds and blowing sands. Even if Annaleah had been a man, it would not have been possible for her to manipulate the dead weight of a body to the top of the cliff on her own. She would have to go back for help, although she strongly doubted, in the time it would take her to reach the house and tell them what she had discovered, that the sailor would still be here when she returned.

The tide was inching higher up the shingle even as she took another step back to avoid staining her shoes with salt-water. Farther out, beyond the jagged breakers, the surface of the sea was a calm, undulating sheet of liquid pewter beneath the hazed sky, but she knew that calm could be deceiving. Many a ship had made the mistake of sailing too close to shore and having its hull cracked open when the currents pulled it into the rocks.

Knowing she had to make a decision, Annaleah wiped her hands on the folds of her muslin skirt and ventured close to the body again. She jumped as the icy water of the Channel scrabbled over her shoes, but there was nothing to be done for it. The hem of her dress was dragged backward and, as uncharitable a thought as it might have been, she felt a momentary surge of resentment toward the unmoving body.

"Some time away with your great-aunt Florence will do you good," she muttered to herself, misquoting her mother's words of a week ago. "The sheer calmness and boredom of the seaside should help sedate your thoughts."

Bracing herself, she reached down and gingerly curved her hands beneath the man's shoulders, testing his weight. She was not a frail wisp of a creature by any measure, but he seemed gigantic by comparison, an utterly limp mass of bone and muscle. It took three grunted attempts and a near spill headfirst into the encroaching waves before she discarded the notion of dragging him out of the sand by his arms. By then her feet were squeaking inside her soaked shoes and a good half measure of her skirt was wet and clinging.

"Damnation, hell, and bother!" she said, citing three of her brother's favorite oaths.

With one eye on the next wave scrolling over the breakers, she slogged around beside the body and tried pushing him, rolling him front over side over back until he was a few feet higher on the shore.

She stopped, her hands braced on her knees, to catch her breath, and noticed for the first time the ugly bruise at the back of his skull. The skin was swollen almost to bursting, mottled blue and black, riddled with spidery red veins. It must have taken quite a blow to cause such a lump and Annaleah, feeling even more helpless than before, knelt gingerly beside him. Her hands hovered over the contusion several more seconds before she found enough nerve to lift the tangled mass of wet black hair off his neck. Assured the skin was not broken and his brain was not leaking out, she took an additional moment to study his profile but was no further enlightened. She did not recognize him, though that was hardly a surprise. In all of her nineteen years, she had paid perhaps ten visits to Widdicombe House, none of them with the intention of retaining any memories of the local fishermen and farmers who gawked openly at the well-heeled visitors from London.

It was Annaleah who gawked now, however. She had deliberately avoided acknowledging his state of near nudity and tried not to think of where her hands were placed each time she grasped his hip and shoulder to roll him. But now her gaze had wandered far below where any sense of modesty should have allowed. He was on his side facing her, and while his whole body had become sugared with a fine coating of sand, the linen of his drawers clung in a shockingly sheer layer to his lower anatomy. Her eyes, bluer than the sky above, widened and gazed appreciably at the shapes and contours molded by the wet cloth. She had heard whispers of such things, even seen a crude sketch drawn once in a parlor full of giggling females, but to actually see such a thing, to realize what an awkward burden a man carried between his legs . . . well, it was no wonder they often looked discomforted—sometimes even in pain.

A slap of cold water against her ankles served to break the spell and, with her skin hot and her breath dry in her throat, she pushed and rolled and heaved again until he was lying in the soft, powdery sand well above the scalloped tidewater mark. With a final shove, her hands skidded onto his chest and she fell forward, sprawling half across his body.

It had the same effect as falling over a rock, and the air left her lungs with a loud *whoomf.* Conversely it left his mouth in a small fount of seawater, followed by a shallow gasp and a much larger rush as his body began to violently reject the notion of drowning. Annaleah grabbed his jaw and turned his head as the first mouthful of foul liquid fell right back into his throat, then held him while he retched and spewed saltwater through his mouth and nose. His eyes remained closed and his body clenched around each spasm, but eventually the effort drained him and he collapsed limp on the sand.

He was now able to draw unimpeded breaths again, and a faint hint of color began to seep back into his skin. His lips remained blue, but the dreadful yellow cast began to fade, revealing the true shading of his bronzed skin. The sand had caked over much of his face and as Annaleah brushed some of it off his eyes, the long lashes shivered and opened a slit. For the briefest of moments she found herself staring into his dark eyes. She held her breath, for there was so much anger and pain in their depths, she almost missed hearing the harsh croak of words that were forced through his lips.

"They have to know the truth."

"Wh-what? What did you say?"

A hand, with fingers like iron bands and a grip that threatened to snap the fine bones in her wrist, reached up and grabbed her. "*They have to know the truth. Before it is too late.*"

"I . . . do not know what you mean, sir," she stammered, shocked by the strength of his hand, shocked by the power of his eyes boring into hers. "What truth, sir? Who has to know?"

His lips moved again, but there was no breath left to give substance to the words. The pressure around her wrist eased enough that Annaleah was able to pry his fingers loose one at a time and free herself. By then, his eyes had shivered closed and his head had lolled to the side.

Thoroughly shaken now, Annaleah pushed to her feet. She glanced one last time at the rising level of the waves, then turned and began running across the soft sand toward the base of the cliff. Yards of wet muslin tangled around her ankles, weighing her down, and her shoes squelched like sponges with every awkward step. At the bottom of the steep path she paused to brace herself, then climbed as quickly as she could, heedless of the brambles that tore the flimsy folds of her skirt.

At the top she paused again, her chest burning, her cheeks flushed red, and wondered that she had not noticed how truly far her great-aunt's house sat from the edge of the cliffs. Once regal and elegant on its perch overlooking the sea, Widdicombe House had seen its crumbling brick facade eroded by the same sands and winds that had worried away at the rocks. The windows were scarred and pitted, most of them opaque on the seaward side. The steeply canted roof, with its rows of gables and forests of chimneys, showed patches of cracked and missing slates.

None of this impacted much on Annaleah at the moment as she hoisted her skirts and started running through the long, windswept waves of sea grass. She passed the gnarled skeleton of the tree where she had left her bonnet hung on a branch, and wondered if she should go first to the stables to see if old Willerkins was up and out yet, tending to his prize beauties. He was nearing eighty, as ancient and weather-beaten as nearly everything and everyone else at Widdicombe House, so she dismissed his usefulness and stayed on the path to the house, hoping against hope that the waterman—a comparatively young bulwark at the age of fifty—would be in the kitchen hunched over his morning meal.

All of the utility rooms, she discovered as she blew through the rear door, were empty. There was a crusted tureen of porridge on the kitchen table and a wooden trencher littered with crumbs to suggest someone had been there recently, but her breathless shouts drew no replies.

This came as no debilitating shock either, since her great-aunt Florence Widdicombe retained only a handful of servants to tend to the upkeep of the entire household. Apart from Willerkins there was a housekeeper, cook, and maid of chambers, a footman, a yard man, a waterman, and a boy to run errands and do light chores around the estate. On the less useful end of the employment scale, there was Throckmorton, the timekeeper, whose only task so far as Annaleah had been able to determine was to keep all the clocks in the house wound and to ring a small brass gong three times a day. There was also Ethel, the chicken-plucker, a woman who had so impressed her aunt at a fair some years back—she could kill, eviscerate, and pluck a chicken clean in under two minutes—that Florence had taken her home and employed her ever since for the exorbitant sum of three shillings a month.

Most of the locals in the nearby town of Brixham were being gentle when they referred to Florence Widdicombe as "eccentric." She was well into her seventies, a spinster with a vast personal fortune who, while she could not see the justification in paying an army of servants to upkeep a house that was falling apart around her ears, could also not justify collecting more than a token rent—and that mostly in liquid form—from the dozens of families who worked the rich vineyards and apple orchards attached to the estate. Annaleah's father regularly sent envoys to his wife's aging aunt insisting she come live with them in London.

Unfailingly those envoys returned alone, their noses red from sampling her wines and ciders, their shins bruised from Florence's tendency to apply her cane when she wanted someone's attention.

Annaleah's limbs felt bruised now as she ran up the stairs to the main floor. She was out of breath, nursing a stitch in her side, and still shedding a good deal of seawater with each step she took. A glance at a well-wound clock told her it was just past nine as she hastened to the morning room, hoping against hope her aunt would be at breakfast.

This time, collapsing with relief against the oak doorjamb, she was not disappointed.

"Auntie Lal . . . Auntie Lal . . ."

Florence Widdicombe looked up from the soft-boiled egg she was stabbing with a wedge of toast. She was tiny as a wisp and looked as if a strong gust of wind would carry her into the next parish. She wore her fine gray hair in a nest of curls on the crown, usually covered by a delicate lace cap with the lappets trailing over her shoulders. She rarely wore any other color but black, and seldom any other expression than a frown that suggested she could not quite remember what she had done five minutes ago.

"Good gracious, Anna dear, you look rather damp. I should have thought it far too early in the day to go wading in the ocean."

"Auntie Lal . . ."

"Come, come. Have some hot chocolate, or try the sweet cider. Yes, do try the cider. The Wilbury brothers fetched a new barrel of it over this morning and I must say it is one of their best efforts."

"Please, I do not want cider or chocolate." Anna gasped and caught her breath. "I have found a man."

Her aunt smiled and waved her piece of toast. "Your mother will be pleased to hear it, dear. I gather she was beginning to fret over your lack of interest in the opposite sex."

"No. No, I mean . . . I have found the *body* of a man. Down on the beach. I thought he was dead at first, but he coughed up a great deal of water and now he seems to be breathing."

The toast remained poised over the egg, a large glob of yellow yolk oozing back into the cup. "Oh dear. Is he one of ours? I do not know how many times I have told young Blisterbottom not to go oystering in the dark. He is barely larger than the bucket he carries, and in truth, I find the creatures he catches to be unpleasantly slimy and salty, reminiscent of . . . oh well, never mind. Suffice it to say, after all these years, I have never acquired the taste. Young Billy tries so hard to please me, however, that I seem plagued to eat them by the plateloads anyway."

"It is not Billy Bisterbom," Annaleah said, using his given name. "It is not anyone I recognized, in fact. But he *is* badly hurt. He has cuts and scrapes and a lump on his head the size of a turnip. He was in the water when I found him, nearly drowned, but I pushed him up into the sand and—hopefully—he lies there still and has not been dragged back down by the surf."

"And no one has come to claim him? How ever did he get there?"

"I saw no one else on the beach. I think he must have fallen off a ship, for he is . . . he is missing most of his clothes."

"Missing his clothing? How very insensible indeed. There are crabs in the cove, you know, and they are not too particular about what they pinch." Florence finished the mouthful of toast and picked up a little silver bell. The tinkle it emitted sounded far too inadequate to bring forth a mouse, let alone a houseful of half-deaf old servants, but within a few moments the door to the breakfast room was pushed open and Mildred the cook waddled through.

She curtsied as best she could with four hundred pounds of excess flesh rolled around her girth, and smiled in Annaleah's direction. "Mornin', miss. Will ye be takin' yer break-fast now?"

"Mildred," her aunt said. "It seems my niece has found a naked man on the beach. Probably some scoundrel from town who had one tot too many and fell off the rocks. Will you fetch Broom and send him down at once to determine if we know to whom the fellow belongs."

The cook's cheeks dimpled with another smile. "Naked, ye say?"

"*Hurt*," Annaleah reiterated with an exasperated glance from the cook to her aunt. "He was nearly drowned when I found him, and could well be dead by now."

"Yes, well, if he drank so much as to lose his clothing as well as his senses, he hardly deserves a kinder fate. Undoubt-edly a prank has been pulled on him and we will discover the culprit hiding nearby. Mildred—?"

"Yes, milady. Right the way, milady."

Another ponderous curtsy took the cook back out the door, and it was all Annaleah could do not to follow. For some reason she did not believe the man she had found was a local drunkard, nor did she think, after having stared into those dark, soulless eyes, that anyone would be so fool-hardy as to play a prank on him.

"You are leaking, dear."

"Wh—what?"

"Your dress," her aunt said, indicating the dark stains on her skirts. "It is making a frightful mess on the floor. If you must drip, at least step to the side and drip on the carpet where it will not be so hazardous to a misplaced footstep."

Though the logic escaped her, for the carpet was from Persia, and worth a small fortune, Anna did as she was told.

"Good heavens." Her aunt raised a large, square quizzing glass, and trained a magnified eyeball on her niece with the intensity of a detective. "You are shivering!"

"I . . . had to wade into the water in order to drag him free."

"Indeed." The glass was laid aside. "And while I applaud your charity, your mother will froth at the mouth if I send you home with a red nose and chilblains. Off you go now and change out of those wet things. By the time you are dry and presentable again, Broom will have fetched the rogue up from the beach and we can have a good look at him before we decide what needs to be done."

Chapter 2

*A*S ANNALEAH HURRIED up the stairs, she worked the buttons free on her spencer and had the short, fitted jacket removed and flung over an arm before she arrived at her room. She had no great expectations of finding Clarice, her personal maid, inside but she called her name anyway, already half out of her gown as she did so.

The dress was ruined. Torn, full of sand and seawater, it was cast aside. Her underpinnings were damp and stained as well; they joined the dress, shoes, and stockings in a crumpled pile in the corner of her dressing room. Naked, Anna quickly rubbed a towel across her feet and between her toes to dry them, then sat on a low velvet chair to don a clean chemise and stockings.

Clad in a sheer layer of silk, she searched through the dozens of dresses she had brought from London. She had not known how long her banishment was to be and had come prepared to spend weeks if need be, waiting for her father and mother to realize that she was no longer a child, that her mind, once set upon a course—especially this particular course—was not likely to be turned about or swayed.

"No," she had said flatly. "It was 'no' yesterday, and it was 'no' last week. It will be 'no' tomorrow and next week and the week after that."

"Annaleah Marissa Sophia Widdicombe Fairchilde"— her mother had recited all five names with her eyes closed— "your father and I are only thinking of what is best for you."

Percival Fairchilde, earl of Witham, sat hidden behind a freshly ironed newspaper, the rustling of a corner the only indication he had noted his inclusion in the conversation.

"Best for me?" Annaleah queried. "In the matter of

choosing a husband with whom I am expected to live out the rest of my days, do you not think I am at least partially capable of deciding what is best for me?"

"Not when that decision threatens to make us the laughingstock of London. You have had three proposals of marriage in the past two years! One from a viscount, one from a baron, and now, for pity's sake, an offer from a marquess who needs only to hear that his invalid uncle has gasped his last breath to be named the next Duke of Chelmsford!"

Annaleah had sighed and closed her eyes briefly, for they'd had this conversation a dozen times . . . in the last week alone. "The viscount was a drunk and a boor—you said so yourself. The baron was at least forty years old and reeked of the garlic and onions he chewed constantly in hopes of living forty more."

"I have no doubt you could have undermined those efforts by at least half, sister dear, with very little trouble taken on your part."

Anna glared at her sister, Beatrice. She was older by three years, staunchly married with one young child wobbling against her skirts and another well on its way. Her husband, Alfred, Lord Billington, was strutting, belching proof that Beatrice had wed for all the right reasons, and her high-pitched, sanctimonious whines of advice warned that she expected no less from her younger sibling.

"I would not marry Lord Barrimore," Anna said evenly, "if he was the last bachelor left in England."

"He may well be," her brother Anthony drawled from his chair by the fire. "Unless, of course, you have a yearning to reward one of the sturdy young bucks returning from the war. I should think there will be a few thousand soldiers who have not seen a member of the fairer sex in a year or more who would be willing and eager to forgo garlic and onions in order to win your favor. Whether or not you could survive on an income of ten shillings a month . . ." He shrugged. "Well, you never were the one to refuse a good challenge, what?"

Anna scowled. "You are hardly one to talk about surviving on a stipend, brother dearest. Ten shillings a *day* barely keeps you in handkerchiefs. A speck of dust on your sleeve and the jacket must be changed. A minute lack of starch in your cravat and all of Bond Street can hear you howling at the incompetence of the laundry. Moreover, you should be the last one standing to Lord Barrimore's defense. Did you not say, just last week, that the man was an uncivilized barbarian?"

Anthony Fairchilde, Viscount Ormont, arched a meticulously shaped eyebrow. "Tch. I said his *bootmaker* was an uncivilized barbarian, unable to apply a shine that lasted from the storefront to the coach."

"Perhaps we are approaching this the wrong way, *maman*," Beatrice interjected with a sigh. "Perhaps, instead of pointing out that Winston Perry, marquess of Barrimore, is devastatingly handsome, stands on the cusp of inheriting a grand title and estates as old as the kingdom itself, and has every eligible beauty and her mother scheming and falling over themselves to catch his eye . . . perhaps we should be asking Annaleah where he fails in striving to meet her exactingly high standards?"

With mother and sister united to present a formidable front against her, Annaleah laced her fingers together in her lap. "He makes me uneasy."

"Uneasy?" Her mother's staunch resolve gave way to a hint of shrillness. "In what way does he make you uneasy?"

"Well . . . for one thing, he never laughs. Never. I am beginning to believe him incapable of even smiling with any genuine emotion. He is offensively rude to those he considers to be his inferiors, which includes nearly everyone below the level of king and regent. He criticizes the smallest word, the paltriest gesture, yet does not see a single fault in his own stiff-necked, self-righteous demeanor. Why, just the other day he crowded a poor flower girl off the pavement and when she went ankle-deep in mud, and spilled all her violets, he just stood there glaring at her as if she deserved to be fed poison on top of her humiliation."

"And so it should be," Lady Witham declared. "These costermaids have been *warned* not to block the walkways when gentlemen and ladies are on parade."

"She was not blocking it, Mother. She was keeping to her own side of the boards. When I offered her five shillings by way of compensation—it was all I had on my person at the time or I should have given her more—the admirable Lord Barrimore looked like he wanted to put me in the mud beside her. I have strong suspicions that, were I his wife and chattel, he would have done so without a wink of hesitation."

"Come now, you judge Barrimore too harshly." Her brother yawned. "I've known the man for half a dozen years. He may, at worst, be judged a little dour, but in the clubs and in general company he is regarded to be an out-and-outer."

"Why?" Anna asked dryly. "Because he is a four-bottle man? Because he can drink all day and carouse all night and still boast enough stamina to tup his favorite mistress before morning?"

"Annaleah!" Her mother's hand flew to her breast. "Wherever do you hear such things?"

"It is difficult *not* to hear them, Mother. The identity of his current mistress, how long it took him to cuckold her husband, and how quickly he is likely to tire of her is one of the more lively topics of conversation during afternoon tea."

"Do you not think, if he had a wife, it would tame his wandering eye?" Beatrice asked.

"If he had a wife—whom he would not hesitate to push in the mud—I rather doubt his habits would change overnight. I shudder to think what a pitiable lump of suet the gossips would make of her."

"There is simply no reasoning with you today, is there?"

Lady Witham bemoaned. "You are determined to spoil my mood for the entire evening. And what are we to do about this?" She held up an engraved card and waved it emphatically in the air. "He has generously applied to send his landau around at eight tonight to escort us to Lady Worthingham's assembly. His *new* landau, mind you. You know what this means, do you not?"

Anna sighed. "I expect it means he has recently taken delivery of a very large, ridiculously expensive carriage that he wishes to flaunt in public."

"It means he is making his intentions known, chit! He is expressing his admiration and his resolve! When you alight from his carriage tonight and he escorts you into Lady Worthingham's assembly on his arm, all of London will know he has chosen you to be the future Duchess of Chelmsford!"

Annaleah dug the points of her nails into her palms. "In that case, all of London will be sadly lacking for news, for I have no intentions of going anywhere in Lord Barrimore's new landau tonight . . . or any other night, for that matter. Nor do I intend to be led around on his arm like a prize heifer purchased at auction."

"I strongly suggest *he* would be considered more the prize," Beatrice remarked through thinned lips.

"In a game I have no interest in playing or winning," Anna countered. "It is all Mother's doing anyway. She has been the one encouraging his attentions all along, not I."

"Regardless of who has been encouraging whom, you are expected at Lady Worthingham's assembly—"

"I am not going."

"Not going? *Not going?*" The exclamation was piercing enough to cause her father to rustle the newspaper again with displeasure. "How can you *possibly* say you are not going? The Regent himself is expected, and such a snub would severely jeopardize the likelihood of our receiving a warm welcome at the masquerade ball he is holding at Carlton House a fortnight hence! You know full well Lady

Worthingham has the Prince's ear! One whisper from her and we shall be off the lists. One breath of scandal and—" Her hand wafted to her brow and she wilted dramatically back in her chair, unable to even complete the thought.

Beatrice set aside her needlepoint and glared hollow-eyed at Annaleah as if she had just condemned them all to death by social ostracism. "You cannot be serious about not attending."

"I assure you, I am."

"Percival," Lady Witham gasped. "Do something."

Her husband's response was to turn the page and sigh. "What would you have me do, Wife?"

"Tell your daughter to forsake this nonsense at once, of course. Tell her she must attend Lady Worthingham's assembly tonight, and she must do so with every ounce of grace and charm she possesses!"

Her father lowered the paper enough for an eyebrow to show over the top. "Annaleah?"

"If I am forced to attend, I shall swallow ipecac and henbane and contribute a good many ounces of charm and grace, all over Lord Barrimore's fine new landau."

Lady Witham wailed and threw her hands up in a gesture of dismay. "There! You see what I am forced to deal with? She is stubborn and headstrong, callous and unfeeling—"

"Mother, I am only trying—"

"*Callous and unfeeling!* I declare you are trying to send me to an early grave! Any girl in possession of half her sensibilities would see what a splendid opportunity this is. The Duchess of Chelmsford, for pity's sake! 'Tis rumored he is worth twenty thousand a year *before* he even inherits the title, and God knows how much after! Well, I'll not have it, do you hear me! I'll not have it! I will *not* go to my bed every night with my stomach bubbling like water spigots and my heart suffering such palpitations it is a wonder I can even close my eyes against the envisioned horrors of what might greet me upon arising the next morning! You have been allowed far too many liberties, that is the trouble. We have been far too lax with you! Percival!"

"Yes, my dear?"

"Call out the coach at once. She refuses to attend the assembly tonight? Fine. Then she will simply not be here to attend it. Beatrice, fetch Mrs. Bishop. Tell her she is to pack Annaleah's trunks at once, that she is leaving immediately for an indeterminate stay at the seaside."

Anna's bravado momentarily deserted her. "The seaside?"

"Your great-aunt Florence is as old and moldy as the house she lives in. Perhaps a few weeks in her company, where the most exciting thing you can hope to see is mortar crumbling from the bricks, will convince you that your life here in London is not as dreadful as you would make it out to be."

Anna leaned forward in her chair. "I never said it was dreadful!"

Lady Witham bent forward an identical amount to glare across the room at her recalcitrant daughter. "Will you attend the assembly tonight?"

Annaleah tensed her jaw. "No."

"Then you will attend upon your great-aunt Florence until such time as you come to your senses."

In desperation, Anna appealed to the raised newspaper. "Father?"

"Percival . . ." Her mother's voice sounded like nails on a slate. "You know very well how hard I have worked to bring this marriage about, what a brilliant coup it would be, and if you say one word in her defense, I shall instruct Mrs. Bishop to pack your trunks as well. Or mine—no matter. Simply be assured that one of us will not be under this roof tonight."

The *Gazette* came slowly down onto his lap. The familial blue eyes studied the firm jut to his wife's chin for a moment before casting an annoyed glance in Annaleah's direction.

"You say he makes you uneasy because he does not laugh? My dear girl, I have had very little to laugh about in nearly thirty years of marriage, and it has not been such a taxing hardship. One simply goes about one's own business and gets along. Now do as your mother says. Stop this nonsense and accept the fact that you are either going to marry Lord Baltimore—"

"Barrimore," Anthony provided.

"Whatever. You are either going to marry him, live in considerable luxury on any one of his thirteen estates, and generally do whatever you want to do for the rest of your days without any more interference from any of us . . . or you are going to spend the remainder of the afternoon packing your trunks to go to Brixham, where you will quickly find yourself wishing you were right back here helping your mother and sister plan your wedding day. Anthony—?" He waited until his son's head swiveled in his direction. "Have you read this morning's paper? Can you believe the House is *still* locked in debates over what should be done with that bounder Bonaparte? They granted leniency once by exiling him to a gentleman's prison on Elba, and look what came of it. A hundred days of war and tens of thousands of good English lives squandered at Waterloo, and for what? An honorable surrender with no penalty? I'll wager my braces it is that idiot Casterleagh, our vaunted foreign minister, simpering loudest for clemency, for on the same page Wellington says, and I quote: 'He is an outlaw beyond the pale of civil and social relations, the enemy of humankind.' Damned fine words too! Hang the bastard, I say, and good riddance."

Without waiting for or, indeed, expecting an answer, he snapped the paper upright again and carried on reading the latest speculations as to where the English ship, *Bellerophon*, was going to land with the surrendered Corsican general.

Annaleah had barely paid attention to the diatribe. She was thinking furiously of what could be done to avoid her own exile to the wind-driven coast of Devonshire, but apart from surrendering her pride and her convictions to her mother's demands, there was nothing to be done but stiffen her back and prepare to maintain her resolve. How long could they keep her in Brixham anyway? A week? A fortnight? Any longer than that would give rise to giddy rounds of whispers pertaining to much more damaging and ruinous reasons for whisking a daughter away in the middle of the night.

Remembering this, thinking of this, Annaleah finished drying her feet and glanced sidelong at the tall cheval mirror beside the bed. The thick, windblown waves of her hair surrounded her face in curls of deep mahogany brown with streaks of sun-kissed gold. Her cheeks were flushed from her exertions and she knew that if she had been at home in London, her mother would have ordered a compress of milk and cucumber water to blanch out the effects of sun and wind. She would have been equally horrified to learn of her daughter's early morning walks along the beach without so much as a wide-brimmed bonnet to guard against freckles. And the mere thought that a young lady of genteel breeding had seen, let alone touched, a half-naked sailor would have required purges and leeches, at the very least, to drain away the shock.

Yet this was the same mother who insisted the dressmaker cut Annaleah's necklines alarmingly low, that the gowns be made of silks and muslins so sheer the shape of her legs showed through. It was she who, after decrying the lack of shame in the beauties who rouged their nipples to betray a shadow beneath their bodices, insisted that her own daughter carry only the skimpiest of shawls to ward off the evening chills in order that every male eye might be drawn to the charming effect arctic air had on her breasts.

A shiver reminded Anna that she was all but naked now. Hastily, she pulled on a clean dress, one made of a more substantial weight of cotton that did not betray the slightest hint of skin-tightening beneath. Cut high in the waist, it was of a style that flattered her long, slender body, and of a color—soft mignonette green—that brought out the rich auburn highlights in her hair. A few strokes of the brush served to tame her tresses as much as her patience would allow, and, after slipping her feet into dry shoes, she hurried down the hall toward the stairs that would take her back to the second-floor dayrooms.

Her aunt was still in the breakfast room, her bony fingers diligently stalking the last smudges of bacon grease with a biscuit. She saw Annaleah and dabbed her mouth with a napkin, then reached for the gnarled stem of her walking cane.

"I have just been informed your naked man is in the kitchen," she said, rising. "He is still breathing and, according to Mildred, quite the forthright specimen. Shall we go and have a look?"

Anna offered a steadying hand to her aunt, who was wearing a high-necked black bombazine gown that was at least twenty years out of style, with rows of jet beads sewn around the cuffs and collar. She carried a black lace shawl draped over the crooks of her elbows, and wore heavy jeweled rings on nearly every finger, some so loose they were rarely turned the right way around and often became flying missiles during animated conversations.

Annaleah recalled how terrified she had been of her great-aunt Florence when she was a child. Now her movements were slow and measured, and her hands looked barely strong enough to hold her cane. The skin was paper-thin and so pale the blue webbing of veins glowed through.

Florence had also stubbornly refused to marry the man her father had chosen for her, and it made Anna wonder if that was not another of her mother's less than subtle motives in sending her to Brixham: to see what could become of someone too proud and willful for her own good.

"We'll take the shorter way, shall we?" Florence said, waving her cane toward the serving doors.

Anna felt the returning warmth of curiosity make her

steps impatient, but apart from lifting her aunt and carrying her, she had no choice but to make a slow, cautious descent in her wake. On one of the landing turns, Florence paused and thumped the wall with the end of her cane, saying casually over her shoulder, "This was where I caught your mother eating an entire cherry pie when she was younger." She gave a soft cackle of laughter and whacked the wall again for emphasis. "Fat as a bullfrog, she was. Always sneaking food from the pantry and blaming it on the servants."

Startled, Anna stared at the wall, then at her aunt, who merely offered a wrinkly smile back. "She quite dislikes me, your mother does. You must have done something excruciatingly dreadful to have wound up here. She sent a letter, of course, but I find her sentences tiresome. For every worthwhile word there are twenty nonsensical ones crouched about it, and I get genuinely fatigued attempting to decipher it all. In this particular instance, I could barely read past the opening salutation, for there appeared to be even more tripe than usual."

It was the first time in the week Annaleah had been there that her aunt had broached the subject of her banishment, and although it seemed odd to want to hold such a discussion in the intimacy of a stairwell, Anna found herself answering with a sigh.

"She wants me to marry."

"All mothers want their daughters to marry. And all daughters usually want to marry."

"You didn't."

The words were blurted out before Anna could stop them, but her aunt only sighed. "No, I did not. A very bold piece of impertinence at the time too, I can assure you, for it was generally presumed that all women were incapable of retaining any thought in their heads more important than which color of thread to apply to their embroidery."

"Those presumptions have not changed much over the years," Anna murmured.

"Nor, I suppose, has the maxim that the parents know

far better than the child who they should and should not marry?"

"Mother has decided, yes."

"And you do not agree with her decision? Well, no, of course you must not or you would not be here having to endure my silly questions."

Her aunt's wry chuckle echoed slightly as she turned and continued down the stairs. At the bottom, she pushed through the door to the kitchen and announced her arrival with a sharp thwack of her cane.

"Well, where is he? What manner of fish has my niece caught for us? Still alive, you say? Good gracious heavens, and still spewing water on my floors? If there is rum in that mix, and I find out he has lost his clothes in a waterfront brothel, why—"

The door swung shut, cutting off the last half of the threat, and in the few seconds it took Anna to catch up, her aunt was standing at the foot of a long pine chopping table studying the unmoving body of the man lying facedown on the boards. The waterman, Harold Broom, who had obviously been attempting to pump the remaining water out of the man's lungs, was at the head of the table, his thick arms hanging like tree trunks by his sides. Behind him, craning his head higher on an already stretched and scrawny throat, was the houseman, Willerkins.

"Go ahead," Florence ordered, rapping her cane on the floor. "Turn him over."

Broom nodded and rolled the unconscious man onto his side first, then his back. There was still a considerable amount of sand clinging to various parts of his body, and enough moisture remained in the skimpy shield of linen to cause Florence's eyebrows to fold upward into her wrinkles. She said nothing for a moment, then a somewhat reluctant wave of her cane brought forth a towel to drape across his waist and upper thighs.

His modesty thus restored, she frowned and took a step

closer to the table. "All that hair," she said, giving her cane another impatient wave.

Broom nodded again and used the edge of one hamlike hand to scrape the wet black waves off the man's face.

Florence stared, and it took another full minute for the smile to fade off her lips. "Good and gracious God," she whispered.

"Do you know him?" Annaleah asked.

A spotted hand, all knuckles and glittering rings, rose to clutch her throat as Florence bent over the body. "I pray God I am wrong, but . . . I believe it is the vicar's brother: Emory Althorpe."

"A gentleman?"

Florence straightened. "Oh, hardly that, my dear. He is a scoundrel, a rogue, an adventurer. And if I am not mistaken, the last I heard, he was wanted by the crown for treason."

"Treason!"

"Indeed. By all accounts, his last great adventure was to help Napoleon Bonaparte escape from Elba."

Chapter 3

A NOTE WAS DISPATCHED in short order to the vicarage, summoning the Reverend Mr. Stanley Althorpe to Widdicombe House at his earliest convenience. There was some discussion about sending for a doctor as well, but because Willerkins had learned a considerable amount about physicking in the army and had even operated on a horse the previous summer, Florence decided it might be more prudent to let him treat Emory Althorpe until his brother arrived and assumed responsibility. In the meantime, the patient was transferred to an upper bedchamber, where charity dictated that he be washed free of sand and saltwater and the more serious abrasions be treated with liniment and bandaged.

It was during this washing stage that Willerkins made a somewhat disturbing discovery. The marks on the man's back and limbs that Annaleah had assumed had come from being scraped to and fro in the surf were in fact older wounds that had been inflicted by a knife or some other man-made instrument. They were precise enough in length and depth for Willerkins to further surmise that Althorpe had been subjected to a particularly insidious form of torture as recently as two, perhaps three weeks earlier, to judge by the degree of healing that had occurred.

Unsettled by this new information, Anna and her aunt retreated to the day parlor to await the arrival of the vicar. Finding it undeniably more exciting than watching mortar crumble out of the bricks, Annaleah kept one ear tuned to the hallway while her imagination formulated all manner of possible intrigues. A man wanted for treason and sedition had been tortured—by whom, and for what reason? How

had he ended up in the cove unconscious and unclothed?
She had never been this close to a genuine criminal before
and had no idea how one might react upon wakening. Her
aunt had ordered Broom to remain in the room as a precaution, but—to put it kindly—Broom was only slightly less
fearsome than an angry puppy. A loud shout would send
him cowering into the corner. Not knowing this, Althorpe
could easily overpower him and then, if he was desperate
and cold-blooded enough, proceed to kill them all to avoid
being handed over to the authorities.

"Are you overly warm, dear?"

Anna started and glanced across at her aunt. "Pardon me?"

"You seem a little flushed. Perhaps you are sitting too
near the fire?"

"I am . . . a bit warm," she agreed in a broken whisper.
"How long does it take to get to the vicarage and back?"

"The way Throckmorton drives? Half the afternoon, I
expect."

Anna stood and paced to the open door. "Are you not
worried? Having him in the house, I mean? Is it not . . . dangerous? Might he not resent waking and finding Broom
standing guard on his door?"

"I expect he will resent it a good deal less than finding
himself in a gaol cell. And if you are asking if I am afraid
Emory Althorpe is going to perpetrate some act of violence
upon us, my answer is gracious me, no. Despite all the
wicked stories that have arisen about him over the past few
years, I was always rather fond of him. As a boy, he used to
ride out here from his family estates at Windsea Hall and
help Willerkins exercise the horses—we used to have quite
a fine stable until the army interfered. After most of our
stock was commandeered, young Rory continued to visit,
although I always suspected it was as much to remove himself from his father's company as to seek mine, and with
good reason I daresay. The Earl of Hatherleigh was such a
dreadful man. Cruel and brutish." Her voice hardened a
moment with the memories. "He believed in using harsh

measures to discipline his four sons, even when they were just babes in arms. In fact, I suspect it was because Edgar Althorpe continuously smacked Poor Arthur on his head that the boy was never quite right in later years. Suffice it to say Emory escaped Windsea at any opportunity or with any excuse. He would bring me books and read them aloud and we would have jolly long discussions about the author's intentions, or the story's purpose. And he was such a handsome boy. Handsome as the devil. Some might say he was a little too wild for their liking, but I always envied wildness in a man. Nothing worse, you ask me, than a primping, preening fop who capers about in a froth of lace, moaning that his cravat is lacking starch or his newspapers are not ironed perfectly flat."

Anna hid a faint smile as she recognized traits her father and brother shared, along with half the men in England.

"On the other hand"—Florence gave the leg of the nearby table a little rap with her cane—"every now and then a storm blows in off the sea and the only man left standing on the cliffs is the one who defies the elements, who chooses to live by his own rules and scoffs at anyone or anything that would dare set boundaries. Emory was like that, deliberately resisting all attempts to fit him into a mold. Even when he knew there was a savage beating waiting for him when he went home, he would sooner sit on the docks and listen to the old salts tell of their adventures in foreign ports than learn how to write the alphabet in Greek. It came as no surprise, to me anyway, when he ran away to sea one day. He told me he wanted to see what lay beyond the other side of the horizon; he wanted to visit the bazaars in Madagascar, and search for gold in Hispaniola. He wanted to hunt elephant in Africa, and he promised to carve me a new walking stick out of ivory. He wanted . . ." Florence's gaze, having drifted out of focus, snapped clear as she looked at her niece. "Well, he wanted a lot of things, most of all adventure. Apparently he found it."

"You said he is accused of helping Napoleon Bonaparte escape Elba?"

Florence nodded. "Not a fortnight ago some wretched man came to Brixham—Ramsey, I believe his name is—claiming to have proof it was Emory Althorpe who sailed to Elba some months back and whisked the little beast out from under the noses of his English guards."

"You do not believe it?"

"Oh, I absolutely believe he would be quite capable of doing such a thing. But it would be for the adventure, you know, not for money—which he always held in such admirable disdain. Nor would it be out of any misguided regard for the Corsican. In fact, he held a commission in the British navy several years back. He fought as a young lieutenant in Admiral Nelson's fleet. But that was, oh, ten years ago. Since then there have been rumors of him throwing in with pirates, of him fetching up his own ship and running the blockades around France and Spain. I do know for a fact the vicar has been trying in vain for the last year or more to contact him and bring him home."

"Surely not to stand trial?"

Florence shook her head. "Family business, I believe. Emory was the third son, you see, and having no prospects of inheriting more than an annual pension someday he never really concerned himself with the daily affairs of the estate. All of that was conferred upon the oldest boy, William, who was groomed as a matter of course to become the Earl of Hatherleigh when their father passed away. Next in line after William was Poor Arthur—and we always called him Poor Arthur, even when he was a boy—but as I said, he turned out to be . . . mmm . . . not perfectly right in the head," she whispered, tapping her forefinger on her temple. "He insisted from an early age that his arms were wings and his fingers were feathers. He actually ruffles them when he talks, and makes these rather peculiar clucking sounds in his throat when he is agitated. On the whole, however, he is quite harmless and spends several weeks in a sanatorium each year, which, if nothing else, curbs his urges to fly.

"None of that would have mattered had nature followed its course. Cousins do insist upon marrying cousins, so there are always a few madmen locked away in the attics of the finest houses. Unfortunately, however, just the winter before last, William caught some childhood disease—a swelling in his stones, I believe—and died. His wife succumbed of grief a few months later, and because they were childless that left Poor Arthur next in line to inherit, which was both impractical and imprudent, to say the least. Stanley was urged to apply to the courts for guardianship, but was unable to file any further petitions regarding the estate without consulting Emory first, and Emory, of course, has been banging about in the Mediterranean, well out of touch. I have lost count of how many times Poor Arthur, claiming he would fly across the Channel to fetch him back, has fallen off the roof of the stable and broken his wings." She sighed and clucked her tongue as if to suggest only that he try launching himself from a lower height.

"Stanley has been coping, of course, but it is an awkward arrangement to say the least. Nor is his burden lightened any by his wife—a thoroughly witless chit, in fact, who would undoubtedly enjoy nothing better than seeing Arthur declared insane and Emory executed for treason. With both impediments out of the way, Stanley would then inherit Windsea and she would become the Countess of Hatherleigh."

"How very cold-blooded."

"Yes, well, the vicar is a sensible and practical man in all other areas, but is as addled as a newt when it comes to pleasing sweet Lucille."

"You mean he would turn his own brother over to the authorities? A wounded and helpless man? But that is terrible."

Florence's eyebrow twitched upward. "A moment ago

you were worried that same wounded and helpless man would waken and shoot us over our porridge."

Anna's cheeks warmed. "That was before you spoke of him so fondly. *You* obviously do not believe him capable of violence."

"I never said that, my dear," Florence corrected her softly. "He is his father's son, after all, and there have been several episodes when his temper has—" She stopped suddenly and tilted her head toward the door. "Ahh. Voices. Perhaps that is the vicar now."

Annaleah was about to dismiss her aunt's unreliable hearing when she caught the faint clip of boot heels echoing in the corridor outside the withdrawing room. A moment later, a somber-faced gentleman in a long black frock coat appeared in the doorway and, after thanking Willerkins for the escort, bowed formally in Florence's direction.

"Dame Widdicombe. I came as soon as I received your message."

The face above the white starched collar was that of a young man, no more than four and twenty, with soft brown eyes and a direct, square chin. He was not much taller than Annaleah, nor was he typical of most vicars of her acquaintance, who were portly and overbearing from so many hours spent lecturing their flocks against sin and seduction. Reverend Althorpe looked more like a bank clerk—in this instance, a harried bank clerk, for he came straight to the point.

"I understand you have seen my brother?"

"Seen rather more of him than gentility allows, actually," Florence agreed.

"You found him on the beach?"

"My great-niece found him. Miss Annaleah Fairchilde . . . the Reverend Mr. Stanley Althorpe." She waved her cane by way of completing the introduction, then thumped the end soundly back on the carpet. "Annaleah is visiting from London and takes long walks in the morning to avoid having to endure the company of a black-busked crone at the breakfast table."

"Auntie! That is not the reason at all!"

The reverend turned anxious eyes to Florence again. "Am I also to believe my brother is wounded?"

"Cuts and scrapes mostly, and a horrid big gull's egg on the back of his head. He was senseless when Annaleah found him and has not recovered his wits yet or I should have been told."

"May I see him?"

"Of course you may. Anna will take you straightaway. I'm afraid these old bones do not move as swiftly as they once did, but I shall be as close upon your heels as Willerkins's arm will allow."

The reverend bowed again, then followed Annaleah out of the room and along the corridor to the main staircase. Arriving at the top, he fell anxiously into step beside her, obviously too agitated to make any attempts at banal conversation.

The door to the room where they had moved Emory Althorpe stood open. The curtains were drawn and the inside of the chamber was notably darker than the hallway. It was furnished similarly to Anna's, with a large canopied bed occupying most of the space, a nightstand to one side, a mirror, washstand, and two wing chairs flanking either side of the fireplace. Harold Broom looked formidable enough standing guard by the door with his arms folded across his chest, but when he saw the vicar, and especially Anna, he grinned and nearly squirmed with shyness.

The air was sharp with the conflicting scents of soap and liniment. Two beeswax candles glowed inside glass hurricanes on the beside table; another pair sent feathers of black smoke drifting over the sconces that hung above the fireplace.

It was the first time Annaleah had seen Althorpe since he had been removed from the kitchen. Not nearly as frightening or imposing as he had appeared on the beach, he lay perfectly still in the middle of the wide mattress, his hair a splash of black across the pillow, his arms on top of the blankets, resting flat by his sides.

The vicar slowed when he approached the side of the bed. His expression altered slightly for an unguarded moment—crumpled, in actual fact—then cleared with a determined breath. Calmly, he leaned over and touched a hand to his brother's forehead, his cheek, then pressed his fingers against the side of his throat to feel the strength of the pulse.

"He has not wakened? He has not moved?" The questions were directed at Broom, who shook his head in the negative.

The long, gentle fingers continued to probe the back of his brother's neck. When he located the huge lump at the base of the skull, his mouth twisted into a grimace.

Annaleah, standing at the foot of the bed, had followed the movements of the vicar's hand on his brother's forehead and cheek, but remained to linger on Emory Althorpe's face when the probing fingers moved on. With that face now cleaned of sand and the long, dark hair brushed back off its brow, Anna found herself thinking that her aunt had not exaggerated when she said he was handsome. Exotically lush, dark lashes lay in black crescents on his cheeks, complemented by the bold slash of eyebrows above. A nose that was straight and prominent lured the eye to a mouth that was wide and generous in shape, a square jaw, a neck that was more of a column rising above the powerful bands of muscle that shaped the upper breadth of his shoulders.

"I used to say in jest that he had a hard head," the vicar murmured. "With such a blow as this must have been, I wonder that the crack has not gone straight through. I am no doctor, but should he not have moved by now, or at least showed some signs of stirring?"

"He did open his eyes on the beach," Annaleah offered. "Very briefly, to be sure, but he did open them. And . . .

while I cannot be absolutely certain . . . I think he may have even been trying to tell me something."

"He spoke to you?"

"His voice was very low and difficult to hear above the surf, but I believe he said: 'They have to know the truth.' He said it twice, in fact, and the second time he was most adamant, adding the words: 'Before it is too late.' "

"Too late? Too late for what?"

"That was the exact question I asked, but he did not answer."

Before the vicar could question her further, Florence Widdicombe arrived in the room, slightly out of breath and leaning heavily on Willerkins's arm for support.

"Well, now that you have seen him," she said from the doorway, "what do you propose to do with him?"

"D-do?" The vicar straightened and looked genuinely taken aback. "I . . . I am not sure. Naturally, I have no wish to impose upon your hospitality any longer than necessary—"

"Pish." Florence cut him off with a wave of the cane. "Just tell me if it is true: Has there been a warrant issued for his arrest?"

The vicar's expression crumpled again. "Yes. Yes, it is true. The envoy from London showed it to me himself."

"Rupert Ramsey? That black-beaked toady?"

"He comes straight from the foreign office, from Lord Westford himself."

"He could come straight from Lucifer and I would still question his intentions. I would question anyone who would dare enter a church in the middle of service and glare about the congregation as if he suspected them all of wanting to *take* coins from the alms basket, not add them."

"Yes, well, there have been soldiers at the vicarage half a dozen times in the last week alone, and each time they insist upon searching the premises. My wife is nearly beside herself with fright."

"I can well imagine," Florence said wryly. "But surely

you do not believe any of this rubbish about Rory being a Bonapartist, do you?"

The vicar seemed to know better than to be startled by Florence's candor. "Whether I believe it or not is of no consequence. A witness has reported seeing him in Rochefort the night before Napoleon surrendered to the captain of the *Bellerophon*. There was also a report that his ship, the *Intrepid*, slipped through the blockade a few evenings later and was bound for England."

"Why the devil would he be so foolish as to come here if half the country is looking for him?"

"This Ramsey fellow is convinced there will be another attempt made to rescue Bonaparte. He is further convinced that Emory will be involved."

The vicar paused and looked down at the still form. "This is my first glimpse of him in nearly three years," he said softly. "I have not even known where he was or how to reach him, so there was no need to lie to the authorities when they questioned me."

Florence's eyebrow crept a little higher, and seeing it, the vicar flushed.

"I have always stood in staunch defense of both my brothers, even when it seemed the pair of them were determined to take flights of fancy. But if what this Ramsey chap says is true, if Emory has been working for the Bonapartists, then this was no minor act of familial rebellion. The charges are real, the warrant is real, and I am a minister of God as well as a loyal citizen of the crown. It would be my bounden duty, in both capacities," he added hoarsely, "to send for the constables and turn him into their care. If he is innocent, the courts will clear him."

"And when they find him guilty?"

"If he is guilty, I—"

"I did not say *if* he is found guilty," Florence pointed out, thumping her cane on the floor for emphasis. "I said *when* he is found guilty, which he surely will be when all of those licentious fat fools who sit in Parliament decide they need someone to hang in Bonaparte's place."

Annaleah stared at her great-aunt in surprise. Old and withered and eccentric though she might be, there was a hard light in her eyes that betrayed a keener intelligence than she obviously cared to show the world.

"Because of their misguided sense of noblesse oblige," Florence continued, "the vaunted House of Lords will undoubtedly decide they cannot justify taking the axe to Bonaparte's throat. All the same, they will be desperate to spill someone else's blood in his stead, and the man accused of unleashing the plague upon the world a second time will suit their needs perfectly. Regardless of Emory's guilt or innocence, therefore, he will be condemned, executed in a public place, and his remains left there for months afterward so the people can spit and jeer and throw spoiled fruit at the rotting corpse. It will not be a fair trial. It will not be a trial at all, but a monkey court, with that carrion-eater Ramsey leading the parade."

The vicar blanched, and a visible tremor brought his hands together in a tight clench. "What else can I do? If I take him back to the vicarage, they will find him the next time they come to search. If I take him to Windsea Hall and they find him there, Arthur will suffer for it."

"We could keep him here, could we not?" Anna heard herself say. "Widdicombe House is probably the last place the soldiers would search for dangerous criminals."

The vicar and her aunt both turned in surprise.

"At least until he is able to defend himself," she added in a self-conscious murmur.

Florence pursed her lips and agreed with another thump of her cane. "My niece is absolutely right. This is the safest place to keep him for the time being. Few of the villagers have reason to come here, and none of my people have ever been accused of having loose tongues. Mr. Broom will see he behaves and Willerkins will shoot him if he does not."

The vicar shook his head. "I cannot ask you to put your-selves at such risk."

"You are not asking, dear boy—I am offering. I am all for justice and loyalty, and I would kiss the King's feet if they let him out of Bedlam long enough. At the same time, I will not condemn a good man on rumor and speculation. I would be curious to know what this proof is they claim to have against him; I should think you would be too."

The vicar drew a large white square of linen out of his pocket and dabbed it across his brow. "I suppose it would only seem natural for me to make inquiries. I shall have to do so with the utmost discretion, however, for I would not want Lucille to become more alarmed than she already is by all this fuss. She has been pleading with me to let her go to London; perhaps this would be a good time."

"I trust she was not at the vicarage when Throckmorton fetched you away?"

"No, she was taking lunch with the ladies of the Found-lings Society. She has become quite involved with chari-table works of late. I believe the time she has spent with Poor Arthur has opened her eyes to the need for compas-sion and kindness in the world today."

"I am sure it has," Florence murmured dryly. "Which is why you are probably right, Vicar. It might be best to send her on a little holiday until this matter is resolved. 'Twould be a pity to involve the poor child in a moral dilemma of such magnitude."

Chapter 4

*E*XACTLY SIXTY-TWO hours passed without so much as a twitch or flicker from the still form on the bed, and Annaleah began to wonder if she had just imagined seeing his eyes open on the beach. She had tried not to show too much interest in the patient's progress; after all, it was hardly proper to linger in a bedroom with a naked man, regardless if he was awake or not. But her aunt, who had taken the precaution of removing Emory Althorpe to a chamber under the eaves, was not able to maneuver the steep and narrow stairs. Anna was dispatched in her stead and after the first dozen or so trips, when his condition remained unchanged, she began to grow resentful as well as impatient.

By the end of the second day, her travels up and down the stairs had become so tiresome, Annaleah offered to relieve Harold Broom while he caught up on some of his household chores. It was midway through the third day, while he was away refilling all the large water kettles in the kitchen and fetching his noon meal, that she looked over at the bed and found Emory Althorpe looking calmly back at her.

She was sitting on the window seat, her legs curled beneath her, a finger idly tracing a pattern in the grime on the glass pane. The shutters were opened wide and where the sunlight poured around her shoulders, it turned the flown wisps of her dark hair into a fiery coppery halo. Her gown was white muslin and the combined effect of the bright sunlight and the streamer of sparkling dust motes caused her body and skin to glow with an almost unearthly, blurred luminescence.

Annaleah was blithely unaware of this. She was only conscious, suddenly, of eyes as deep and dark as the blackest of sins staring at her.

For a very, very long moment, that was all she and he did: stare at one another. Anna could actually feel the blood draining out of her face and the strength melting out of her shoulders, her arms, her legs. She turned instantly cold, was completely paralyzed, to the point where she forgot she had to breathe.

"Am I dead, then?" he asked in a rough whisper. "Is this the end of it?"

Anna's lungs emptied on a gust and she tore her gaze away from the bed long enough to glance at the door. Broom had been gone over an hour and should have been back by now, but he was not, and she was entirely alone with a dangerous criminal, three long flights of stairs away from a smattering of old servants who were too deaf to hear her scream, and too old to wobble to her rescue if they did.

"No." Her voice sounded equally cracked and ragged and she had to swallow to make her throat work properly. "No, you are not dead, sir."

The long black lashes closed and opened slowly again. He blinked a second time, then a third, as if he still did not believe that the soft, glowing vision before him was real. In the next instant, when he tried to turn his head to identify the rest of his surroundings, any lingering doubts were removed as his lips parted around a grunt of pain so pure and involuntary it brought Anna jumping to her feet.

"You should not try to move, sir. Not until you are fully apprised of your injuries."

"Injuries?" His left hand moved with the ease of a hundred-pound weight, inching up off the bed to grope clumsily at the lump on the back of his neck. The swelling had gone down considerably over the past two days, but it was apparent by the look on his face that the pain was excruciating.

"Wh-what happened?"

"You were found half drowned on the beach. My great-aunt, Dame Florence Widdicombe, had you carried up here to the house, where you have lain for the past two . . . nearly three days without moving. We were beginning to wonder if you were ever going to waken. Your brother has stopped by at least twice each day and is quite beside himself with worry."

"My brother?"

"The vicar. Reverend Althorpe. S-Stanley," she stammered finally, not knowing exactly how much familiarity was permitted under the circumstances.

He frowned again. "*How* long did you say—?"

"We found you early Monday morning, and today is Wednesday, not quite noon. Of course, we have no idea how long you lay on the beach, or floated in the water, or"— she was starting to ramble desperately as the bottomless black eyes searched her face again—"or if you fell off a ship in the Channel, or if you took a tumble off the docks, or the cliffs. . . ."

Her voice trailed off as, thankfully, he looked away. This time he seemed to brace himself for the pain, meeting it with a clenched jaw. He scanned the bare walls, the high-peaked roof, the lamp that hung from a long chain off a wooden beam. His inspection halted briefly at the open door, then went on to locate the rail-backed chair, the washstand and painted china pitcher, the cluster of towels hanging on a wall peg. There was more, including a bottle of tincture and one of laudanum that drew forth another frown, but his gaze skimmed them quickly before flickering back to Annaleah.

"When you said I was brought here, may I ask . . . *where*, exactly, is 'here'?"

"Widdicombe House." It was Anna's turn to frown. "My aunt tells me she knows you very well; you used to visit here a great deal when you were younger. She has been almost as anxious as the vicar to speak with you. In fact—" She took a nervous step toward the door. "She wanted to be told the minute you came to your senses."

"Wait . . . please!"

The genuine note of panic in his voice stopped her.

"Please, Miss . . . Widdicombe?"

"Fairchilde," she corrected him in a whisper.

"Please, Miss Fairchilde—"

"My father is the Earl of Witham, my mother is a Compton, by way of the Somerset Comptons, and niece to Lady Widdicombe." It was an awkward and pretentious introduction at best, but for some reason she felt compelled to establish her position and stature quite clearly. At the very least, she had no intentions of being mistaken for a poor relation relegated to the position of companion to an old woman. At best, she would not be ordered about by a treasonous rogue, regardless if his head was broken or not.

"Miss Fairchilde," he said, licking dry lips, "if you would be so kind as to bear with my ignorance a moment longer? Since you appear to be well enough informed, I would be grateful if you could tell me who the blazes *I* am."

Anna started, shocked again. "Who *you* are? You do not know?"

"My head is"—he stopped and appeared to look inside himself, with no happy result—"utterly and completely blank. A void. Entirely empty, except for the bastard who is pounding the inside of my skull with an iron pike."

A shudder rippled the length of his body as he fought to cope with both the pain and the sudden anxiety. "Please," he said through clenched teeth, "if you can tell me something . . . anything that might help jar a thought or memory loose? I don't mean to frighten you, and can only hope it is just a temporary impediment, but—"

"You remember nothing at all? Not how you came here, or how you ended up on the beach?"

"Nothing. I remember nothing. Water, perhaps. A great deal of water and hot sun, but other than that . . . I have no recollections at all." His arms, his legs, his entire body began to tremble beneath the blankets, and the look in his eyes was frantic enough for Anna to abandon her caution and hasten to the side of the bed. There, she had to place her hands on his bare shoulders to restrain him from struggling to sit up.

"Mr. Althorpe, please. You must not overtax yourself. I am certain you are right. I am certain it must be a temporary thing, a result of the blow you took to the head, but you will do yourself no good trying to force something that is not quite there yet."

He slumped back, all but exhausted by such a feeble effort. "Althorpe?"

Anna pressed her hand over his forehead, but it was cool. "Emory Althorpe. That is your name, is it not?"

"I don't know—is it?"

His teeth were beginning to chatter and his eyes, when she looked into them, had the terrified, uncertain look of a trapped animal.

"Your name is Emory Althorpe, sir. You have two brothers; one of them is the Reverend Mr. Stanley Althorpe, who is, I believe, five years your junior. You also have an older brother—" She paused and reached for the stoppered bottle of laudanum on the bedside table, pouring what she hoped was a safe measure of the pale blue liquid into a glass before mixing it with equal parts of water. "His name is Arthur, and I think my aunt said he was thirty-one . . . or perhaps it was thirty-two, I am not sure. There was a fourth brother, William, but he has passed, as have your father and mother. Your father was Edgar Althorpe, and he was the Earl of Hatherleigh," she added, trying to remember what her aunt had told her about the family. "Your mother's name was Eugenia. You have no sisters, but you do have a sister-in-law, Lucille—the vicar's wife. Your family home is called Windsea Hall and is located some five miles north and east of here, above Torquay."

His eyes were squeezed tightly shut. "I do not recog-

nize any of those names or places. I do not even recognize
the name you tell me is my own."

"Here," she said, leaning over the bed. "Take a sip of
water—you must be thirsty. I've put some laudanum in it,
which may help ease the pain."

He reached out eagerly but his hand was still too shaky
to hold the glass steady against his lips. Anna slid her arm
under his shoulder to support him while he took several
deep swallows, and when he finished, he fell back against
the pillows, trapping her arm beneath. The motion brought
her forward and she found herself practically sprawled
across his chest, her nose a mere inch or two from his face.

His eyes were closed again and she watched as a trickle
of water ran down his chin, leaving a shiny path of liquid
between the taut cords of his neck. The hand he had placed
over hers while she held the glass to his lips had slipped
lower until it was around her wrist, and although it was
warm and dry, Anna felt a cool, prickling sensation skitter
up her arm and down her spine. It was not nearly as fierce
a grip as the one he had held her with on the beach, but
even so, the size of his hand, the strength in his fingers
made her wrist feel as fragile as a matchstick.

"I really should fetch my aunt," she whispered. "She
will know much better than I what to do."

"Just one more question."

"Truly, sir, my aunt knows far more about this than I.
I have only been here a week myself, on a visit from
London."

"Please," he said, the softness of the word sending another shiver through her body. "You said I was on the beach?
Who found me?"

"As it happened . . . I did. I was the one who found you."

He had not yet opened his eyes, for which Anna was particularly thankful. She was wriggling her arm to free it, but
it was a slow process, not helped any by the fact that there
was not an inch of her own flesh not burning with mortification. It was bad enough that she already had a more intimate

knowledge of his body than any books on social etiquette allowed. Now, to feel all that hard, smooth muscle sliding against her hand . . . well, it was almost more than she could bear and hope to survive with her modesty intact.

Making matters infinitely worse, she was close enough to count the individual stubbles of his beard if she were so inclined. The lashes she had admired earlier were so long and thick they would have been the envy of any woman. The eyebrows above were black and smooth, the left one marred by a tiny white scar that cut through the arch. The waves of hair that framed his face were blacker still, far too long and undisciplined to comply with strict London fashion—but then she doubted if a rogue and adventurer cared much for the dictates of Beau Brummell. His mouth was blatantly, shockingly sensuous as well, and if he ever smiled the effect would be, she imagined, quite heart-stopping.

"You have no idea how I came to be on the beach?"

"What?" She was still staring at his mouth when she realized his eyes were open again. She quickly pulled her arm the rest of the way free and straightened. "Oh. No, none at all. We were hoping you could tell us, for you were in a rather . . . unusual state of undress."

"Unusual? How so?"

The color that had been riding high on her cheeks flamed even darker. Undergarments of any kind were most definitely never to be mentioned in polite conversation, especially not when the memories of the ill-concealed shapes and shadows they were intended to protect were still shamefully clear in one's mind. "You were not . . . *completely* without coverings, sir, but . . . what there was . . . suffice it to say, they could not have been worn in any public place."

He said, "I see," though she doubted he did, then added, "I am truly sorry to be the cause of so much trouble."

"You have been asleep most of the time and therefore

no real trouble. My aunt, as I said before, is quite fond of you, despite"—her breath caught and held for as long as it took her to bite back the words she had been about to say—"despite the fact that you leaked a great deal of saltwater onto her carpets."

He said nothing. If he realized she had been about to say one thing and at the last moment had said another, there was no indication of it in his eyes. He was just studying her face, feature by feature, in the same fashion she had been studying his a few moments ago.

"When I first saw you sitting by the window . . . I thought you were an angel," he murmured, "I thought I was dead and you were waiting to take me away."

Annaleah reacted with an involuntary smile. "I expect my family would be vastly amused by your misimpression, sir. For that matter, I always imagined angels must be dressed in long flowing robes, with wings, and halos, and a shining cascade of long golden hair spilling down to their knees."

His own smile was crooked, a little wistful. "Whereas I will forever more imagine them as dark-haired beauties with eyes the color of a stormy sea."

Anna raised a hand self-consciously to touch a glossy chestnut spiral that had tumbled over her shoulder. It was by no means the first compliment she had ever received in her life, and yet . . . delivered through those lips, accompanied by those eyes, it was almost a physical caress.

"I really must fetch my aunt," she whispered.

"Please—" He held his hand out palm up in a hesitant plea. "Will you not sit with me just a few minutes longer?"

There was a shadow of desperation in his eyes, and helplessness. It occurred to Anna that she could imagine feather-winged angels with perfect ease, but she could not for a single instant imagine what it must be like to waken in pain, in a strange place, with no memories, not even a name.

She looked at his hand, trembling visibly with the fear of rejection, and she reached out, slipping her cool, slender fingers into his. The thrill that traveled up her arm this time shot straight down into her knees, and having already broken more rules of decorum than she could count, she shattered a few score more by sitting down on the edge of the bed.

"You said this was your aunt's house?"

"My great-aunt, actually. Florence Widdicombe."

"And . . . you have been here a week visiting?"

He seemed so pleased with himself to have remembered such a trivial thing, she smiled. "Yes. I came out from London eight days ago, actually."

"Alone?"

"Yes," she said slowly. "Alone."

"Your family is not with you?"

It was on the tip of her tongue to retort that if she was alone, then by definition her family was not with her, but then she realized he was no longer even looking at her. He had turned to stare at the beam of sunlight streaming through the arched window, and she realized that he had not really cared about the answer, he had just wanted to hear her voice so that he would not be left too long with his own thoughts.

It was a feeling she could well understand, for the silence was forcing her to look at the way the cords of his neck stood out when he turned his head, and the way his hair lay like a wave of silk over his cheek. The blanket had slipped down below the first hard plates of muscle that formed his chest, and the hair there was smooth and black as well, covering the skin like a dark breastplate. It was much finer on his arms, allowing a clear view of the veins that flowed down to his hands, to the fingers that were wrapped with easy possession around hers.

As far as making casual conversation, what could she say? You, sir, are a fugitive charged with treason. There are soldiers patrolling the roads, searching inns and taverns on the waterfront, watching the vicar's house, the church, even questioning Poor Arthur's nurses to see if he has been visited by his notorious brother.

"My family lives in London during the season," she said, clearing her throat softly, "and spends their summers in Exeter. I have a sister, Beatrice, and a brother, Anthony, both older. Bea is married, Anthony is not. I am . . . I am engaged," she added awkwardly, wondering why she had felt the need to throw up such a petty defense. Especially when the addition caused him to turn and stare at her through a frown.

"Do you happen to know . . . if *I* am married?"

"No," she whispered. "I am afraid I do not. According to my aunt, you have been out of the country for several years and no one really knows what you have been doing."

She saw the next question forming in his eyes, but before he could ask it, the sound of loud, scraping footsteps on the stairs put her hastily on her feet and prompted her to take several precautionary steps away from the side of the bed.

"That will be Broom," she explained. "He has been watching over you while you slept."

"Watching over me?"

"Yes. In . . . in case you woke up. Now I really *must* go and find my aunt. She will want to send for the vicar at once, and between them, perhaps they will be better able to answer some of your questions."

"Will you come back later?"

"Later?"

"Later," he said with quiet intensity, "when you can tell me what it is you are too frightened to tell me now."

Again there was no time to answer—if indeed she could have thought of something to say—for Broom was at the door, snatching the crumpled felt hat off his head and bowing as much to clear the lintel of the doorway as to extend the formal courtesy to Annaleah.

"Mr. Althorpe is awake," she explained needlessly. "I was just going to find my aunt."

"Aye, miss. She be in day parlor, miss, wi' visitors."

"Visitors?"

"Aye. An 'ole flock o' them. Two fancy toffs come first in a big black rig wi' four 'orses!" To a man who measured wealth in livestock, it was an impressive testimony of importance. "They was 'ardly 'ere long enough for 'er ladyship to settle 'em in the parlor afore anither coach pulled up wi' Colonel Ramsey an' a brace o' redcoats."

Chapter 5

*A*NNALEAH DID NOT even want to entertain the notion that Reverend Stanley Althorpe had faltered in his resolve and alerted the authorities to his brother's whereabouts. But as she descended from the attic to the third floor, then hurried along the corridor to the main staircase, she could not think of any other plausible reason why soldiers would be in the house. Her own brother, Anthony, irritated her almost beyond endurance at times, yet she could not fathom a crime so heinous as to make her willingly betray him. Beatrice often made her clamp her hands to her sides to keep from reaching up and tearing out locks of her sister's hair, but there too, at the slightest hint of trouble, Anna would defend her unto the death.

By the time she arrived outside the day parlor, her cheeks were warm with indignation, her temples steamy, and her jaw set for battle.

The two scarlet-clad soldiers stood with Willerkins just inside the doorway, rigid in their official capacity, and were the first persons Anna saw when she entered the room.

The next visitor, whom she recognized from a brief introduction at Sunday mass, was Colonel Rupert Ramsey, retired from active service by a shattered elbow, and more recently attached to the garrison at Berry Head to oversee the demobilization of the army. He was short and wiry in an ill-fitting uniform, with a pointed face and thick curly hair more suited to a sheep than a man.

She sought her aunt immediately, hoping to take some clue from Florence's expression as to why Ramsey was here, but her gaze had barely touched upon the diminutive gray-haired figure in black bombazine when it was jolted abruptly over to the second pair of "toffs" seated by the fireplace.

Both balanced delicate cups and saucers on their laps, which they set aside at once as they rose in deference to her arrival.

"Anthony!" Annaleah gasped, and her gaze shifted again. "Lord *Barrimore*?"

Their formal bows executed, it was her brother who spoke first. "Anna. Good show. You have saved old Willerkins the need to hunt you down."

Anna was too stunned for cleverness or subtlety. "What on earth are you doing here?"

Her brother coughed into his hand. "A rather blunt greeting, I must say. To which the equally blunt answer would be the obvious: We have come to fetch you home."

He was impeccably dressed, as usual, in a charcoal jacket, green striped waistcoat, and pearl gray trousers. Winston Perry, marquess of Barrimore, made for a rather somber contrast in black superfine from head to toe, with the only break in severity being the white collar and cravat. He was taller than Anthony by an inch or more, with precisely clipped and curled brown hair surrounding a handsome face that might have been considered irresistible were it not for the fact that his expression was usually as tight as his collar. At the moment, only the two brittle green points of his eyes showed any animation as they assessed her loosely combed hair and simple muslin dress.

"Do come in, Anna dear," her aunt invited, "and take some tea with us. You remember Colonel Ramsey? He has no time for tea himself," she added, "but has come to warn us to be on guard against any strangers lurking about."

"Strangers?" Anna's voice came out suitably hesitant.

"Yes. You have not seen any, have you, dear?"

Instead of answering directly, she looked at Colonel Ramsey. "Has there been trouble in the village, sir?"

Ramsey stopped undressing her with his eyes and looked up into her face. "We have reason to believe there may be some trouble brewing, what with Bonaparte due to arrive in port any day now."

"Bonaparte is coming here? To Torbay?"

"Why yes," Anthony said, parting the swallowtails of his coat to resume his seat. "The most recent sightings put the *Bellerophon* less than a week out of port. Plymouth will not have him, and London wants no part of the circus he is expected to draw. It was decided, quite rightly so, that he should be kept as isolated from the general population as is possible. They do not even intend to land him, merely let him sit on board the ship at anchor."

"What does that have to do with us?" Anna asked.

"Nothing directly, of course," the colonel said carefully.

"It would seem, Niece," Florence interjected, "they are also looking for a dangerous criminal. A gentleman by the name of Althorpe."

"I would hesitate to call Emory Althorpe a gentleman, dear lady, since he is wanted for a host of crimes, none of which carry less than a penalty of hanging."

"Yes, well, I only vaguely recall the boy," Florence said, waving her cane absently, "and thought him dead long ago of a shrunken head in Borneo. At any rate, you say there is a reward being offered for his capture and arrest?"

"Five hundred pounds." Ramsay nodded. "Authorized by Lord Westford himself, as Lord Barrimore will no doubt confirm."

Anna glanced at the marquess with renewed astonishment. "You know this man, the one they are looking for?"

"I have never met him personally, but I have run across his name a time or two through my dealings with the foreign office. As a privateer—which is a roundabout way of saying he was a mercenary—he was apparently recruited some years ago to provide information about the movements of the French navy. In light of the charges that have been brought against him in recent months, one can only presume the French offered him more money to turn his coat and work for them instead."

"For the five hundred pounds being offered for his capture, I would turn my coat," Florence stated flatly, drawing focus back to the reward. "It is an astounding sum of money in and of itself. One that will be bound to draw the worms out of the woodwork."

"We have had several false sightings already," Ramsey admitted. "One from a fisherman who claims he saw someone who resembled Althorpe floating toward shore on a piece of driftwood."

"In that case, please do tell my niece what the scoundrel looks like that she might be on her guard next time she is walking by the beach."

"This was several days ago and well south of here, but we are taking no chances and have printed up a likeness we are in the process of posting in all public areas."

Ramsey reached out awkwardly with his stiff arm and snapped his fingers at one of the redcoats, who in turn produced several sheets of paper from a leather dispatch case. He handed one to Florence first, then to Anthony. Barrimore barely glanced at it before waving it away with a small frown, at which time it was passed to Anna. She took the sheet and braced herself before looking down. Considering that it was only a rough sketch in smeared black ink, it bore a startling likeness to the man lying upstairs. The hair was wilder, embellished by the kind of braids depicted in stories about pirates. The eyes were close-set and mean, and more license had been taken etching the scar in his eyebrow; far from being the slim nick it was in reality, the artist suggested it dragged across his brow and distorted the entire temple.

But it was him. It was Emory Althorpe, and the huge blocked letters beneath his picture declared he was wanted for "Treason! Sedition! Piracy! Murder!"

Anna glanced at Florence, who was studying the sketch as if it were of no more importance than the evening menu.

"Have you seen anyone like that in the vicinity, miss?" Ramsey asked. "Privates Dilberry and Ward may be able to help with additional information, as they were familiar with the rogue in his youth."

One of the soldiers touched a forelock. "Aye. I know'd 'im, miss. Big man, 'ee is. Stands near seven feet tall, wi' a scrint eye, scarredlike, an' shoulders this wide." His comrade nudged him on the arm and he amended the distance between his hands, increasing it beyond Broom's impressive bulk. "Aye, more like this wide."

"In absolute honesty, sir," she said, addressing Ramsey, "I have not seen anyone who would match that description."

"Nor is she likely to," Lord Barrimore said dryly, "since there is some doubt as to whether he is even still alive. A report received in the foreign office stated there was some trouble in the harbor at Rochefort shortly after Bonaparte's surrender and Althorpe was killed by one of the general's own men."

Colonel Ramsey shook his head, obviously not convinced. "He has been reported dead before, only to appear like a bad dream some months later. I have heard nothing that would convince me this time is any different, and until I see an actual body, I will not believe it."

"You sound as if you have been looking for him longer than a few short weeks," Florence said.

"I have had a personal interest in following his career these past three years or more," Ramsey admitted. "The man is as elusive as smoke and twice as hard to catch."

"Then I bid you the best of luck in your hunt, Colonel. Wild geese have never appealed to me, personally."

"Too gamy by far, Auntie," Anthony agreed, dropping the warrant sheet on the table beside him. "Especially if they have been dead for over a month. Was there anything else, sir? Any other bogeymen we should be on the lookout for?"

"I'll not take up any more of your time," Ramsey said, bristling slightly at the sarcasm. "Be advised, however, that there will be increased patrols along the coast roads and at every tollbooth on the turnpikes leading in and out of

Torbay. If you are planning to return to London anytime soon, you might want to spare yourself any unnecessary aggravation by allowing for the additional delays."

With that, he nodded curtly at Florence and Anna and, after snapping his fingers again at his two men, stalked out of the room, following Willerkins down the hallway.

"Such an unpleasant man," Florence said after a moment. "But can it be true? Is that dreadful little French general coming here to Torbay?"

"It has been in all the newspapers, Auntie," Anthony said. "But of course, you would have no reason to read one. Not to worry, however. Barrimore tells me there is more than enough room in his berline to carry you home to London with us. We shall consider it an adventure, shall we?" He leaned forward to rest his hand patronizingly on her knee. "A grand adventure to London town."

Florence looked like she wanted to give his shin a sharp whack with her cane, but she smiled sweetly instead. "How thoughtful of you to worry about me, Nephew, but I do not often venture out of the house these days. My poor bones are so brittle, I fear even a brief journey in any manner of moving vehicle would likely crack my spine in two. No, no. It is kind of you to worry after my safety, but sadly, I must decline your offer."

"But you heard what Ramsey said. Disregarding for the moment the rabble that will be swarming to the coast to catch a glimpse of Bonaparte, one should not be so cavalier in dismissing the possibility of a dangerous criminal being on the loose."

"Pish. I knew Emory Althorpe when he was a boy, and if he has retained half the common sense he had back then, I should think Brixham would be the last place he would come. Not when there would be a very good chance he would be recognized, and certainly not with a reward on his head worth twenty times what most of the fishermen hereabout will earn in their lifetimes!"

"Nevertheless," Anthony argued, "I cannot say I am

comfortable with the notion of you being so far out of town. It could take hours for one of these creaking old servants to fetch help if it were required."

"I am fine. We are all of us fine. There is a young boy in the house—Blisterbottom—who runs like the wind, and we have Willerkins. He was a member of the King's Royal Guard back in the '45 and is still a crack shot. Indeed, the locals—not to mention the field mice—are quite terrified of his prowess with a blunderbuss."

Anthony looked dubious. "Mother will not be pleased when we return home without you."

"Your mother will survive the disappointment, I am sure."

"Both disappointments," Annaleah said, "for I am not leaving either."

"What?" Anthony had started to lift his teacup but stopped. "What did you say?"

"I said . . . I am not leaving either. I am staying here with Aunt Florence."

She might well have said she was taking up a gun and turning highwayman for the look he gave her in return. And were it not such a serious breach of parental authority she was proposing, she might have laughed out loud at his expression.

But this was no laughing matter. She could not leave Florence alone in the house with a notorious criminal. Moreover, she had not changed her opinion of Winston Perry, Lord Barrimore, and she knew if she left Widdicombe House and drove back to London with him, her fate would be sealed. Her engagement would be announced, the marriage date settled, the banns read.

"Not leaving?" Anthony said again. "What nonsense is this?"

"I . . . I cannot leave," she insisted. "Not while Auntie still needs me."

Anna hastened to her aunt's side and settled beside her in a soft swirl of white muslin. Taking up one of the gnarled hands, she gave it an imploring squeeze. "I know you are determined to put forth a brave show for my brother and Lord Barrimore, but I could not live with myself if I left you alone, knowing that you are in such terrible pain."

"Pain?" Anthony frowned at his aunt. "You are in pain, Aunt Florence?"

"I am?" Florence gasped as Anna's fingers dug into her hand. "I am. Well, not so much that you would notice."

"There, you see," Anna declared, looking at her brother. "She would never tell you so, but dear Auntie can barely walk from one chair to the next without assistance. Her legs are so weak . . . why, she nearly took a dreadful tumble just this morning, and would have fallen head over heels down the stairs had I not been there to catch her."

"My dear child, you exaggerate." The canny blue eyes narrowed into their wrinkles. "I will have you know, it has been nearly a whole week since the last time my feet went up in the air. And the pain is not so very dreadful; my ankle can almost bear the weight."

"The doctor said you were not to overtax yourself."

"He did? Oh, of course he did. And you have been such a help to me, hovering about like a lovely little butterfly, at my elbow day and night to attend to the smallest request I might make. But I could not impose upon your sweet nature, child. Not if your dear mother wishes you to return home."

"It was my mother who sent me here to help you and I shall remain here to help you for as long as you need me."

"Anna," her brother protested. "Mother's concerns are genuine—"

"Her concerns were equally genuine when she hastened me out of London on a moment's notice," Anna said, conscious of Barrimore's eyes boring into the back of her neck. She had wondered exactly what he had been told in regard to her abrupt departure from the city, but because she doubted it was anything near the truth, she gambled it was more than likely her elderly aunt's health that had been used for an excuse. "Can you not see I am still needed here? How cruel and cold a person do you think me that I would simply walk away and leave our aunt alone and helpless in her pain?"

"I have Willerkins to help me," Florence said in a brave, quavering voice. "And Ethel, of course, though it is sometimes difficult to tolerate the smell of chicken that always clings to her."

"You do not have to rely on either Willerkins or Ethel, Auntie. I am here, and here is where I shall remain."

"I do not want to be a burden on anyone, even for the short time I have left." Florence took up a crumpled lace handkerchief and touched it to the corner of her eye as she offered up a watery confession in Anthony's direction. "The doctors, you see, have already said it will be a true miracle if I live to see another Michaelmas Day, not two full months hence. They apply leeches and open veins every time I have a spell, but . . . the relief is only temporary."

"You have spells?" Anthony asked, clearly concerned.

"Spells." Florence nodded solemnly. "And then there is the chaos in my bowels. It erupts at the most inopportune moments."

"I see. Well, ah, I suppose I could send Mother a post, explaining the situation." He glanced around the room, at the aged furniture, the dark walls, the musty shadows, and shuddered visibly. "Naturally," he added with no attempt to conceal his reluctance, "I shall remain as well to offer what assistance and comfort I may."

Florence dabbed her eyes again and smiled. "You are more than welcome, of course. There are at least a dozen empty bedrooms that have not been used in, oh, several years. But I am certain a few hours with soapy water and carpet brooms should make one or two of them presentable. And as long as it does not rain at night, you gentlemen should be quite comfortable. The bats, as your sister has discovered, are not so very great a problem if you remember to keep the curtains drawn and rags stuffed in the windowsills. And you, sir—forgive me, but I have quite forgotten your name—?"

"Barrimore," said the marquess, looking even more appalled than Anthony, if that was possible, at the prospect of rags and bats.

"I knew a Barrimore once. He used to steal the oranges out of the children's Christmas boxes. He was the butler, I believe, or perhaps the dustman—it was so long ago; the faces all crowd together—but of course he would have been your grandfather's age, and I daresay your grandfather was not a dustman, was he?"

"No, madam. He was not. Nor would I would dream of imposing upon your hospitality at such a trying time as this. Fairchilde," he snapped. "A word, if I may?"

Anthony sprang to his feet at once. "Of course. Ladies, you will excuse us a moment?"

He offered a brief bow and retreated with Barrimore to stand before the window.

Anna bowed her head and her lips barely moved. "I am so sorry, Auntie, but I did not know what else to do."

"There is no need to explain anything to me," Florence murmured. "Would I be mistaken in presuming to guess Lord Barrimore is the paragon your mother has chosen for your future husband?"

Anna tilted her head up, her huge blue eyes shining with confused emotions. "She insists he is a fine catch."

"Mmm. No doubt he is rich, titled, handsome, and she has told you you should be grateful he has even deigned to consider you a marriageable prospect?"

"A thousand times," she agreed dully.

"And you have said no a thousand times and so she has sent you here to me as your punishment?" Florence's hand tightened over hers. "Only say the word and I shall send Willerkins to fetch his fowling piece."

"I . . . just need some time to think," Anna said.

"Then you shall have it. And a wise choice, all things

considered"—Florence winked, obviously enjoying the conspiracy—"for in truth, the old fool damned near shot his foot off the other day endeavoring to clean a pistol for Broom."

As anxious as she was about her own situation, Anna had not entirely forgotten their other "guest." In low tones she said, "Mr. Althorpe is awake, Auntie. We spoke for a few moments and"—she cast a cautious glance over her shoulder to ensure that the men were far enough away not to be able to hear her words—"and he claims he does not remember anything."

"He does not know how he came to be on our beach?"

"He does not know *anything*," she reiterated. "Not where he is, or who he is; nor can he remember anything about his . . . his *activities* before he washed up on the shore."

"How extraordinary. I have never heard of such a thing. Well, no, that is not exactly true, for I have heard of it—a sailor once claimed to have lost all memory after suffering a high fever at sea, but I suspect it was more because his wife in Plymouth discovered he had a wife in Portsmouth. You say he remembers nothing?"

"He did not even know his name."

"How extraordinary," Florence murmured again, leaning back in the chair just as the men rejoined them.

"Barrimore has suggested a brilliant compromise," Anthony began. "If it meets with your approval, that is. He says he has often stayed in Torquay while tending to his business affairs and knows of a perfectly respectable villa overlooking the bay. We would be but five miles away, close enough to respond to any emergency should one arise yet far enough not to inconvenience you with our presence. In the meantime, I shall dispatch a post to Mother at once, explaining the situation, begging her leave to remain in attendance a few days more."

Florence responded with a dotty smile. "You do not have to rush off right away, do you? You will stay to lunch, will you not? With my teeth falling out at such an alarming rate, I usually have little more than a bowl of mashed turnips and soup, but I have no doubt Mildred could catch a plover to boil for you."

"Ah . . ." Anthony caught a glare from Barrimore's eye. "No. No thank you, Auntie. As it happens, we partook of a rather large breakfast this morning. And we really should see to the post for Mother. The sooner sent, the sooner received."

Florence raised her hand to accept Anthony's buss. Over his head, she smiled at Lord Barrimore. "It was a pleasure to make your acquaintance, milord. I trust we will have occasion to meet again."

He took her hand and bowed over it, but did not trouble himself to kiss more than the air. "I shall not draw a happy breath until we do, madam."

"Anna." Anthony extended his hand in her direction. "Can you be spared long enough to walk us to the door?"

She accepted his assistance and rose to her feet. The two men made a last, formal bow at the door and, with Annaleah walking by her brother's side, descended the wide staircase to the main floor.

"You do realize this will put Mother in a fine mood," Anthony groused. "And I shall somehow be made to shoulder the blame."

"Lucky then, that you have such fine, broad shoulders."

"And what do you know of this business the colonel was telling us about?"

"I know what you know. They are looking for a villain seven feet tall with a scar over his eye."

"Treason is no laughing matter, Miss Fairchilde," Barrimore said stonily. "Neither is the nature of Emory Althorpe's crimes."

"I promise you I am not the smallest part amused, milord," she countered and turned to look at him. Up close, his eyes were a cold, clear green, their gaze steady and unblinking. She'd had occasion before to wonder if he ever laughed, but now she began to question if he even knew how to smile. She could not for an instant imagine Barrimore's hand shaking when it touched hers, or his mouth relaxing into a crooked, wistful smile when he told her he would forevermore envision angels as being dark-haired beauties with eyes the color of stormy seas.

She so startled herself by thinking of Emory Althorpe that she had to ask her brother to repeat the question he had just asked.

"I said: I am a trifle uneasy leaving you here. Are you sure you will be all right?"

"I have been perfectly fine for the past week, but if you are concerned, you can always stay. Auntie said you were more than welcome."

"With the mold and the bats? No thank you. I am driven to wonder how you have held up this long."

"My room is quite pleasant. I have everything I need for my personal comfort."

"Yes, well." Anthony sighed and gave his head a little shake. "I fear I would be so intrigued by my surroundings, I would not be able to properly digest my mashed turnips."

Anna smiled for the first time. "You have not even met Ethel, the chicken plucker, or Mildred the cook, who claims there is a ghost in the kitchen who tastes her food and tells her if it needs salting or sweetening. And there is Broom, who is as large as a mountain and keeps a pet mouse in his pocket. And Throckmorton, the gong man, who—"

"Say no more," Anthony pleaded, holding up a hand, "lest I am persuaded, out of sheer fascination, to change my mind."

He glanced over at Willerkins, who had glided up on silent feet behind them with hats and gloves in hand.

"I will be fine," she assured him with a light kiss on the cheek. "We will all be fine. And you know as well as I do that as much as Father protests, he would be here himself if he could to have a firsthand accounting of Napoleon Bonaparte's arrival in port. Imagine what the ladies will make of you back in London the instant they learn you were standing on the dock when the *Bellerophon* dropped anchor."

His expression brightened somewhat, in direct contrast to Barrimore's, which grew even more bleak as he gave his large gold signet ring a twist around his finger.

"You are not curious to see the famous prisoner?" Anna asked him.

"Considering my time would be better spent back in London helping to bring an end to the debates in Parliament, I am not curious in the least."

"I am sorry to be the cause of any inconvenience," she murmured, feeling the warmth rise in her cheeks.

"With an eye toward catching the afternoon post," he said to Anthony, "we should make haste for Torquay. Perhaps it would be possible, Miss Fairchilde, to have a word with you in private at a later time? If not today, perhaps tomorrow? It concerns a personal matter that your father and I have already discussed and I would like to have settled before we return to London."

If there was a warmer, more romantic way to suggest he wanted her alone in order that he might propose, she could not think of it. The fact he had already discussed the arrangements with her father sent the fine hairs across the back of her neck rising.

She looked up, aware of Barrimore's cool stare as he waited for an answer.

"Yes. Yes, of course you may call," Anthony said. "Let us away now before all the rooms in Torquay are taken by French pilgrims."

"I will send my card," Barrimore said, bowing again.

Anna stood under the portico and watched the gleaming black berline roll down the drive, the sound of the wheels on the crushed limestone remaining long after the coach itself disappeared around a tree-lined bend in the road. Having nothing better to look at, Anna gazed out to where the sea was a shining expanse of blue across the horizon. It was so open, so vast, so endless. . . . Why did she feel, suddenly, as though she could not breathe?

"Miss Annaleah?"

She turned and found Willerkins standing beside her.

"Milady said to tell you she would be going upstairs to visit with our other guest."

"Thank you, Willerkins. I will assist her directly."

"No need to hurry, miss. She can be as spry as a hare when it suits her."

Chapter 6

*H*IS BODY WAS DRENCHED *in sweat. The scent filled his nostrils with a sour-sweet odor that nearly overpowered the stink of the harbor air. It was dark. Too dark to see more than the glint of the blade as it teased the air in front of him. The steel was long and needle-thin, seated in a carved ebony hilt. It reminded him of an icicle and each time it touched his flesh, the first sensation was always cold, followed by an incredible stinging heat. He did not have to see his back to imagine what it looked like. The hand wielding the knife was practiced and efficient, cutting only deep enough to inflict pain and to make it last a very long time. . . .*

Emory Althorpe lunged upright in an effort to break the ropes that were binding his arms, and his hand smashed hard against the edge of the bed. His eyes popped open and his legs kicked out, thrashing the blankets into a tangle of wool. He made a sound in his throat, low and guttural, for he had vowed not to scream, no matter how deep the knife carved into his flesh . . . and it emerged in the form of a curse that clearly shocked the women who stood by the side of the bed.

One was old, swathed neck to toe in black bombazine with skin like wrinkled parchment and a knot of white curls supporting a lace caplet. The other was younger. Much younger. And as he blinked the sweat and panic out of his eyes, he realized she looked familiar, with her dark chestnut hair and deep blue eyes.

It was the angel he had seen before. He remembered she had cool hands and a soothing voice, and she had sat with him and smiled and he had wanted to drown in her eyes.

"Well." The old lady visibly relaxed the defensive grip

she had taken on her cane. "I must remember not to touch you again while you are sleeping. I meant no harm, I assure you. I only wished to see if you had developed a fever."

Emory's heartbeat began to slow, his rate of breathing began to return to normal, and the images of his nightmare—or whatever the hell it had been—began to fade into the background, taking the memory of incredibly blinding pain with it.

"I . . . must have been dreaming," he managed to rasp.

"It must have been quite the dream," the old woman remarked, looking down at the twist of covers.

He followed her bemused gaze and saw that he had kicked the blankets with enough force to pull them well below his waist.

"Forgive me," he muttered and reached for the edge of wool, drawing it high up beneath his chin.

"For what?" The old woman chuckled. "You have grown into a fine specimen of a man, Emory Althorpe. The last time I saw you, why, you were no wider than a sapling and still ignorant of the use of a razor."

"You must be"—he glanced briefly at his angel, but she had not yet composed herself enough to look at the bed—"Florence?"

"You used to call me Auntie Lal, but I suppose 'Florence' will have to do. Unless, of course, Rory dear, you are feeling better? My niece told me yesterday that you were having difficulty remembering what happened."

"Yesterday?" Emory frowned. "Was it not just this morning—"

"It seems she was a trifle enthusiastic administering the laudanum," Florence said dryly. "We sat about all afternoon waiting for you to waken again, but alas, apart from a few stirrings and mumblings, you remained asleep through the night. A grave disappointment to your brother, I might add, who was exceedingly hopeful last evening of finding you fully awake and recovered."

"My brother—" Emory glanced briefly at his dark-haired

angel of mercy, who had not once looked up since averting her eyes from his naked body. "Stanley?"

"Yes." Florence beamed. "Do you recollect him now?"

"No. Nothing more than the name."

"Oh dear. I was so hoping with an extra night's rest and all, you would have gained back some of your faculties. I was so hopeful, in fact, that I did not tell your brother there were some, ah, complications in your recovery."

"It is as if someone has taken a cloth and wiped all the writing off the slate," he said honestly. "I see blurry images, an occasional picture of something. I get impressions of things flashing through my mind, but I do not know what they mean."

"Do you get an impression of hunger?" Florence inquired solicitously. "You have been here nearly three full days without eating a morsel of food and only drinking what little sustenance Annaleah could pour through your lips."

Annaleah, he thought. She had told him her name yesterday. She had been prim and formal . . . and frightened.

"I think I am a little hungry," he admitted, attempting a faint smile.

Florence waved her cane to indicate the small banquet that had been laid out on a table behind them. "Do you feel strong enough to get out of bed, or shall we bring a tray to you?"

"I feel strong enough to try," he said. "If I had some clothes . . . ?"

She rapped the end of the cane on a nearby chair. "Shirt, breeches, stockings. You came with your own drawers so we did not have to scrounge about for them, but the rest came from whoever could spare it. My niece and I shall remove ourselves to the hallway while you dress, and then, if it is agreeable to you, we shall return and take tea while you replenish your strength."

The cane gave off a muted thump with every footstep as Florence took Annaleah's arm and retreated toward the door. Emory caught a quick glance from the celestial blue eyes, but he had no time to respond to it before the door closed behind them. She had not said a word, had barely raised her gaze above the level of the bedskirt, and it made him adjust the covers again, wondering just how long he had kicked and thrashed before he had wakened himself.

Long enough to set the devils hammering in his skull again, that much was a certainty, and he raised his hand, probing gingerly at the lump at the back of his head. The pain was still bad, but it was something he could control. The images and flashes of things, people, places that came and went through his mind had no rhyme or reason, nor could he hold one long enough to identify it. The nightmare had been all the more alarming for not knowing if it was a real event from his past that he was reliving, or something his mind had conjured to torment him. If it was real, what did it mean? His wrists had been tied to a beam in the ceiling and someone had been deliberately cutting him . . . but why? He had wakened the day before with nothing more than an impression of water, vast expanses of water. Now there was distinct memory of pain, but no reason behind it. Unless, of course, it hadn't really happened.

Emory ran his fingers over the tops of his shoulders, and at first felt nothing. But when he reached farther back, they were there: thin raised lines in his flesh where stripes had been cut in the skin.

Searching farther afield, he peeled the covers aside and stared down at his naked body. All of his parts appeared to be there, in ample enough quantities to explain why a modest young lady would blush herself almost crimson. There were, however, other scars on his arms, his legs, his hip, his belly and ribs, some more obvious than others, and most able to be attributed to other kinds of violence. There was a deep, puckered welt he surmised to be an old saber wound on his thigh, another on his arm. A mark on the back of his left buttock drew a frown when he fit the pad of his forefinger into the center of the ragged pock and realized it was a healed bullet wound.

At some point in his life, he had been shot in the arse—surely a painful and embarrassing occurrence—yet he could not remember it. He had been shot, slashed by swords, and God knew what else, but he could remember none of it! His skin was weathered and tanned from the waist up, suggesting he was no stranger to sunlight and ocean breezes. His arms and legs were like oak, tempered with strong bands of sinew and muscle. There was strength in his hands as well; enough for him to know he was not a man who squandered his days in idle dicing and dancing.

Feeling the pressure beginning to build behind his eyes again, he forced the panic aside and, after swinging his legs over the side of the mattress, used the wooden bedpost to lever himself gingerly to his feet. The room spun sickeningly for a few moments but he persevered until he was upright, swaying like a drunk, but standing on his own with only the fingertips of his left hand resting against the post for support.

His success sent another flush of heat surging through his body and he savored the sensation of knowing that not only were all his parts intact, but they were functioning normally. He searched around the floor of the bed for a moment and found what he sought, and after relieving himself in the chamberpot, he inspected the assortment of clothes that had been left neatly folded on the chair.

With modesty his first priority, he dragged a long white shirt made of rough homespun over his arms and shoulders. It was several sizes too big and fell well below his hips—he guessed it was a donation from his giant watchdog—in contrast to the knee-length breeches, which were a stretchable but exceedingly tight fit. There were stockings but no garters, and leather shoes with thin wooden soles. On the washstand, he found a brush and used it to tame the unkempt black waves of his hair. Noticing one glaring omission in the toiletries, he rubbed a hand over his jaw and discovered it was smooth. Someone had already shaved him, either not trusting him to do it without cutting himself, or simply not trusting him with a razor.

He shrugged the question aside and bound his hair with a length of black ribbon. He had been staring at another object on the table for a few moments, and when his hair was tamed and his hands ran out of things to do, he lowered them and ran his fingertips over the raised pattern of silver swans that graced the back of the oval mirror.

He must have stared at it for two full minutes before he finally persuaded himself to simply pick it up and turn it over. It was a strange sensation, slowly angling the polished surface upward, not knowing what to expect, not knowing what he would see or feel when he saw the face that was reflected back at him.

He did not recognize it. Not the wide brow or the smooth, dark eyebrows. Not the bold jut of the chin or the straight ridge of his nose; not the brown eyes that were nearly as dark as the lashes that surrounded them. He had ears, a mouth, most of his teeth, but he could have been looking at a stranger on the street for all the comfort and familiarity he felt. The pressure, the panic, the sense of sheer frustration made him tighten his fist around the metal handle, and with a cry that welled up from deep in his soul, he turned and hurled the mirror across the room, shattering the offending image into a hundred bright shards of glass.

Out on the tiny landing, Annaleah was in the midst of trying to eradicate an image of her own—that of Emory Althorpe's body with the blanket twisted down around his waist. An inch or two more and he would have revealed everything she had been trying so diligently to forget since finding him on the beach. Unfortunately, her mind was fertile enough to put the two images together, with the result that she had been afraid to meet his eye, certain he would sense her discomfort and know that she was not particularly thinking of her own shattered modesty. Rather, he would know she was thinking he was the simply the most spectacularly beautiful man she had ever seen in her young life. Beautiful, dangerous, and as her sister Beatrice would have said with succinct and justifiable emphasis, the kind of man who represented Instant Ruination to any woman with a modicum of sensibility to see it.

The cry of anguish, followed by the sound of the mirror crashing on the wall beside her, made Anna literally leap to one side and mash her shoulder sharply against the opposite wall. Her aunt, who was used to gongs being struck with little or no advance warning, merely turned from the tiny garret window and arched an eyebrow.

"Dear me. Do you suppose he does not like the breakfast we have prepared?"

"Auntie, wait—" Annaleah held out her hand to stop her aunt from reaching for the doorknob. "Perhaps we should call Broom."

"Whatever for, child? A broken platter?"

Anna bit her lip and watched as her aunt opened the door. She could not very well let Florence go back inside unattended, and so she followed, but each step was cautiously placed, with every sense on prickling alert. She saw the mirror lying in a spray of broken glass beside the door, and a few feet away, Emory Althorpe was standing in front of the washstand, his broad back to the door, his hands braced against the wall, his head bent forward between his shoulders.

"I gather you have met another stranger?" Florence asked gently.

"Was it a test of some sort?"

"A test?"

"Yes. To see if I was telling the truth, or if, for some reason unknown to me, you believed I was faking this loss of everything I am, everything I was."

When he straightened and turned around, both Anna and Florence had cause to hold their breaths, for the composition of his face had altered completely. Not the physical look of it, but rather the impression as a whole, changing from a countenance full of confusion and uncertainty to one of blackness, mistrust, and anger.

"It was not a test, Rory," Florence said carefully. "It was merely an old woman's thoughtless attempt to help you jar your memory."

The accusation remained cold and brittle in his eyes for a long, silent moment, then gradually began to melt, like candle wax collapsing toward a flame. His shoulders sagged and his arms fell limp by his sides, the muscles no longer straining with tension.

"I . . . I'm . . . sorry," he said haltingly. "I just don't . . . I can't—"

"Come," Florence said, interrupting his attempt to explain something neither she nor Annaleah could have understood anyway. "Sit and have something to eat. I always find it difficult to concentrate when my belly is rumbling and my tongue is dry. Eat and we can pick our way through the maze together."

He spread his hands in a helpless gesture of apology. "I suspect I have a temper," he said lamely.

"You did not tolerate fools or foolishness lightly," Florence agreed. "Not even as a boy. Now come. Sit."

The command was emphasized with two forceful raps of her cane. There were only two chairs, which Althorpe held for Anna and her aunt, but the table had been set up in front of the window, providing for a third seat on the recessed ledge of the casement. He sat with his back to the sun, the light turning his hair into gleaming ebony and silhouetting the shape of his torso beneath the loose folds of the shirt.

Anna nearly shook her head as she imagined all the Fates conspiring against her, for she sat opposite him, her hands folded primly in her lap, her back straight, her gaze deliberately averted. She was determined not to look directly at him, not with his shirt unlaced and an immodest expanse of his chest bared through the gap. At the same time she could scarcely fail to be aware each time he looked at her—which he seemed to do with alarming frequency. Her cheeks remained continuously warm and her mouth stayed dry no matter how many times she moistened her lips. There were subtle reactions elsewhere in her body as well. A slow, rhythmic tightening chilled the skin across her breasts, while a strange throbbing low down in her belly made her wary of moving, or even breathing too deeply.

Florence whacked her cane against the leg of the table.

"I said, shall we have tea or cider? Cider, I think. Much more restorative to the blood, do you not agree?"

Annaleah fumbled for the jug and poured out three glasses of the sweet apple cider for which Widdicombe House was moderately famous. While she did so, Florence encouraged Althorpe to help himself to the heaped mounds of cold sliced ham, mutton, cheese, and bread. At first he protested, there being only one plate and one set of cutlery, but at Florence's repeated insistence, and after the first mouthful of tender ham, he literally attacked the platters and assaulted the hillocks of food until there was not one single crumb left for an ant to carry away.

While he ate, Florence casually expanded upon what Anna had told him about his family members, the estate at Windsea, the years he had spent growing up in Torbay. Anna listened intently as well, finding it increasingly difficult to resist glancing across the table. Each time he shifted or moved, the sunlight winked through a lock of his hair, drawing her attention to the slope of his neck or the noble outline of his profile. She tried to compromise by watching his hands, but there too, the movement of his long, strong fingers sent tiny shivers down her spine and made her remember how warmly those fingers had curled around hers the previous day.

Another wink of light made her look up, and this time her heart all but stopped in her throat. He was grinning at something Florence had said, and the effect on his face was even more devastating than she had imagined it could be. His mouth evoked sinful thoughts at the best of times, but when he smiled it caused a squirming flutter of pleasure where she should have been ashamed to feel such a thing. She found herself avoiding his glances less and less, meeting and holding his eyes for longer and longer periods of time. She was still not completely at ease doing so, but when she was caught the first time and did not burn up in flames, the second was easier. The third time she even returned his smile with a shy imitation of her own.

She should have known that, as soon as they were comfortable exchanging pleasantries, the Fates would interfere again.

"The vicar," Florence was saying, "is naturally anxious to speak with you."

"So anxious," Althorpe said carefully, "that he has left me here, in your care, instead of taking me home?"

"When we first found you on the beach, we had no way of knowing if anything had been broken, most particularly your head. We all agreed it would best not to move you too soon."

"And that is the only reason?"

Florence's face remained remarkably blank. "Whatever do you mean?"

Emory drained his fourth glass of cider and set the empty goblet carefully aside. "I mean . . . I may have lost my memory, but I have not lost my sight or my wits. You both look as if you are sitting on broken glass, wary of my asking a wrong question or venturing onto a subject you would prefer not to broach. And this room. It is under the eaves, is it not? Rather a peculiar choice of accommodations if I am, as you say, an old family friend. Furthermore, since I have been here, there has been a guard on the door."

"Broom? Why, Broom is hardly—"

"I can only assume he was put there for one of two reasons: either to keep me in, or to keep everyone else out. And since he is a fairly large brute, and wears a proportionately large pistol tucked in his belt, I am inclined to believe it is the former."

"We are not holding you prisoner in this room, Emory. You are free to come and go as you please."

He searched Florence's face for the truth, then the dark eyes flicked in Anna's direction. Obviously not as skilled at concealing her reactions as her aunt, she could feel the heat flooding up her neck again, but it was too late to look away. He had laid his trap well, for she could not have broken his hold if she had wanted to. Moreover she was left with the distinct sensation that he had climbed right inside her thoughts and had a thorough look around before he finally relented and turned back to her aunt.

"Fair enough," he murmured. "If I am free to come and go as I please, you'll have no objections if I borrow a horse and ride over to Windsea? Maybe if I see my old home it will jog some memories clear. For that matter, a ride into Brixham, or Paignton, or Torquay might accomplish the same thing. If, as you say, I spent a great deal of time on the docks and in the harbor, someone there might know what happened to me three days ago. I could post a notice, or offer a reward for information."

The side of Florence's mouth curled down the same measure of distance that her eyebrow inched upward. "All things considered," she said on a sigh, "I doubt that would be your wisest course, Rory dear. I should not think you could offer as high a reward as the King's Bench has posted for information concerning your whereabouts."

He studied her without moving for several long moments, then slowly folded his arms over his chest and leaned back against the window casement. "Have I committed some crime?"

"You have been accused of committing one," Florence conceded. "There has been no proof offered, however, and quite frankly, without absolute proof I cannot bring myself to believe any of the charges laid against you."

"*Any* of the charges?" he asked softly. "Implying there is more than one?"

Florence waved a hand with some impatience, sending one of her gold rings flying off her finger. "All unfounded, so far as your brother has been able to determine. On sheer rumor and speculation alone they are claiming you conspired to help the enemy, committed treason, even that it was your ship that assisted Napoleon Bonaparte in escaping his prison on Elba."

Emory had started to lean over to retrieve the ring, but at the mention of Bonaparte's name, he froze. His hands rose to his temples and his fingers squeezed until the veins in his arms stood out like thin blue ropes.

He lowered the spluttering length of fuse to the touch hole and watched the small puff of powder explode against the charge. A split second later the huge cannon reared back in its carriage, the breeching tackle straining against the force of the shot as it was expelled in a huge cloud of white, acrid smoke. He had covered his ears, as had every other man in the gun crew, but the concussion rocked the deck under his feet and shook every bone in his body, and after more than a dozen such horrendous impacts, he could feel blood beginning to trickle down the sides of his neck. Already the men were loosening the tackle lines, reeling the heavy gun back on board. At his shout of encouragement, one man was there waiting to swab the smoking barrel, another to load fresh powder and packing, a third to ram the charge in place while a fourth lifted a thirty-two-pound ball of lead into the muzzle. It was a dance they had done many times before, practicing and drilling with precision until they could fire two deadly rounds per minute.

"What is it, Emory?" Florence's anxious voice cut through the smoke and haze. "What is wrong?"

He opened his eyes. He was on his knees and Annaleah was beside him, her arm stretched out across the front of his shoulders to prevent him from pitching forward onto the floor. Her face was only inches from his, and without thinking he reached out and took it in his hands, staring at it, focusing on her eyes, the soft bow of her mouth.

"Emory?"

He heard Florence's voice, but he dared not take his eyes off Anna's face, dared not lose his only link with reality.

"Guns," he rasped. "I saw heavy guns. Cannon. We were on board a ship, we were firing full broadsides over and over. My hands"—he briefly eased his grip on Anna in order to verify the thick calluses on his palms—"they were scalded. Burned from the heat of the barrel. There were men screaming and shouting all around me, but I couldn't see through the smoke, it was too thick. Something was on fire . . . something behind me. We had been struck. A shot had hit some powder cartridges and exploded."

He stopped and swallowed hard, choking back the words that would have described the bloody horror of seeing a man crushed to death on the deck beside him. That was why he had been manning the gun: because one of his crew had fallen. One of *his* crew. On *his* ship. He had stepped in, as he done before, to take the place of a man wounded or killed. And Seamus had been right beside him. . . .

"Seamus?"

Startled, Emory looked into Anna's clear blue eyes. "What?"

"You said the name . . . Seamus."

The burning scent of gunpowder grew less pungent, the acrid white clouds of smoke blew away, and the screams faded until they were only a distant echo. He turned his head to try to catch the image before it dissolved completely, but he was too late. The brilliant light was gone, leaving only a strident throb behind his eyes.

"What the devil is happening?" he whispered.

"I suspect it was something I said," Florence offered. "It must have triggered a memory."

"You said . . . I helped Bonaparte escape?" He braced himself, expecting another violent rush of images, but nothing happened.

"You recognize his name?"

"Bonaparte is . . . *was* the emperor of France," he muttered. "The Duke of Wellington fought him at Waterloo. And won."

"How positively extraordinary," Florence mused. "You can remember that, yet you do not remember your own name."

Emory seemed to become aware that he was still holding fast to Anna, still cradling her face between his hands. He eased his grip, not really wanting to let go, but he could see that he had frightened her. Hell, he had frightened himself.

"I am sorry, I . . ." He faltered in his effort at an apology, and once again it was her eyes that saved him. They drew him in, held him, calmed him like a cool hand on a fevered brow, and for one wildly irrational moment, he wanted just to drag her forward, wrap his arms around her, and hold her until neither one of them ever had to fear anything again.

"Let me help you up," she murmured.

Feeling as weak and foolish as a child, he was grateful for her support as she assisted him. Only when she was certain he could stand on his own did she ease her arms away and put a few discreet steps between them.

For Annaleah, a few hundred steps would not have been enough. The heat of Emory Althorpe's body, the scent of his skin, even the faint tang of cider that clung to his breath had affected her senses, had tightened the skin everywhere on her body and made her feel, for a few seconds at least, that she had been as helpless on her knees as he had been. Even worse, he had not been the one able to read thoughts this time. She had read his enough to know he was floundering. He was lost, confused. He was like a drowning man reaching for a lifeline. . . .

Chapter 7

*I*T WAS FOOLISH. Completely and unconscionably foolish to be standing there flushing like a schoolgirl over a man she did not know, and should probably not want to risk knowing. But the awful truth was that Anna could still feel the imprint of his hands where they had cradled her face. She had not wanted him to go. Her skin was glowing, her knees were wobbling enough to make the folds of her dress tremble, and she was grateful for her aunt's presence; she was not certain what might have happened had Florence not been there to carry on the conversation.

"Do you think you are strong enough to venture down the stairs to the parlor?" she was asking.

"If I had boots and a horse," Althorpe answered quietly, "I would ride away from Widdicombe House and spare you any further trouble."

"In your present condition, I doubt you would get more than a mile. As for sparing us trouble, we will hear no more of it. This is the safest place to keep you, for the time being. Now then, Anna dear, if your feet have not grown roots into the floor, you may offer me your arm and escort me as far as my bedchamber. I should like to lie down for an hour or so."

"Are you not feeling well?"

"My dear child, I am seventy-seven years old. I no longer enjoy the luxury of a full night's uninterrupted sleep. I must snatch it in what increments I may, lest I fall into my cabbage at suppertime. While I am resting, however, perhaps you can use the time to reacquaint Rory with the house and grounds."

Anna curled her lower lip between her teeth and avoided

glancing at Althorpe. "If you think it would help, of course I should be happy to do so."

"We do not know what will help, do we? But staying in this wretched little room all day can only hurt. I will speak to Willerkins about moving you again. Somewhere you might feel less confined. I believe there is a larger room across from Annaleah that might be more to your liking. No bats, I promise you. Well, not recently anyway."

Florence's bedchamber was located directly at the top of the main staircase, and after descending the narrow passage from the attic rooms, they followed the wide central hallway until they arrived at her door. There, where Anna would have accompanied her inside to see her settled, she shooed the pair of them away with a sleepy yawn.

Emory had said nothing along the way, and he said nothing now as they descended the wide central staircase to the second floor. Enormous life-size portraits of ancestors were hung in gilt frames on the walls, and Anna imagined their shocked eyes following her, their glowering silence attesting to the impropriety of her keeping company with a known brigand.

"I presume you have no burning need to see the kitchens or the pantry or the great dining hall, do you?"

"Not if you feel I can survive in ignorance."

She faltered a bit at his gentle mockery, but saw no point in challenging it or in taking him to the lower floor, where most of the rooms, with the exception of the utility areas, had been boarded up for the past half century or more.

"You might remember the library," she said, putting on her best touring voice as she led the way toward a large set of double oak doors. "Auntie said you used to spend a great deal of time here."

She swung the doors open and stood to one side to let Althorpe pass through. The windows and the heavy velvet draperies were closed against air and sunlight. The twenty-foot-high walls were lined floor to ceiling with shelves, the shelves filled with row upon row of leather-bound volumes that added their own peculiar musk to the gloomy room. There were chairs and settees placed in ghostly groupings, and against one wall an enormous fireplace, stacked with wood that had gone unlit for so long there were cobwebs linking the iron arms of the grate. Set in front of one windowed alcove was a desk and chair, before the other a scrolled brass music stand.

Althorpe walked to the middle of the room and made one complete, slow turn before meeting Anna's eyes. She did not have to ask. He recognized nothing.

He was about to rejoin her by the doorway when he apparently glimpsed something that caught his attention. He veered over to Anna's left and, when she edged farther inside to see what he was looking at, she could once again feel her heart slowing to a dull thud in her chest.

It was a gun case. Glass-fronted and crisscrossed with a diamond pattern of leaded panes, it contained several long-snouted muskets and a shelf displaying half a dozen assorted pistols nestled in pockets of green baize. The cabinet boasted a stout lock cut in the design of two rearing griffons, but its purpose was rendered moot by the present of a key jutting from the mouth of one of the beasts.

Annaleah said nothing as Emory turned the key and opened the door. She stared, not knowing quite what to think, when he reached inside and picked up one of the flintlock pistols, testing its weight and balance in his palm, checking the condition of the firing mechanism. He did not miss a step breaking open the large S-shaped cock to see if there was flint inside, or in sliding open the frizzen to see if there was powder in the pan. An agile thumb pulled the hammer into half-cock, then full-cock position while the finger he curled around the trigger squeezed to release the mainspring.

Anna jumped when she heard the distinct click of the striker hitting the pan. Her father and brother were avid hunters and she was familiar enough with weaponry of many kinds to know how to load and prime a full charge. She was definitely *not* comfortable with Emory Althorpe's obvious expertise, nor with the glance he cast over his shoulder when he heard her gasp.

"They are not loaded," he assured her. "In excellent working order, however, and exceptionally well-kept compared with the rest of the contents of these shelves." He raised the gun to his nose and took a delicate sniff. "Cleaned regularly, I would guess."

"Willerkins," she said, clearing her throat to remove her heart. "He is a fine shot. An expert huntsman."

Though she could not be absolutely certain, she thought she saw a wry twinkle in his dark eyes as he carefully returned the gun to its compartment. He closed the door again and turned the key in the lock, removing it after a moment's hesitation and presenting it to Annaleah when he joined her at the doorway.

"Careless habit, leaving keys in locks."

He bowed casually to indicate she was free to continue the tour, and when he straightened, his eyes held hers for a long, dragging moment.

"You have remembered something else, have you not?"

"Not really," he said with a dismissive shrug. "It is more like small flickers of lightning that cut through the darkness for a split second . . . 'and doth cease to be ere one can say it lightens.' "

Her eyebrow quirked upward. "You can quote Shakespeare?"

"Can I?"

"*Romeo and Juliet*. I have read it a hundred times."

"A hundred times?" He smiled. "You enjoy reading about doomed lovers?"

"They were victims of cruel circumstance," she whispered, conscious of her belly starting to make the slow downward slide into the region of her feet. He was standing close—too close, really. And almost touching her. If there had been a wall behind her, she would have gladly leaned on it to prevent the rest of her body from melting into a hapless puddle at his feet.

If he was aware of her discomfort, he did nothing to alleviate it. His gaze, in fact, drifted down to her mouth, which she was in the process of moistening. Seeing where his attention was focused, her tongue froze halfway across her bottom lip, then curled slowly inward, leaving a moist shine behind.

He looked up into her eyes again and tipped his head slightly to one side as if he was contemplating exactly what her reaction would be if he drew her into his arms there and then and kissed her.

"Sh-shall we try another room?" she stammered.

He bowed again, obligingly, and moved slightly to allow her room to pass through the doorway. She felt like running, but she managed a regal enough walk to the next set of double oak doors, which opened into a huge drawing room.

The interior was similarly steeped in gloom and neglect. It had never, in all of Anna's memory, been opened to guests or used for entertaining, and the furniture, though dusted and polished on an irregular basis, was in the same general condition as she imagined it had been in her great-grandfather's time. There were no guns, no lazy streamers of sunlight stirring the dust motes to offer distractions, and Althorpe dismissed the antiquated elegance with another nonchalant shrug.

The only remaining room of any consequence on this floor was the conservatory, another sadly moldering chamber that, as a child, Anna had thought to be the most beautiful, awe-inspiring place in all the world. One entire wall was a glittering array of stained glass. Row upon row of tall colored windows reached up to a gilded ceiling painted with cupids and fairies and beautiful women with long flowing hair. The floor was marble, and with the noon light pouring through the squares of red, blue, green, and yellow glass, it created a kaleidoscope pattern on the stone, on the sheer white muslin of Anna's dress, on the front of Emory's shirt.

Tall french doors led out onto a wide terrace that over-looked the slope leading down to the cliffs. Althorpe opened them and walked outside, but Annaleah did not immediately follow; she stood in the doorway and just watched his reactions.

As always, the pounding of the surf was a low rumble of thunder in the background. The breeze, blowing in off the ocean, carried a faint tang of salt and wet sand and brought the sound of gulls crying in the distance. An ornate stone balustrade fronted the terrace, with open stairs at either end leading down to paths and little gardens, but here too, everything was choked with ivy and weeds that had gone wild.

Althorpe went to edge of the terrace and braced his hands on the stone rail. "It is a shame this place has gone to ruin. It must have been quite magnificent at one time."

Seeing he was not in any haste to return to the musty smell of the interior rooms, Anna stepped outside. "If it is any consolation to you, sir, I do not remember Widdicombe House looking any other way. It was always big and empty and unused, and as a child, I was convinced there were ghosts waiting around every corner. My brother, in fact, used to hide in my bedroom and wait until I was almost asleep, then he would rustle the curtains and make dreadful, low moaning sounds."

"He sounds like an amiable fellow."

"I did think of giving him poison a time or two over the years," she confessed.

Althorpe turned his head slightly and offered a half smile.

Even that much charity was unsettling, and Anna felt the goose bumps rise along her arms. His profile reminded her of a statue of a Roman centurion, powerful and clean. Wisps of his hair were slowly working their way free of the ribbon. Strands of it curled against his nape, the ends black as paint strokes over the collar of his shirt, and she had a sudden, preposterous urge to free the rest of it and run her fingers through the inky waves to discover if it was as soft as it looked.

Giving herself a little inward shake, she turned to gaze out across the sea. The sun was nearly straight overhead, a colorless ball in a bleached sky, the distant horizon distorted by a gray haze.

"There's a storm coming our way," he predicted. "We will have heavy rain before the day is through."

Anna scanned the horizon and saw not a single cloud anywhere. She turned to say as much, but the words died in her throat. He was looking at her. Not just looking, but *looking*, as if he had not had the chance to do so before. His eyes traveled slowly along her hairline, touching on her cheek, her mouth, her chin, eventually following the spiral of a dark curl where it trailed over her shoulder and lay against the gentle swell of her breast. The end of the curl held his attention for the length of two stilted breaths, then he was looking into her eyes again, an intimacy more shocking than any mere pressing of flesh against flesh could have been.

"How badly do I frighten you, Miss Fairchilde?"

"You do not frighten me at all," she said on a whisper. "Well, perhaps a little. Should I not *be* frightened of you?"

"That would depend," he said, widening his smile, "on how loudly you can scream, and how safe you would feel walking with me to the cliffs."

"The cliffs?"

"Yes. I would like to see exactly where you found me, if it would not be too great an imposition on your time."

Annaleah glanced hesitantly over her shoulder at the open doors to the conservatory. His allusion to how loudly she could scream was another mockery, for she doubted a volley of gunshots would carry up from the beach. Once again he was putting her in the awkward position of having to bend the accepted rules of conduct, for an unchaperoned, unmarried woman simply did not traipse off somewhere with a man.

On the other hand, it was ludicrous to keep applying rules of behavior to the situation with Emory Althorpe. He was a man without memory, a man struggling to regain his identity, and she knew she should be doing what she could to help him instead of worrying what a few singularly peculiar servants might think if they saw her out walking along the cliffs without a maid and a parasol.

"We can go this way," she said, pointing to one of the wide staircases.

Emory fell easily into step beside her, adjusting his long strides to her smaller, more compact ones. They walked in sunlight and silence across the lawns and along the worn path Anna had taken on her early morning excursions to the shore. She had not ventured down to the cove since the morning she had found Althorpe lying in the sand, nor was she particularly eager, when they reached the end of the path and stood looking out over the escarpment, to do so now.

"There," she said, indicating the cluster of rocks near the midpoint of the shingled crescent. "That was where I found you. The other side of those large boulders."

He nodded. "Wait here. I will only be a few minutes."

"There was nothing else washed ashore with you," she assured him. "Broom went back and made a very thorough search of the entire cove."

"It is not so much a case of what I want to *see*," he tried to explain. "More what I hope to *feel*."

Anna watched him start down the steep path. After a moment she lifted her hands away from her thighs in a gesture of frustration and followed, wondering if there were varying heights of foolishness to which one could aspire and reflecting that if so, she must surely be nearing the zenith.

When Althorpe reached the bottom, he set off immediately toward the rocks, noting as he passed the scallops of dried seaweed that marked the high tide. Anna trudged across the gritty sand behind him, resenting his stubbornness almost as much as the midday heat. She had not worn a bonnet, of course; no gloves, no shawl, nothing to protect her skin from the harsh effects of the sun save for a skimpy lace fichu worn around the shoulders and tucked into the front of her bodice. There were scant patches of shade along the base of the cliffs where overlapping seams of limestone jutted out, and, after five minutes of watching Althorpe search for goodness only knew what along the edge of the water, she retreated there to wait him out.

He walked back and forth at least half a dozen times. He went down on his knee at one point and turned over several smaller rocks and pebbles; he poked the toe of his shoe into the thicker grains of shingled stone, but found nothing. Three days and nights of active tides would undoubtedly have removed anything Broom might have missed, yet it did not stop Althorpe from climbing onto the top of the largest boulder and balancing precariously on the slime and seaweed. With both hands raised to shield his eyes from the glare of the sun, he searched the shallow depths. Anna was on the verge of losing her patience and was about to start the long climb back without him when she saw him drop his hands suddenly and in two nimble leaps splash into the water and wade knee-deep into the foaming surf.

The waves were stronger than they had been the day she had found him, and he had to wait until a swell passed before he was able to bend over and pluck something off the bottom. He stood, letting the water swirl around his legs while he turned something over and over in the palm of his hand.

Curiosity brought Anna out of the shade to stand at the water's edge again. "Have you found something?"

He did not answer right away. He turned and started walking back to shore, but halfway there, a spasm brought him doubling over and cause his eyes to screw tightly shut against a searing hot flash of pain.

The street was narrow and dark, the gutters overflowing from a recent rain that had done little more than bring a million worms rising out of the cracks in the cobbles. The air smelled slimy with them. Each footstep crushed the elongated bodies to mush.

Emory stood in the shadows, his torn and bleeding back pressed against the damp bricks. He waited there a moment, listening for the scrape of a heel on stone, the snap of a hammer being cocked, ready to fire. He could not hear anything, but that did not mean he was in the clear. The fact he had escaped at all was a miracle, that he had made it this far a triumph of strength and sheer willpower. But his vision was beginning to blur and the world was starting to skew at a sickening angle that would make it feel as though these last hundred yards were all uphill.

He could not afford to wait any longer. Seamus was either there, or he was not. He had either waited or he had decided Emory was dead and it was better to take the ship out of port and save the rest of the crew.

He drew a deep breath into his lungs, wondering if it would be his last. He doubted he could outrun a bullet and he was vaguely curious about how it would feel tearing into his back, ripping through his heart, bursting out his chest. At least there would be an end to the pain. It would be over.

With a final, desperate heave, Emory pushed himself away from the rough stone wall and ran. He ran like a thousand-year-old man, bent in half, his feet dragging as if they hauled iron balls behind them. He saw the expected flash of powder in the shadows to his left and a fraction of a second later heard the sharp report of a pistol. The shot whistled past his ear and likely would have gone in it had he not stumbled and gone down hard on the cobble-stones. The air burst out of his lungs on a sob and he saw a shadow detach itself from the side of a building and start to walk toward him. He passed briefly under the gaslight and Emory saw his face, long and pointed like that of a bloodhound. It was Le Couteau, and he was grinning. It was a sick, evil grin, and Emory was determined it would not be the last thing imprinted on his mind before he died.

With a groan of pure agony, he rolled to the side of the wharf. An instant before he fell over the side and splashed into the greater agony of the saltwater, he caught a glimpse of something bright and shiny that had been clutched in his hand. Now it would die with him, the key to everything, to all the secrets, the truths, the lies. . . .

"Mr. Althorpe! Mr. Althorpe! Emory . . . *please*—!"

Emory forced his eyes to open. Someone was calling his name. . . .

"Emory!"

He looked up and saw Annaleah. Her eyes were impossibly wide, impossibly blue, and her hands were clasped into small white fists, pressed over a mouth that was crumpled with concern.

"Emory?" she cried softly, lowering her hands. "Are you all right?"

He blinked and swallowed hard several times in an attempt to fight back the wave of nausea rising in his throat. The pain in his head, the cramps in his belly began to subside and he was able to slowly straighten. "Yes," he gasped. "Yes . . . I think so."

His voice sounded like a dry croak, and he waited until he was fairly confident his legs would not give out beneath him before he splashed forward the remaining few steps to shore. Anna reached out and took hold of his arm, then guided him over to a seat on a nearby rock.

Finding nothing else to use in its stead, she untucked her fichu and dipped it into the surf. She twisted most of the water free, and then used the moistened lace to bathe away the sweat that glistened across Emory's brow and temples. Before she could finish, his hand closed gratefully around hers.

"There was no warning," he said haltingly. "It just . . . happened."

"Another one of your lightning flashes?"

"More than a flash. It was a bloody great bolt." He leaned forward without thinking, without conscious intent, and pressed his forehead into the soft juncture between her breasts. Anna stood breathlessly still for a moment, her hands hovering just above his head, the dampened ball of lace dropping forgotten into the sand.

Slowly, so very slowly she could scarcely believe she was doing it, she rested one hand in his hair, then the other, cradling him against her while she stroked the gleaming black waves with her fingertips.

"W-were you on the ship again?"

"No. No, I . . . I was near a wharf. It was dark but I could hear the water, and there were ships nearby riding at anchor."

"Was it here, in Torbay, do you think?"

"No." He was very firm in this as he tipped his head up. "It was a French port. I could tell by the smell."

Anna's hands were still in his hair, though they had stopped moving. Emory's hands had somehow found their way around her waist, and although he was barely touching her, she could feel the heat through the scant layers of muslin and silk she wore. As much as her fingers had moved of their own accord, his did the same now, molding gently to the curves, daring even to inch upward so that his thumbs rested just below the ribbon separating the bodice from the Empire skirt.

"H-how can you be sure it was a F-French port?"

"I don't know. The same way I knew Napoleon was emperor. It was just . . . familiar somehow." He frowned and focused on her mouth. "Like I had been there many times before. And I was trying to get back there again."

"Trying . . . why?"

He started to shake his head again, but then he remembered something else and lifted his hand away from her waist. In his palm were the pooled links of a gold chain. When he held it up, it glittered like liquid sunlight, a stark contrast to the plain iron key that dangled at the bottom of the loop.

He straightened and frowned as he turned it over in his

palm and Anna, not knowing what to do with her own hands, carefully lowered them and clasped them together behind her back.

"Do you recognize it?"

"I recognize what it is," he said. "A key to a strongbox. The kind you find in the captain's quarters on most ships."

"Is it yours?"

He shook his head. "I don't know. I saw the flash of gold through the water and—" He paused to draw another calming breath. "I don't know. It could be. Or it could have been there a couple of months, years. . . ."

Anna pointed out the faint orange stain it left on his skin. "I set a hairpin on the windowsill one night, and in the morning, it had turned completely red and was stuck fast to the wood. I suspect, had this key been in the sea much longer than a few days, there would be rather more rust on the iron than you see here. What is more, young Blisterbottom comes almost daily to dig for clams and mussels. He would have found it long before now."

Althorpe nodded, if a little reluctantly. "The last thing I saw before I fell into the water was a key. This could be it."

"You fell into the water?"

"I rolled myself off the edge of the wharf," he said. "Deliberately. I was trying to get away from someone. From whoever had been cutting on my back . . ."

He looked up again, suddenly.

"I saw the marks," she said, answering the unasked question in his eyes. "Willerkins said he thought the wounds had been deliberate. That someone had made them with the purpose of causing you great pain."

He had neither answer nor explanation. His frustration was echoed in the soft oath that came through his lips as he squinted up at the sky. His eyes, catching the direct rays of sunlight, changed from an almost soulless black to a rich amber-lit brown, and Anna wished she had the nerve to reach out and take him in her hands again. To draw him against her breast and comfort him until, in the same way his eyes just had, the pain on his face changed to something else.

"If I ask you something, will you oblige me with an honest answer?"

She refocused her attention and moistened her lips. "If I can, yes."

"Do you believe I am guilty of the charges laid against me?"

"My aunt, clearly, does not."

"That was not what I asked."

"I do not know you well enough to form an opinion of what you are and are not capable of doing, sir," she said truthfully. "Up until these last few days, I did not even know my aunt well enough to say whether her judgment was creditable or not. I always thought . . ." She stopped, not wanting to betray too many confidences, but he looked at her again, his eyebrow raised in gentle amusement, and she continued with a faint smile. "I had always been led to believe she was a little addled."

"And now?"

"Now . . . I think she is eccentric, certainly, and definitely set in her ways. I also believe she takes great pleasure in letting the rest of world *think* she is addled, though she is far from it. She is strong-willed, stubborn, tenacious. If it does not suit her purpose to do or say what other people think she should do or say, then she simply does not do it."

"You sound as if you envy her."

"I envy her courage. And her freedom. And the fact she has no one to answer to but herself. That makes a great deal of difference."

He bent over and retrieved the scrap of lace off the sand. "Everyone has that choice, Miss Fairchilde. They can please themselves or they can try to please everyone else."

"It is a choice that is much easier for a man to make, sir, than a woman."

"You just said your aunt was able to do so."

"My aunt was able to do many things because she was very wealthy and did not have to rely on anyone else's good grace to support her or keep her. Nor did she feel any oppressing need to heed the opinions of others in order to form her own. Moreover, I am coming to believe she is a very astute judge of character."

This last was said softly enough to bring a surprisingly unguarded smile to Althorpe's lips. It held long enough to play havoc with the texture of the skin across her breasts and for a not so subtle flush of hot color to flood into her face.

"We should go back," she said, retrieving her fichu from him.

He did not release it fast enough—or at least, his hand came with the lace and somehow ended up holding her arm, then her shoulder.

Once again, she had nowhere to look but up into his eyes.

"Perhaps it would be safer if you were the keeper of both keys," he murmured, slipping the gold chain over her head. She could feel the cool weight of the key sliding down between her breasts and the warmer presence of his long fingers carefully lifting her hair to ease the curls free of the links. He seemed rather more meticulous than the circumstances warranted—a suspicion that was confirmed when his thumb brushed along the curve of her chin and in the process forced her head to tilt higher.

Anna held her breath. His mouth was slightly pursed in contemplation and he wore much the same look as he had in the library when she thought he was going to kiss her. The desire to do so, the longing to do so was as plainly etched on his face as it was in the subtle shifting of his frame forward.

Exactly what stopped him, she did not know. He was there, bending toward her one moment, stiffening and moving awkwardly away the next. It was certainly nothing she did or said, for she had felt herself bracing for the touch of his lips, her entire body trembling in anticipation. But something made him pull back at the very last heartbeat and when she opened her eyes, he was bending over and taking off his shoes, tipping them one at a time to empty them of seawater.

He had the grace to pretend not to notice the flush darken her cheeks. He also made very sure he shook every minute droplet free before he put each shoe back on again, and by the time he had done so, Anna was halfway back toward the base of the escarpment. He let her run well ahead before he followed and made no effort to close the gap between them.

At the top, she paused to catch her breath and the wind caught her hair, sweeping it over her face, blinding her briefly behind a dark silky cloud. Her emotions were still raw and singing when she heard the soft crunch of Emory's footsteps coming up behind her, but she was distracted from whatever he might have offered in the way of an inept apology by something in the distance.

Where a gap in the trees allowed a view of the curving drive in front of the house, an elegant, gleaming black berline was just rolling to a stop. A smartly liveried postillion jumped down from the back of the carriage to open the door and drop the stair and a moment later, Winston Perry, marquess of Barrimore, stepped out into the sunlight.

Chapter 8

" SWEET MERCIFUL HEAVEN!" She gasped and turned quickly away. "I completely forgot. He sent his card this morning to inform me he would be calling just past noon."

Emory looked toward the house and saw the tall figure of a man dressed all in black beside the coach. The pale blot of an aristocratic face was angled in their direction; he must have seen the splash of Anna's white muslin gown outlined against the sky.

"Is he a friend of yours?"

"His name is Barrimore. Lord Barrimore. He has come to Brixham with my brother to take me home. At least . . . it was their intention to take me home, but I refused to go. Now they have taken rooms in Torquay and . . . and . . ." She stole a quick peek over her shoulder. "Oh dear God, he has seen us. He is coming this way. What *must* I do to convince him I do not want any part of his marriage proposal! That is why he has come, I know it is."

"Proposal? But I thought you said you were already betrothed?"

Anna looked up and vented an exasperated sigh. "My mother assumes we are as good as betrothed, as does my father, my brother, my sister. . . . I have no doubt his lordship presumes it as well, though I have given him absolutely no encouragement whatsoever. I have, in all truth, been the closest thing possible to downright rude whenever I am in his presence and simply cannot understand why he would even *want* to marry someone so horribly disagreeable."

The corner of Althorpe's mouth twitched at this first

explosion of fire in her eyes. He had begun to suspect it was there all along, but up to now she had been remarkably adept at holding it in reserve. It was to his own credit that he managed to keep a straight face. "I confess I cannot see much of him at this distance, but he looks a stalwart enough fellow. Rich, to be sure. A confident stride. I am no expert on the subject—at least I do not think I am—but he does not appear to be the type of man who would be irreparably crushed if you simply said no."

Barrimore was three hundred yards away and temporarily hidden by a copse of trees as Anna glared at Althorpe in amazement. "*Simply say no?* To a man my mother has groomed for the altar these past six months or more? To a man who is a friend and confidant of the Prince Regent and goodness knows who else in government, and who will eventually be one of the most powerful and influential dukes in England? Why, I could no sooner 'simply say no' to the Marquess of Barrimore than you could simply say 'yes, by all means old chap' to someone wanting to turn you over to the magistrate's office."

As soon as the words were out of her mouth she could have bitten her tongue off at the root for the smile they put on Althorpe's face, but there was no way to retract them. There was nowhere to hide, either. They were standing on the edge of a cliff, for pity's sake, with nothing but endless sea and boundless sky surrounding them. She was with a man who had no memory, no constraints on his conscience, no reason to question his own ill-conceived belief that everyone had a choice whether to please themselves or to please others.

"Perhaps," he murmured, "I should, ah, retreat back to the beach and leave the two of you alone."

"No!" she cried. Then in a calmer, more determined voice she added, "No, he has already seen you and it would look twice as suspicious if you were to suddenly just vanish over the cliff."

At the word "suspicious" she had another terrible thought.

Barrimore was still on the other side of the trees, but once the path rounded onto the grass, he would have an unobstructed view. And if he came close enough to distinguish Althorpe's features, might he not remember the sketch on the warrant Colonel Ramsey had been waving about the previous afternoon?

"Dear sweet God," she muttered. "For both our sakes, sir, I . . . I think you should kiss me."

The dark eyes widened. "I beg your pardon?"

"Will you please kiss me! And will you please do so with all good haste before he realizes that *we* have seen *him*."

Emory opened his mouth to question her intentions. Then closed it. The wind was whipping her hair again and she had dispatched a hand to gather it against her nape; her eyes were so intense, so determined, that he gave a little shrug and bowed forward, obliging her with a brief, clingy meeting of the lips.

In and of itself, the contact was not particularly shocking. She had been kissed by prim-lipped suitors before, and while she was by no means an expert, her first reaction was disappointment for she had certainly not expected such a chaste, timid peck. Her second was to glance surreptitiously along the path. Barrimore had emerged from the trees. It seemed as though his pace had slowed—as if he had seen something, but not quite well enough to give it credence. And he was still coming their way.

In a blaze of frustration, augmented by the sheer unparalleled audacity of what she was doing, she twisted her hands into the loose folds of Emory's shirt. "Was that your best effort, sir?"

"My best . . . ? Miss Fairchilde, I do not know what your game is but—"

"I assure you this is not a game, sir. Putting aside for the moment the fact that he was shown a perfectly handsome sketch of you yesterday, would *you* continue to press suit upon a woman you found in the arms of another man?"

"A sketch?"

"On the warrant Colonel Ramsey showed my aunt. Now will you please kiss me—if not for my sake, then for your own? And do so as if you mean it this time! Surely the loss of your memory should not have resulted in the loss of *all* your abilities."

Again, she could have bitten off her tongue and swallowed the offending pieces, but whether it was because of the threat of recognition or the challenge to his vanity, his eyes darkened to the color of chocolate and his arms slid around her waist.

"My best effort, then," he mused, pulling her forward against his body. "As you command."

When he bent his head again, Anna was just expecting more of the same. Perhaps a little more firmness, more authority. More care to hold his arms the proper way to give the whole of it the appearance of unbridled passion. She did not expect his arms to crush her close enough to almost lift her off the ground, nor did she anticipate that his mouth would come down upon her as heatedly as one of his flashes of lightning.

Startled, she made a soft, stifled sound in her throat. The heat and pressure increased and the next thing she knew, he was inside her mouth. His lips had worked hers apart and his tongue had intruded past the barrier of her teeth and, after smothering her initial gasp of surprise, he was beginning to explore her mouth in earnest. Instinctively she tried to pull away, but one of his hands raked into the dark tangle of her hair and held her fast. She tried to refuse the intimacy, to turn back his every prowling, provocative stroke, but he paid no heed to her protests. He only held her tighter, plunging and lashing and venturing deeper with each thrust until her cries turned to whimpers and her shock was swept away in waves of disbelieving pleasure.

A loud drumming filled her ears, drowning out the sound of the surf. Her hands were still curled in the folds of his shirt, and she used them to pull herself closer. Inch by inch they crept upward, her fingers spreading over muscles tempered to the strength of steel, over sinews that tightened and rippled with each movement he made. Every drop of resistance drained out of her body, leaving her limp and completely at his mercy. All her senses were focused on the lush heat of his lips, the brazen seduction of his tongue. Her legs were useless, quivering from the tops of her thighs to where her toes curled within her shoes. Her skin was tight, tingling with shivers and tremors that responded to every sleek, slippery pattern he made on the inside of her mouth. And when he would have begun to ease away, to withdraw and set her firmly back down on the ground, she drove her hands up into his hair, parted her lips wider, and thrust her tongue after his, demanding more, demanding everything he had to give her with all the raw innocence of newfound pleasure.

Dimly, she heard a groan that did not come from her own throat and realized it came from his. His breath was expelled in a gust against her cheek, and his body shifted, threatening to arouse even more of her ingenuous yearnings. He wrapped both arms around her, holding her impossibly closer than he had before, and his hands . . . his hands curved up and around her rib cage, his fingers caressing the sides of her breasts. This time when she gasped, it was not to protest his boldness but to mark the rush of lightheadedness that told her she had to break free if only to catch hold of her breath and wits before they deserted her completely.

Stunned, shocked beyond comprehension, she tore her lips away from his. The dark eyes, clouded with a similar sense of confusion and incredulity, searched her face a moment. Unable to answer the questions she knew must be mirrored in her own eyes, she bowed her head, too shamed, too shaken to even push out of his embrace. His arms eased their grip but did not relinquish their hold completely. Nor did he seem behooved by any sense of propriety to do so.

With her brow touching his chin, and her body churning with all manner of unfamiliar sensations . . . Anna remembered Barrimore. She gasped and turned to check the path, but he was nowhere in sight. A further small twist and she could see the drive, the berline, and the haste with which the driver and liveried postillions were clambering into their seats. A moment later, the huge wheels spun into the crushed stone and the matched fours were galloping away under the urgent crack of the whip.

She closed her eyes and melted weakly against the heat of Althorpe's body. The deed was done and could not be undone, and for some reason, though she knew she should be falling away in a dead faint, she wanted instead to stay within the protective circle of Emory's arms.

Indeed, the only faintness she felt was inspired by the overwhelming need to feel his hands rake into her hair again, to feel him tilt her head up to meet his mouth once more in a devouring passion.

But of course, he did not do that, and by slow, reluctant inches she lowered her arms from around his neck and eased her body away from his.

"Your strategy appears to have worked," he murmured.

Anna touched her fingers to her lips. They were tender and more than slightly puffed. She felt raw and vulnerable, aching in places she did not know she could ache. And because she could not think of a single solitary thing she could say in response to the slow smile that was spreading across his face, she whirled around and started running back along the path, her hair snapping out in a dark wake behind her.

She ran until a stitch in her side forced her to slow down. Her heart was pounding relentlessly in her breast and while she attributed some of the weakness in her legs to the mad dash from the cliffs, she knew that was not the only reason for it.

Once again she heard the faint crush of footsteps approaching along the path, and she pushed away from the trees without daring to glance back. She could not have borne it if his smile had turned into a crooked grin. Or if his eyebrow was raised in mockery of her staunch declaration earlier that it was easier for a man to fly in the face of convention than a woman.

Fly? She had fairly launched herself off a cliff, and the cold reality of what she had done struck her like a sharp hand. She had shielded Althorpe, but at what cost to her own reputation? She had discouraged Barrimore's advance, but how would he react to the affront of watching his carefully selected fiancée throw herself into the arms of what could only have appeared to him to be a muscle-bound, ill-dressed common clod?

Annaleah returned to the house the same way she had exited, through the conservatory. Her shoes made hurried clipping sounds on the marble floor and she would have gone directly up the staircase and locked herself away in her bedroom for the rest of her natural life had she not been halted in the hallway by Willerkins's tall, officious presence.

"Ah. There you are, miss. Milady asks that you join her upon the instant."

"Tell my aunt . . . I will join her as soon as I am able."

She took a step to one side, intending to dart past the old butler, but Willerkins took a matching dance step and blocked her way.

"She did say, upon the *instant*, miss." He leaned slightly forward to rub a shin that often bore the brunt of his mistress's impatience. "Both she and her walking stick were quite adamant on the point."

Anna pushed the straggled and windblown locks of her hair off her face and followed Willerkins's outstretched hand toward the open doors of the day parlor. A mortifying thought nearly finished off what strength remained in her knees—had her aunt been standing at the window and had she witnessed the same scene that had sent Barrimore driving off in a spray of crushed gravel?

But no. The parlor faced south and east. Her aunt could not possibly have seen the cliffs from any of the windows. The driveway, yes. She might have seen that. She might have seen Barrimore's coach pull up, then drive off again without its passenger so much as paying his respects.

Wilting inwardly, she dutifully followed Willerkins to the parlor. Out of the corner of her eye, she saw movement farther along the hallway as Althorpe emerged from the conservatory and closed the doors behind him.

Florence was, to her dismay, indeed standing in front of the window. A fire was blazing in the hearth and spirit lamps flickered on the tables, but Anna's blood was burning far hotter when her aunt turned and raised a snowy eyebrow.

"Gracious, child, where have you been? There is a coach coming up the drive. We can expect a visitor at any moment."

"Dear Lord," Anna whispered, pressing her hand over her belly. "He has come back."

"Who has come back?"

"Lord Barrimore. The marquess. I . . . he . . . he must have been so enraged he turned his carriage around."

"Enraged? Have you said something to anger him?"

Anna waved her hand, but the words floundered in her throat, impeding her efforts to catch a deep enough breath to clear away the stars spinning in front of her eyes.

Althorpe came through the doorway just then, and the dark eyes barely touched on Anna before seeking out her aunt. "I'm afraid I am to blame for our tardiness. I asked Miss Fairchilde to show me the beach where she found me and, while it was a pleasant enough walk down to the shore, the wind picked up considerably on the way back. A storm is likely on its way."

"Yes, well, another kind of storm may well be approaching even as you stand there shedding sand on my floors again. It might be best for the pair of you if you tuck yourselves away until it passes. No, no, Willerkins has already gone to answer the door, it is too late to go out that way—you would be seen before you reached the stairs. Come. You can remove yourselves through here."

She pulled on an ornamental carving on a section of the wall and a wide panel swung silently open. "All of the rooms in the house connect one to the other with secret passages and niches," she explained rather blithely. "Quite clever, actually. I suspect there was an ancestor somewhere in our past who did not like surprises. Quickly now. And watch your step, it is very dark."

Having no choice but to obey, Anna allowed herself to be ushered through the opened panel and into a narrow, cramped passageway that appeared to run between the two rooms. Without light it was difficult to confirm, but she thought she could see an equally narrow flight of wooden stairs midway along the wall leading up to the third floor on the one side and down to the first floor on the other.

"I'll be damned," Althorpe murmured, squeezing his broad shoulders in behind Anna.

"Just be very quiet," Florence warned. "And when the time comes"—she reached past Emory's shoulder to point out a corresponding latch on the opposite wall that would open a secret door into the adjoining room—"go through there to the library."

Before either of them could object to being closed into the confining space, the panel swung shut, smothering them instantly in darkness. They heard the click of the latching mechanism, and for the next few seconds there was nothing but silence and absolute darkness.

Althorpe was beside her. Anna could not see him but she was all too aware of his big body close by. Gradually, as her eyes adjusted, she began to see little cracks and slivers of light where molding was attached to the walls or age had caused the wooden panels to shrink at the seams. Somewhere up above she heard a faint scuffling sound and it occurred to her that there were probably creatures, of the four-legged variety, that had been drawn to the seclusion of these narrow passages.

"I hate mice," Emory muttered, giving voice to her thoughts. "I would rather be locked in a hold with a nest of snakes."

Before Anna could answer, he was touching her arm, cautioning her to silence.

She heard them too. Voices. At least two of them, one distinctly female as Florence was greeted with a gush of delight.

"Dame Widdicombe! How positively wonderful to see you again. I was just saying to my dear husband . . ."

It was not Barrimore! He had not come back to confront her. He had not returned to challenge Emory Althorpe to a duel or to condemn her to social hell with his icy condescension.

The weakness in Anna's knees was complete, and when she felt Emory's hands on her shoulders, she simply sagged back against him, assuming he shared her sense of relief.

"Forgive me," he whispered. "There isn't much room to maneuver in here."

"Wh-what? What are you doing?"

"Trying to change places, but I seem to be stuck on something. . . ." After the distinct sound of a tear set him free, he shifted sideways again. "There we go. And there it is."

Anna was almost beyond registering any further surprise as he reached up to where a small pinhole of light was showing through the wood. A flick of his thumb dislodged a disk of wood, revealing what turned out to be a large peephole bored into the wall. He leaned forward and pressed his eye to the hole, then moved aside and guided her into place that she might also take a peek.

"Do you know them?" he asked, his mouth pressed against her ear.

Anna blinked at the cool draft that blew against her eye. She offered a small nod, then realized he could probably not see the gesture. She turned her head in order to whisper the information in as low a voice as he had used, but instead of finding his ear, she managed, quite to their mutual surprise, to find his mouth. The contact was brief and quickly broken, but it was made nonetheless, and the shock of it caused her to jerk back and bump her head hard against the edge of a beam.

Emory muffled her cry with his hand, his reaction as swift as it was instinctive. But instead of releasing her right away, he merely eased his hand to one side and rested his fingers against her throat, angling her head so that her lips were where she had originally intended them to go: next to his ear.

"It is your brother Stanley," she said in a strained whisper. "And his wife, Lucille."

He straightened and peered through the peephole again. After a moment, he dropped the little disk back into place and, cautioning her unnecessarily to silence, wormed his way behind her again and located the latch Florence had shown him. When the panel—which turned out to be a section of shelving—swung open, he took her hand and led her out of the passage into the library.

With the shelf pushed securely back into place behind them, he inspected her skirt, brushing dust and shreds of cobwebs off the folds of muslin. He had lost the ribbon from his hair back on the cliffs and the unkempt black waves hung loose and shaggy around his shoulders. Thanks to a protruding nail in the wall, there was now a considerable gash in the sleeve of his shirt; when combined with the salt-water stains on his breeches and the sodden condition of his shoes, it did not add up to the best impression he might have wanted to present to a brother he had not seen in several years.

Something else struck Anna as she watched him comb his fingers through the wild black locks of his hair.

"How did you know about the peephole in the wall?"

"What?"

"The hole in the wall—how did you know it was there?"

Althorpe frowned. "I don't know. I just . . . did," he said, and suddenly she thought she saw a small smile.

Anna relinquished her own frown less willingly as she

glanced at the door. "I suppose it would look odd if I did not join them. The vicar seemed quite adamant about not wanting his wife to know you were anywhere near Brixham, and if that is still the case, if she has only come with him by accident, you may have to remain out of sight until they are gone."

Althorpe nodded, somewhat reluctantly she thought, although she could appreciate his disappointment, for Stanley was not only his brother, but possibly the strongest bridge to his vanished memories.

"Wait here. If it is safe, I will come back and fetch you."

He nodded again, but before Anna took half a step, he reached out and caught her arm.

"I am sorry."

"For what?" she asked in a whisper.

Though there were undoubtedly a multitude of sins for which he could have sought penance, he merely offered up another crooked smile. "For having washed up on your beach."

Emory waited until the library door closed before he released his pent-up breath.

His gaze flicked over to the locked gun cabinet. He had given Annaleah the key earlier that morning and had watched her slip it into an inside pocket of her skirt. It had been a simple matter to retrieve it while brushing past her in the passageway, but why had he felt the need?

Did he have reason to doubt his own brother's loyalty? Did he have reason to fear his brother might have betrayed him to the authorities? A more nagging question concerned the Marquess of Barrimore. Who the devil was he and why had the hairs on the nape of Emory's neck stood on end when Annaleah identified him? Emory had not recognized him, had suffered no spontaneous flashes of memory, but that was not to say the marquess suffered from the same handicap. Annaleah assumed she had driven him off by throwing herself into the arms of another man, but what if

Barrimore had recognized him despite their most enthusiastic efforts and had ridden off posthaste to fetch the constables?

Granted, he had been a fair distance away and Barrimore would have no reason to suspect his fiancée of passionately kissing a fugitive from the law. He likely had no reason to suspect her of wanting to kiss anyone at all, passionately or otherwise, and would have been too unnerved to make the connection anyway.

Emory had been pretty unnerved himself. Then, and again just now when their lips had touched, he had felt the shock of it shoot clear through his body.

His frown stayed in place as he loaded and primed four of the five flintlock pistols, discarding the last as being too archaic not to blow up in the face of whoever shot it. He set the guns back in their baize pockets and left the cabinet unlocked, checking to be sure there was extra shot and powder within easy grasp.

These were, he realized with a newfound grimness, the actions of a guilty man. But was he a traitor? Had he committed crimes against his country, his King? And if so, how long would he be safe here at Widdicombe House before someone came searching in earnest?

Chapter 9

"WELL, OF COURSE you must believe that I am simply too, too appalled at the very notion of Stanley visiting a house where there might be an infestation of the plague. While I certainly support him in his efforts to save as many souls as possible before they venture on to a more heavenly plain, I do regard festering pocks and delirium to be a rather steep price to pay for benevolence."

"Lucille, my dearest, there is no plague in Brixham."

The petite blonde beauty glared at her husband. "I distinctly heard you say there was fever and a bloody flux."

"In the houses of two parishioners, yes, who may or may not have contracted some stomach ailment from eating rancid meat."

"May or may not?" She sighed and appealed to Florence. "You see why I insisted upon accompanying him on his rounds today? He simply cannot be trusted to place his own health—and mine—before that of his flock."

The reverend cast a sheepish glance in Florence's direction. "My sweet wife is determined to wear me down until I agree to allow her to visit London. Yesterday it was the rumor of a French army invading to rescue Napoleon that made this particular area of Britain unsafe. Today it is the flux."

"Well, it *is* unsafe," Lucille insisted. "The garrison is bristling with soldiers. The roads are positively clogged with thieves and cutthroats who are filling the villages in anticipation of the crowds the wretched man will draw. All this before there is even any confirmed announcement of his final destination. I am surprised, Miss Fairchilde," she added, turning to Annaleah, "you would voluntarily choose to remain here under the circumstances."

"London is ten times as crowded," Anna pointed out. "And there are always thieves and pickpockets in the streets."

"Yes, but you travel under the protection of your brother, Viscount Ormont, and the Marquess of Barrimore. The latter, especially, is reputed to be one of the most dangerous duelists with pistol or sword in all of England. I daresay a thief would have to be entirely witless to approach *you* with mischief in mind."

"Lucille made the acquaintance of both gentlemen yesterday," the vicar explained.

"Yes, and I could have sworn that was the marquess's berline we passed not five minutes ago on the road. I also had the pleasure of riding in it yesterday, you see."

To answer Annaleah's startled look, the vicar went on to further reveal, "The marquess, as it happens, stopped at the North Fort on a matter of government business, where my wife and several ladies of the Foundlings Society happened to be taking lunch."

"I recall you mentioning it." Florence nodded.

"Indeed." Lucille picked up the story. "We had been invited by the regimental commander, Colonel Huxley, to watch both the infantry and cavalry on parade. Your brother and the marquess arrived just as one of the ladies was inquiring if the soldiers might not fire one of the big cannons. The colonel declined—rather churlishly, I thought. He claimed his balls were not to be squandered on casual amusements."

"Having suffered Colonel Huxley's acquaintance for some thirty-odd years," Florence said dryly, "I can attest to the truth in that."

"As if *any* of us are amused by the notion of Napoleon Bonaparte invading our shores," Lucille added. "I have no doubt that was why the marquess took it upon himself to inspect the defenses himself. He is attached to the foreign office in some capacity, is he not?"

Annaleah managed a smile. "I believe he works closely with Lord Westford of the foreign office."

"Dispatching spies and such? How exciting. No wonder he seemed most anxious to speak with Colonel Ramsey, what with all the talk of—"

"He met with Colonel Ramsey again?"

"Indeed. They had a fairly long discussion, though what they said could not be overheard. But he is quite the dashing gentleman, I must say. And completely charming. When I commented that I had not seen such a handsome coach and four in too many years to recount, he insisted on my accompanying him on the ride back to Brixham. That was why I was sure I could not be mistaken when I saw his berline pass the vicarage this morning, and again, just now, on the road. How very disappointing to have missed him by so few minutes."

Truth be told, she sounded more than simply disappointed, and Anna could not help but associate her pretty pout with the pouts of innumerable other women who had worn their lowest-cut bodices and set their bonnets on a tilt for the marquess. More alarming, however, was the revelation that Barrimore had not gone directly to Torquay yesterday, but had followed Colonel Ramsey back to the garrison, and that they had engaged in a lengthy private discussion.

Florence, who like Lucille must have been wondering why the marquess had left in such a hurry, drilled Anna with a pointed glance. "I, too, am sorry I missed him when he called."

"He did not stay long," Anna murmured. "He . . . had to return to town almost right away."

"Oh, la. The next time, perhaps." Lucille toyed with a bit of lace on her cuff, obviously piqued to have rushed all this way for nothing. "I would have insisted on accompanying Stanley regardless."

Florence smiled. "Visits are always a pleasant surprise, I assure you." Her gaze flicked past the vicar's shoulder as she murmured, "Though I daresay it is not the only one in store for the day."

Stanley Althorpe turned to follow her glance and saw his brother standing silently in the doorway. The blood had not completely drained from his face before he managed to slowly rise to his feet, but it was a near call.

"By God's grace," he whispered. "You are alive." .

Emory smiled briefly before he replied. "God's grace had little to with it, I am afraid. It was Dame Widdicombe's tender nursing that brought me back from the brink."

The vicar started forward, a smile breaking out across his face. "By God. By God, I say! When first I saw you, your flesh was so gray and cold I did not hold out much hope for recovery. But here you stand, alive and well, looking exactly as I have pictured you in my mind's eye all these long years!"

Emory endured the younger man's enthusiastic hug as well as a few stout claps on the shoulder, before he gently disengaged himself.

"Not so completely recovered as either one of us might hope," he said quietly and glanced at Florence. "You have not told him?"

"I have had little chance, what with all the talk of plagues in the village and cutthroats on the roads."

The vicar's boyishly handsome face lost none of its happy excitement as he searched for broken bones, missing digits. "Told me what? You look in perfect health to me."

"The damage," Florence said gently, "is not immediately visible. It is here," she added, tapping a finger on her temple, "for you see, he has no memory of what happened. No memories at all, for that matter."

"No memories?" The vicar frowned. "You mean you cannot recall how you came to be washed up on the beach?"

"He means," Florence sighed, "he has no memory whatsoever. He does not know who he is, or who I am, or my niece . . . not that he should know her, of course, for he never met her before this week. But he is quite without any recollections whatsoever. The blow on the head, we can only surmise, must have been severe enough to bruise his brain, for when he does remember something, it comes to him piecemeal and not without a measure of pain."

Stanley expelled a gust of air. "But that is . . . that is absurd! How can you not know who you are?"

"I promise I do not," Emory said. "And as absurd as the idea may seem to you, it is doubly so for me. I have been walking about this past hour like a child in a strange and terrifying place. I am told I have been here many times, that this house, these rooms should all be familiar to me, but"— he spread his hands wide—"I doubt I could find my way to the front door without assistance."

Stanley's mouth worked a moment to form words that eventually had to be forced through a strained whisper. "You do not recognize me?"

Emory did not have to answer; the look in his eyes was eloquent enough to tighten the younger man's jaw with disbelief.

Annaleah could see the obvious resemblance between the two men; there could be no mistaking they were brothers. It was not so much a physical similarity they shared, though there were definite likenesses in the line of the chin, the shape of the nose, the width of the brow. One was more weathered, his face more deeply etched by the broader scope of his experiences, and his body harder, shaped by the more physical nature of the life he had chosen. The other was softer, more the scholar and less like a dark storm cloud on the horizon, but there was still an underlying hint of steel in the way he thrust out his hand and clasped it firmly to Emory's shoulder.

"Then we shall have to do our best to reacquaint ourselves in the time we have."

Lucille, all but ignored on the settee, cleared her throat with a delicate cough. "I presume this is somewhat of an awkward moment, but I believe more than one of us must lay claim to a measure of ignorance here today."

Stanley dropped his hand and looked over at his wife. "Of course. Forgive me. In the confusion, I seem to have forgotten my manners. Lucille . . . dearest—" He moved haltingly to stand by his wife's chair. "I have the very great pleasure of introducing my brother, Emory St. James Althorpe. He has been away from England lo these six years, but now, as . . . as you can plainly see, he has returned."

Emory had started to offer a polite bow in Lucille's direction just as her chin dropped and her little bow-shaped mouth popped open with a gasp. "Emory Althorpe! The traitor?"

Utter and absolute silence followed the blurted pronouncement, and when Florence rapped the leg of a table with her walking stick, it earned the same skin-jumping response as a gunshot.

"We will have no mention of unfounded accusations under this roof," she declared fustily. "He is your husband's brother, as well as a dear and valued friend of mine. As such, he will be treated accordingly."

Lucille's hand had flown to her throat when the cane cracked against the wooden leg. It remained there as, fearing another strike, she shrank back in her chair and fumbled to grasp her husband's hand.

Stanley caught the fluttering white fingers and held them tightly in his. "Lucille, I realize this is rather sudden and certainly awkward, but . . . it *is* a somewhat blunt charge to make. Especially under the circumstances."

"It is all right," Emory said. "I am already aware of my status as persona non grata in these parts."

"Non grata?" Lucille squeaked. "The soldiers at the garrison have been given orders to shoot you on sight!"

Florence whacked the table again and this time, a lamp and two porcelain figurines jumped in unison with everyone else in the room.

"Well, they have!" Lucille insisted. "There are patrols

everywhere and as of this morning, the reward for his capture, *dead or alive*"—this last phrase she added with suitable dramatics—"has been doubled to a thousand pounds!"

Florence looked quickly to Stanley for confirmation.

"I am afraid so. Colonel Ramsey questioned the fisherman again and showed him the warrant poster. He is convinced the man he saw and Emory were one and the same. Further, he is now speculating openly that there may be a plot afoot to rescue Bonaparte from the *Bellerophon* when it arrives in port, and if so"—he paused and looked at his brother—"he believes Emory is the mastermind behind it."

"Sweet Mary, Mother of God," Florence muttered. "Has he nothing better to do with his time than invent intrigues? Are there not enough bodices to fondle or skirts to sniff after to keep him amused?"

"Wait." Emory put a hand to his temple and rubbed. "Wait. The man is a prisoner on board an English warship, bound for an English port, under heavy guard by English soldiers. How am I supposed to accomplish this feat of magic?"

"The same way you accomplished it on Elba?" Stanley suggested bitterly. "There were three thousand English soldiers guarding him on that occasion, yet we are told you somehow sailed into port one night and whisked him away."

"Rory's involvement has not been conclusively proven," Florence reminded him.

"Ramsey claims there are witnesses—men who swear it was the *Intrepid* they pursued and came close enough to to exchange several rounds of shot before losing her in a squall."

Emory frowned. "The *Intrepid*?"

"Your ship, blast it. Your damned ship! The vessel in which you chose to sail around the world in search of adventure instead of staying at home and seeing to your family responsibilities!"

No sooner were the angry words out of Stanley's mouth than his jaw dropped and his mouth slackened. When he saw the stunned expression on Florence and Anna's faces—Lucille, on the other hand, seemed on the verge of offering applause—his hands came up in a gesture of contrition.

"Oh dear God, Emory . . . I am sorry. I . . . I don't know where that came from and I had no right to say it. It is absurd to hold you to account for matters of which you could not possibly be aware a thousand miles away. Even more so now, when . . . when you barely recall your name."

Emory seemed to sway and even stagger a bit. Anna jumped to her feet and rushed to his side, fearing he might have another of his spells.

"No." His voice was ragged, his jaw tense. A tiny muscle shivered in his cheek, but he managed a puny imitation of a smile as he laid his hand over the cool fingers she placed on his arm. "I'm all right." He looked at Stanley. "It is all right. There is no need to apologize. If I am a bastard, I suppose it is best to hear it from my own family first."

"Will you at least sit down?" Anna said. "Perhaps take a glass of wine, or brandy?"

Florence swung her cane up, more than passingly familiar with the height and distance needed to strike the bell that hung on the wall beside her. "A splendid idea. We could all use something stronger than tea at the moment. Once we have calmed ourselves we can discuss the situation without any silliness or histrionics. Stanley—did you bring clothing? I daresay those breeches your brother is wearing, while giving him the appearance of a fourteen-year-old stripling, could make sitting almost as painful a prospect as prostrating himself on the ground and begging pardon for all the sins known thus far to mankind."

"I, er . . . yes," Stanley said, nodding. "I did bring a selection of garments and boots. They are in a small trunk in the carriage."

"You knew?" Lucille said, gaping up at him. "You knew he was here all along and said nothing?"

"I have only known since Monday, when Dame Widdicombe first sent for me. And if I said nothing, my precious, it was because I did not want to alarm you. I am aware of how delicate you are, how genteel your sensibilities. I also recognized how upsetting this might be for you, what with Colonel Ramsey and his men at the rectory nearly every other day."

Florence's blatantly indelicate snort put a spot of color in the translucent white cheeks.

"Colonel Ramsey has been most civil of late," Lucille protested. "And while I may find his presence exceedingly intrusive, I should hope you would not misinterpret that to mean I would do anything disloyal to our family."

"No, of course not, my dearest. I would never—"

"My first loyalty is always to you, Stanley. And if I sound upset, it is only because you did not think you could trust me with the truth. I am surprised, yes. Who would not be in the same situation? Nevertheless, I do think Dame Widdicombe's judgment of me is perhaps a little harsh." She pulled on her lower lip to draw attention to the visible tremor affecting her ability to speak. "I am not silly. I am only concerned. For your welfare *and* that of your brother."

"But of course you are, my dear," Stanley cried, going down on one knee before her. "And I would never suggest you were anything but loyal and trustworthy. I . . . I only sought to spare you any needless worry."

Barely mollified, Lucille turned to address Emory, her chin held high enough to strain the cords in her neck. "I meant no ill will, dear brother, and hope that you will forgive me my unthinking cruelty. I am naturally and immeasurably pleased to make your acquaintance after all these years, and you must know that, if it were at all possible, I should insist upon you coming home with us this very minute."

Florence was on the verge of lifting her cane again when Willerkins appeared in the doorway. "Thank goodness. I was not sure if you had heard the bell."

"I heard the walking stick, milady. Quite clearly."

"Yes, well, if you would be so kind, the vicar has left a small trunk in his carriage which needs to be fetched. Will you also inform Mildred there will be five for supper tonight—you are staying for supper, I assume?"

Stanley dared do nothing else but nod his thanks, in spite of the grip Lucille took on his arm.

Willerkins bowed. "Will there be anything else, milady?"

"Indeed yes. I believe that old rascal Dupré left us a keg of very fine French brandy the last time I allowed him to hide from the revenuers in my bay. A bottle would not go unwelcome at the moment. And some small cakes to tide us over until the chickens can be plucked and the hares stuffed."

When he was gone, Florence crossed her hands over the head of her cane and glared about the room.

"I grew quite fond of French lace before the war," she explained, though no one asked, "and saw no reason to do without it for twenty years. For that matter, I doubt there is a house anywhere between here and Cornwall that does not have a storage room filled with black-market goods of one nature or another. And I would defy you to explore any one of the caves beneath Berry Head and not find evidence of transactions conducted with the garrisoned soldiers. Why, I recall . . . Well, never mind what I recall. It is what Rory recollects—or does not recollect—that is the more pressing concern at the moment. He is much better today compared with yesterday and I'm sure he will improve twofold by tomorrow if we all make the effort to help him remember *happier* times."

Anna had not moved from Emory's side, nor had he taken his hand away from hers. Whether he sensed her watching him, or whether his gaze just happened to stray in her direction, she found herself suddenly looking deeply into the dark eyes. His face wore no expression, betrayed no emotion. She could not have said how she knew what he was thinking, but it came to her as clearly as if her aunt had struck another limb with her cane: He did not plan to be there tomorrow. Regardless if his memory came back or not, he intended to leave Widdicombe House at the first opportunity.

Anna lowered her lashes in an effort to hide her sudden dismay. It made perfect sense, of course, that he should want to leave, that he *should* leave before too many people discovered he was here. Lucille Althorpe did not exude a sense of discretion. If anything, she reminded Anna of the kind of woman who crowded the ballrooms and assemblies in London and who would raise her fan and "in strictest confidence" tell a complete stranger some twisted piece of "truth" she had heard whispered by someone who had sworn her to secrecy.

And if her aunt was right, if dearest Lucille had grand designs on becoming the next Countess of Hatherleigh, it would only require the right whisper in the right ear to remove one of the barriers standing in her way.

Chapter 10

*T*HE STORM EMORY had predicted struck with full force less than two hours later. It came on swift, green-bellied clouds swollen with rain, driven by winds that gusted so hard at times the windows rattled and the trees outside were bent in half. Willerkins was dispatched to gather extra candles and lamps, to stoke the fires in the parlor and bedrooms, and, where required, to set out buckets and towels to collect the water that dripped from ceilings and ran down walls.

During those same two hours, Stanley monopolized most of the conversation, earnestly convinced it was possible, if he recounted enough events from their youth, to fully restore Emory's memory before Throckmorton appeared to ring the six o'clock gong. To Annaleah, who found herself an equally rapt listener, it was a tale of a misspent youth, the wild and undisciplined adolescence of a third son who saw no earthly benefit to learning philosophical theories or memorizing long passages of Latin scripts.

Florence had already intimated that Emory had not got on well with his father, that there had been beatings and violent arguments. Most of the former came from stepping in to defend Poor Arthur from the earl's belief that if his having repeatedly boxed his son's ears had brought on the boy's avian fantasies, they could be cured in the same manner. Stanley speculated it was only because of Arthur that Emory had not run away long before his sixteenth year.

But in that year, the earl died of a burst vein in his head. With their older brother William now the head of the family, Arthur was safe, and within a week of their father's funeral, Rory was on a ship bound for the Indies. He spent the next six years sailing to parts of the world most people only knew as vague names on a map, and when he returned, he came to Windsea Hall laden with bolts of exotic silk and jars of spices no one could name. He had been to the American colonies, to Mexico and Peru. He had even sailed to the Far East and walked along the Great Wall. He had brought back tiger skins and Chinese porcelain, and a wondrous curved sword that had belonged to a famous samurai warrior.

For Arthur, he had brought a solid gold cage made in many tiers and layers, containing tiny yellow birds that sang so sweetly they brought tears to his brother's eyes.

Even though William had welcomed him home, Emory had barely lasted out a month in the quiet countryside before his blood grew restless again. He answered England's call for experienced seamen and went off to join the war against France. He served as a lieutenant in Nelson's fleet, but after the victory at Trafalgar, he parted company with the navy and engaged in several private ventures that eventually won him the *Intrepid*. During those same years, Stanley had answered his own calling and been given the parish in Brixham. Three years ago, he had married Lucille; thirteen months ago, William Althorpe had died unexpectedly, leaving Poor Arthur next in line to inherit the titles and estates.

Annaleah had watched Emory's reactions carefully to see if he responded to anything his brother said, but he might as easily have been listening to a stranger's mixed tales of woe and adventure. In the end, she abandoned the pretense of studying him for purely clinical reasons and found herself studying the man himself. She had startled herself—and her aunt, she suspected—by rushing so quickly to his side earlier. After the episode on top of the cliffs, she thought she would rather be trampled under a runaway coach than ever have to stand face-to-face with him again. She had challenged him to do his best, and by heaven, he had done it. He had kissed her with his entire body, not just his mouth, and the smallest flicker of a smile, the slightest warmth in a glance that came her way—and there were many—started that melting feeling all over again.

When Willerkins had fetched the trunk from the vicar's coach, Althorpe had excused himself to change. The clothes had once been his and had been stored in the attic of the vicarage; even so they were, sadly enough, not much of an improvement. He was no longer the gangly youth who had gone off to sea in search of the seven wonders, nor was he the righteous young officer who had stalked off to war. His shoulders were considerably broader and strained the seams of the royal blue velvet jacket Stanley had brought. The high white collar of the linen shirt seemed to constrict his throat, and the buttons on the cream silk waistcoat tested the strength of the embroidery around the holes. The nankeen breeches were a somewhat better fit, though his thighs were so taut with muscle, the lightweight fabric molded to them as immodestly as had the wet linen drawers that, try as she might, Annaleah would likely never eradicate from her thoughts.

He looked very much like a pirate. With his gleaming black hair, his weathered complexion, she could easily envision him on the rolling deck of a tall ship, his hands braced on the wheel, his smile as gleefully ominous as the skull and crossbones flying overhead.

Yet as easily as she could picture him as a pirate, she could not envision him a traitor. If he was a sneaking, conniving, treacherous malfeasant, would not some of that sly cunning show in his eyes? His manners? If he was a cold-blooded murderer, would he not betray some degree of lethal impatience with Lucille Althorpe, whose flirtatious entreaties for him to elaborate on his lightning glimmers of shipboard life sent Florence's hand curling longingly around the silver head of her walking stick time and again.

By the time Throckmorton appeared to ring the six o'clock gong, the storm was in a full-blown rage. Willerkins reported that the vicar's coach had been taken to the stables to prevent its being blown into the sea, and that he had taken the liberty of having an additional bedchamber prepared for overnight guests. Lucille had looked aghast at the very notion of having to spend the night at Widdicombe House, but when the wind started to howl and the rain began to pelt the windows like sprays of pigeon shot, her misgivings were replaced by alarmed whimperings.

Out of deference to Florence's age, supper was served early, at eight. Throughout the meal of boiled chicken, mutton pie, and stewed kidneys, Anna merely pushed her fork around the plate, building a small hillock out of her food, then flattening it again. She kept one eye on the lightning and thunder crashing outside, one eye on Emory Althorpe, and if she had time between she glanced at Stanley, who now felt it was his duty to point out the fact that Emory had never liked kidneys, was not overly fond of pickled eel, and did not tolerate the gastric effects of cabbage well. Lucille had begun to seriously grate on Anna's nerves, laughing in a high, tinkling falsetto at nearly everything Emory said. Or interrupting her husband to add something completely irrelevant and usually vainglorious to the conversation.

When supper was over, they returned to the parlor, where brandy was brought in on a tray alongside a small teak box. Before Willerkins went to the men, he opened the box for Florence, who helped herself to one of the cigars inside, clipped the end with her teeth, and spat the nub in the general direction of the hearth.

If nothing else, it had the effect of finally rendering Lucille speechless, especially when Emory struck a match and lit the cigar for Florence, then casually strolled back to his seat and lit one for himself.

Annaleah's father and brother both indulged in tobacco, and while she had never in all her years seen a women do so, she had heard rumors that the Queen was known to enjoy a dinner cigar on occasion. In polite London society, of course, it would have been considered the height of rudeness for a gentleman to smoke in front of a lady. But they were in a house atop a storm-swept cliff in Devonshire, and because it was a lady herself who had drawn the first puff, that particular rule, like so many others that had been cast upon the wind thus far, seemed a bit absurd.

Anna was tempted to take one herself, and might have done so had Lucille not clapped her little hands and declared it such fun to be so wicked. Against Stanley's solemn advice, she entreated Emory to light a cigar for her, and when he did so, she coughed herself into a blinding fit of tears. When the fit passed, it left her face wavering between ash gray and a rather spectacular shade of green.

Florence and the men were able to enjoy their brandies with little interruption save for the ragings of Mother Nature.

"I expect we shall see the kidneys again at breakfast," Florence remarked as she stubbed out the last smoldering inch of tobacco. "Mildred is not one to waste good viscera. Lift the crust of a pastry at one meal, you are bound to find remainders of another, usually disguised with mustard or fennel. I cannot remember the last time she was pressed into cooking for more than one guest at a time, however, so there will either be sufficient fare to feed ten in the morning, or barely enough to fill a hole in your tooth."

"You have already been generous beyond the pale, Dame Widdicombe. I only regret that circumstances force us to make further intrusions on your hospitality."

"Nonsense, Vicar. I have not had two such handsome gentlemen staying under my roof in too many years to recount. To that end, I believe I shall retire to my bed and spare all of you the need to look politely at your hands."

She accepted Emory's help out of the chair and walked stiffly to the door. "Willerkins will show you to your room, Vicar, when you are ready. He assures me he has prepared one of the more civilized bedchambers for you. Rory dear, you have been brought down out of the attic again and put in a room with a water closet and a real tub for bathing; I trust you'll not get the two confused," she added with a wink. "Anna, you may walk me to the stairs, then return and take my place as hostess. Everybody please carry on as long as you like. I doubt I shall get much sleep with this thunder crashing all about us, but I have had three brandies and should find my bed well enough with Willerkins's help."

After Florence bid her last good night, Annaleah accompanied her across the hall, carrying a three-tined candelabra to augment the light cast by the scattered wall sconces.

"Well?" Florence leaned close to whisper. "What do you make of the evening thus far?"

Anna glanced over her shoulder. "I think Reverend Althorpe is genuinely happy to see his brother. He is trying very hard, at any rate, to help restore some memories. As for Lucille . . ."

Florence chuckled. "I think if sweet Lucille stares any harder, poor Rory will have scorch marks in his breeches."

"Auntie!"

"Never you mind 'Auntie.' I am not too old or dry to appreciate the healthier attributes of a man's body. Nor should you be playing the gulled innocent with me, young lady. I was not the one dueling with the rogue's tongue out on the cliffs this afternoon."

Annaleah stopped cold, letting her aunt walk ahead several paces into the shadows before she found her voice. "You saw us?"

"Good gracious, if I could still see across the *room* with any clarity, I would not have conversations with my coat tree each morning. It was Ethel who saw you. She told Mildred and Mildred told Willerkins and Willerkins"—Florence half turned and raised an eyebrow to where Willerkins hovered in the shadows—"tells me everything. Not that I would not have guessed something was amiss, young lady, for there has been a fine blush in your cheeks all evening, and it suits you. From the sound of it, I wish I *had* seen the kiss. Willerkins says you gave your fiancé quite an eyeful."

"Oh . . . Auntie . . . It was not on Mr. Althorpe's initiative.

It was mine. Entirely mine. I was desperate to discourage Lord Barrimore's proposal and all I could think to do on the moment was—"

"Throw yourself in the arms of another man? And Rory obliged, of course—how gallant." Florence pursed her lips. "I expect if you wanted to discourage the marquess, then you have succeeded. As related by Ethel, the poor man's back was so stiff with indignation, she heard it crack when he clambered up into his carriage. It is a wonder he did not appear on my doorstep tonight demanding a real duel, and lucky for all of us the storm closed in so swiftly. On the other hand, I would not be surprised if, as soon as it departs, your brother is the one who appears—with a warrant to remove you from this house of shameless debauchery."

Anna groaned softly, for she had never even considered that the repercussions might extend to her aunt. The candelabra seemed to grow inordinately heavy. It tipped and splashed wax on the floor, and she would have dropped it had a familiar hand not reached past her shoulder and gently relieved her of the burden. Emory had come up quietly behind them and stood beside her now with his face bathed in the bright yellow glare, his eyes reflecting tiny sparks of light from the flames.

"If blame is being apportioned, ladies, I will bear my share. I believe it takes two to give an eyeful."

He left Anna gaping after him as he passed the candelabra to Willerkins and walked over to where Florence waited at the bottom of the stairs. She gave him a crinkly smile and rested a gnarled hand on his cheek.

"And such a devilish handsome eyeful you are too," she whispered. "If I were sixty years younger, or even forty . . ."

He caught up her hand and pressed it to his lips. "You would likely still be too much for me to handle."

Her smile held a moment longer, then gave way to a slow sigh of resignation. "I do not imagine we shall have the pleasure of your company much longer, will we? But you'll not leave without saying good-bye?"

"On that you have my word, though I am at a loss to know what I could ever do or say to thank you."

Florence chuckled again. "Would that I were wicked enough to tell you."

She reclaimed her hand, took Willerkins's arm, and turned to climb the stairs. Emory stayed by the balustrade until they arrived at the top, then watched a few seconds longer as the bloom thrown by the candlelight wavered away into the darkness.

Anna was standing exactly where he had left her. The white muslin of her dress glowed softly against the shadows; her skin was so pale the circles of color on her cheeks stood out like paint.

"Why would she think you would leave without saying good-bye?"

"Because if I had any sense I would go now and use the storm to my advantage."

"Advantage? Since when would a soaking and a fever be to anyone's advantage?"

"When it is one's own health at risk and exposes no one else to harm."

His voice was as soft and dusky as the shadows, and Anna tried not to notice how his eyes were following the curve of her throat, her shoulder, the low décolletage of her bodice while he spoke. She had changed clothes before dinner and foolishly discarded her first choice of a high-necked cotton day dress for a shiny froth of silk that left her breasts no room for error.

"Where would you go? With no memory of who might be a friend and who a foe, how could you possibly travel anywhere with any confidence? Would you not be exposing yourself to the far greater danger of walking blindly into a trap?"

He drew closer. "I am flattered, Miss Fairchilde, that you show so much concern for my well-being."

"I am not concerned," she protested softly. "I . . . I am merely attempting to be practical. Do you not think it

ludicrous for a man with no memory to be in such a hurry
to depart the only place he knows he is safe?"

"No more ludicrous than a young woman inviting complete social ruin upon herself instead of simply refusing a
man's offer of marriage."

Anna flinched as a particularly loud crack of thunder
seemed to shake the foundations underfoot. Her blush had
spread down her throat, had shivered across her skin and
tightened it into visible peaks beneath the silk.

"A gentleman," she whispered, "would not mention the
incident again."

He was close enough to pluck a stray lock of dark hair
off her shoulder and let it slip through his fingers. "You
have heard what my brother has been saying about me all
evening. If nothing else, I think we can safely assume that
I am not a gentleman, at least not in any refined sense of
the word. As for forgetting the incident"—he caught up the
silky strand of hair and started to wind it slowly around his
fingers—"I found myself thinking of little else each time I
looked at you tonight."

"A simple solution, then," she said without breath,
"would be not to look at me."

"That would be like telling a man not to look at sunlight
when he has been stumbling around in absolute darkness."

He smiled, and the floor beneath her turned to quicksand.

It was his eyes, she decided. Darkly magnetic, full of
secrets and mysteries—she could not escape them. Tonight at dinner, each time he looked at her she felt compelled to reach down and grip the sides of the chair to keep
from being physically pulled across the table. Later, in the
parlor, she had tried fixing her attention elsewhere—at the
sheets of rain blurring the window, the blue and orange
flames in the fire, the remarkable two inches of ash that grew
at the end of her aunt's cigar—but each time her guard
slipped, she was drawn to the silent figure by the fireplace
again.

Emory Althorpe had been ten feet away, on the opposite side of the room, but he might as well have been sitting right beside her, his thighs pressed to hers, his arms around her shoulders, his lips nuzzling hot patterns along the curve of her throat.

He was standing less than ten inches from her now, yet it felt as if he was inside her skin. The air was crackling between them and it felt as though the storm had moved inside the hallway and the slightest touch would ignite a flame and burn them both to cinders.

And his smile was widening, as if he knew exactly what she was thinking.

Using the lock of imprisoned hair to gently coax her forward, Emory bowed his head and pressed his lips over hers. Anna's eyes remained wide and fixed for a moment, but there was no burst of bright light, no instant incineration. The consummation was more gradual, beginning at her lips and ribboning downward in a warm spiral. As the heat and raw sensuality engulfed her, her lashes fluttered closed and she leaned willingly forward into his enfolding arms. Her lips parted with little persuasion and she met the slow, sensual thrust of his tongue with a sigh that carried with it all the longing, the loneliness, the confusion of her awakening emotions.

The door behind them opened, but neither of them noticed. Nor did they notice the Reverend Stanley Althorpe when he stepped out of the parlor and came to such an abrupt halt, his wife walked up his heels and slammed fully into his back.

"Stanley, what on earth—!" Lucille's jaw dropped open as she too saw the embracing couple.

Annaleah sprang out of Emory's arms and muffled a gasp with her hand.

"What indeed," Lucille murmured, her eyes as round and bright as newly minted coins. "And only two days recovered, you say? Another two days I daresay we would be conducting a hasty wedding service."

A small, strangled sound escaped through Annaleah's

fingers and for the second time that day, she whirled around and ran. She heard Emory's voice calling out to her as she flew up the stairway, but she did not stop. She hoisted her skirts and ran in a flurry of belled silk and pounding heartbeats, not daring to glance back at the accusing faces, not even slowing when she reached the gloom of the upper landing.

There were only two sconces lit along the long hallway. In the dark spans between, there were slippery stretches of flooring and corners of carpets to snag a careless foot. But she made it to the far end safely and, once inside her room, swung the heavy door shut with a resounding bang.

Chapter 11

WHEN THE TAPPING eventually did come to her
door, it was so low and apologetic, Annaleah almost
credited it to her imagination. Nearly two hours had passed
since she'd locked herself in her room with only the thunder and several glasses of her aunt's fine red claret to offer
comfort.

Her initial response was a determination to ignore the
knock and anyone who dared intrude on her private
humiliation.

When it came a second time, it was not noticeably
louder, yet somehow managed to convey the impression
that whoever was applying knuckles to wood would do so
again and again until she relented. Approaching on bare
feet, she leaned her mouth to within an inch of the jamb
and whispered, "Whoever it is, go away. I am sleeping."

"Forgive me for disturbing you, but I must see you for
a moment."

Anna straightened and stared at the door. "Whereas I
have absolutely no desire to see *you*, sir."

"Please. Only for a moment."

"Please," she countered firmly, "go away."

"It is important that I speak with you," Emory insisted.

"You are speaking with me now, are you not?"

"Actually, no. I am speaking with a door."

"Oh good sweet gracious heaven!" she exclaimed and
gave the knob a savage twist. "How can you possibly"—she
yanked the door open a hand's width and glared out at
Althorpe with one blazing eye—"have the nerve to disturb
me? How *can* you, sir, when even the most imbecilic low-
born turd farmer should realize he was the last person on

this earth with whom I would wish to have any manner of intercourse at this precise moment?"

Emory, dressed only in breeches, boots, and cambric shirt, took a guarded step back, uncertain of what might come flailing out of the darkness at him. By the time he recovered, the door had shut again with an angrily hissed "Now please . . . *go away*!"

For added emphasis, Anna twisted the key in the lock and removed it, making enough noise to leave no doubt that the discussion was over. She waited, listened, half expecting to hear him knock again—fully prepared to ignore him to perdition if he did so—but after several minutes of silence she relaxed her vigil and smugly turned away.

Emory Althorpe was standing directly behind her, a tall blur of white against the shadows.

He reached out and caught her around the waist before the surprise could send her stumbling painfully back against the door.

"Once again, I would beg your pardon. I did not mean to startle you."

"Wh-where did you come from? H-how—?" Annaleah remembered what her aunt had said about hidden passages and doorways in most of the rooms, and she glanced wildly at the walls and shelves to see if there were any secret panels standing ajar. *"How did you get in here?"*

"Your room connects to another through the dressing room," he said calmly.

"You came through the dressing room?"

"It is a little damp outside to be climbing up the ivy."

His dismal attempt at humor caused her to raise a hand to her temple. "Mr. Althorpe, I am very tried. I believe I have expressed my wish to be left alone. . . ."

"Why? So you can pace the night away worrying about what my sister-in-law might say or do in the morning?"

"She can hardly shred my reputation into any smaller pieces than Lord Barrimore," Anna said on a sigh. "But of course, if you feel as though you must fulfill some moral obligation, then by all means, tender your proposal. I will reject it and the social graces will have been served."

"Tender my proposal? Of *marriage*?"

"You did say it was important that you speak with me."

"Well yes, but . . . I assure you it had nothing to do with a marriage proposal."

He looked so genuinely taken aback that Anna was able to quickly cover her own blunder by pretending to mock his. "Ah. May I therefore assume there has been no miraculous recovery of either your memory or your conscience? Pray enlighten me, then, as to what other possible reason you could have for forcing your way into my bedroom in the middle of the night?"

"I wanted to make certain you were all right."

"As you can plainly see: I am fine. I have not thrown myself out the window or branded my cheek with the symbol of a harlot. To be sure, however, if they made one for a fool, I might be sorely tempted, since that is what I have been making of myself all day long. Still and all, for the comparatively small sin of two misguided kisses, I am not about to don a horsehair shirt and flay myself raw with a willow switch."

"I am relieved to hear it," he mused.

"I am relieved that you are relieved. Now will you please take yourself away before someone hears us or sees us here alone in my bedroom, in which case you would indeed be forced to extend the protection of your name and I would be forced to accept it, and we would both be miserable for the rest of our natural lives."

A gust of wind blew against the windows, sending a corresponding draft through the open dressing room door. It carried enough force to whuff out the candle that was burning on the nearby table, leaving only the light of the fire to penetrate the shadows. Feeling justifiably uncomfortable in such close surroundings, Anna brushed past him and returned to the window to relight the smoldering wick.

Emory followed her with his eyes only at first, for she

looked quite magnificently disheveled in a long, flowing robe and night rail of whisper-fine lawn. Her hair was loose and scattered over her shoulders. Bare pink toes peeped out from the hem of the robe, and when she crossed in front of the fire, the light made short work of any speculation over the other shapes and curves that lay beneath the flimsy shield of cloth.

"Actually, I came to say good-bye. Your aunt rises with the first cock's crow, so I can be fairly confident of seeing her before I leave, but I was not certain of your own sleeping habits and did not want to go without at least thanking you for everything you have done."

Anna did not turn around but continued staring out the window.

"I have not done much, sir."

"No." He came up behind her. "You only found me facedown in the water and dragged me up into the sand, where you emptied the sea out of my lungs and undoubtedly saved my life in the process."

"Anyone would have done the same thing," she said, dismissing the deed with a small shrug. "It should not cause you to pace the night away thinking yourself an ingrate."

On the table beside her was a half-empty decanter of wine and a glass with a finger's depth of claret glittering red in the candlelight, confirming the sweet scent Emory had detected on her breath. The brass key from the gun case was lying alongside—he had taken the precaution earlier of slipping it back into her pocket. He had also caught a glint of gold at her throat and knew she was still wearing the key to the strongbox around her neck.

"You asked me what I would do when I leave here," he murmured, "where I would go. Would it be intruding too much if I asked you the same thing?"

"Me? That is hardly a mystery, sir. When my brother comes to fetch me—as he surely will do the moment the weather clears—he will make it quite clear that I will be returning to London without further ado." She paused and raised her hand to massage the sudden tightness across the nape of her neck. "Once there, I shall again be expected to attend the endless rounds of assemblies, balls, masquerades; to smile and curtsy before the new parade of sallow-faced suitors my mother will invite to inspect me. And I shall in all likelihood be pressed into marrying the one she decides has the most to offer by way of wealth and influence. I shall bear his children without complaint, and raise them to take their proper place in society."

"It sounds very . . . tedious."

She closed her eyes. "Most people's lives *are* very tedious, Mr. Althorpe. We cannot all be pirates or adventurers."

He let the bitter gibe pass. "You are not worried that your erstwhile fiancé will vent his wounded pride back in London?"

"I have given the matter some thought, and while he is an arrogant, pompous prig, I do not believe it is in Lord Barrimore's nature to embarrass himself by admitting he could not hold my attention. And I strongly doubt he will pursue the matter of a union between us any further."

"Then you have accomplished at least one thing you set out to do."

"Yes. I suppose I have," she conceded softly.

There were sporadic flickers of lightning outside, most of them too far away to cast more than a brief glow across the underbellies of the clouds. Between flickers it was pitch black, and the inner surface of the window became like a mirror, reproducing the candlelit images of Annaleah and Emory. It only took a moment for both of them to realize they were studying each other's reflection.

With her eyes warily following his every move, he reached up and gently grasped her wrist, guiding her hand down by her side. He skimmed his hands up beneath the dark, glossy fall of her hair and took up the task of kneading the knotted muscles across her shoulders, using his thumbs to stroke the tension out of her neck.

"An imbecilic turd farmer?" he mused.

"It . . . is my brother's fondest term of endearment for our prime minister, and it was the best I could think of on the moment."

"Well, at least I am flattered you searched for an endearment."

Anna's wits were beginning to desert her; her belly was starting to flutter. She curled her hands into fists by her sides and tried to will her flesh into remaining indifferent, but it was no use. Far from his actions easing the tension in her body, she could feel her flesh growing tighter and tauter with every stroke of his thumbs. When he gathered a gleaming handful of hair to one side and lowered his mouth to within a breath of her ear, it was all she could do not to gasp out loud.

"Believe me when I say that if I thought there was the smallest chance these charges against me were just a terrible nightmare, if I thought I would waken tomorrow and discover I was just another wastrel devotee of the ton . . ." A shallow sigh of frustration tickled her ear. "If I even knew for certain I was not already happily wed to some sloe-eyed vixen, I would not hesitate to offer you the protection of my name or my body."

Anna watched his mouth settle into the curve of her throat, her every sense focused on the warmth of his lips, the gentle kneading of his hands, the solid wall of hard muscle crowding against her back.

"What if that tomorrow never comes?" she asked in a whisper. "What if you never regain your memory? What if you are caught and imprisoned and hung . . . and you never learn the truth of who or what you are?"

He captured the velvety lobe. "Then I suppose I shall curse myself for having missed the opportunity to take advantage of a beautiful young woman who could have sent me to my grave with enough memories to last me a lifetime."

Anna stared, frozen in a welter of shimmering sensation. His thumbs were no longer caressing her nape, but his hands were still resting on the curve of her shoulder as if they had a perfect right to be there. His mouth, having met with no resistance, roved down her neck again, tracing a slow, nibbling path to the collar of her dressing gown.

Anna feared that the tremors in her legs would prevent them from supporting her much longer, and she leaned her head against his shoulder, using the hard wall of muscle to brace her as she arched her neck and invited his lips to trace even warmer, more erotic patterns on her skin. He painted a wet, swirling path to her ear again, then back to her shoulder, and when her whole body shuddered with the pleasure, he curled an arm around her waist and held her close against him.

Her dressing gown had not been belted tight to begin with, and it took only a small, careless flick of his hand to tug the satin sash out of its loop. The edges of the robe fell open and Emory's lips slowed their assault as he contemplated not only the reflection of her face in the window, but the full, rounded swell of her breasts where they pushed against her nightdress.

Annaleah Fairchilde was lonely and confused—not to mention gently fuddled by claret—and he knew that only a bona fide bastard would take advantage of her vulnerability. Only a bastard would bury his lips in the thick, glossy crown of her hair, and only a bastard would slide his hand down, inch by treacherous inch, until his fingers were curved around the lush ripeness of her flesh.

He felt her body stiffen in astonishment, but she did not push him away. Nor did she offer more than the softest whimper of resistance when he brushed his thumb across her nipple, stroking and teasing the already well defined circlet until the peak was hard enough to draw a groan from his own throat. With the worst done, it was a trifling matter to pluck at the ribbons that bound the bodice closed and to slide his hand beneath the feather-soft lawn so that it was flesh against flesh, incredible silky heat against roughened calluses that he knew, instinctively, had not felt such exquisite beauty in a very long time.

Emory cursed softly as heated blood surged through his veins, transforming what had begun as a modest stirring into a hard and needful swelling that strained him to the point of agony. Emerging from the lawn again, his hand smoothed over her belly and slid downward, his fingers curving into the juncture of her thighs. The cloth was sheer enough for him to feel the buffer of downy soft curls, sheer enough for him to trace the contours of the two distinct mounds of tender flesh and the sensitive cleft between. He expelled another soft oath against her throat and stroked his fingers to and fro, parting the delicate folds of flesh wider on each pass. He probed as deeply as the fabric allowed, until it was damp and Anna was no longer whimpering with the pleasure, but gasping and shuddering and pressing herself eagerly against his fingers.

Emory murmured something in her ear, but she was too distracted to understand what he said. Her body had never known such erotic stimulation before, and although she had heard whispers of the wicked pleasures that could be had by such sinful manipulations, she had never dared explore them herself. She could scarcely believe she was allowing a man—a veritable stranger she had barely known two full days—to take such shameful liberties, but shame was suddenly and unexpectedly the last thing that concerned her now. It was only the press and drag of his fingers she cared about. The skillful and deliberate incursions that were urging her toward the brink of some unknown ecstasy.

Her eyes shivered open, and her vision, at first blurred by the candlelight, cleared when she saw the image of her writhing body in the window. Her robe was hanging open, her night rail pushed aside over a bared breast. His head was bent over her shoulder, his lips were still plundering the curve of her throat, while lower down his fingers were moving between her thighs, indenting and straining the lawn with each appallingly explicit thrust.

A harsh cry broke from her throat and she twisted frantically out of his arms. Her knees buckled even as she grabbed at the length of velvet draperies to prevent herself from stumbling. She knocked against the edge of the table, jarring it enough to tip the glass and startle the candlestick. Quickly, she scrambled farther into the corner, hauling the thickness of the velvet drapery with her to use as a shield. She stood there, gasping and panting, staring in utter horror at the pale outline of Emory Althorpe, who had used his catlike reflexes to catch the wineglass before it toppled onto the floor and shattered.

When it was righted, he searched out the pale figure cowering in the corner.

"Anna—"

"Don't come near me!" she cried, cringing even more and raising the clutched velvet panel higher when he took a step toward her.

Emory stopped. "Anna, I'm sorry. I did not mean to frighten you."

"No, you only meant to ravish me? To . . . to *take advantage of me* so that you might carry the blissful memory to your grave?"

Her sarcasm stung, but the shot was not entirely off the mark and he admitted it. "You are right. Of course you are absolutely right, and I can only say again: I am sorry. I am a cad and a miscreant, and I would not blame you for calling me every filthy name your brother ever thought to devise, although you must also believe that I would do nothing to hurt you or compromise you in any way."

"A n-noble declaration," she stammered, "having done just that."

Not knowing what else to do with his hands, he raked them angrily through his hair and paced to the foot of the bed and back.

Anna watched him, trembling from the strength of the pulsations between her thighs. Her skin felt as if it had been rubbed raw everywhere by a coarse towel and the slightest touch might cause her to faint.

"I will admit," he said finally, "to the present circumstances being somewhat more compromising than a couple of misguided kisses."

"*Somewhat* more compromising?"

"All right, yes. Significantly more so. But still not enough to emblazon your breast with the mark of a harlot and pillory yourself on a stockade."

"Not in your opinion, perhaps. Not in the opinion of a self-proclaimed cad and miscreant who, although he cannot even remember if he has a w-wife, blithely attempts to seduce his way into another woman's bed anyway."

He looked away for a moment and when he turned back, he shook his head. "I am not married."

"How can you be so sure?"

"I cannot swear it unequivocally on a Bible, of course, but if there *was* a woman in my life that I loved enough to marry"—he paused to expel a small gust of air—"I doubt very much I would be damn near coming out of my skin every time I was close to you."

Anna was not sure if that was meant as a compliment or a means of excusing his behavior. In any case, she did not want him coming out of anything. In the past week she had broken more rules, flaunted more conventions, found herself asking more questions about who she was and what she wanted out of life than she was likely ever meant to ask. She had deceived her brother, lied to the authorities, actively conspired to conceal a criminal, and destroyed her chances for a potentially brilliant marriage. Yet here she stood, trembling with an incomprehensible lust—and it was lust, she was not deceiving herself by calling it anything else—for the last man on earth for whom she should be feeling such urges. The knowledge that he had been fighting a similar attraction was hardly reassuring. On the contrary, it was frightening and unsettling.

"The timing and circumstances are no better than they were ten minutes ago," he added, misinterpreting her silence. "But if it will set your mind at ease and bring you out of that damned corner, we can go down the hall now and waken my brother."

"Waken your brother?"

"He is a vicar, is he not? Licensed to perform marriages. I am sure we could persuade him to forgo the standard formalities."

"Is *that* your idea of an apology? A proposal of marriage? Or is it just another means of getting what you wanted in the first place?"

Emory's eyes narrowed with the first hint of a threat. "Madam, if I truly wanted what you are protecting so valiantly with your draperies and your pride, I could take it in a heartbeat and there would be nothing you could do to prevent it or stop me. I do not offer marriage for the mere convenience of taking you to bed. Indeed, I would not be offering it at all if I thought there was the slightest possibility it might hinder my speedy departure from these premises."

"Nothing is hindering you from leaving now, this instant," she gasped, the resentment flooding her cheeks, making her want to lash out and hurt him.

He stared at her through the darkness for a long moment, then offered a curt bow. "No indeed, there is not. Again, I thank you for your solicitude these past few days and beg your forgiveness at my unwanted intrusion here tonight. I would also wish you the very best of luck for the future, whatever it may bring."

She watched him stride across the room and disappear into the darkness of the dressing room. A few seconds later she heard the muted click as the door to the outer hallway was shut firmly behind him, and she knew he was gone. He was gone and she was left with only her draperies and her pride for comfort.

Chapter 12

ANNALEAH DISCOVERED THE loss in the morning. She had deliberately remained in bed much later than her normal hour and for added insurance ordered a tub to be filled, that she might steam away the chill which had settled in her flesh since Emory Althorpe's brusque departure. It was when she was removing her night rail that she noticed the key was gone. The chain had been around her neck since Althorpe had put it there on the beach, but now, although she searched the floor in front of the window and in the corner, she could not find it. Nor could she find the key to the gun case that she had left beside the wine decanter last night.

When Broom came to the door she sent him lumbering—and grumbling—back to the kitchens with his unwanted buckets of hot water. She dressed unaided in a simple high-waisted gown and gave her hair a rudimentary brush before twisting it into a tight coil and pinning it haphazardly on the crown of her head. She left her room and hurried along the hallway, heading straight for the library when she descended to the second floor.

The key was in the gun cabinet, jutting out of the lock as it had been the previous afternoon. But instead of five pistols seated in nests of baize on the shelf, there were only three. And of the compartments designed to hold flints, shot, and powder flasks, half were empty. A further, panicked thought sent her to the huge cherrywood desk, where she knew her great-aunt kept her household records and accounts. She yanked open the top drawer and lifted the lid of the handsome enameled box in which Florence had placed a hundred pounds in rents and sales from her cider at the beginning of the week, and was stunned to see that it too was empty.

"Dear God, he robbed us," she whispered.

"Borrowed a few pence, more's the truth," Florence said from the doorway. "And even then I had to force him to accept it."

"Auntie! He has taken guns and—"

"A horse, a saddle, and a haversack full of Mildred's biscuits and cold chicken. Willerkins contributed a compass and supplied the name of a posting house along the Excter turnpike whose proprietor would not ask too many questions of a stranger. That, of course, proved to be a gauntlet thrown in Broom's face, whereupon he spilled forth a veritable list of inns, taverns, and brothels of various repute where a coin or two would guarantee anonymity."

"But where will he go?" she asked softly.

"Anywhere but here, in Torbay. The *Bellerophon* slipped into the harbor sometime during the night, you see. Napoleon Bonaparte has arrived and the crowds will be pouring in like herds of sheep and cattle, though frankly, I cannot see the attraction. I always thought him an unctuous little snipe in too-tight breeches, and knew that eventually the bad blood would out. Just because a pig knows how to root out truffles, it does not change the fact that it is still a pig."

"Speaking of refined snouts," Florence added. "Your Lord Barrimore is in the parlor with your brother. I have been suffering genuine bouts of chaos seeking to intercept you before you barged into the room unawares."

Anna's head took another terrible spin and she sat down heavily in the desk chair.

She had not even considered the possibility of facing Barrimore so soon after humiliating him. Nor did she want to speculate on what form of greeting he might extend, how sharp the daggers in his eyes or how thick the frost on his tongue. She could deal with her brother's anger, even his contempt, but the thought of being upbraided for her hoyden behavior while Barrimore stood witness was enough to drain the blood from her face with the speed of an opened vein.

"We could always say you were so stricken with guilt, you threw yourself off the cliff and are too distraught to receive visitors," Florence suggested with a dry wit. "But I daresay that would only delay the inevitable a day or two. And besides, it could be much worse."

Annaleah shook her head. "I cannot imagine how."

"Well, for one thing, the vicar and his annoying little wagtail could still be here, and Willerkins would have had to fetch the constables to arrest me on a charge of murder. As it was, having to listen to her incessant natter over breakfast, I came perilously close to striking my own head with my cane just to give myself something more painful to contemplate."

Anna's eyes were silvery with tears as she looked up at her aunt. "Oh, Auntie, I wish I could stay here with you forever."

Florence clutched her hands together. "I wish you could too, dear, but . . ." She braced up and attempted a smile. "Good God, child, in a month you would be as addled as the rest of us. We have had a bit of an adventure together, though, have we not? And you have discovered—I trust— that I am not nearly as frightening or as peculiar as your mother would make me out to be."

"You are sweet and kind and generous to a fault."

Florence trembled and looked down at her hands, trying to remain constant, but failing miserably. "I'll thank you not to repeat that anywhere, young lady, for it would seriously dent my reputation as a dotty old hen. Now come along." She stiffened her shoulders and thrust out her chin. "They would not dare cast stones, verbal or otherwise, in the presence of a feeble old woman."

Anna blew out a resigned breath and pushed to her feet.

Arm in arm, they walked out of the library and turned in the direction of the day parlor.

"By the by, his face was as long as a pike this morning too," Florence murmured. "Not that it is any of my business, of course, but I had the distinct impression his mind was not on guns or horses or mad flights into peril. Dear Lucille, in her earnest zeal to be helpful, was only too eager to expound on what occurred after I retired."

"Auntie Lal, I'm sorry, I—"

"Do not be sorry, dear." Florence patted her hand. "I only wish you would do your kissing where I might judge the attributes for myself, firsthand. Lucille was quite breathless in her recounting, but it is not the same as actually seeing it with one's own eyes, is it?"

Anna was too startled to do more than glance sidelong at her aunt as they walked through the doorway and into the parlor. Nor did she have a chance to fully recover her wits before her brother and Lord Barrimore marked their entrance and ceased their murmured conversation to turn and offer polite bows. They were both standing by the fireplace, Barrimore in his usual staid funereal black from head to toe. Anthony displayed a fashionably more colorful splash of green satin in his waistcoat and buff trousers, and oddly enough, wore a cheerful expression.

"Dash it, Anna m'dear, if you have not cost me half a crown in a trifling wager with Barrimore." He pointed to the clock on the mantelpiece. "I was convinced you would sleep until noon. In truth, I must say, if it were not for the clamor of the hordes outside our window this morning, I should still be abed myself. All this sea air. The sun burst rudely through the curtains before anything remotely resembling a civilized hour . . ." He waved a hand to emphasize the injustice of it all. "Far too countrified for me, I am afraid. Too many bumpkins hawking apples and wanting to haul you by wagons into the sea. Frankly I cannot see why the Regent would find the place the least bit endearing, since he is never off his pillows until late afternoon. As for him paddling out with codfish, well, I just cannot see the charm."

"No doubt he has heard that a swim in the saltwater is extremely beneficial for his health," Barrimore explained. "That it enriches the blood and clears the mind."

"Not to mention dampening any interest he might take in the daughters of the local gentry, what?"

Anthony laughed at his own jest, but Barrimore's cold eyes did not betray the slightest flicker of humor as they fastened on Annaleah. "I am exceedingly sorry I could not keep our appointment yesterday, Miss Fairchilde. As I explained in my *note* . . . I was detained somewhat longer on business matters than I had anticipated."

Anna sensed a warning in his voice, and although she had seen no such note—and knew, indeed, that he had not sent one—it was apparent he had not said anything to Anthony. He had not betrayed her indiscretion and was relying on her to reciprocate by not making him the laughingstock of the ton. In this way, they could both return to London unscathed and cheat the gossips of a delicious *scandalum magnatum*.

Her relief was almost as draining as her approbation.

"Thank you," she breathed. "And yes, the delay was perfectly understandable."

For the first time ever, she thought she saw a visible easing of the tightness around his formidable jaw, and she realized with a further start that Winston Perry, marquess of Barrimore, was probably quite unused to being in the position of having to depend upon the charitable acts of others.

"As it happens, I also find I must start back today. The *Bellerophon*, having run ahead of the same storm that struck us last night, has arrived in port two days early, and no doubt the debates in the House will accelerate accordingly."

Florence settled into her chair with a scowl. "Surely there are enough soldiers garrisoned at Berry Head to form a firing squad."

Barrimore held Anna's gaze a moment longer before addressing her aunt's remark. "Undoubtedly there are, madam, and I would be among the first in line to pass out the powder cartridges and shot. Unfortunately, there are those of a more lenient nature who feel he would pay a higher price if we returned him to exile and made him eke out his days knowing he was roundly defeated."

"You sound as if you do not believe he would accept it."

"He escaped from prison once; he can do it again. Especially with the proper help."

"Are you still on about this renegade Bonapartist that Ramsey seems bent on resurrecting from the dead?" Anthony arched his brow as he inspected the small platter of cheese, paté, and toasted bread triangles Mildred had brought in earlier. "In truth, he is probably in the right place to do so, for there have been sightings of ghosts in the caves hereabout for centuries."

"Really? Then perhaps I was not just imagining that I saw such an apparition on these very cliffs." Barrimore's cool green eyes settled on Florence. "A man presumed to have died long ago of a shrunken head in Borneo."

To her credit, Florence did not even blink. She held Barrimore's gaze, and though they both knew he was making an oblique reference to Emory Althorpe, they might have been discussing something as trivial as the weather.

"Ghosts are quite prevalent in the area," she said. "They come and go, and harm no one."

"Then I trust this one has gone?"

"Oh yes. I doubt you would see him again if you waited a month of Sundays."

Barrimore's eyes narrowed and he looked directly at Annaleah. "The once was enough, thank you."

It took a massive effort for Anna to refrain from clutching her aunt's hand. She had no idea what the penalty was for harboring a traitor to the crown, much less kissing one.

Anthony, who had been busy spreading foie gras on a piece of toast, missed the innuendo altogether and chuckled.

"As I recall, I had Annaleah thoroughly convinced there were ghosts in every room here at Widdicombe House. Do you remember the incident, Anna, when we were children and came for a visit? You annoyed me to such an extent during the day that by night I had you screaming and running out of the room in terror for your life?"

"Yes," she said. "I remember."

"God a-mighty!" He pinched his face around a sour pucker and looked at his aunt. "What the devil do you feed your barn fowl? This goose liver tastes like bog moss."

Florence did not take her eyes away from the earl as she answered. "We do not have any geese, Nephew. It is probably yesterday's kidneys from a rather old ewe."

Anthony swallowed with obvious difficulty and wiped his mouth on a hastily produced handkerchief. "Yes, well. I expect my palate has been spoiled by the chefs at Whites. Which reminds me, Anna dear, I am much relieved to see Auntie's ankle is improved, for I must insist *we* leave for London today as well. Mother will have received my note by now and has likely dispatched one back in the next mail coach, and it would be best if neither of us were here to accept it. Quite apart from the overcrowding in town— we could not even hire a hackney this morning to bring us out; we had to use the berline in all this mud!—Barrimore has reminded me the Regent's masquerade ball is Friday next and we would both be flayed alive if we were not in attendance."

This time Anna did reach out and grip her aunt's hand for courage. It was one thing to avoid Barrimore's cold stare in a cluttered parlor; it was entirely another to endure it for three days within the tight confines of a traveling coach.

"A masquerade ball," Florence said. "How lovely. Yes, I suppose it is time she went home. I shall miss her, of course"—she gave Anna's chilly hand a little squeeze— "but will hold her to her promise to visit again soon."

"We were hoping to be away as early as this afternoon—?" Anthony looked from one to the other. "Really, you need only pack the essentials. The rest can be sent on later."

"I shall have Willerkins find Clarice at once to pack what is required. And if the gentlemen can spare our company for another few moments, I will go up and fetch that lovely ring you were admiring the other evening, Anna dear—the one that matched your eyes so exquisitely. It would be a shame for you to have to wait until I died to enjoy it. 'Tis only a bit of paste," she added, winking at the men, "but it is pretty, and pretty girls deserve pretty things, do you not agree?"

Anthony offered a complacent shrug, while Barrimore only flexed a muscle in his jaw.

"Then if you will just help me up, dear—?"

Anthony moved forward to assist her to her feet, but Florence whacked him smartly on the shin and reached for Anna's arm instead. At the door, she paused and glanced over her shoulder.

"Please, do help yourself to the cheese and kidney paste. I shudder to think what Mildred will invent next if the tray is returned untouched to the pantry."

They progressed along the hallway with only the muted thump of Florence's cane to break the silence. At the bottom of the stairs, Anna drew back and opened her mouth to speak, but her aunt raised a finger and pressed it against her lips.

"These old hallways, you know. Full of echoes."

Anna bit her lip and waited until they were well along the upper hall in the direction of her aunt's bedchamber, then could bear it no longer.

"He knows. Barrimore knows Emory was here."

"He suspects," Florence corrected her. "He saw you with a man who fit the general description of Emory Althorpe, and because he has been in the company of that oaf Ramsey and other gentlemen who have undoubtedly been engaged in endless rounds of debate concerning Rory's purported crimes, he has considered what he saw and arrived at a breathtaking conclusion. The fact you were *kissing* the bounder when he saw you would only make him more susceptible to suggestion.

"But what if he repeats what he saw, even if he only *thinks* he saw it? Will that not bring on every constable and soldier within fifty miles of here? Will they not search the house top to bottom and question you endlessly?"

"If they search the house, what will they find? Dusty carpets and a thousand spiders spinning webs of intrigue. I will have you know I was once questioned by the Duke of Cumberland himself, when those pesky Jacobites were inviting the French to help restore their Catholic king to the throne. For a full month they kept me in a damp prison cell because they had heard some silly whispered rumor that I allowed smugglers to land guns and exiled Scotsmen in my bay. I merely played the innocent fool, weeping and wringing my hands, swearing on my virginity that I had no knowledge of anyone engaged in such activities."

"And did you?"

"Did I what?"

"Have knowledge."

Florence glanced over with a wry chuckle. "I had carnal knowledge in trumps when I lost my virginity to a handsome groomsman at fourteen. And I made enough profit off the smugglers to buy and breed some of the finest horseflesh in Devonshire. Come to think of it, I sold some of those same horses to the English army a few years later for twice what I paid for them."

Anna expelled a soft breath. "You are a far stronger woman than I could ever be."

"Nonsense. You do not know the depths of your strength until you find yourself in a crisis worthy of it."

Anna held out her hands to show how they trembled. "Would you not call this a crisis?"

"The tauntings of an arrogant nobleman who has had his pride cuckolded?" The snort Florence released would have better suited Broom. "A mere irritation, child. Something on which to hone your feminine skills. Despite the stiffness of his neck, I vow the man is clearly smitten with you. What is more, I would stake my new whalebone busk that a few well-fluttered glances would have him on bended knee again, offering all he possesses for the charity of your smile."

"But I do not want him on his knee," Annaleah insisted. "Nor do I want him offering me anything, not even his escort to London."

"Be that as it may, you will have to find some way to endure it. Now come here a moment and let us choose a trinket that will inspire the appropriate awe in any future suitors."

She led the way into her bedroom—a cavernous chamber filled with mementos from the past eight decades, including a huge carved oak tester bed that could easily sleep four. Its canopy and curtains were made of scarlet velvet swagged with fat gold cords and fringed tassels, a color scheme that was also prevalent in the carpets and the brocaded silk wallpaper. The ceiling was painted with cherubs and cupids peeking through a forest of red and gold leaves. Everything seemed old and dusty at first glance, but it was just because there was so much clutter crammed into every nook and corner. Paintings, books, chairs, a hundred figurines and objects collected over the years vied for space with tables, a tapestry stand, even a small pianoforte buried under another mound of well-worn books.

Anna had never been invited inside her great-aunt's bedroom before; she had always been left standing at the threshold like a tinker hawking wares at the kitchen door. Part of the reason for that, she suspected, was the full-size painting of a naked woman reclining on a scarlet fainting couch. The woman was young and beautiful, with full, lush breasts and generously rounded curves; the portrait had obviously been painted with an eye to the smallest, most erotic detail. Her hair was a cascade of thick chestnut brown waves spilling over the cushions and trailing over the side of the couch; finer, silkier curls were clustered at the top of her thighs, where one of her hands, with its long delicate fingers, was placed with the teasing suggestion of an invitation.

"I was just about your age when I posed for that," Florence said proudly. "I had every stallion in the parish rearing up on his hind legs to show off his potential, driving my father mad day and night with their flowers and poetry. I recall one persistent fool used to read sonnets outside my window late at night, until Father could not take it anymore and had the servants empty all the thunderpots onto his head at once."

"You never answered me as to why you never married."

"Not for lack of wanting to, my dear," she sighed, "but because the man I loved was as proud as he was stubborn. He was just a lowly groomsman, you see. A stable boy. Regardless of how high he climbed through the ranks, he always considered himself a servant and respected my father, my family too much to besmirch my blood with his. I called him every kind of fool I could think of; I even tried my damnedest to get with child, hoping that would shame him into relenting, but alas, that was not to be either." Florence gazed up at the portrait and chuckled. "I had this painted and hung in his room so that every time he awakened in his wretched little cot he would see what he was missing. Oddly enough, though, when I gave it to him, it had clothes on. The scoundrel had them painted off."

"He sounds very much your match," Annaleah said. "You must have loved him a great deal."

"Yes," Florence said softly. "Yes, we did have our love, and I would not have traded that for all the princely titles in the world. You deserve nothing less, Annaleah Fairchilde," she added firmly. "And you should not settle for anything less either."

"My . . . situation is somewhat different."

"Why? Because your mother has set her sights on a

grand block of ice like Barrimore and because your father is too involved with his son's political aspirations to see that his daughters are equally precious commodities? Sad to say, your sister shares the same temperament as your mother and would not have questioned their decision to marry her to a wooden post—which, as it happens, her husband handily brings to mind. But you. You have a sparkle in your eyes, my dear. Do not let them blot it out."

"How can I possibly prevent it? You give me too much credit, Auntie, for in truth I have no more wit than my sister."

"If that were the case, you would not have lasted an hour in my company. And I would not already be missing you even though you are not yet out the door. Now come, help me move this rubble."

Florence led the way to an old, ironbound sea chest sitting against a profusion of scarlet silk. It was piled high with books and papers, which her aunt had Annaleah move and stack upon another half-buried vessel. On a further wave of the cane, she leaned over and lifted the heavy lid of the chest, then removed several layers of what looked like smallclothes, corsets, and stockings yellowed with age. Buried beneath them was another, smaller chest, this one made of polished wood secured with a brass lock plate.

"Bring it over here," Florence ordered, pointing to a dainty Louis XIV vanity table. "I lost the key about forty years ago, so it is not locked. Go ahead, open it. There should be a sapphire ring inside, along with a matching set of earrings if I remember correctly."

Anna lifted the lid and her eyebrows at the same time. The ring was one of dozens tangled carelessly among webs of gold chains. She found three sapphires in the midst of all the rubies, diamonds, and emeralds, but each was waved away with the cane. A fourth ring, a huge glittering thing with a dozen blue gemstones surrounding a diamond the size of a thumbnail, won a smile and a nod.

"That should do nicely," Florence said. "Put it on, put it on."

"It is lovely," Anna agreed, slipping it onto her finger. It was a tight fit and she had to force it over the second knuckle. "I would never guess the stones were paste."

"Then you would be exhibiting good sense, my dear, because they are not. They are very real, I assure you, as are all the other pretties in my little treasure box."

"But downstairs you said—"

"I know what I said, but if I had said I wanted to give you a trinket worth several thousand pounds, how long would it have taken for your mother to declare me an incompetent old frizzen and come searching out the rest? Now, I want that to remain in *your* possession," she added with a grumble, "to wear or not to wear, to ferret away for a little nest egg of your own, or to sell as need be."

"Sell? I would never sell it!"

" 'Never' is a word that should be used sparingly, and only after a great deal of thought. In any case, the ring is yours to wear, to sell, to toss in the privy if the shine disappoints."

"I . . . do not know what to say."

"Say thank you and remember we are only here for one go-around. Fifty years from now we will all be dust and no one will remember our names, much less the scandal of who we chose to love and who we did not. Now, run off to your room and pack. It is nearing the noon hour, and Mildred will walk out the door if she is forced to cook for any more guests."

"Thank you." The whispered words came with an impulsive hug that left Florence's chin quivering, her eyes damp.

"I will expect a letter the instant you arrive back in London," Florence insisted, clearing her throat. "I will want to know every word that passes inside that coach. And naturally, if you should happen to hear anything of that young rogue you keep kissing without my permission, I would want to know of that too."

"Oh, Auntie," she whispered. "We parted on such

dreadful terms, I am sure he would never want to see me again."

Florence tucked a hand under Annaleah's chin. "You just remember what I said about the word 'never.' I suspect it is one that rarely passes Emory Althorpe's lips."

Chapter 13

*F*OLLOWING THE NIGHT of heavy rains, there was only one main road that was maintained well enough to support a carriage the size of the berline. From Widdicombe House, it followed the coastline, passing Berry Head, a wide raised promontory of rock bordered on three sides by two-hundred-foot limestone cliffs. The town of Brixham, smallest of the three that skirted the harbor of Torbay, was built around the base of the promontory, and on top, because the summit presented the ideal strategic location for monitoring naval traffic moving to and fro in the Channel, there were four batteries of heavy cannon, two garrisoned forts, and a naval hospital.

Normally a speedy journey, on this day it took nearly an hour to traverse the mile from Berry Head to Brixham. Not only was the road thick with mud, but the distance was clogged with coaches and horses carrying men and women to the best vantage points along the cliffs for them to observe the huge warship newly anchored in port. The deeper the berline drove into the narrow streets of the town, the worse the congestion, because now there were pedestrians and enterprising pie-sellers filling every corner and lane that converged upon the waterfront. Most of the buildings were narrow wooden structures that seemed to lean one against the other for support, and from these the windows were flung wide and more people hung over the sills shouting, waving, chattering excitedly.

Only the constant cracking of the whip by Barrimore's driver, combined with the threat of the four matched geldings, kept the path before the berline clear. Two liveried postillions walked in front of the lead team, adding their shouts and threats to the snap of the lash. Two more coachmen in the rear suffered the indignity of being pelted by the occasional piece of rotten fruit tossed from a window or alleyway, but in the end, they rolled through Brixham and followed the coastal road down and around through Paignton and on to Torquay, where wealthy patrons came to rent villas and take the sea air. Here too there were crowds on the boardwalks and beaches. The harbor held a forest of masts swaying to and fro with the motion of the tides.

Barrimore and Anthony had taken rooms in a hotel overlooking the harbor. Because it had made little sense to burden the berline with their belongings, it was necessary to make a brief stop in order to collect their cases and strap them into the boot.

Annaleah was grateful for the chance to stretch her legs. Apart from the muddy, rutted roads and the berline's constant lurching to bypass obstacles in the roads, she was suffering from the strain of having to ignore Barrimore's brooding silence. Anthony, who barely lasted long enough to make a final comment about the unhealthy effects of so much fresh air, had fallen promptly asleep when they departed Widdicombe House and remained so until the wheels rolled to a halt outside their hotel. As for Barrimore, while he had not exactly stared at her for the entire length of time, she had felt his eyes boring into her more than once, not believing for an instant that although she kept her eyes closed, she had, like her brother, slept through the bouncing and jostling.

Annaleah was offered tea in the small cafe that fronted the hotel, but she chose instead to walk across the street to a small, shady park where visitors strolling along the boardwalk could enjoy the stunning view of the harbor below. The benches along the tree-lined walk were all full, the walk itself crowded with men in tall beaver hats and women in airy summer gowns. Waving once at Anthony to indicate her intention, Annaleah followed the boardwalk to a more promising stretch of grass and was there afforded her first clear view of the HMS *Bellerophon*, anchored well out in the middle of the great harbor.

She was a big three-masted ship-of-the-line, with an ornately carved and gilded gallery of windows across the stern and two gun decks painted with black stripes running the length of her hull. Her captain, Frederick Maitland, had set out perimeter guards, for there was a circle of smaller boats tethered to her sides, presumably manned by soldiers who warned away the flotilla of fishing boats that swarmed around the outside of the ring like bees buzzing a hive.

Napoleon Bonaparte, France's most fearsome general, self-proclaimed dictator, emperor, master of the continent of Europe . . . was now reduced to an insignificant dot on the deck of a ship. She remembered the stories her nurse used to tell her about "Old Boney." To most children, he was an ogre with one flaming red eye in the middle of his forehead and long teeth protruding from his mouth with which he tore to pieces and devoured naughty little girls who did not learn their lessons.

"Would you care to take a closer look, miss?"

A young gentleman standing beside her offered Anna the use of his small brass spyglass. It was bound in leather and fit neatly into her hand, but when the various sections were telescoped and the eyepiece held against the eye, it brought the warship close enough to distinguish the various clusters of officers and seamen standing on deck.

Anna lowered it, and the ship shrank to the size of a walnut again.

"He was on deck not two hours ago, miss. Napoleon himself, I warrant, for he wore the green uniform of a colonel in the Imperial Guard and the naval bicorn with the tri-colored cockade."

Anna closed her left eye and peered through the spy-glass again, counting at least a dozen men in green uniforms on the deck, most of whom wore bicorns. There were a dozen more in blue coats with gold trimmings, scarlet tu-

nics with white crossbelts, black and brown jackets with
white breeches, and still more men in frock coats and
trousers who were either not attached to the military or who
were not accorded the same courtesy as the prisoner of
being allowed to maintain the appearance of a ranking officer.
She did not see any with flaming red eyes or long fanged
teeth, nor would she have known Napoleon Bonaparte had
he looked straight back into the glass and waved.

With a polite smile, she thanked the obliging young
man and returned the spyglass. Her amused expression
remained in place for several moments after the gentleman
had bowed and moved away, but her glance had flickered
back to a nearby tree, her heartbeat had slowed to a dull
thud, and her breath was suddenly coming out in a long, dry
rasp through parted lips.

There was, indeed, a single flaming eye looking straight
into hers, but it was not red—it was a deep, dark brown.
And its mate was hidden under a swath of white bandaging
that was wrapped on an angle across the face of the last
man on earth she'd expected to see standing less than ten
paces away.

Emory Althorpe spared a quick glance in the direction
of the black berline before he left the shelter of the tree.
He was wearing a multicollared greatcoat draped over his
shoulders, the sides of which flared like bat wings when he
walked toward her. He had a rucksack slung over one arm,
and when the coat flared open—before a prudent hand
snatched it close to his body again—she caught a glimpse
of a pistol barrel stuck into his belt.

Anna's mouth dropped open wider with each step that
brought him closer. Her skin had turned the color of cold
ashes and she was genuinely in danger of fainting by the
time he reached her side. He quickly took hold of her arm;
then, without saying a word, he lifted the edge of the bandage and showed her the covered eye, as perfectly whole
and dark and cocoa brown as the other.

"What—" Her breath came in a rush and she raised a

hand, pressing it over her breast to keep her heart from bursting out of her chest. "What on earth—?"

"A necessary ruse, I am afraid," he explained in a low voice. "I was not half a mile from Widdicombe House when I discovered the colonel's warrant sheets were tacked to every post and pillar along the side of the road. You were right. They bear a strikingly accurate sketch of my face. A bandage was the only thing I could think of upon the instant."

Annaleah shook her head. "But . . . what are you doing here?" she managed to gasp. "How did you find me?"

"I did not find you," he said. "I followed you."

"You *followed* me?"

At a curious glance from one of the pedestrians, he took hold of her arm and hooked it through his, then started walking casually along the boardwalk, leading her back beneath the canopy of trees.

"Actually, I followed your fiancé's coach. It was not very difficult with all the crowds, and it is a rather impressive conveyance."

"You are mad," she declared. "You should be a hundred miles away by now."

"In truth, I was no more than two when I was forced to turn back."

Annaleah tilted her head in amazement as she looked at him. "But why? Why would you turn back?"

"Because someone took a shot at me."

Anna stopped abruptly. "Someone shot at you!"

Emory's one dark eye warned her to guard the level of her voice as he urged her to walk forward again. "It was just the act of an overzealous guardsman, but he was clutching a copy of the warrant when he went running back into the tollhouse for reinforcements. I circled around for a while to lose them and was keeping to the trees, not exactly sure where to go next, when I saw the berline rolling by in the distance."

"So you followed us . . . expecting what? That Barrimore might offer you a ride to London?"

Her unintentional wit won a smile from him, but it was hardly the devastating, breathtaking kind of expression that had affected her sensibilities the previous afternoon and evening. It was a thin flat line that was as ominous as the steely glare in his eye, and unnerving enough to make Annaleah twist around and glance back over her shoulder.

The hotel was no longer visible through the trees. Neither was the berline.

"I dare not go too far or my brother will come looking for me."

Althorpe kept walking. If anything, his pace increased.

"The other thing is, I have been remembering things. The flashes of lightning I told you about? Well, they have been coming closer together; sometimes it is more like a burst of light behind my eyes, and other times, I just look at something—like the spyglass you were holding just now—and I remember what my own looked like, where I kept it, the gold initials on the case."

"Then your memory is coming back?"

"Not fast enough," he said grimly. "There are still enormous gaps, and I have visions I do not understand, but some of them I do, and I am not too full of myself to say that they alarm me."

"Alarm you in what way?"

"As I have no easy way to say it, Miss Fairchilde, you must bear with my bluntness, but I believe I was indeed responsible for Napoleon's escape from Elba, and that my services were bought and paid for by the Bonapartists working to arrange his freedom."

"Dear God, you are admitting—!"

"I am admitting nothing. Not when I keep seeing myself bound by my wrists to a ceiling beam, being cut with a hundred stripes while someone is asking me what I know, what I saw, what I suspect. Does that sound like the treatment they would give to someone who is working on their behalf?"

"What are you suggesting?"

He shook his head. "I don't know, but I am convinced it has something to do with our guest out in the harbor."

Anna bit her lip. "Colonel Ramsey is convinced you are here to arrange another escape. Perhaps he has learned there is a plan afoot to rescue him."

"Perhaps so. But I was tortured in France, by a member of Bonaparte's inner circle."

"How can you be so sure, if you cannot remember—"

"I remember the knife. I kept thinking of the knife, kept seeing the knife. And then it came to me that it wasn't a *thing* I was seeing and remembering at all, but a name. The Knife. Le Couteau. He is an assassin, a man by the name of Cipriani, and if he was cutting me, asking me questions, torturing me for information, then I sure as hell was not working for Napoleon Bonaparte."

"Then . . . who *were* you working for?"

"Damned if I know. But listen—" He stopped walking a moment and faced her. "When you found me on the beach, you said I spoke to you. I mumbled something."

"Yes. You said something like: 'They have to know the truth before it is too late.' "

"That was it, that was all I said?"

"That was all I heard."

He stared past her shoulder, at a sliver of blue water visible through a break in the trees. Something about the *Bellerophon* had been bothering him since his first glimpse of the ship in the harbor, and it was there again now, an elusive shadow of a memory hovering just out of reach. Naturally, when he wanted the damned flashes, they would not come. When he did not want them, they came with sudden, debilitating fury.

"If you said 'They have to know the truth' and you claim the French were the ones who bound you and tortured you for information . . . it would suggest to me that perhaps you were not working for them at all," Anna said thoughtfully. "It might even suggest . . ."

The single dark eye came slashing back and his grip tightened almost painfully on her arm. "Suggest what?"

"That this knife person had discovered you were actually working against them?" she offered hesitantly. "That perhaps you had seen something, or heard something you should not have seen or heard and they wanted to know exactly what it was before they killed you. I mean . . . is that not why they torture people? To find out what they know, or who else they might have told?"

Emory's eye seemed to go out of focus as he considered her words for a moment. In the next, he reached up slowly and fished beneath the edge of his coat. His hand emerged with the iron key, which he stared at for another dozen heartbeats before curling his fingers tightly around it in a fist.

"It was my ship that took him off Elba," he whispered tautly, nodding his head slowly as he did. "But I did so on orders from Whitehall."

"*Whitehall?*"

"The foreign office." He looked down at the harbor again. "Westford."

"Are you suggesting Lord Geoffrey Peterson, the Earl of Westford, ordered you to help Bonaparte escape prison?"

A muscle shivered in his cheek. "I am suggesting I was acting with the full knowledge—even the full approval— of someone inside the British Naval Office."

"You mean . . . like a spy? An agent working secretly for the government? For *our* government?"

He heard the skepticism in her voice and his mouth pressed into a thin line. He turned and started walking again, taking one long stride to each of her two.

"If that was the case," she said, "why has someone not come forward to clear your name? Why is half of England looking for you?"

"If I knew that, I would not need your help."

"*My* help? What can I possibly do to help?"

"I have to get to London. The answer, the explanation is there."

"London! You just said you could not get two miles out of Brixham without being shot at."

"Yes, well, I did not have a trump card then, did I?"

"Trump card? What do you mean, trump card?"

When he did not answer right away, she glanced back and saw that even the trees had been left far behind. They were no longer on the boardwalk, either. He had led her into a narrow alleyway, and Anna had been too distracted to notice. He was turning into another laneway now, taking her farther and farther away from the hotel with every hurried step.

"Wait," she cried. "Wait! Where are we going? Where are you taking me?"

"Just a little ways farther—we're almost there."

"Almost where?" She tried to slow down, to pull back on his arm, but despite a second tug and a second protest, there was no visible break in his long stride. "I have to go back! Anthony and Barrimore will notice any moment that I am missing and they will come after me!"

"No doubt they will, which is why I would appreciate your hastening your steps a little."

"Not until I know where you are taking me!" she insisted.

When he started down yet another dark, evil-smelling alley instead, she dug her heels into the ground and yanked with all her strength. Her wrist slipped enough that she almost succeeded in wrenching herself free, but in the next instant she was recaptured, swung around hard, and pushed into the recessed niche of a doorway, with Althorpe's big body planted across the opening to block any chance of escape.

"Listen to me, please," he said in a chillingly low voice. "I do not wish to make a scene, or force you to do anything you do not wish to do, but at the same time, I am insisting that you come with me. I promise I will explain everything when we get to the inn, but at the moment, we are a little pressed for time."

"Inn? What inn?" she demanded.

"I will know it when I see it, and I have not seen it yet, so I would appreciate it if you would keep moving."

"I am not going one step farther!" Anna's eyes widened. "Have you completely lost your senses, sir? Apart from the sheer impropriety of accompanying you to an inn of any kind, for any reason, the mere *presumption* of even *imagining* that I would do so is . . . is . . ."

He leaned closer and turned up the edge of the bandage so that she felt the full impact of both forbiddingly inky eyes. "I have no doubt you can think of a hundred terms to apply to my character, and perhaps there is some merit to all of them, but regardless of the impropriety or presumption, you *are* coming with me."

Anna's hand flew up and lay trembling against the base of her throat. "Are you kidnapping me?"

"I prefer to think of it as taking advantage of an opportunity," he explained gently. "I am sorry, but I need to get out of Torquay, and I cannot do it without your help."

"Well, you will not get my help this way, sir," she said through her teeth. "Moreover, I shall make a poor hostage when I scream at the top of my lungs—which I am about to do at any moment."

The dark eyes narrowed. "I would not suggest you do anything half so foolish, Miss Fairchilde. For reasons you are undoubtedly aware of, I had little sleep last night and my head is pounding like the very devil. I am hungry, thirsty, and rapidly running out of patience, so unless you agree to come quickly and quietly by my side, you will leave me no choice but to render you speechless here and now, then pick you up and carry you over my shoulder like a sack of grain."

"You would not dare!" she exclaimed with breathless disbelief.

"Please do not test what I would or would not dare, Anna. Not now. Not today."

He held her gaze a moment longer before lowering the edge of the bandage over his eye and stepping back into the open lane. Anna remained in the niche until she regained a measure of composure, then gave her chin a small tilt upward and started to follow him. A sharp noise farther down the lane startled his gaze away for a split second and without thinking, without pondering the consequences, she gathered up her skirts and darted past him, running as fast as she could back up the street.

She did not even feel him catch her. One instant she was running, the next her feet were flailing the empty air and she was being hoisted up and swung around, landing over his shoulder with enough of a jolt to drive all the air out of her lungs.

For the full ten seconds it took for this appalling new affront to register, she hung with her arms and head dangling halfway down his back. When her wits returned, she tried to scream, but the effort was little more than an outraged splutter, most of it smothered against the wool of his coat. She tried pummeling him with her fists, but her hands became tangled in the long ribbons of her bonnet and by the time she freed them, the bonnet was so loose that it fell off, the steel hairpins began to spring out of the neatly wrapped coil of her hair, and with each long stride he took another thick brown curl tumbled over her eyes.

From somewhere nearby she heard a shout of laughter, and she struggled desperately to lift her head, hoping to catch the eye of a gallant who would come to her aid. But the laughter had come from a second-story window, where a woman dressed in an hourglass corset and silk drawers was sitting on the sill swinging a bare leg in the sunlight. To her further horror, Anna saw there were more open windows, more women in various states of undress laughing and pointing. The few men she did see, when she managed to push the straggled curls off her face, were surly unshaven creatures who leaned on the sides of buildings and grinned when Althorpe passed. One of them even had the audacity to ask if he needed assistance.

"Dear God," she gasped. "Where are we?"

"We are in an area of town best suited to a genteel woman's ignorance," he said over his shoulder.

"Will you please put me down!" she hissed, pounding her fist on his back.

"Will you promise to behave if I do?"

"No!"

"Then enjoy the ride."

He turned another corner, and Anna's senses swooped with the sickening motion.

"Oh, please. I am going to be ill. I swear I will not make a scene. I swear it on my honor."

Althorpe's steps slowed, then stopped. His hands were hooked over the back of her knees and as he bent forward, they moved up to her hips, climbed to her waist, and finally came to rest just beneath her arms. Anna wobbled for as long as it took her head to stop spinning, then batted furiously at his hands until he let her go.

"How dare you," she gasped. "How dare you manhandle me in such a beastly way! Is this how you show your gratitude? Is this how you repay my aunt for the faith she had in you, for the risks she took in order to *save your life?*"

"Anna, if there was another way—"

"I have not given you leave to all me Anna!" she cried. The frustration and the sting of unwanted tears caused her to stamp her foot, a childish gesture that she recognized as one, and which resulted in yet another unpleasant surprise: She had lost one of her shoes.

The anger that had fueled her spirit for battle slowly began to give way to the realization that he did not care. He did not care that she had lost her shoe or her bonnet. He did not care that her brother would be frantic and her aunt would feel horribly betrayed. He did not care that she had also lain awake most of the night tossing and turning, reliving the sensation of his hands on her body, the caress of his mouth on her skin. Nor would he care that until this very instant, when his threats and promises took the choice away from her, she might actually have been willing to help him.

Slowly, the blaze in her eyes faded. The bloom of indignation in her cheeks turned to a ruddy stain of hurt and disappointment.

"You may believe me when I say, sir," she said softly, "that I enjoyed your company more when you did not know who or what you were."

Unmoved even by the shine of tears in her eyes, he held out a hand, indicating the direction in which he wished her to proceed. She turned quickly, her heart crushed, and did not see the tremors that forced him to curl his fingers into a tight fist to stop them from shaking.

Chapter 14

WHILE EMORY ALTHORPE was arranging accommodations at a tawdry, nondescript inn halfway across town, Anthony and Barrimore were searching the length of the boardwalk in both directions. They were not alone in the hunt. Colonel Ramsey had arrived at the hotel moments after Barrimore, and while Anna thought her brother and the marquess were settling their account, they were, in fact, being questioned by the colonel in the presence of a half dozen armed redcoats.

Neither Anna nor her aunt had allowed for the speed with which Lucille Althorpe had gleefully hastened to Colonel Ramsey with the information that her husband's brother had been hiding at Widdicombe House. As soon as Stanley had driven her home that morning, she had pleaded a migraine and taken to her bed, insisting she wanted nothing more than darkness and utter quiet. A note had been delivered to the rectory during the night concerning the condition of one of his parishioners and Stanley, having been told by his brother and Florence, and again by a swanning Lucille, that the best thing for him to do was to go about his business as usual, did exactly that. The moment his carriage pulled out of the drive, the fair Lucille had her shawl and bonnet on and was hurrying through the rear door.

It took Lucille well over an hour to reach the barracks at the North Fort, where Ramsey had taken a temporary office. There were five other people waiting in the anteroom to see him when she walked up to the young adjutant and gave her name. He was polite enough in directing her to take a seat, which was instantly made available by one of the gentlemen, but she merely stared at the adjutant, her pale blue eyes shimmering with tears, and was ushered, amidst a flurry of sincere apologies, into Colonel Ramsey's office.

Less than ten minutes later, Ramsey was shouting orders to muster the guards and an armed detachment was immediately dispatched to Widdicombe House. At almost the same instant, a courier was arriving from the tollhouse with the report that shots had been exchanged with a man matching the description of Emory Althorpe. He had escaped, but the guards had chased him back into the vicinity of the coastal plain and were confident he was now trapped somewhere between the villages of Paignton and Torquay. Copies of the warrant with Emory's face were distributed among the rest of the garrison and they were dispatched in pairs, threes, and groups of six to scour the roads and turnpikes leading out of all three towns.

Ramsey, who prided himself on the network of spies he had created in the two short weeks he had been in Torbay, was also informed as a matter of due course that a berline belonging to Winston Perry, Lord Barrimore, had been seen on the road to Widdicombe House with the marquess and another gentleman identified as Anthony Fairchilde, Viscount Ormont, on board. It had returned along the same route an hour later carrying an additional passenger, Miss Annaleah Fairchilde, the viscount's sister.

"She was the one," Lucille had insisted excitedly. "She was the one who was throwing herself in the rogue's arms last night and kissing him as if it was neither the first nor the last time! I daresay if anyone knows where he is now, or where he is going, it will be her—if, indeed, it is not already part of her plans to meet up with him wherever that may be!"

"Surely you are not suggesting that the daughter of Percival Fairchilde, Lord Witham, is involved in some way with the Bonapartists?"

Lucille expelled an audibly impatient breath. "My dear

Colonel Ramsey, I am telling you only that they did not kiss like strangers. Had the little glances and sly smiles they stole throughout the entire evening not been enough of an indication of familiarity, I had occasion to require a glass of warm milk later that night and saw Emory Althorpe emerging from Miss Fairchilde's bedroom! Her bedroom! And he was without a coat or boots!"

Rupert Ramsey needed no further convincing. He called for his coach and gave orders for a patrol to ride on ahead and detain the marquess's berline until all three occupants could be questioned. As it happened, with the muddy condition of the roads, the heavy congestion of traffic, and the time it took for the larger vehicle to maneuver its way to the hotel in Torquay, Colonel Ramsey was alighting and adjusting the wrinkles in his jacket just as a tall fellow with a bandage around his head—not an unusual sight in an area that boasted a busy naval hospital—was vanishing through the trees with a lovely young woman on his arm.

"The hell you say!" had been Anthony's reaction when Colonel Ramsey had explained the reason for their delay. "Annaleah made no mention of any criminal being harbored on the premises, nor would she tolerate his presence if there were one! As for her having any prior knowledge of the fellow, I can assure you she has not so much as clapped eyes on him before, much less engaged in any manner of prolonged communications."

"I have been told, by a rather reliable source, that your sister seemed extremely . . . friendly . . . toward Althorpe."

"She has been known to be friendly toward stray cats too—does that earn her a turn in the stockade?"

"It would if one of those stray cats was known to have committed treason against King and country," Rupert answered easily.

"And how would he do that? By pissing on the crown?"

"By aiding and abetting the Corsican general in his escape from Elba. By whisking him away to France to meet and lead an army of loyalists on a path of death and destruction. And by landing here, in Torbay, days before the prisoner is slated to arrive so that he might organize and implement a second attempt to free the bastard and carry him to safety in the Americas, where God only knows what manner of war and havoc would be wrought in his despotic quest to conquer the world!"

In his zeal, droplets of spittle had flown from Ramsey's lips, several of which had landed on the front of Anthony's lapel. The latter looked down in disgust and with greatly exaggerated care removed a handkerchief from his cuff and blotted them dry.

"My sister would not even know how to go about making the acquaintance of a man engaged in the activities you describe, and in the event she did so—by purely accidental means, I assure you—she would most likely faint dead away from the shock. She is a very proper, very genteel, extremely cultured young lady for whom such weighty matters as politics, war, and the intrigues you describe would be as distasteful as walking through dung. She would no sooner give the time of day to a bounder like Emory Althorpe than she would to a common guttersnipe. And if you doubt me, sir, you can ask her yourself. She is waiting outside, no doubt as impatient as Barrimore and I to remove ourselves from this rarefied air of fish heads and villainy."

Barrimore had contributed nothing to this point, nor did Ramsey, his fervor notwithstanding, dare to interrogate such an important member of the peerage. He was also wise enough not to relate what Lucille had said about seeing Althorpe embracing his fiancée or paying a late night visit to Miss Fairchilde's bedchamber, not in the presence of a man said to be one of the finest duelists in England.

"Yes," the marquess said at this point, flexing the long fingers in his hands as if the conversation was beginning to irritate him. "Let us ask Miss Fairchilde if she has any knowledge of any desperate criminals, and then I really must insist we be on our way."

One of the hotel clerks was sent across the park to find Annaleah, and when he returned more than ten minutes later to report that no one matching her description was to be found, it was Anthony who strode outside with a curse of impatience, and who came back after another fruitless search along the boardwalk to announce she must have wandered into a nearby shop or cafe.

Ramsey dispatched his men to expand the search while Anthony and Barrimore each took a section of the boardwalk and followed it to its end. It was not until they began to question the occasional passerby that a young man with a spyglass recalled seeing a lovely young woman dressed in blue standing alone by the iron fence. She had not remained alone for long, however. A tall, broad-shouldered gentleman in a black greatcoat—a wounded veteran, he had surmised from the bandage covering half his face—had joined her in short order and led her off down the boardwalk.

"Led her off?" Anthony said with a frown.

"Well, yes. It seemed that way. He had her by the arm, as I recall."

Ramsey had quickly taken a poster out of his pocket and unfolded it for the young man, who studied the sketched features a moment before holding his hand over half the face and nodding thoughtfully, admitting it *could* be the same gentleman.

Ramsey crumpled the sheet in his fist and looked wildly around the street. "He is here. By God he is here and I have him."

"Do you not forget he also has my sister!" Anthony hissed.

"I am not forgetting, sir. Nor am I discounting the possibility that the meeting was prearranged and she went with him willingly!"

"Sir! Sir!"

A pair of soldiers came running along the boardwalk, one of them carrying a blue silk bonnet with long dangling ribbons and a cream-colored veil. The other clutched in his hand a small gray leather shoe. Anthony, blanching as white as his collar, identified both as belonging to Annaleah.

"Found 'em a few blocks from 'ere, sir. Shoe were just lyin' in the gutter, but we 'ad an 'ell of a time gettin' the bonnet back; it were already on the head o' one o' the 'ores struttin' up an' down the lane."

"Did you say . . . a whore?"

"Aye. Down on Gropecuntlane. Brothels one end t'other. Girls don't usually talk to sojers, but one o'them, she were drunk as a newt an' shouted she saw a gent carryin' a proper lady over his shoulder, her kickin' an' squealin' an' the like. Said 'ee looked like a pirate with 'is 'ead all wrapped up. Said it looked like 'ee caught himself a bit o'fancy lace t'take on board 'is ship wi' 'im, cuz 'at's where they was bound: t'the wharfs."

"Dear God," Anthony whispered. "He has abducted Annaleah."

"You will not get far with me, sir," Annaleah was saying, "if that is your intention."

Emory glanced up from lighting a pair of oil lamps and saw that she had once again sought refuge in a shadowy corner and was pressed as far away from him as possible without actually molding herself to the wall.

"You will be pleased to know that is not my intention at all." He adjusted the wicks on both lamps, enlarging the circle of light each threw to its brightest peak. He left one on the side table and carried the other to a rickety wash-stand by the window, where he stood for a moment gazing out at the street below. The sun was well below the distant promontory of Berry Head and the purplish haze of dusk was growing thicker by the minute. There was still a good deal of pedestrian traffic moving to and fro. Lamps were being lit over the doorways of taverns and brothels. They were a stone's throw from the waterfront and the establishments here were frequented by fishermen, sailors, and journeymen—plus thieves and rogues as well—who'd put in a long day of hard labor and wanted nothing more of an evening than to drink their ale and fondle a willing breast.

The inn was one of the ones Broom had named, and the proprietor had extorted a celestial twenty pounds from Emory for the privilege of renting a small, squalid room under the eaves.

"Might I ask just what your intentions are?"

He turned away from the window. "I plan to wait another hour or so, then leave under cover of darkness."

"And you plan to take me with you? Slung over your shoulder like a sack of grain?"

Emory smiled faintly. "Actually, no. I was going to leave you here, with this for company." He picked up the haversack and from it withdrew a small leather-bound book. "I'm afraid I could not find a copy of *Romeo and Juliet* in your aunt's library, but I thought *A Midsummer Night's Dream* might prove equally engaging."

She gaped at the book, then at him. "You want me to read a damned play?"

"Tut-tut, Miss Fairchilde. Language. And yes, I want you to amuse yourself for a couple of hours."

"Why?"

He dragged the angled bandage off his head. He had tucked most of his hair beneath the linen binding and had to give it a vigorous raking with his fingers before it fell soft and thick around his collar again.

"Why, indeed," he murmured. "Can you think of a better diversion in a town swollen with cutthroats and thieves than for a young and beautiful heiress to go missing? Within a couple of hours at most, every soldier and constable within five miles will be pulled off their other duties and ordered to search for you instead."

"How very clever," she said, staring at his broad back. "But what makes you think I will sit here calmly reading Shakespeare after you have gone? What makes you think I will not run out into the street at once and tell the constables exactly where to look?"

He leaned slightly to the side and pulled the heavy greatcoat off his shoulder. "I suppose I was not thinking clearly."

"I suppose you were not," she said slowly, the words fading as she watched him shrug his other arm free of the coat and toss the heavy garment on the bed. The upper half of his coat sleeve was stained around a long gash in the wool. When he took the jacket off, she realized the stain was red and the linen of his shirtsleeve was soaked with blood.

"Dear God," she whispered. "What happened?"

"It's nothing. A lucky shot. Barely a scratch."

"You have been *shot*! You might have told me!"

"I did. I told you the guard at the tollhouse shot at me."

"You did not say he hit you. Oh, dear gracious me!" This last exclamation brought her out of the shadows as he peeled down the sticky layer of linen and bared the damaged flesh beneath. The wound was, as he had said, not very deep, but it had bled a good deal and ungluing the congealed bits of the torn sleeve caused it to start weeping again.

Anna searched around for a towel, but although the innkeeper had supplied a jug of brackish water and a chipped washbowl, it was apparently left up to the guest to provide his own toiletries. She spied the haversack and after rummaging through the contents, produced two handkerchiefs and a large square napkin that had been wrapped around some of Mildred's biscuits.

She pointed him to a chair and removed her short blue spencer jacket. "Sit down and let me look at it."

"It isn't necessary—"

"Oh, do shut up and sit down before I pinch some sense into myself and let you bleed to death."

Emory frowned, but did as he was told, pausing first to tug his shirttails out of his breeches and peel the bloodied garment over his head. Annaleah was tipping water into the bowl while he was doing this, and when she turned, she drew up short for a moment, startled to see him bare-chested before her.

She had not seen him without some manner of modest covering since he had first wakened at Widdicombe House, and with the light from the lamp burnishing his shoulders, it brought a hint of fire to life in her belly—heat that was most unwelcomed and unwanted at a time when she needed to rely on anger to maintain her composure.

Determined to look at nothing but the wound, she soaked the napkin in the washbowl and twisted the excess water free. Working quickly, she washed away the blood that had leaked down his arm first, gradually wiping and blotting her way closer to the actual injury. She was not squeamish by nature, and had seen her share of cuts and scrapes—even a horrid long laceration in a groomsman's leg after a stallion had kicked half the flesh off his calf. It surprised her, then, that she should feel queasy bathing a mere cut on Emory Althorpe's arm, and downright light-headed when he obeyed her instruction to lift his elbow that she might clean the smear over his ribs.

Somewhere between one stroke of the cloth and the next, she lost the battle not to notice the powerful muscles across his back and shoulders. His neck, where the fine curls of hair clung to his skin, held a particular fascination, as did the dark smooth mat that covered his chest. From there, it was only logical to look at his back, at the dozens of raised white lines that had been painstakingly carved into his flesh. Knowing what they were, how they had been caused, the pain he must have endured, sent her belly sliding even lower.

She cleared her throat and rinsed the napkin. "You should have told me you were hurt," she said again.

"Would it have made a difference?" he asked. "Would you have been more obliging?"

"No," she admitted after a brief pause. "But it might have explained some of your belligerence."

"*My* belligerence?"

"Your behavior was downright rude and ugly, sir. I am not accustomed to being treated like a common trull, or being pawed or ordered about. Nor do I take kindly to any man who threatens violence against a woman."

"Did I hurt you in any way?"

"I am likely bruised, yes."

"Only your pride."

The napkin slipped on the wound, causing Emory to suck an involuntary hiss of air between his teeth.

"You took it upon yourself to presume a great deal," she said.

"You are absolutely right: I did."

"And you acted with an unconscionable lack of consideration, not only for me but for my family. Father is a respected member of the House of Lords. You just do not go about kissing the daughters of noblemen in a public street."

He glanced up and murmured, "I was not kissing you."

"I meant *kidnapping*. You do not go about kidnapping daughters of noblemen! Should so much as a whisper reach his ear that I allowed myself to become entangled in such intrigues, why—" She waved the cloth a moment, searching for a way to convey the trauma it would cause, but the only thing she could think of was that it might put him off his newspaper. "Well, my mother, at any rate, would be humiliated beyond words."

Emory watched a small frown crease her brow. Her eyes flickered up from his arm and met his, then sank slowly down again, as if she was only just then realizing where she ranked in her family's priorities.

He reached around and gently grasped her hand.

"Forgive me," he said with genuine regret. "I realize that by all accounts I make a better villain than hero, but I had hoped—and yes, perhaps even presumed—that you believed me. Perhaps even trusted me a little."

She stared at the long, tapered fingers where they were wrapped around her wrist and felt their heat ripple all the way up her arm, spread through her breasts, and bristle across the nape of her neck.

"But if I cannot even convince *you* of my innocence in all this," he added softly, "what chance do I have of persuading anyone else?"

Slowly, her eyes rose to meet his, and in the prolonged, breathless instant that followed, she wanted to tell him how very wrong he was. She did believe him. And although he made it exceedingly difficult to justify, she did trust him. Far more than she should. She had been raised not to think or act on her own, not to believe anything that was not dictated to her over her morning chocolate. In turn it was expected that she would be the dutiful daughter, the obedient wife and mother who would raise her own daughters to parrot the rigid standards of behavior dictated by her superior class. But in less than a week, her faith in all that social stricture had been shaken. Florence Widdicombe had shaken it, for she was proof that someone could break the rules and live quite happily ever after. Emory Althorpe had shaken it. He had shattered every rule, broken every covenant, scoffed at every social protocol . . . yet even helpless, wounded, and lacking any memories of who and what he was, he was more alive, exciting, and appealing to her than all the staid, draconian Winston Perrys in England.

She wanted to believe him. She did believe him. And because she believed him, the full measure of her disillusionment and confusion passed like a shadow through her eyes. Emory saw it. Even more, he could see that by admitting it, even just to herself, she felt more lost and isolated than ever.

His eyes narrowed a fraction, enough to cause her to turn her head away in embarrassment. But she was not as quick to move, and when he stood, she was still beside him. He grasped her shoulders and forced her to look up at him again, but she could only shake her head in a feeble attempt to deny the emotions that were suddenly raging through her veins.

"Anna—" He cradled her face between his hands. A muscle shivered in his cheek as he studied the melting blue depths of her eyes, the trembling softness of her mouth. "Anna, forgive me for what I have done to you."

"You have done nothing I did not let you do willingly and freely."

"Ahh, but given the smallest chance, I would have," he whispered. "Another moment or two in front of that window, with the lightning outside and the heat inside . . ."

Her lashes fluttered closed with the sensation of his thumb's brushing gently at the wetness that had gathered at the corner of her eyes. "Given another moment, I . . . I might not have stopped you."

His smile wavered, then faded altogether as his body reacted to the tremors in her voice. "You don't mean that. You would have wakened this morning hating me."

"I do mean it." Her eyes were huge and fierce with conviction when she opened them. "I mean it now," she added in a faltering whisper. "I . . . I . . ."

The pads of his fingers brushed quickly over her lips, preventing her from finishing the thought. He was not even certain he wanted to know what that thought might be. Not here, not now at any rate. He saw the subsequent movement in her throat as she swallowed the rest of her words and he felt the warmth rising in her skin, burning with the shame of showing him just how vulnerable she was. He leaned forward, pressing his lips over the residue of a tear. He kissed her eyes, her temples, the pink tip of her nose. Her hair was in disarray, catching the lamplight on its dark, tumbled strands, and his hands moved almost with a will of their own to bury themselves in the silky waves, drawing her closer, holding her while his mouth covered hers and urged her lips to part, to let him in.

She did it willingly, tilting her head higher, feeling no need whatsoever to pretend she did not want him to kiss her, or that she did not want to kiss him in return. Her one lingering concession to modesty was that she did not groan aloud with longing when her hands slid up the bare heat of his chest and curled around his neck. In the end, the sounds all came from him: a throaty warning when her body pushed eagerly up against his, a husked, breathless curse when her mouth, once again, would not settle for anything less than his very best effort.

"Stop me," he gasped, his hands trembling around fistfuls of her hair. "Stop me or I will not be able to stop myself."

She pulled herself higher and wrapped her arms tighter and kissed him like she had never kissed a man before, never known it was possible to kiss, with her whole body and soul.

Emory's groan turned deep and guttural, his lips demanding and possessive. Her breasts were crushed against his chest, and his hands moved restlessly to explore what had kept him awake and tormented through most of the night, but there were too many barriers, too much silk, too many fashionably pert satin ribbons. He swept aside the tumbled waves of her hair, his fingers searching blindly in the delicate pleats a moment before he found the upper lacings. A few quick tugs and the gathered folds of the bodice were slack enough for him to ease the sleeves of the dress and the underlying chemise off the top of her shoulders. A further stroke of his hand brushed the flimsy shields down to her waist and he breathed another oath, soft and warm against the satiny-smooth flesh as he dragged his mouth downward and claimed the pink crown of her nipple.

Anna gasped and arched her head back. Her fingers curled into his hair and her body swayed with the sensations pouring through her, a flood of sweet, hot shivers that responded to every rolling thrust of his tongue. She felt deeper, more urgent contractions in her belly and between her thighs, but it still came without warning—the hot, shuddering rush of exquisite pleasure. Desire for more spread through her body and weakened her knees; it brought her down beside him, then beneath him as he lowered her onto the crush of her skirts. His lips continued to plunder her breasts, then descended, following the path his hands blazed as he pushed her gown lower to bare her hips, her thighs. When the last filmy layer of silk was tossed aside, he lingered over the smooth plane of her belly, his breath as hot as his mouth where it teased the indented vee above her thighs. His hands skimmed to her knees, coaxing her limbs gently apart, wide enough for him to ease his fingers, then his mouth into the dark patch of curls.

Anna did not know where to look or how to respond to the intimacy. The shock of feeling his fingers sliding back and forth over her flesh was devastating enough; the realization that it was his mouth now, and his tongue lapping at her, devouring her like she was some exotic delicacy, nearly sent her skin up in flames. Surely this had to be the ultimate violation of every moral and chaste rule that governed the behavior of a proper young lady, but for some inexplicable reason she wanted to laugh out loud with the joy of it. It was pleasure. Simple, raw, sensuous pleasure with a magnificent rogue who saw no shame in her cries and who did his very best to elicit more.

When the pleasure became almost too acute to bear, she tried to pull herself away, but his hands were there to catch her, to hold her by the hips and brace her while he proved she could indeed withstand more. His tongue lashed furiously at her few remaining shreds of modesty and Anna did not even have a chance to draw a full breath before the light and heat and fury burst within her. It sent her arching up off the floor, her hands clawing at his shoulders, his neck. It sent her fingers twisting frantically into the waves of his hair, holding on for dear life as streak after streak of unimagined ecstasy brought her writhing and lurching against him.

When the tumult passed, she lay quivering and shaken beneath him. He lifted his mouth from her body, but only for the few brief seconds it took to strip away his boots and breeches. Then he was back, his lips chasing the shivers that raced across the surface of her belly while his hands stroked and caressed and urged her thighs to part again, this time to welcome the heat and heaviness of his own naked need.

Emory forced himself to move slowly, to introduce himself inch by agonizing inch. She was lush enough, slippery enough to accept the increasing pressure with hardly more than a startled gasp. Yet she clutched at his arms, his shoulders, even his hair, until he began to fear that perhaps she was too small, too frightened to accommodate something so swollen and inflexible, so rigid he almost did not recognize it as part of his own body.

In some ways, he shared her thrill and uncertainty. Lacking any memories of previous experiences to fall back on, he did not know if all women tasted this sweet or felt this sleek and luscious; if it was just pure instinct or something else urging him to thrust and thrust and thrust until there was nothing between them but friction and heat.

The fact he could do barely more than ease half of himself inside her posed a slight impediment to all this unbridled thrusting, however, especially when he heard Anna whimper softly in his ear and knew he could push no farther, not without tearing into her like a plundering barbarian. He stopped, his stomach clenched, his whole body shuddering with the effort it took, just to calm himself and count his heartbeats, one thunderous measure at a time. She was a virgin; of course she was. She was tense, tight as a fist, and he had her on the hard wooden floor like a twopenny strumpet, with her thighs spread and her eyes glazed with fear over the size of what he was trying to push inside her.

"Dear God . . ."

"Wh-what is it? What is wrong?"

"Nothing," he rasped. "Absolutely nothing."

"Am I hurting you?"

"Hurting *me*?" He lifted his head off her shoulder and

gazed down with a combination of disbelief and curiosity. "I am barely holding on by the skin of my teeth, trying not to make a complete damned fool of myself, and you want to know if *you* are hurting *me?*"

Her eyes were indeed glazed, but not with fear over any discomfort he was causing her. They were bigger and bluer than any ocean he had ever seen, and were looking up at him almost apologetically as she gently untwined her fingers from his hair. It was only then that he understood: She was afraid she had tugged too hard on the bruised back of his scalp and that the pain was what had made him stop and pull back.

He laughed in sheer self-defense, then kissed her full and hard on the mouth. "No. You are not hurting me. But you *are*," he added gently, "killing me."

"I am?"

"You are a virgin, are you not?"

An instant flush of mortification darkened her cheeks and he kissed her again, quickly, then said, "No. No, I . . . I was not asking, I was . . . I was trying to explain why I had to stop. Why I am being . . . cautious . . . and trying not to hurt *you.*"

She curled her lip between her teeth and considered what he said, weighing it against the swollen, throbbing presence inside her. "You do seem very . . . big," she admitted on a whisper."

The innocent acknowledgment was too much for Emory, and he groaned. He slid his hands down to her waist, then beneath her hips, and lifted her, breaching her so hard and fast she had no time to register anything but a little cry of surprise. A ripple of tension passed through her body, but he only held her closer and buried himself deeper until there was nothing between them but damp skin. Nothing but heat and a rising sense of urgency that bade him whisper reassurances against her mouth, against the strained arch of her throat.

He need not have worried. The sting of penetration was

all but forgotten as her body shuddered and melted around him. Waves of tiny contractions began to turn all the tension inward so that she gripped him harder, tighter, adjusting to his size and thickness. The pleasure began to build again, gathering in upon itself, coiling around him in a series of fierce little clutches that had him gasping, shaking like a schoolboy on his first foray into the realm of sin. Her entire body began to burn with an intuitive impatience that made her tilt her hips higher, wriggle herself closer, implore him by her actions if not her ragged breaths to move, to do something to ease the terrible, wonderful pressure.

Emory complied with his hands, his body. He began to move inside her with slow stretching strokes, displaying a level of skill and restraint he did not know he possessed. He slid into the soft, sucking wetness as deeply as he could bear it before he withdrew, judging the impact of each thrust by the way she lifted her body to receive him, by the soft sounds of awe that vibrated in her throat. She turned liquid around him, molten and silky, and he started to surge into her with greater speed, greater power, more ferocious urgency, knowing by the way she trembled and pushed herself feverishly into each rhythmic beat that the brilliant release of a shared orgasm was just a breath away. It was there, flaring white-hot and brilliant, just a stroke . . . two . . .

"Wait," she cried. "Stop!"

Emory's spine was arched, his chest a wall of bulging, corded muscles above her, his hips an aggressive blur of movement below. He bared his teeth in a snarl and shook his head, unwilling to stop, unable to stop or to believe she could ask it of him now, not now when he could feel the pleasure about to break within him.

"Do you not hear it?" she gasped. "*Listen!*"

Blood was pounding through his veins, drumming in his ears, and if he could have made a coherent sound he would have asked her what she possibly expected him to hear when his entire body was screaming like an open nerve. But then it came to him, and he blinked the blindness out of his eyes. He turned his head and his gaze flew to the window and with a single fluid motion that was as breathless as any that had gone before, he pulled out of her and was on his feet, moving with catlike speed across the room to extinguish both lamps.

No sooner were they smothered in darkness than the authoritative clumping of a dozen or more booted feet passed by on the street below. Emory went to the window and rubbed a circle in the grime while Anna wobbled to her knees, holding up a fistful of crumpled clothing to shield her nakedness.

"What is it?"

"Soldiers," he said. "An entire bloody detachment, from the look of it."

"Soldiers?" The word was scarcely a breath. "What do they want? They could not possibly be looking for us already!"

"I would not want to wager the fate of my soul on it." He hurried to where he had draped his greatcoat over the foot of the bed. While Anna watched in increasing dread, he took a pistol out of one of the deep pockets and checked to ensure it was primed.

"What are you going to do?"

"They appear to be starting their search at the far end of the street, and with luck it will take them a few minutes to work their way here to the inn."

"But what are you going to *do*?"

He glanced at her as he reached for his drawers and breeches. "I am not going to trust the landlord to keep his mouth shut for a mere twenty pounds."

She glanced down, her nude body pale against the shadows. Quickly she separated her chemise from her dress, pulling both garments over her head and fumbling with the drawstrings around her bodice and waist. Her arms were shaking almost too much to accomplish the simple task, and she could see she was not alone in her predicament—Emory seemed to be having difficulty buttoning his breeches. When he saw Anna watching, he frowned and turned aside.

"It doesn't just go away as easily as all that," he muttered.

No, it doesn't, she thought, barely able to keep her teeth from chattering in the sudden chill that claimed her. There was blood on her thighs, proof that something was gone, but she was still tense and trembling inside as if there was something more, something not quite achieved before it had been swept away.

She noticed more blood on her hand and wrist and realized that Emory's arm was bleeding again. A smeared trickle of red ran from the wound to his elbow, threatening to drip onto the floor. She fetched the two large handkerchiefs she had found in the haversack and folded them into a bandage.

"Keep still," she ordered when he tried to scowl her away. "The shirt you were wearing is ruined, and you only have one spare."

"I did not pack this morning with an eye to comfort."

"Well," she said, wrapping and tying the bandage in place, "I am sure we will be able to manage without extra clothing for a day or two, but how I shall get along with only one shoe is another matter entirely."

"*We?*"

"I am going with you."

"You absolutely are not."

"I absolutely am."

"Anna—"

"And if you try to stop me, or order me to stay behind reading a foolish play about forest nymphs, I shall lean out the window the moment you leave and scream at the top of my lungs."

"You would not do that."

"Yes I would. My father knows some very good solicitors in London. If you are innocent, they will be able to prove it."

He grasped her by the shoulders and gave her a little

shake. "This is not a parlor debate, Annaleah. Those are real soldiers with real guns and they intend to kill me, if they get the chance, not take me to court."

"Then we mustn't give them the chance, must we," she said softly. "And besides, at the moment they are most likely searching for *me:* a terrified, kidnapped heiress who they believe has been snatched off the street by some nefarious brigand of unknown origin."

"I don't—"

"There is no earthly reason they should suspect it was you. Not yet anyway; not until they have searched everywhere and found no one tied to any chairs awaiting the delivery of a ransom note. Was that not your goal all along? To keep them busy searching for a stolen heiress while you slipped away unnoticed? If so, it will be a very short distraction if they find me in the next ten minutes; I doubt you would get farther than the first crossroad.

"On the other hand," she added, shoving her arms into her spencer, "I would happily wager the fate of *my* soul that we could walk out the front door of this inn, arm in arm like husband and wife, and they would not glance at us twice."

Outwardly she looked calm enough to be convincing—there was even a hint of a lift in her eyebrow. Inwardly, she was holding her breath, refusing to acknowledge the more sensible side of her conscience as it shouted at her to pick up the book and tie herself in the chair if need be.

His dark eyes narrowed. "I grant you may be right. But what if you are wrong?"

"If I am wrong . . . then you will be shot and I will be sent back to London in disgrace and we will be no better off than if we stand here and argue about it for the next hour."

His fingers tightened a moment on her shoulders. "As soon as we are safely out of Torquay—the very first town—we will find a respectable hotel and leave you there."

"As soon as we are safe," she countered, "I will write a note to my brother telling him that I have *not* been kidnapped and that all will be explained at the earliest possible convenience."

"Do you honestly think that will make him stop looking? And how will he know I did not force you to write the letter with a knife against your throat?"

"I will word it in such a way that he will know that I pen it willingly and truthfully."

He continued to stare, waging his own private war with his common sense, but in the end, the noise out in the streets and the determination in her eyes made him mutter an indecipherable oath. "Why do I have a feeling I am going to regret this? Hurry up then. It would not do for them to get close enough to have too good a look at you."

At her wary frown, he smoothed a handful of tousled curls off her shoulder. "Because at the moment, you look far too thoroughly ravished to be any man's wife," he murmured, "and I would not want them sniffing after us for those reasons either."

Chapter 15

ANNALEAH WAS STILL fumbling with the buttons on her spencer when they hurried down the steps to the ground floor of the tavern. The taproom was full of thick-limbed men and blowsy women, many of whom turned and gave their neighbor a snickering nudge as Emory and Anna passed through their midst. The air was close with the smell of lamp oil and unwashed bodies, and the first thing Anna did when they were out on the street was gulp at a mouthful of fresh air. The second was to expel it in a rush, for there were soldiers not a dozen paces away, emerging from the establishment next door.

Emory calmly cradled a hand beneath her elbow and started walking down the street in the opposite direction. Ten more paces, then twenty added enough distance for them to breathe and for Emory to risk a casual glance over his shoulder. The soldiers seemed to be ignoring them, intent upon holding their lanterns up to the faces of the three men they had brought out of the tavern with them. The trio were all tall and dark-haired. One had a black patch tied over his eye, and at a barked order from one of the guards he lifted it show a hideously puckered scar above the empty socket.

The street itself was eerily devoid of pedestrians. The regular citizens not sidled up to a jug of ale already had scurried away into the cracks and crevices of buildings like cockroaches at the first sound of military boots on the cobblestones. The few stragglers who were left were either too drunk to hear anything or too belligerent to care.

The sound of clopping horses and carriage wheels sent Emory melting into a shadowy doorway now, drawing Anna after him. A carriage reined to a halt outside one of the more raucous brothels along the street and two gentlemen alighted. They tossed a coin to the driver and promised another if he would wait, then staggered up to the door and pounded good-naturedly until they were welcomed inside.

The wheels of a second carriage echoed hollowly along the near-deserted street. It pulled around the hackney and rattled past the niche where Emory and Anna stood, the glow from its riding lamp casting a brief flare of light over their faces before leaving them in shadow again. The driver stopped where the three men were being held at musket length by the soldiers. When the door opened, a man in a dark blue uniform disembarked and paused a moment to glance both ways along the street, the light winking off his silver lapel buttons as he did so.

"What have you found?"

Colonel Rupert Ramsey's voice was abrasively loud and carried easily enough for Emory and Anna to hear.

"These two gentlemen," said one of the soldiers with obvious sarcasm, "were attempting to scarper out the rear door when we entered. The other kicked over a bench to block our path when we gave chase."

Colonel Ramsey looked over all three men carefully before dismissing them with a wave of his hand. "Keep looking. The bastard is here somewhere, by God, and I intend to find him. There are another forty men on the road behind me; they should be here any minute to help you broaden the search."

"Forty soldiers?" Anna hissed. "Should we not move away from here before they arrive?"

Emory did not answer. He did not respond at all except to sag slightly against her shoulder.

Keep looking! The bastard is here somewhere. He has to be. If he has drowned, I want to see the body. . . .

"Oh dear God," Anna said. "Not now!"

The water was icy cold and the salt stung his wounds, turning his back into a sheet of fire. He had opened his mouth to scream when he first fell over the side of the wharf, but the water swirled down his throat, choking off anything other than the rush of bubbles that were expelled. He sank all the way to the bottom— probably twenty feet, no more—and when his feet struck the soft ooze there, it was purely an instinctive reaction that made him bend his knees and kick off with all his strength. He came up beneath the stinking planks of the docks, only long enough to grab another breath before he sank again and swam to the next wooden pylon. In truth, it was easier moving through the water than trying to run onshore, and it was almost beautiful to look up and see the lights shimmering on the decks of the ships.

A brighter light struck the water a dozen feet behind him, cutting streamers through the murky depths like a starburst. They were searching for him. Cipriani would be furious he had escaped. He had been looking forward to gutting him that night, showing him his own intestines as he disemboweled him inch by inch.

Had he told Le Couteau where he put the letter? He didn't think so. Even if he had, Seamus had already taken the Intrepid *out of port. The Irish bastard must have known something had gone wrong and had had the presence of mind to save the ship and crew, to get them out before the blockade trapped them in port.*

Would he look in the strongbox, though? Would he know what to do with what he found there?

No. No, he wouldn't. Which meant it was still up to him to save the bloody world. Damn Westford anyway. He never wanted to be a fucking hero! And damn Seamus for kicking the shit out of that insipid little limp wrist. Damn the King, the Queen, the whole bloody country for not even letting him die in peace, without pain. . . . If he just let go, he could sink to the bottom again. He could sink into the blackness, the peace, the silence. . . .

"*Emory!* Emory, can you hear me? Don't you dare do this now. You have to walk. You have to put one foot in front of the other and you have to walk!"

Emory groaned and staggered out into the street, his hands holding his head, his body doubled over in pain.

Anna ran after him, glancing fearfully over her shoulder,

hoping the soldiers were still distracted and Ramsey was back on board his coach.

As luck would have it, however, the colonel was just in the process of boarding. He had the door open, his hands on the rail and a foot on the coach step, when he caught a glimpse of the commotion farther along the poorly lit street.

"What the devil . . . ? Who is that? What is going on?"

One of the soldiers crossed the road and stood beside Ramsey at the coach. "Looks like a gent and 'is doxy is havin' a go at each other."

The colonel raised a hand to shield his eyes against the glare from his riding lamp. "Does that dress she is wearing look blue to you?" he said slowly. "Never mind. Fetch them both here."

The redcoat shrugged and shouted, "You there! Hold up. Colonel wants a word!"

Anna cast another panicked glance over her shoulder as the soldier started walking toward them. She twisted her hand around the lapel of Emory's greatcoat and gave it a violent shake. "Please," she cried. "Emory . . . please speak to me!"

He tried to push her away and in desperation, she swung up hard and fast, slapping the side of his face with her open palm. His chin jerked up and his eyes rolled a moment before snapping back into focus, but the pain was still blinding enough that he had to grasp hold of her shoulders to steady himself.

"They're coming," she cried softly. "The soldiers. They have seen us and they're coming. What should we do?"

He blinked, squeezing his eyelids tightly together for as long as it took him to reach down and snatch up the haversack he had dropped. He took hold of Anna's arm and started leading her swiftly away from the approaching soldier.

"You there!"

Anna risked a quick look over her shoulder and saw the soldier unsling his musket from his shoulder.

"I said *hold up*!"

Emory stepped swiftly behind Anna's back, hooking his hand around her waist as he made a hard turn to the right and pulled her after him. She had not even noticed the narrow throughway before he dragged her into it, and before she could cry out in disgust at the horrible spongy debris she felt beneath her one shoeless foot, they had run the length of it and emerged on the other side, onto another cobbled street. She heard shouts and the loud report of a musket behind them, then Emory was leading her down another alley, urging her to as much speed as she could muster.

They veered left and ran half a block before the sound of shouting and pounding bootsteps turned them around mid-stride. There were more shouts off to the right and a solid wall of buildings to the left, which left them only one direction to run, up a steep and relatively well lit section of road that kept them exposed long enough for some of the soldiers to spill out of the alleyway, spot them, and sound the alarm to the other guardsmen converging on the street.

Anna ran as she had never run before, but she still felt as though she was being dragged along by Emory's longer, faster strides. She was frightened, desperately short of breath; her skirts were hindering her movements, her foot was pricked raw by pebbles and jagged edges of cobblestones. She did not know how much farther she could run, or if it was even fair of her to hold Emory back when he was barely winded and could probably fly like a gazelle and be away, free, before the fastest soldier reached the crest of the hill.

"Leave me," she gasped. "Go! Get away!"

He glanced over at her once, but his hand only tightened on hers. "Come on. A little farther. Just a little farther."

They went that little farther and heard the sound of a carriage coming up the road toward them. Right before they ran around a twist in the road, they saw the gleam of a riding lamp and the black silhouette of Ramsey's head and shoulders where he leaned out the window. He was shouting orders at the soldiers to move out of the way, screaming at the driver to whip the horses into more speed.

"Leave me!" Anna cried. "You can still get away if you leave me!"

Emory snarled and dragged her in the direction of a side street, where a hackney was just about to make the turn onto the main road. He had his gun in his hand as he vaulted up into the box and pushed the startled driver off the other side. In an unbroken movement, Emory flung the haversack into the back and swung Anna into the passenger seat, then took up the reins and slapped them on the rump of the startled horse, who jumped instantly into a trot.

Ramsey's coach came thundering around the bend. He was still hanging out the window, still shouting orders when they drove by. He glanced quickly at Emory as the light passed over the smaller vehicle, then swiveled around again with a red-faced scream when he saw the ousted driver staggering to his feet yelling, "Thief! Thief!"

Emory snapped the whip over the horse's flanks, stinging it into a gallop. Many of the soldiers who had been following on foot were still pressed against the fronts of buildings in response to Ramsey's perilous dash past. Those who thought to venture boldly into the path of the oncoming vehicle dove ignobly back into their nooks and crannies when Emory took aim and fired his pistol over their heads. One or two had the presence of mind to shoulder their muskets and fire after them, but the majority were too stunned to do more than stare in disbelief at the escaping carriage.

Holding the reins in one hand, Emory balanced precariously on the boards of the seat and swung around, using the butt of his pistol to shatter the small coach lamps that hung on either side of the hood.

"Are you all right?"

"I think so," Anna gasped. "Are *you*?"

"We will find out in a few minutes. Find something to hang on to. We might be in for a bit of a wild ride."

He flashed a devilish grin and cracked the whip in the

air again. It had cost Ramsey's heavier coach valuable time to turn around, and by the time Emory saw the yellow eye of the coach lamp, he had gained three or four hundred yards. With the next crack of the whip, he turned the hackney down a narrow street on his right, pelting past dimly lit doors and swaying tavern lanterns until he came to a second, even sharper turn onto a winding lane.

Anna clutched at the leather hand strap and held on for dear life as the carriage seemed to career around each corner on a single wheel. There were shouts from startled pedestrians as they galloped past, and curses from men who had to scatter to one side or the other to avoid being run down. Emory was shouting as well, cracking the whip at everyone who moved too slowly to suit him. He sent frequent glances over his shoulder, and each time he did his hair blew back in the windstream, all but covering his face.

Anna did not have to look through the tiny rear window to know that their pursuers were gaining. The sudden hail of musket fire told the tale.

"Hold on," he shouted again and pulled the reins, commanding the horse to take a hard left. The body of the coach pitched sickeningly to the right, slamming Anna against the far side and nearly ripping her arm out of its socket.

"Do you know how to load a gun?"

Oh dear God, she thought! "Yes. Yes, I know how."

"There is powder and shot in the haversack," he shouted, leaning back to hand her the spent flintlock, "as well as a second pistol. Load them both for me if you can."

"What are you going to do? You cannot possibly shoot them all!"

"I don't particularly want to shoot any of them," he said. "Just scare them back a little. Quickly now. Another turn coming up on the right."

Anna ground her teeth, clutched the strap in one hand, and clamped the other around the gun in her lap while the coach roared around another impossibly abrupt turn in a road never built for breakneck chases. When the wheels settled again she groped at her feet for the haversack and found the round tin powder horn, the canvas sack of shot, and a thin strip of silk wadding. She loaded both pistols and was about to call out to Emory when a curlicue at the upper corner of the carriage hood disintegrated in a shower of wooden splinters. A second shot thudded into the back of the carriage alarmingly close to Anna's head.

Emory reached around. "Give me the guns!"

But Anna was already on her knees, aiming the snout of one pistol out the narrow window above her seat. She thumbed the hammer into full cock and squeezed the trigger, shutting her eyes tight against the flare of powder igniting in the pan followed by the almost instantaneous kick and blast from the gun as it discharged. The recoil sent her sprawling in a painful heap against the back of the driver's seat, where she might have remained wedged if Emory had not hauled her up by a fistful of crushed blue silk.

"You little fool! Give me the other gun!"

"You just drive, dammit," she cried, climbing back onto the seat. She snatched up the second gun, cocked, aimed, and fired it, this time braced for the sparks, the *pooft* of acrid smoke, the explosion and recoil. The shot did not come within twenty feet of the pursuing coach, but it did zing off the side of a wrought-iron rail and ricochet back into the street, where it found the arm of one of the soldiers clinging to the boot of Ramsey's vehicle. The unlucky fellow screamed and lost his grip, falling to the side of the road and rolling away in a blur of red and white.

"I need time to reload," Anna gasped.

Under any other circumstances, Emory might have laughed at the irony of a kidnapped heiress's loading and firing guns to keep her rescuers at bay. But all he could see was Anna's pale face and huge dark eyes, and he knew he would never laugh again if so much as a hair on her head was harmed on his account.

"Get down on the floor," he commanded. "Wedge yourself against the seat."

"Why? What are you—"

"Just do it!"

Anna caught a glimpse of his grim expression and asked no more questions. She did as she was told without a second to spare as he sent the carriage slewing sideways off the road and onto the manicured green of a park. Clods of dirt and sod flew out behind the spinning wheels. Without regard for the rows of flowers and neatly planted gardens, Emory steered the horse through the fragrant beds, blazing a new trail across the soft earth, aiming, as near as Anna could see, for a solid black line of trees. Her mouth dropped open and her stomach lurched into her throat as the carriage hurled toward what looked like certain doom at breakneck speed.

But Emory had seen what she could not: a paler shading of black that indicated what he hoped might be—in daylight—a riding path, the entrance marked by a stone archway. He had to slow the charging beast by a hair until he could be reasonably certain, but a glance back at Ramsey's coach told him he could not afford to veer away and look for a more plausible route. The bigger vehicle had followed them onto the parkland, the two-horse team gaining ground as their hooves found greater traction on the earth. Moreover, the soldiers were reloading, firing as soon as they were able, and Emory heard whoops of triumph as someone on board guessed that they had trapped the fleeing carriage against the trees.

Seconds later, the whoops turned to curses, then screams as the driver was forced to rein sharply back and throw his full weight on the brake. The smaller, slimmer carriage vaulted through the arch, the axle caps scraping both sides of stone and sending a shower of sparks into the darkness. There was no heavenly way Ramsey's coach could squeeze through without slicing off all four wheels and likely one side of the conveyance. They pulled to a rolling stop instead, and at the occupant's screamed orders the soldiers discharged their muskets at the rapidly disappearing carriage, several of the shots finding their mark and chipping holes in the wooden frame.

Emory was not lulled into thinking his pursuers would be deterred for long. He suspected that the moment the soldiers were back on board, the wheels of their coach would be chewing into the earth again and they would circle the park, hoping to pick Anna and him up again where the path emerged from the trees.

They had to get rid of the carriage. He did not like their chances on foot, but the horse was unaccustomed to such mad dashes and was starting to blow like a bellows. One of the wheels was grinding on the axle as well and would not bear much more strain over uneven cobbles.

"When we break through these trees," he said, leaning back to help Anna onto the seat again, "we are going to abandon ship. Be ready for it; we will only have one chance to jump clear."

"Jump?" she gasped weakly. "We are going to jump?"

Emory saw the edge of the trees and drew back on the reins. The carriage scraped through a second arched gate and rolled onto the square of another well-maintained garden. Ahead were the winding terraced streets populated by the more respectable hotels and cafes, and higher still, the elegant villas owned by the wealthiest residents of Torquay. An image came into Althorpe's mind and this time he did not try to shake it away. He tried to concentrate on it instead, to focus on landmarks that seemed vaguely familiar.

"Hold on!"

Anna was beginning to dread the sound of those two little words, but she gritted her teeth and did as she was told. The wheels bounced once, twice, over a graduated stone gabion, lifting her clear off the seat by a foot or more before crashing down on the cobbled road again. The carriage landed with a loud, bone-shaking crack that sent leaves and broken branches spraying in every direction. The wheels held, however, at least long enough for the horse to haul them another twenty yards or so before the lost nuts and bolts became a genuine threat.

Emory looped the reins around the brake stick and turned, grabbing the haversack with one hand and Anna with the other. He tossed the sack overboard, caught Anna around the waist, and jumped, with her body cradled against his. He landed first to cushion her fall, then rolled with her into the soft grass by the side of the road. The last glimpse they had of the carriage, it was wobbling off down the slope of the street, the wheels teetering in and out, screeching in protest.

"Are you hurt?"

"I . . . don't think so," Anna said.

Emory ran his hands along her legs, testing her knees, her calves, her ankles for any signs of injury she might be too numbed or shocked to feel. She was fine. Remarkably fine for a woman of delicate sensibilities who had been chased, shot at, and forced to accompany a madman on a wild dash through a dark forest. He refrained from laughing and kissing her, but only just.

"What do we do now?" she asked, looking around.

He tipped his chin to indicate the lighted facade of a hotel at the top of the hill. "If my mind is not still playing silly buggers, that should be the Mannington House. They will have coaches out front for hire."

"A marvelously civilized notion," she agreed dryly, letting him help her to her feet. "But where shall we hire it to take us?"

"Somewhere we will be safe, I promise. Can you manage to walk a little ways farther?"

She straightened her skirts and brushed the bits of grass off her sleeves and smiled at him as if he had asked her to take a walk along Bond Street. Her cheeks were flushed from the excitement, her eyes shining as she looked up at him, and despite his best efforts, he could not stop himself from cupping her face between his hands.

"I think I can say with confidence that I have never known anyone as brave and beautiful as you, Annaleah Fairchilde, and I swear that when this is over"—he kissed her with equal amounts of pride and fierce determination—"I will make it up to you somehow."

"I intend to hold you to that promise, sir; see if I do not."

He offered her the support of his arm, but she shrugged it aside. After a few limping footsteps she even paused to discard her remaining shoe, finding it more of a hindrance now than a help. Her hair was a flown disaster, but she combed it as best she could with her fingers, then did the same for Emory's dark, shaggy waves.

Five minutes later, at the Mannington House, they hired a closed coach, and after Emory gave the driver directions, they settled inside, dousing the small candles that burned in their brass sconces. This time of the evening, the traffic was building nicely, with carriages taking passengers to dinner or to parties. There were also signs of a commotion farther down the street, for some of the coaches were starting to back up and the drivers were sending postillions ahead to see what was causing the stoppage.

They were not safe yet, nor could Emory afford to let his guard down until they had left the streets of Torquay far behind. But for the moment, with his arm around Anna's shoulder and her head resting in the crook of his neck, it was enough to just to let his muscles unwind and his heartbeat return to something verging on normal.

Chapter 16

*A*NNALEAH STOOD JUST inside the heavy iron gate where Emory had left her nearly twenty minutes ago, her back pressed up against a thick spread of juniper bushes, her toes fidgeting nervously in the wet grass. It was so quiet she could hear herself breathing. It was so still she could hear the residual heat of the day rising off the damp earth and curling around the bases of the nearby trees. Overhead, the sky was a vast, endless black expanse of space pricked by a million tiny pinpoints of light. Behind and well below her, the harbor was ablaze with lights strung on the masts of the ships in port, with the heaviest and brightest concentration clustered around the daylight-bright beacon of the *Bellerophon*.

She moistened her lips and looked back up at the looming silhouette of the house. It stood on one of the higher levels of the terraced crescent surrounding Torbay, on a street populated by elegant houses set back against the hillside. The nearest neighbor on either side was five hundred yards or more away, their lights scattered and broken by the dividing barrier of trees. And it was probably just as well.

Emory had ordered the driver to take the hackney around the back, where there was a small carriage house. When the man had disembarked to open the door, Emory had, with unexpected violence and swiftness, rapped him over the back of the head with the butt of a pistol. He had then bound the unfortunate man hand and foot and stuffed him back into the coach before driving the vehicle into the carriage house and closing the doors behind him.

"What did you do that for?" Anna had gasped.

"As soon as the colonel finds our coach he will have

assumed we either stole or hired another one. I would prefer our friend in there not ride back to town with a tale of carrying two bedraggled passengers—one of them shoeless—to an abandoned house on the hill. I have tucked a twenty-pound note in his pocket; that should ease some of the pain of the headache he will have when he wakens in the morning."

He had then ordered her to wait by the junipers and gone into the big house alone, where he seemed now to have been for hours, not minutes.

Anna heard a faint noise—a bang followed by a dry scraping sound—and pressed farther back into the junipers. She was beginning to have serious doubts about her sanity—and his. Hers, because she was standing here in the dampness and dark instead of running away as far and as fast as she could. His, because he was trusting her to remain where he had left her and not listen to a conscience that was screaming at her to take this one last chance to undo at least some of the harm that had already been done.

A few seconds later she saw Emory striding out of the shadows, relieved of his greatcoat and haversack and looking quite jaunty as he approached.

"As empty as the Sahara," he announced. "Everything just as I remember it. And believe me, I only just remembered it, or I would have brought you here at the outset."

"You know this place?"

"I do indeed. I own it."

"You do?" She frowned and tried to keep her teeth from chattering.

"I believe I won it in a game of billiards. I never actually stayed here for more than a few days at a time—or nights, as the case may be—so I doubt anyone would even think to search it."

She looked at the hand he extended but did not take it, and in the end he merely beckoned her to follow and led the way back to the house. He did not enter by the front door but circled around to a small rear entrance that was half hidden by overgrown bushes. Once inside, he lit a small candle and hooded it with his hand.

"Come," he said. "We will have to be careful not to let any lights show in the windows."

Anna rubbed her arms, the chill seeming even worse than outside, the air as musty as the lower chambers of a crypt. She followed him through several doors and up a narrow staircase. At the top, a pale reddish glow emanated from one of the open doorways, and it was with an honest sigh of relief that she saw he had drawn heavy damask curtains over the windows and started a fire.

She stumbled directly over to the hearth and held her hands out before the flames, turning them and wiggling her fingers in order for some of the ice in her veins to thaw. There were streaks of dirt on her skin and the sleeves of her jacket; she did not even want to look too closely at her skirt, her hair, or God forbid, the shredded, blackened ruin of her stockings. She would, she decided, commit murder for a bath, a long hot soak in bubbled water with the steam so thick it fogged the windows.

"Here," Emory said, sliding a chair in front of the fire. "Sit down. I managed to draw a few inches of water out of the well. Not much, and certainly not very warm, but I have more boiling on the stove downstairs."

She looked at him wordlessly.

"I am not completely uncivilized," he said gently. "Now sit. Let *me* take care of *you* for a change."

Shivering too much to argue, she obeyed the stern guidance of his hands as he directed her into the chair. A flick of his wrist had her hem folded up over her knees, and although she could not see them herself, she saw him shake his head and cluck his tongue over the condition of her torn stockings and blackened soles. He rolled down her stockings—she had donned them so hastily they were below her knees anyway—and tossed them over his shoulder into the fire. The silk caught with a hiss, each stocking melting in a cloying sizzle of thick black smoke. He reached back and dragged over the washbowl he had set by the hearth, warming the contents further with a hot iron he took from the fire.

"What are you doing?"

"Cleaning your feet."

"What?" She drew them back, tucking them under the chair.

"You may have cut yourself on the road," he explained patiently. "And God only knows what kind of muck we ran through. You don't want or need an infection right now."

"I am quite capable of washing my own feet," she insisted.

"I'm sure you are," he said. He reached out and took one foot by the ankle, and when the move to bring it forward met with more resistance, he looked up and frowned.

That was all he did. Just frowned. Anna bit her lip and relaxed her leg enough to allow him to hold her ankle and foot over the shallow bowl.

"Is all this not taking up valuable time?" she asked, watching him soak a scrap of toweling. "Earlier, you said that time was an important consideration, that the sooner you reached London, the sooner you might find the answers to some of your questions. I should think that would mean traveling by night as well as day."

"I think we have both had enough excitement for one day, would you not agree?"

She felt the water being squeezed gently over her ankle and foot, heard it trickle softly back into the basin. It was barely above ice cold and her toes curled in response, but when he started lathering her skin with a small chip of soap, it was all she could do not to curl her entire body with sensual gratification.

"Besides which," he carried on, "if the other hacks at the Mannington report that they saw two people matching our description get into a carriage shortly before the commotion on the road, and if our driver cannot subsequently be located, Ramsey will assume we—*I*—forced him to take us out of town posthaste. I doubt it would ever occur to him that we drove a mere half mile then stopped for the night."

The lather had made his hands slippery as he massaged it into her sole, between her toes, around her ankle and partway up her calf. She watched his lips moving, heard his voice rumbling somewhere in the distance, but for all she cared, he might have been explaining the deductive reasoning behind the Pythagorean theorem. Her every sense was focused on the movement of his hands; every smooth, massaging stroke evoked a veritable glut of sensations that had very little to do with logic or reason.

Finished with the one foot, he held it over the basin again and rinsed the lather free, patting it dry with a soft towel before he turned his attention to the other.

Anna's hands gripped the edge of the chair and she closed her eyes, willing herself not to faint or otherwise make a complete fool of herself. Naturally, he had left the dirtier foot for last, and by the time he finished soaping, rubbing, rinsing, and soaping again, she was flushed from the top of her hairline to the tips of her toes.

Oddly enough, for a man who seemed to take nefarious delight in reading every thought she had in her eyes, he appeared not to notice. He meticulously toweled the second set of glowingly pink toes dry, then pushed to his feet and took the washbasin away to empty it. Anna collapsed back against the chair, not sure whether to laugh or cry or throw herself out the window in frustration.

He was gone long enough for her nerves to partly settle, for her eyes to even drift closed in the lulling heat of the fire. When he came back, he was carrying a round, shallow tub and a large metal bucket full of water, both of which he set in front of the hearth. He filled the wooden bath to a depth of several inches, then took up the additional hot irons he had set against the grate and plunged them, hissing, into the water.

"Better," he pronounced, testing it with his hand. "Up you go now."

"Up?"

"Stand up, please. Unless you would like me to bathe you like Cleopatra, reclining on a couch."

"Bathe me?" The words came out on a whisper of breath.

"It is the least I can do, since I have been too inconsiderate to supply you with a maid."

He said this with a smile, but Anna's silence was horrified enough to quash it.

"Look, you're cold, you're shivering, your clothes are damp, and frankly, they don't smell any too pleasant either. I found some spare shirts and things in one of the armoires—not the height of fashion, I will admit, but at least they are warm and dry and clean."

Anna followed his glance and saw a shirt and a pair of men's breeches flung over the back of a chair. *Breeches!* It was too much, and she jumped up, nearly stumbling in her haste to put the width of the chair between them.

"I think not, sir. I think I have endured quite enough for one night without being bathed by a stranger and turned out into breeches like a child."

"A stranger?" His mouth curved up again at the corner. "I hardly think, after this afternoon—"

"Yes, well, I really do not care what you think. As for what happened earlier this afternoon, it was a mistake. A very big mistake. In fact, these past few days"—her lower lip began to tremble again and a shiver overcame her entire body—"I have done things I never expected to do in my wildest imaginings."

"And now you regret them."

"Of course I regret them! How could I not regret them? I have been chased and shot at, kidnapped and threatened. I have undoubtedly caused my aunt a terrible embarrassment, not to mention my entire family. I have squandered my virginity on the rough boards of a tavern floor and . . . and . . . now you expect me to wear breeches!"

"Death to the Philistines," he murmured softly.

"What? What did you say?"

Her voice was shrill, on the edge of cracking, as Emory rose slowly from his crouch. Her lips were blue with cold and her eyes shone with a fever brightness that did not bode well for the state of her health if he did not soon get her warm and dry.

"I said: One way or another, you are coming out of those clothes."

Anna gasped and stumbled back a step. "I most certainly am not!"

He came around the side of the chair, and the intent in his eyes was clear enough that she whirled around and bolted for the door. He was there in a heartbeat, one arm around her waist, the other around her shoulder, effectively trapping her against his body.

"No," she cried. "No, let me go!"

"I am only trying to save you from a heavy chest and a dripping nose."

"Then build the fire higher and that will suffice."

"You have not seen what I have seen clinging to the hem of your skirts. The heat, I fear, will only make it worse."

She released her breath on a gust and curled her fingers over the tautness of his forearm. "Please. Please let me go."

He guessed she was not just talking about the prospects of a bath, and his arms tightened, rather than loosened.

"Not like this. Not until you have calmed down."

"I *am* calm! I am *perfectly* calm! So calm, in fact, that I have finally come to my senses! This is madness! You will never get out of Torquay with me in tow. You will be caught and anyone with you will be caught as well! We will be sent to prison, both of us, you because you are a madman, and me because I was witless enough to think that I could just walk away from everything and everyone and not suffer the consequences. But I was wrong. I am not strong enough. Everything I said at the inn was foolishness and I just want you to *let me go!*"

"All right." He let out a huff of breath and his arms

sprang open so suddenly she lurched forward. "Fine. Go. No one is stopping you, if that's what you want. I will even roust the hack driver and he can take you back to the Mannington . . . or back to Barrimore, the devil I should care. I am sure he will welcome you with open arms."

She looked back, her face ghostly white against the shadows. "Do you honestly think I could go back to him now? That he would *take* me back now?"

"Why ever not? From what I have seen of your Lord Barrimore, I suspect he will respond magnificently to the challenge of proving himself the better man." Emory paused and his eyes hardened with speculation. "Unless, of course, that has been your intent all along."

"I d-don't know what you mean."

"Do you not? That fine little act on the cliffs was for his benefit, was it not? Kiss me, anger him. Prove you were not like all the other rich little heiresses that have been shoved in front of him for his consideration."

She shook her head. "No. No, that wasn't why—"

"And today, at the inn. Was that another performance? Would the game have ended too soon if I had left you behind? Would he not have suffered enough, appreciated you enough, had you been returned too soon to the bosom of your family?"

Her eyes grew rounder, brighter. "You cannot believe that. You know very well what it cost me to stay with you."

"Your reputation? Your 'squandered' virginity? Believe me, madam, not one bride in twenty goes to the altar as pure as the blush on her cheeks, and most men are grateful to be relieved of the burden."

Anna drew a startled breath and instinct sent her hand swinging up to slap him. He caught it, easily, and for a long moment his eyes glittered and his jaw remained tight and square. "You do not want to do that," he warned.

"Why?" she asked, her voice shaking with resentment and betrayal. "Would you strike me back?"

"No." He drew the word out into a silky threat. "But I

might be tempted to return you to Barrimore with more experience than either one of you bargained for."

"You would rape me again?"

His eyebrow crept upward. "I was not aware I had raped you before. Of course, if that is the story you were planning to tell him, we could arrange proof of that as well."

Anna curled her free hand into a fist and aimed for the crest of his cheek. This blow was blocked as easily as the first, and he caught it with a snarl and yanked it down, twisting it around to the small of her back. He brought his face within an inch of hers, close enough that she could see the sparks of anger exploding in his eyes. She could taste it too, when he kissed her, for his lips were hard and bruising, his tongue thrusting with a savagery that robbed her of the smallest ability to resist.

But then, as quick as lightning, his anger turned into something else. It could have been brought on by the sob in her throat, or it could have been the result of her body pushing fiercely up against his, but whatever the cause, the fury was transformed into passion and the need to hurt her with words became an urgent need to mend the wounds they had already caused. Anna's response was less than a heartbeat behind, for she opened herself to his punishment, sucking him into her mouth and holding him hostage until he released her wrists and put his hands to better use. He held her, cradling her by handfuls of hair, turning her this way and that to reach every part of her mouth. When that was not enough, he tore at the delicate row of buttons down the front of her spencer, popping them onto the floor like a broken string of beads. The laces on her bodice fared no better, and when they proved to be knotted and stubborn, shreds of blue silk came away in his hands.

He pushed the gaping edges of her gown and jacket off her shoulders, then worked the fastenings of her skirt free. His hands molded around her breasts, and rode the curve of her hips, and when they ran down her thighs, they returned with fistfuls of her chemise.

Anna clutched at his arms. She reached up and clawed her hands into his hair, holding him against her, her breath as ragged and broken as the cries that shivered up her throat. The embrace was fueled by hunger and desperation and Anna reveled in it, responding with a need that was as raw and ungovernable as his. His hands went between them and he fumbled a moment with the fastenings of his breeches, then he was lifting her against his body and she could feel him hard and straining, sliding between her thighs.

She was already wet enough, slick enough that he needed no helping hand to guide himself along the silky cleft, no muffled cry of consent before sheathing himself completely in the heat of her. Anna took him deep, deep inside, stiffening slightly with the shock of all that flesh impaling and filling her, but she was as determined as he, and within the span of a few forceful thrusts willingly obeyed his hoarse command to wrap her legs around his waist, to trust that he would not drop her, to take the initiative and ride each powerful stroke until the lust for more, for everything he had to give, became increasingly violent, ruthlessly urgent.

Emory's arms, his legs, his entire body shook. There was no bed in the room, no couch large enough to hold them, and he was buried too deeply inside her to withdraw for even as long as it would take to lower her to the floor. The wall was only a few staggered paces away, and when he had its support behind her, he surged upward, driving into her with a ferocity that caused them both to groan with the explicit shock of pleasure.

Anna had thought she had experienced the ultimate ecstasy back at the tavern, but her memory of it paled compared with the incredible, shattering orgasms that ripped through her now. They splintered her body into a thousand bright-hot fragments and caused her to throw her arms wide, to almost tear the draperies off the wall. They made her arch her hips into each of his thrusts so that when she heard the roar of his voice in her ear and felt the heat of his long, throbbing release, she gripped him as tightly as she possibly could, her own spasms matching each pulse and shudder that wracked his body.

The fury ebbed slowly, leaving them panting together in a frozen embrace. His hands were clamped around her buttocks, the fingers splayed, the tips pressed deep into the pliant flesh. Her legs were locked around his waist, her feet crossed at the ankles, and she did not think she had the strength or dexterity to even unhook them. Nor did she have the desire, as she felt his lips move across her shoulder and up beneath her ear.

"Forgive me," he gasped, the words fighting with the need to draw a clear breath. "Forgive me, that was . . . crude and inexcusable, and . . ." He stopped and lifted his head. Her body was trembling in his arms but she would not look up at him. She twisted her chin out of his grasp when he tried to tip it up and she buried her face against his shoulder when he tried to angle his head around to catch her eye. In the end he settled for holding her and waiting until the tears she was trying to keep him from seeing were nothing more than faint, damp blots on his shirt.

"I should not have said those things," he murmured against her hair. "I did not mean any of them. It was pride, stupid and simple, and the challenge to prove myself better—the very thing I was accusing Barrimore of responding to, and . . . if it is what you want, I will take you back," he added, cursing his arrogance. "I'll take you back to Widdicombe House first thing in the morning."

This time she did look up, and her eyes were like two drowning pools.

"No," she whispered. "No, that is not what I want at all."

And it wasn't. She knew that now. She knew it by the hard set of his jaw as he'd watched her face, by the tremors in his arms as he'd anticipated her rejection. It was madness and it was foolishness, but it was also the most exciting thing that had ever happened in her young life. Finding Emory Althorpe washed up on her aunt's beach had turned her world upside down, and by God she was going to see it through to the end, no matter what the consequences.

"You asked me once if I was afraid of you," she said, resting a hand upon his cheek. "I said no, but I meant yes. Yes, you frightened me then and you frighten me now . . . but only because you make me afraid of myself, of who I am inside these silly trappings of silk and lace. I did not mean the things I said either. This is the only place I want to be. Here. With you. Like this. Please," she added in a faint whisper, her lips reaching out to his. "Do not give up on me just yet."

His body responded with one tremendous shudder, and when she realized he was still thick and pulsing inside her she started to move her body again, without shame, without a thought to anything but the melting heat and friction. But this time he had regained enough control of his wits to stop her, to ease her away long enough to strip off his clothes and make the two of them a makeshift bed in front of the hearth.

Annaleah squeezed the excess water out of the sponge and dragged it over the glistening surface of his skin, removing the last traces of soap from the washboard belly. As had happened frequently over the last few hours, his flesh stirred and a calloused thumb and forefinger tipped her chin upward.

"It is only water," she protested faintly.

"Water, hands, lips," he murmured. "They all seem to have the same effect tonight."

"Yes, and this is the third . . . or is it the fourth time I have tried to bathe you, sir, and you are simply not cooperating."

He smiled and smoothed the dark fall of hair off her shoulder. "This from someone who squirms and wriggles each time I reach for the soap."

"My maids," she murmured against his lips, "were

never half so thorough in their washing technique as you, sir."

"I am glad to hear it. I, on the other hand, vaguely recall a valet once who . . . well, who tried to be very thorough while bathing me. I believe I broke his jaw and several ribs for the impertinence. Purely an instinctive reaction, I assure you, and not one I would repeat if . . . if you were to ever express a wish to be that scrupulous."

Intrigued by the sudden catch in his voice, she opened her eyes and stared thoughtfully at the flickering shadows of their silhouettes against the far wall. What further sin could he possibly be enticing her to commit now? she wondered. Her body was no longer flushed with the wickedness of his actions, but humming with anticipation for what might yet come. She was no longer chaste, no longer a virgin, no longer ignorant in the ways of a man and a woman. All that remained now was curiosity and a burning sense of urgency to know this man as thoroughly as he knew her.

At some point, while he had drifted into a brief, exhausted doze, she had donned the shirt he had found her and was wearing it like a nightdress—albeit one he had removed several times already but that kept reappearing with an amusing persistence. The fine brushed cotton was splashed liberally with water, but with her hair a mass of disheveled curls and her legs peeping long and pearly white below the hem, she presented a more enticing picture than if she had remained naked.

"In my own defense," he murmured, bending forward to nuzzle her neck, "it must be said you present a fetching distraction I warrant few men in my condition could resist."

"Your condition?"

"Starved for affection."

Anna's gaze flicked to the haversack, all but forgotten on a nearby chair. "Mildred's biscuits," she declared.

"That is not the first remedy that comes to mind," he said, frowning as she pulled out of his arms.

She opened the canvas flap of the haversack and rooted

in its depths until she found the biscuits as well as a small wheel of cheese, a greasy paper wrapper folded around slices of ham, and, wonder of wonders, a bottle of her great-aunt Florence's apple cider.

Emory scooped up the towel and rubbed himself dry as he watched Anna carry her treasures over to the hearth. A picnic with a near-naked beauty he had spent half the night ravishing was, he thought, unquestionably the last thing he would have seen himself doing with half the military forces in Torbay searching for him. It was also the only thing he wanted to do right now, in spite of the nagging prickle that kept scratching across the back of his neck.

"Glasses?" Anna asked. "Can you find some?"

He took the bottle she handed up to him and unstoppered it with his teeth, spitting the cork into the fire. He took several long, deep swallows from the mouth of the bottle, then grinned and handed it back. "I am feeling a little heathen tonight, aren't you?"

Her gaze flowed down his body, touching on all the burnished muscles, the hard sinews, the rampant maleness he had not shown the slightest inclination to shield from view.

She put the bottle to her lips and tipped it, matching the noisy enthusiasm of his initial mouthful. "Will you eat something with me? You complained as early as this afternoon that you were hungry."

He stared at the bead of amber liquid that clung to her lower lip and smiled. "I suppose we should eat our fill while we have the chance."

She patted a spot on the rug and gave him back the bottle when he sat down beside her.

"Biscuit?"

He shook his head and buried his lips in the curve of her shoulder instead. When all she did was sigh, as if forcing herself to tolerate a recalcitrant child, he set the bottle aside and slipped his hand beneath her shirt, circling and capturing the soft heaviness of a breast.

"If you are not hungry, sir, *I* am."

"You have your banquet laid out before you, I have mine."

"It is very difficult to concentrate with—" She sucked in a small huff of air and dropped the wheel of cheese she had been about to break in two. Emory grinned again and raised his mouth to hers, but stopped when he saw the look of sudden horror on her face. He whirled around to follow her gaze, noting instinctively as he did so that he had left both pistols on a table half the width of the room away.

It had been a stupid act of carelessness, and deserving of the harsh, derisive laugh that came from between the thin lips of the man who was standing in the doorway—a man whose own guns were in his hands, both cocked, both aimed straight for Emory's heart.

Chapter 17

"I AM A PATIENT man, m'sieur," the stranger said, his voice low and raspy, "but even I grew tired of waiting, though I can see now that the reason for your delay was justified."

Emory was on his feet with the swiftness of an uncoiling spring. He stared unblinking at the guns, gauging the distance between himself and the door, calculating the chances he would make it even halfway before having twin holes blown in his chest. The odds were not worth wasting his effort, and he studied the man's face instead: the lean hawklike jaw, the black glitter of his eyes, the cruel twist of a smile that curled his lips.

Emory knew that face. He had seen it in a half dozen painful flashes of memory. He had also seen the guns before, elegant and distinctive in design with octagonal steel barrels, the stocks made of polished walnut with inlaid silver falcons in full wingspread.

They were his own guns, presented to him as a gift by the Dey of Tunisia. And the man holding them was . . .

Emory felt a surge of heat flush through his veins, the threat of light and pain behind his eyes, but he savagely blinked it away. With a startling clarity that nearly stripped him of breath, he knew that the man before him was Franceschi Cipriani, and why he was here.

"How did you find me?"

"I admit it was difficult, my friend. I was almost convinced you were still under the wharf at Rochefort."

"What made you change your mind?"

Cipriani shrugged. "You are like the cat with nine lives, so it came as no surprise to hear you were still alive. Even so, you were very clever, very artful in eluding the soldiers tonight. In truth, they arrived at the inn mere moments before I was about to visit you myself. It was a small matter—and somewhat amusing—to join the chase and watch their ludicrous attempts to catch you. I only managed to keep you in sight because I was on horseback and could follow you through the woods, where they could not." He paused and waved one of the guns absently in the direction of a window. "As it happens, it may have worked out for the best anyway, for nothing rouses the chivalrous blood in you Englishmen so much as the thought of a helpless demoiselle in the hands of a bloodthirsty villain. By morning every able-bodied man within a hundred miles will be armed and scouring the countryside for you. If I thought they could hold you, I would have led them here, but alas—you are too good for them, my friend, and I cannot risk the possibility of you escaping again."

"How did you know I was at the inn?"

"Ahh, now that was sheer luck, m'sieur. Sheer, unbridled luck, I must confess, but then I have the nine lives too, do I not? Once I knew you were here, I simply watched the roads, watched the harbor. As I said, I am a patient man, and today . . . who should I see riding down the road with a bandage on his head?" He paused and shrugged. "What are the chances, m'sieur? A thousand to one? Ten thousand to one? Or simply fate."

"But how did you know I was in Torbay?"

Cipriani grinned. "Now, now. We must all have our secrets, must we not? Keeping them is what sets us apart, you and I, for you were not very good at doing so."

The muscles in Emory's jaw flexed. "The lady is not involved in any of this," he said quietly. "Let her go."

The heavy-lidded eyes glinted with a trace of amusement in Annaleah's direction, prompting her to curl her bare legs tighter to her body and to pull the hem of her shirt lower.

"Setting the definition of 'lady' aside for the moment"—

the black eyebrows inched upward—"she helped you elude a garrison of soldiers and has been rutting happily with you here on the hearth for several hours. . . . I would suggest she is most *intimately* involved."

Emory's gaze went again to the table where his guns lay so carelessly discarded, and he heard the assassin's soft chuckle.

"No, my friend. I would not advise such foolishness, not unless you wish the death of your lovely companion to be the last thing you see."

"Let her go and I will tell you what you want to know," Emory said quietly.

Cipriani chuckled. "Again, so predictable. So noble. Did I ever tell you where I learned to hone my skills? No? It was in the desert, in Morocco, where my teachers specifically used Englishmen to demonstrate the art of inflicting pain. I was constantly fascinated to see that they could have the skin peeled from their bodies in strips, have their raw bodies then stretched out in the hot sand to bake, and they would scream out no more than curses. But put a fair-skinned beauty in front of them and merely touch the tip of a blade to a cheek or a hand or a breast . . . and those same stalwart heroes would tell you far more than you ever wanted to know."

"Let her go," Emory said. "You have me; that's what you came for, isn't it?"

"It was," he acknowledged with a tilt of his head. "But if she has managed to keep your interest up for so long . . . perhaps my priorities could change. You see, it works the other way too. You would be surprised how enthusiastic a young woman can be when she is bargaining for her lover's life."

At a signal from Emory, Anna scrambled to her feet and stood close behind him. The assassin only laughed at the feeble gesture of protection, the sound grating enough to make Anna's skin feel as though there were a thousand maggots crawling over her flesh.

"Let her go. Let her go now or I swear I'll tear your heart out with my bare hands."

The Corsican's smile lingered as he let his thumbs caress the serpentine locks on the pistols. "Many fools have made that same promise, Englishman. I made them all eat their words as they drew their last breath."

"Then make me eat mine," Emory challenged quietly. "If you can."

Cipriani pursed his lips and took a thoughtful step into the room, brushing an admiring toe across the thick pile of an Indian rug before crushing his boot over the delicate design of flowers. "You always were a thorn in my side, Englishman. I knew, you see. I knew you were not to be trusted, not from the very day you came offering your services to the empire. Unfortunately His Excellency was not so willing to discard your apparent friendship, not while he still had some use for it. We all had *some* use for it at one time or another, and to that end I will concede that your skills at the helm of a ship are unparalleled. I cannot think of another man who would have had the audacity to sail into Elba and whisk away an emperor under the noses of a thousand prison guards. But then, you were not expecting to get away, were you?"

"What do you mean?"

Cipriani gave his grating laugh again. "Please, m'sieur, do not play the innocent with me. We intercepted your messages to Whitehall. We knew you had alerted the navy to the escape and we knew you would be expecting to see one of His Majesty's warships hovering off the coast, ready to snatch back their prisoner. We knew, you stupid bastard. We knew all about you, from the very beginning. Do you think your Lord Casterleagh is the only one to have spies in high places? The delicious part now, of course, is that they are calling you traitor and sending the hounds after you. Rather an exquisite irony, do you not think? One of their best spies being hunted for treason?"

Emory felt Anna's hand on his back, but he did not acknowledge the touch. Nor was he given much time to ponder the million questions that came into his mind with Cipriani's confirmation that he was not a traitor.

"I am rather curious to know one thing, however," the Corsican was saying. "Why are you still here? I would have thought you would have run straight to London."

"Why would I go to London?"

"Where else does a dog run, but to its master?"

"But Bonaparte is here, is he not? And so are you."

"You did not actually believe we would allow such a great man to be led off in chains, to be executed, or to be kept in an iron cage as suits the mood of your Parliament?"

Emory folded his arms across his chest. "Since you obviously intend to kill us anyway, would you care to share exactly how you plan to free him?"

"Your ignorance surprises me, unless of course it is a crude attempt to stall." Cipriani's eyes narrowed. "Or unless you were hoping to single-handedly spoil our plans so that you might redeem yourself in your master's eyes. And if that is the case"—his smile turned even more evil, accompanied by a hot, hissing breath—"it means you still have the letter."

"If I do?"

"If you do . . ." The slitted eyes flicked to where Annaleah was peeping around Emory's shoulder. "It would go far easier on everyone concerned if you simply returned it."

"Ah, well, there we have a small problem." Emory uncrossed his arms and spread them wide, his naked body gleaming like marble in the firelight. "As you can plainly see, I do not have it on me. Feel free to search if you like. As well-known as we English may be for some perversions, like honor and nobility, you French are renowned for others."

The hooded eyes blinked once, slowly. "Tell me where the letter is and I make you this promise, Englishman: The moment I have it in my hand, I will kill the girl quickly and painlessly. Lie to me, play me false, and you will hear her screams all the way down in hell."

"Kill me—or her—you will never find it."

"And neither will anyone else, which suits our needs just as well."

"Then why go to all the trouble to get it back?"

"Because I dislike loose ends, and because I have never yet failed to honor one of *my* master's requests. He asked me to fetch the letter back, likely for the benefit of that fool De Las Cases, who insists on documenting every scrap of paper, every message, every conversation for the sake of the memoirs he is writing. This, of course, being the ultimate triumph, must be precisely set down for posterity to show the utter blind stupidity—not to mention humiliation—of our enemies. Therefore"—he held out one of the guns, taking aim at Emory's left knee—"we shall start slowly, taking our time if that is what you prefer. You do understand if I take the precaution of crippling you first?"

"Wait," Anna cried, stepping out from behind Emory's back. "Please don't shoot!"

The reptilian eyes widened slightly. "You have something to offer that might dissuade me?"

"Anna, for God's sake—"

"No," she said, stepping well out of range of Emory's long arms and keeping her own clasped behind her back so he could not reach out and grab her. "Please, m'sieur. I know where the letter is. I can fetch it for you."

"She doesn't know," Emory declared, clearly appalled by Anna's actions. "She has no damned idea."

"I do know," she insisted and moved, seemingly through fear and feminine panic, closer to Cipriani rather than farther. "Please, m'sieur. I can do this. I can help you. I have the key."

"Key?" The Corsican did not take his eyes off Emory, but he was aware of Anna's moving closer and kept one of the pistols trained on the pale blot of her shirt. "What key?"

Emory was about to shout again, but at the last instant caught a glimpse of the wine bottle she held clutched tightly in both hands. He had no idea what she thought she could possibly do against a man with two loaded pistols, but it was a chance. A slim one, to be sure, but he had no choice. He had to let her take it.

He glanced deliberately at the table again. The guns he had taken from Widdicombe House were there, the barrels crossed one over the other, and lying beside them in a puddle formed by the gold chain was the iron key he had retrieved from the surf. At some point during the night, Anna had complained about being struck in the chin with the swinging key and he had removed it, only the second time he had done so in a month. The first had been when he was dragged half conscious into an empty warehouse and hung up by his wrists to a ceiling beam. He had clutched the key in his fist, even gouged the pointed end into his palm, using the self-inflicted pain to distract him from the pain of Cipriani's carving techniques.

The Corsican followed his gaze and saw the glitter of gold, saw the key. His distraction lasted only a moment, but a moment was all Emory and Anna had. At the same instant she swung the bottle around and knocked the aim of one gun aside, Emory was springing forward and diving low, his full weight and momentum crashing into Cipriani's knees and driving him backward. Both guns exploded, the sting of gunpowder searing Annaleah's eyes and nose, blinding her for the few moments it took her to scramble out of the way as the two men went down in a tangle of legs and arms. She had no way of knowing if Emory had been shot, or if he could overpower the wiry assassin.

She had not credited his rage as a weapon, but he used it now to good effect, planting punch after punch into Cipriani's face and throat. With nothing for his opponent to grasp but skin, he was slippery and able to twist himself free to rise up on his knees, and from that position to smash his fist into the long, thin nose, crushing it to bloody pulp. The pistols had flown out of Cipriani's hands in the fall, but he used his fingers to claw for Emory's eyes and throat. Grunts and curses heated the air, punctuated by the sound of flesh pounding flesh, as the two men rolled again, the Corsican briefly gaining the advantage, dripping blood onto Emory's face and chest from his ruined nose.

Anna searched frantically for a weapon she could use, but the two men were between her and the table. She was still clutching the wine bottle, and she grasped the neck tightly, then brought it down hard across the back of Cipriani's neck, but it only thudded dully against the bone, and the jolt did more damage to her wrist and hand than to his head. There was a long iron poker Emory had used to stir the fire and she ran for that, but by the time she brought it back, the men had changed positions again, had twisted apart and were on their feet, crouched and circling like two blooded cocks at a country fight.

They came together in a crunch of flesh and bone, and Anna was close enough to feel a warm spatter of blood on her face. She gripped the poker with both hands, but there was no clear opening. Fists drove first one man, then the other back; a chair went flying and a lamp crashed to the floor in a spray of oil and glass. From somewhere in the depths of Cipriani's wool coat there came the glint of a knife, the blade long and thin and tapered to the width of a needle at the end. It flashed twice, leaving bloody stripes across Emory's chest before he jumped back. The Corsican followed, the knife raised and glittering, his lips drawn back as he muttered promises and threats in a voice that spiked the hairs across the nape of Anna's neck.

The two men moved into the darker gloom of the hallway. Anna threw aside the poker and ran to the table, her hands trembling as she picked up one of the flintlocks. She was shaking so badly she needed to use the pressure of both thumbs to cock the hammer. The end of the barrel wavered back and forth as she turned it toward the door, but there was nothing to see, nothing to aim at but shifting shadows in the darkness.

The panic caught in her throat, but she waited. She

waited until one of the shadows was hurled through the open doorway, and then she closed her eyes and fired.

The recoil jerked her arms back in their sockets, but she managed to drop the smoking pistol and and immediately snatch up the second one, cocking it, aiming it, bracing herself to fire again. She looked up in time to see the startled look on the Corsican's face as he staggered back into the shadows, a hand held up in front of him with four fingers blown clear away. Emory plunged through the door in the next breath, his locked fists catching Cipriani low under the chin, driving his head up and back with enough force to lift the assassin bodily off the ground and send him crashing senseless onto the floor. Emory—his cheeks, chest, and arms splashed with blood—followed, crouching over him again, his fists laced together like a hammer, slugging hard left, right, left, sending more blood, spittle, and sweat across the carpet with each blow.

Anna would have been quite happy to let him beat the Corsican to death if not for the look on Emory's face. The lust for blood was wild in his eyes. She ran up behind him and tried to catch his arms.

"Stop! Stop! You're killing him!"

He shook her hands away with a snarl. "He deserves killing!"

"Not like this. *Not like this!* This is murder, and it makes you no better than him!"

Emory landed one more punch, the effort causing him to sprawl half across the unconscious man's body. His face was still contorted with rage, his chest was heaving for air, his body gleaming wet with sweat and blood.

But he stopped.

After a moment, he pushed unsteadily to his knees, then staggered to his feet, swaying there for the two or three seconds it took for him to realize Anna was beside him, the gun still dangling in her hand. He looked at her, looked at the gun, then reached down and pried it gently from her frozen fingers. At the same time, with what little strength he had remaining, he pulled her forward into his arms and held her tight, and somewhere deep inside his chest, he felt something twist and ache with genuine fear.

"What on earth were you thinking?" he rasped.

"I wasn't thinking," she sobbed. "I just did not want him to cut you again."

He groaned and buried his lips in her hair, drawing several deep, steadying breaths before he looked down at Cipriani's body. Apart from the blood that flowed freely from the twitching stubs of the missing fingers, there was no sign of movement, but Emory knew his enemy as well as his enemy knew him.

"We need something to tie him up with. Some cords off the curtains."

Anna turned her face slightly. "His hand—?"

"You're right," he murmured, "you shot the wrong one. The bastard does his best work with his other hand."

Without any warning, he raised the pistol and fired it again, the bullet taking off the thumb and shattering most of the bones in Cipriani's left hand.

Anna felt her stomach lurch and did not know if she was going to faint or vomit.

"Now get me the cords and a heavy case off one of the chair pillows."

She moved numbly to do as she was told, fetching the long, braided gold ropes that swagged the curtains and a red brocaded pillow slip. She watched in silence as he tore strips off a linen sheet and bound wadding around the Corsican's damaged hands, then she handed him the ropes to tie his wrists and feet together. Halfway through the process, the bruised eyes shivered open and Cipriani started to gasp oaths in a language Anna did not understand. She did not have to listen to it very long, as Emory stuffed more linen between the battered lips, then slipped the brocaded casing over his head. He used another length of the gold braid to tie the case around his neck and fed the rope down and around his wrists and down again around the ankles, pulling his body into a bent figure S. Satisfied the bindings were taut enough to choke him if he moved, he dragged the assassin into the darkest, coldest corner, leaving him in a heap against the wall.

He came back into the light of the fire, wiping the blood off his chest and face with a scrap of linen.

"Are you all right?" Anna asked. "Is any of that blood . . . ?"

Emory checked his arms, his legs, his ribs. "He must have missed." He looked up quickly. "You?"

"No. I'm fine. But . . . how did he know you were here?"

"Franceschi Cipriani could follow a black cat through a coal mine at night." Emory spat, working a loose tooth with the tip of his tongue.

"No, I mean . . . how did he know you were here in Torquay? He said he *heard* you were here, but who did he hear it from? Who told him?"

"He could have seen the posts. He could have heard rumors on the street."

"He also said you had a letter . . . ?"

Emory raised a hand, rubbing bruised, scraped fingers against his temple, and it was clear by his expression that he was as much in the dark as she. "If I do, I don't have a clue where it is or what it contains."

"It must have been important if he tortured you once and was prepared to kill you for it now."

Emory waved his hand in anger. "I'm sure it is, I just . . . *I don't remember.*"

Anna could see his frustration, and bit her lip to keep it from trembling. "At least you know you are not a traitor. He as much as said you were one of England's most valuable spies."

"Small consolation unless I can find some way to prove it." He started to rake his hands through his hair, but stopped when he caught a flash of gold out of the corner of his eye. He snatched the iron key off the table, staring at it as if he could will it into telling him what he wanted to know. "You may not have been so far off the mark. If I do have this letter, it is as likely to be locked in the strongbox on board the *Intrepid* as anywhere else. But where the devil is the *Intrepid*?"

Anna's teeth chattered once in response. She was cold and growing colder by the minute as the shock of the recent violence began to settle into her bones.

"He mentioned Lord Westford," Anna said, giving her arms a little rub. "He and Father are acquainted, and I . . . well, his son, Austin, Viscount Lutton," she blurted out after a brief hesitation, "offered for my hand last year."

"And?"

"And . . . I refused, obviously. He was very personable, but . . ."

Emory tipped his head. "But?"

"I thought he had a reckless nature," she whispered.

Emory had the grace not to point out the irony in her admission. He picked up the spent flintlocks and started reloading them instead.

In truth, Anna needed no one to draw attention to the obvious. She was well aware of the incongruity, although in her defense, there was a vast difference between a man who enjoyed gaming tables and horse races to a man who defied the very devil himself. Emory Althorpe was unlike any man she had ever met before, and there were no comparisons possible. The life he had been leading had made him capable of committing shocking acts of violence in order to survive—that much she had just witnessed. He was also capable of great passion and inordinate gentleness, and he possessed a certain nobility missing from most noblemen of her acquaintance—the kind that belonged to a man who did not give a damn about how something looked to others, as long as it was the right thing to do.

Yet looming over all this for Anna was a certain measure of uncertainty, for with each segment of his memory that returned, he grew stronger, more confident, more in control, and who was to say, when all of his past was fully restored, what he would expect or want from her—or if he would want her at all. Once before he had given up the life she represented. It was possible . . . probable even, that he would not be eager to embrace it again, just for the sake of a few passionate hours in her arms.

It was madness. It was lust and it was envy for his freedom, pure and simple. It was also witless, foolish, and completely absurd to consider taking one more step beside him, and yet . . . she could feel herself growing stronger just by virtue of being in his company. She was smart, she was useful, and she had displayed a rather surprising capability for violence herself over the past few minutes, and truth be told, she would do it again if threatened. Her days of sitting quietly in a corner while others determined her destiny were over.

She squared her shoulders and looked up at Emory. "You obviously have to find your ship, and then you have to speak to Lord Westford. If you suspect there is a plan afoot to rescue Bonaparte, he has to be told."

"I had already made up my mind to go to London," he said quietly.

"And do what? Walk into Westminster Hall and demand an audience with Lord Westford?"

"I had not thought that far ahead," he admitted.

"Well, you will have to, for Parliament is literally under siege—the buildings themselves are surrounded by a dozen regiments of Royal Horse Guard. I doubt you would get close enough to shout a greeting through the iron grate." She paused and focused her attention on the unwound clock sitting on the mantelpiece. "What day is today?"

"Monday." He looked up from reloading the guns. "Actually, the small hours of Tuesday. Why?"

"This coming Friday night there is to be a masquerade ball at Carlton House."

"A ball? With Napoleon Bonaparte on board a ship anchored in an English port and Parliament under siege while they debate his fate?"

"It is Lady Charlotte Carrington's twenty-first birthday. She is a vivacious, beautiful widow, an heiress of considerable fortune, and is currently being wooed by the Regent to be his next mistress. There would be a ball in her honor even if another Spanish armada were in the Channel. Anyone who chooses not to risk the Regent's disfavor, not to mention instant social ostracism, will be there, including Lord Westford. It was the main reason Mother sent my brother to fetch me home."

Emory's mouth wore a wry twist. "I assume you are not telling me this just to keep me apprised of your social calendar."

"I am telling you this because it would present the perfect opportunity to approach Lord Westford. Since you would be in costume, no one would recognize you, and I would imagine the Regent's principal residence would be the last place on earth anyone would expect to find you."

The dark eyes glittered faintly with speculation. "What makes you think it would be easier getting into a royal ball, where the guests and invitations are closely scrutinized, than it would into Westminster Hall?"

"It would be easier because I have an invitation. It would, of course, require my presence for you to be acknowledged."

He stared at her for the whole of one minute with just the hiss of the fire to break the silence. Despite the promise made in the tavern, Emory had not been about to risk her safety even as far as the next village, and he had fully intended to leave her here. He knew he could not do that now. Cipriani would kill her if he got loose, and Emory was not naive enough to believe a few missing fingers would deter him. But the thought of taking her all the way to London . . .

"Do you have any idea what you are suggesting?" he asked quietly. "The risks you would be taking? The consequences if you are caught helping me?"

"I am suggesting that you trust me as much as I trust you. As for the consequences, I think they would be far more devastating to my peace of mind if I did nothing at all. You are not the only patriot in this room, you know. I may not have the flag emblazoned on my forehead, but I far prefer seeing the red, white, and blue flying over England than the fleur-de-lis."

"You might be wise not to put too much faith in me, Annaleah," he warned quietly. "I may not be worthy of it."

He turned back to the guns and Anna stared at his broad back.

"If I were wise," she said on a breath too low for him to hear, "I would never have let myself fall in love with you."

Chapter 18

"*T*HEY WILL BE LOOKING for a fashionable young woman in a fine silk dress," Emory explained, handing her breeches, linens, stockings, a waistcoat, and a plain brown coat he had found in one of the armoires. "We shall therefore endeavor to make you into a homely urchin of questionable fashion sense."

It was not difficult. The stockings and breeches were made of a tight-knit wool that clung reasonably well, but the shirt, vest, and jacket were zealously oversized. A belt solved the problem of keeping the excess linens confined at her waist, while both the shirt and coat had to have the sleeves folded into wide cuffs to allow even the tips of her fingers to show. Emory dressed himself alongside, showing her how each unfamiliar garment was worn, adjusting each layer as it was added, even pruning judiciously here and there with a pair of scissors where it was required. He bade her lift her hair out of the way while he wrapped and tied the neckcloth and cravat, but when it came to actually taming the unruly mass of curls, he backed away and left her to struggle with comb and brush until it was smoothed into a contrite tail at her nape.

While she fought with each crackling strand, he stuffed extra shirts and linens into the haversack and rolled a couple of woolen blankets into a small bundle. The brace of pistols he had brought away from Widdicombe House he tucked into the haversack, along with the extra shot and powder; his own guns went into the belt around his waist. He checked once on Cipriani, but the groaning had stopped and there was no sign of consciousness. After a moment's hesitation, he searched through the assassin's pockets, coming away with a heavy purse and three stiletto knives. Returning to the hearth, he banked the fire, making certain the coals were thoroughly reduced to ash, then stood and shrugged his big shoulders into the multicollared greatcoat.

"Ready?"

Annaleah stepped forward out of the shadows. Her hair had been twisted into a thick coil and was hidden beneath a brimmed felt hat. She had the haversack slung over one shoulder and the rolled blankets tucked under the opposite arm, and for one split second Emory saw a startlingly clear image of himself standing determined and defiant on the wharf in Brixham, frightened near to dampening his breeches as he stared up at the towering masts of the ship that was to take him out to sea and change his life forever.

Anna looked nervously down at herself. "Is anything wrong?"

"No. No, nothing is wrong." He blinked to dismiss the image and relieved her of the bulging haversack. "Cipriani's horse should be somewhere outside, and we have the nag off the hackney. If we can reach Exeter by mid-morning, we can catch a Palmer to London."

"A mail coach? Would they not have a copy of the post with your likeness on it?"

"More than likely, yes, but with any luck, it will simply be thrown into the mail pouch with the rest of the news sheets. The driver's prime concern is taking the least amount of time to travel the distance between two points— which also makes for a damnably uncomfortable ride and therefore attracts fewer passengers than the regular coach lines."

When she did not look like she felt any enthusiasm for the idea, he added, "It would stand far better odds than trying to ride all the way there on two tired horses."

"I suppose," she conceded in a murmur.

"Anna . . ." He tucked a finger under her chin and tilted her head up. "You do not have to do this, you know. I can take you back to your aunt's house; you would be perfectly safe with Florence. I daresay a brigade of the King's Own Rifle could not make it through the door once her mind was set. And your reputation—"

"My reputation be hanged, sir. I am with you, and that is where I shall remain until we see this through to the end!"

Her determination won a resigned sigh. "In for a penny, in for a pound, is it?"

"Please tell me you are not quoting Shakespeare again."

"My first gun captain, actually. And if I recall correctly, we were squaring off against three French frigates at the time."

"Did you win? Well, of course you did—you are here, are you not?"

Emory only laughed softly and doused the candles. The last thing he did before closing the door firmly behind them was to sling the gold chain around his neck and tuck the iron key beneath the folds of his shirt.

It took them eight hours to complete a journey that normally took two. Necessity kept them traveling on back roads and in some cases riding across fields and picking their way through forests in order to avoid towns or villages, where a curious eye might take notice of the two strangers, one wearing bandages across half his face, the other looking sorry and stiff and weary beyond words. When they reached Exeter, they found the posting house where the mail coach made its regular stop and were able to purchase a meal and arrange boarding for the horses.

At noon, when the distinctive blare of the mail horn sounded outside, they gathered up their meager belongings. While Emory paid their fare and arranged transport to the end of the line in London, Anna stood off to the side of the road, her head bowed, the brim of her hat pulled low over her brow.

The Palmer coach was a boxlike affair built for speed and utility. Painted maroon, scarlet, and black, with the royal arms gilded on its doors, it could accommodate four passengers inside, if they did not care that the seats were scantily padded and the journey was unbroken save for the time allowed to change horses and collect mail along the route. The record, Anna had overheard the hostler's wife telling another guest, was sixteen hours from Exeter to London, but with news of Bonaparte flying back and forth daily she expected it would be broken ere the week was out.

If the first leg of the journey was any indication, Anna could well believe the prediction. The team of four horses was driven at a steady gallop over roads that sorely tested the ability of the wheels to remain balanced on the track. Even so, to her great surprise, she was asleep before the first mile had churned away behind them, and because they were the only two passengers, she was able to make use of Emory's shoulder as a pillow.

She slept through most of the afternoon, waking only briefly around three when the driver and guard spared ten minutes to stretch and collect the mail. She fell instantly back to sleep once the coach started up again and did not rouse until Emory shook her gently on the shoulder.

They were at a major crossroads in Bath, where they had to change turnpikes to join the more heavily trafficked West Road into London. Three passengers joined them there, two choosing to ride the roof, and the third, a pork-faced merchant whose buttocks barely squeezed between the supports of the door, clambering inside with Emory and Anna, there to sneeze and cough his way through the next several hours. Without the comfort of a shoulder to lean on, Anna was forced to prop an arm against the hard wooden sides of the coach, and it soon felt black and blue from the constant jostling. By evening, when another brief stop was permitted for a meal, she was ready to cry, to rail at the unfairness of Emory's ability to doze peacefully in his corner, and to gleefully pound the merchant into the macadamized gravel of the road.

"I cannot bear his wheezing and dripping much longer," she whispered. "He stinks of rotten teeth and whatever wretched concoction he keeps eating out of his pocket."

"Courage, mon petite," Emory murmured back. "He is only paid to Reading, which should come at the next change of horses, by my guess. We have made excellent time thus far, and if our luck holds, we should reach the outskirts of London by early morning."

"And then what?" she grumbled. "I'll not be able to walk or sit or stand in any comfort whatsoever. Moreover"—she scratched savagely at the side of her ribs—"I suspect your neglect of the house back in Torquay has resulted in a host of new residents' taking advantage of your absence. I swear these clothes are alive," she added with a final hiss. "I will not need a costume for the ball, at this rate; I shall just be able to attend as a large pustule."

Wisely, Emory kept his smile in check. "Another few hours and I shall personally massage away all your aches and itches, I swear it."

She stopped scratching long enough to shove the brim of her hat higher. "And draw me a real bath? Hot and deep?"

"Scented with rose oil," he agreed.

"Swear it."

"I do, most solemnly."

She groaned and allowed herself to be propelled gently back to where the coach was waiting, its two forward riding lamps casting bright circles of yellow light on the road. Despite Emory's encouragement, she still hesitated at the door, long enough to see a second coach and four emerging out of the darkness. The horses had been driven hard and were flecked with lather. While the driver wore no distinguishing set of livery and there were no arms or emblems to identify the owner, the shape and size of the gleaming black berline were unmistakable.

"Get inside," Emory said, his hand on her back to spur her into moving.

She glanced once, quickly, over her shoulder, but Emory's one visible eye was fastened on the other coach as it rolled to a dusty halt less than half a dozen long paces beside them. He climbed hastily up behind her and pulled the door shut just as the door of the other carriage opened and the Marquess of Barrimore's broad shoulders ducked through the opening.

Anna pressed as far back into her shadowy corner as she could. The small side lamps suspended over the door seemed to flood the interior of the Palmer with light as she counted off the five, six slow thumping heartbeats it took for Barrimore to shake the wrinkles out of his jacket and stretch the kinks out of his long legs. She could *feel* him looking at the mail coach. She could feel him staring, frowning, tipping his head to take a closer look, his eyebrows arching in surprise as he strode over to the open window and . . .

She gasped as the driver called to the horses and the coach jerked forward, kicking up a small spray of gravel in its wake. In the last glimpse she had, she saw there were now three men standing outside the berline and that Barrimore had his back to the road, his arm outstretched to assist a young woman in disembarking. Anna leaned forward, craning her head partway out the window, convinced her eyes were playing a trick, but the angle of the road changed and she could see nothing but the black avenue of trees that flanked the side of the turnpike.

She leaned back, frozen in her seat a moment, then turned to stare at Emory. She had insisted on dashing off a quick note to Anthony before they left Torquay, if for no other reason than to assure him she was alive and well and not to worry, she would meet up with him in London in a few short days. That explained why *he* would be traveling back to town in the company of the Marquess of Barrimore; it was more difficult to think of a reason why Colonel Rupert Ramsey and Lucille Althorpe would be with him as well.

At seven in the morning, there was enough activity stirring among the laundresses, the butchers, the tinkers, the farmers, and the footpads of London for a wounded soldier and a young boy to vanish into the crowds almost as soon as they stepped off the mail coach. They had lost the companionship of the merchant somewhere around midnight, but a light rainfall had brought the two other passengers down from the roof and Annaleah had worried her way through another sleepless night. She was cramped and aching but at least there was terra firma beneath her feet and she thought she could do justice to a large breakfast if a suitable inn could be found. After searching longer than Annaleah thought justifiable, considering that each squalid tavern resembled the next, the alehouse Emory finally entered was far from anything to which she was accustomed. It was small and dark and stank of thievery, but he seemed comfortable enough with his surroundings to remove the linen wrappings from his head and shove them into one of the deep pockets of the greatcoat.

"Do you recognize this place?"

He shook his head by way of denial, but she thought there was something in his eyes that suggested otherwise.

"I have lived in London all my life," she said under her breath, "yet I have no idea where we are."

"There would be no reason for you to know. Not unless you were a thief or a cutpurse or someone who made their living off the misery of others. Or if you wanted to hide and not be found."

Before she could question his cryptic remark, the landlord, a skinny man who stumped along on one wooden leg, was fanning his way through the thick layer of pipe smoke, hurrying over to their table.

"Are ye mad?" he asked, a pair of little piglet eyes popped wide in disbelief. "Comin' in 'ere bold as brass ballocks on a bear. Get up. Get up I say an' get into the back room afore ye bring arf the bulls in London down on us! Whisht! Whisht, up wi' ye!"

Using the hem of his leather apron for emphasis, he shooed them onto their feet and through a grimy curtain, then herded them down a narrow hallway to a smaller room in back. The fact that it was already occupied by a man and woman grappling together on a creaky cot made no impression on the innkeeper. He kicked the man's naked buttocks with the stump of his wooden leg and ordered him out, then glared impatiently at the barmaid as she scrambled to push down her skirts and adjust the gaping laces of her bodice.

"I'll want my 'arfpence fer that," he shouted, drawing the curtain closed behind them. "Been in 'ere the whole blessit mornin', they 'ave, firkytoodlin' like rabbits every time I turns me back," he added in a grumble. "Now then, Cap'n." He looked up sharply at Emory. "I suppose ye did that just to get me old heart pumpin' double fast?"

"I'm, ah, not—"

"N'owt in yer proper senses, aye. Ye got that right. We 'eard tell the Frenchies 'ad kill't ye, but Seamus, now, he know'd better. Wagered me ye'd turn up sooner or later, like a bad rash on a once-'oled flute."

"And Seamus would be . . . ?"

"Down at Peg Powter's, o' course. Only other place he figured ye'd be fool enough to show yer gob." He tilted his head to see around Emory's shoulder. "Who's the lad?"

"A friend. Where's my ship?"

"Eh?" The innkeeper snapped upright. "Ye don't know?"

"I have been . . . out of touch for a few days."

"Well, swive me with a spoon. I'm n'owt 'appy bein' the one to 'ave to tell ye then."

"Tell me what?"

"The *Intrepid*. She's been conferscated."

"Confiscated?"

"Aye. An' her crew be locked in the 'old, waitin' on enough gibbets to be built so's the lot o' them can 'ave their 'eads made into gallows apples."

A telltale muscle in Emory's cheek flickered and his eyes grew dark as inkwells. "What are the charges?"

"Treason. Piracy. Smugglin'. Pick yer poison. Their necks get stretched, one way or t'other. Seamus an' some o' the lads managed to bash a few brains togither an' slip over the side, but most the rest are boxed."

"And the ship?"

"She be at Gravesend waitin' on the court's pleasure."

Emory cursed and raked a hand through his hair.

"Ye'll be wantin' to see Seamus, I warrant?"

"What? Oh. Yes. Yes, I will." His hand stayed at his temple, pressing against the side of his skull. "Can you take us to him?"

"Take ye to 'im?" The innkeeper frowned. "I already told ye, he be at Peg's."

The heavy haversack dropped to the floor as Emory's right hand joined his left in squeezing his temples. Anna touched his arm, then looked swiftly at the innkeeper.

"Can you bring us some water, please?"

"Water?"

"Ale. Rum. Anything."

"Aye." The word came out as slowly as he took in Anna's unshaven cheeks, the too-slender shoulders, the supple shape of her mouth. The tiny piglet eyes nearly popped out of their creases when he noticed the hand resting on Emory's sleeve. She had tried like the devil to remove the ring her aunt had given her, but it was stuck fast. The gloves she had worn since leaving Torbay had come off without a thought and, though the room was small and poorly lit, the facets of the diamond sparked like fiery beacons. "Aye," he muttered. "Ale. I'll fetch it directly."

He was not fully through the curtain when Emory started to fall forward, a groan escaping between clenched teeth.

"It is all right," she said. "It is all right, let it happen."

The ship was a Spaniard, though she had kept her flags down until she had been in position to present her broadside. Seamus stood beside him, the heat of his cheeks almost as red as the blaze of his hair, as he shouted the order to fire. The full battery of heavy guns exploded almost simultaneously, the iron snouts bucking back in their carriages, the winching ropes screaming with the strain. A cloud of smoke and cinder creamed back over the deck rail, blasting the sweaty faces of the crew with heat while they worked to haul the guns back on board, ream, reload, and run them out again.

Seamus, the magnificent Irish bastard, leaped up on the rail and hung by one hand from the shrouds, using the other to direct the gunners' aim. He shouted a warning, broadside coming in, and roared a stream of Celtic curses as shot exploded all around him, blowing through wooden rails, cutting through lines, shattering spars and sail into a burning hail of canvas and splinters. The gun beside Emory took a direct hit down the muzzle, causing it to buckle back against the wheels of the carriage. The tackling lines split like cotton threads and the huge iron barrel reared back and rolled to the side, crushing one of the crew. Emory screamed and ran forward, but it was too late. The boy was dead. He was nothing. He was there shouting and cheering one minute, a slippery red stain on the planking the next. . . .

Emory opened his eyes. He was lying on his back, his cravat loosened, the ends trailing over the side of the cot. Anna had discarded her hat and the thick coil of her hair had unwound and was hanging over one shoulder. Her face was pale, her eyes wide and almost too blue to bear as she blotted his forehead with a dampened cloth. Standing behind her, his back pressed to the wall, his face nearly as white, was the innkeeper.

". . . remembered nothing," she was explaining.

"He didn't know 'is own name?"

"We had to tell him what it was."

"We?"

"My great-aunt and I. Luckily she knew him as a boy and was able to tell him some things about himself, his family."

"Are ye sayin' he 'as the artemesia?"

Anna moistened her lips and dipped the rag in the shallow bowl of water she held cradled on her lap. "I believe the word for it is *am*nesia."

"Aye, the one where he remembers n'owt?"

"He did not even know his own brother," she said softly.

"The wee bird?"

"No, the . . . the other one. The vicar. But he did not remember Arthur either."

"He is remembering things slowly," Emory said, his gaze leaving Anna's face with some reluctance to focus on the innkeeper. "Thomas. Thomas Fysh."

Fysh's brows shot upward. "Aye, that be my name."

"You sailed on the *Intrepid*."

"Aye. Till a surgeon fed me leg to a shark an' gave me a fonder likin' fer drawin' ale than cannonballs."

"You lost it the same time a boy was . . . was crushed under a gun carriage. He was dark-skinned and"—Emory frowned as he traced a finger along his cheek—"had a scar down the side of his face."

The innkeeper nodded. "Johnny Goodenough. Ye caught 'im tryin' to pick yer pocket in a bazaar in Tunisia. He were just ten years old, skinny as a stick o' kindlin', burned all over with sores an' scarred across the back from whippins. Ye took 'im on board the *Intrepid* an' when 'is master come lookin, ye beat the barstard to within an inch o' 'is life an' left 'im hangin' on the dock by 'is thumbs. Boy 'ad some damned Ay-rabb name ye couldn't say without jugglin' a mouthful o' weevils, so ye called 'im Johnny Good-enough an' promised 'im ye would make 'im a good enough sailor to captain 'is own ship one day."

"Apparently I failed to keep my promise," Emory said with quiet grimness.

"He'd not have spit on ye for the lack. Ye kept 'im by yer side for six years, put a few stone worth o' muscle on 'is chest an' set a smile on 'is face would've lit up the sun. Ye were like that, ye were. Always tryin' to save every waif ye come across. Seamus said as 'ow it would likely be the end o' ye one day, bein' so soft in the head." He paused and glanced uncomfortably in Annaleah's direction. "That was what Seamus said, any road."

"I have to speak to Seamus," Emory said. "And we need a safe place to stay for a couple of days. Can you help us?"

Thomas Fysh flushed. "Since yer brain were near squirted out yer ears, I'll not be holdin' that against ye, but I'd not be here at all if ye hadn't pulled my neck out o' worse pinches than this. 'Course I'll help ye, Cap'n. Help ye an' then some, if I can. Give me 'arf a mo' to tell the missus what I'm about, an' I'll be back, quick as a blink."

He ducked out the curtain, leaving Anna and Emory alone.

She waited a moment, then smiled and whispered, "A philanthropic pirate? A dangerous spy, soft in the head?"

"Repeat that at your own peril, madam," he murmured.

"I shall," she assured him, leaning close enough to brush her lips over his. "You may count upon it."

He caught her face between his hands before she could pull away and kissed her thoroughly enough to leave her breathless. When Fysh came back a minute later, he had to clear his throat to break them apart.

"We can go now, Cap'n, if ye're up to it."

"Oh, I am up to it," Emory said, not looking away from Anna's eyes. "Very much so."

Chapter 19

*F*YSH LED THEM through alleyways and along a twisted labyrinth of lanes that snaked through the crowded, narrow buildings. He had taken the weight of the haversack on his own stooped shoulder, and glanced back constantly, his eyes darting along the streets and up to the overhanging windows of the houses and taverns, looking for any sign they had been followed or were being watched.

Anna stumbled behind, with Emory following in the rear. She could not recall a time when she had ever been so exhausted or so miserable. Her poor, battered feet were blistering inside the ill-fitted shoes and she was certain her skin was one large infestation of hives.

Moreover, she was convinced Fysh was leading them in circles. She was no Viking explorer, but she knew in which direction the sun rose and fell and twice now, they had taken turns that doubled back on the route they had just covered. He was likely trying to impress Emory with his conscientiousness, but she just wanted to smack him. Very hard.

When they had about reached the point where she was ready to simply sit down and cry, Fysh signaled them to stop and wait in the niche of an alleyway. He hurried on ahead, crabbing sideways in his uneven gait as he checked his surroundings one last time before darting across the street and into a small recessed doorway. A sign, bearing a carved depiction of a blue sailing ship, identified the establishment as the Jolly Tar.

Anna leaned her head against the wall and closed her eyes. She could feel Emory's presence beside her, but for once she did not care if he saw how weak or weary, or how very close to tears, she was.

The door across the street opened and Emory tapped her on the arm. They crossed quickly, keeping their heads down and their eyes lowered, and because of this, Anna's first glimpse of Seamus Turnbull was of his feet. They were huge, encased in worn brown leather and splayed wide apart as if he was balancing himself on a rolling deck. A wide folded cuff was buckled to his calves and held a knife sheathed for easy access. His breeches were black, molded to the tree trunks he called legs, disappearing beneath a long leather jerkin cut with a flared back and buckled cross-straps in front. A brace of pistols were belted to his waist, along with two more knives, the handles polished smooth from use.

His chest was as wide as the doorway; his shoulders sat like two boulders atop a granite cliff. Looking up . . . up . . . she saw a thatch of the wildest, reddest hair she had ever seen in her life, surrounding a face that was one large freckle broken by a pair of sea green eyes.

While she gaped, the eyes narrowed and the mouth opened over a roar of pleasure.

The volume of the greeting sent Anna cringing to one side as he stomped past and flung his arms around Emory's shoulders, lifting him half off the ground.

"Damme if you're not a sight for sore eyes, boy-o," he shouted, laughing and clapping him on the shoulder. "Pruner and the rest o' the lads were sure that sheep-dipping Corsican had done ye in, but I said no. I said ye had too much of the devil in ye to kill. Stayed in port two days, though, looking for ye. Stayed until the blockade was damn near too tight to squeeze a turd through, and as it happens, it was. Even so, we might have made it if the wind hadn't played us foul. Sailed into a dead calm and a fog so thick you couldn't see your prick to piss. By the time we hauled ourselves out of it, His Royal Bloody Majesty's navy was on us, ports opened, flags up, tellin' us to surrender or say our last prayers." He sobered a moment and scowled. "Fysh told ye what happened?"

Emory nodded. "He said the *Intrepid* had been seized."

"Aye. Happened so damned fast we had no time to run out but one or two of our own guns. A couple, three of us managed to slip over the side before the shackles went on, but the rest o' the lads were tossed in the hold and chained down like black ivory. But Fysh tells me ye've had trouble of yer own. What's this about being thrown down a well?"

"Artemesia," the innkeeper chirped in. "Aye. Knocked senseless 'ee were, an' if ye don't believe me, just arsk the little lady 'ere."

"Lady?" The Irish giant turned and glared down at Anna, who was already melted as far back against the wall as was possible. "Ye were down a well with a lady?"

Annaleah whimpered softly. Seamus Turnbull looked and sounded exactly how she would have expected a bloodthirsty pirate to look and sound. Up to this moment, she had felt quite safe in Emory's company, had even regarded their flight as a kind of noble adventure. But now, pinned against the wall by glittering green eyes and a face so ominous it choked her breath, she could only wish for the strength to dash back out the door and run to safety.

There was no cache of energy left to call upon, though, and just managing to hold her bladder drained the last of her reserves. Her knees wobbled and she could feel herself starting to slide down the wall, sinking into a cool, dark fog of her own. Dimly she heard a voice beside her, and there was a sudden flurry of movement as a strong pair of arms caught her before she actually crashed to the floor. Her lashes stayed open long enough to see Emory's face swim into view above her, then they fluttered closed . . . and then there was nothing. . . .

She awoke one sense at a time. The smells came to her first, a frowsy blend of roasted meat, soap, mustiness, and lamp oil. Somewhere in the distance she could hear voices raised in song: a ribald sea ditty complete with the banging accompaniment of many tankards. These were mingled with street sounds: carriage wheels, shouting pedestrians, the clopping of horses' hooves. There was a faintly unpleasant taste at the back of her throat, salty and harsh, like stale broth, and a swollen feeling to her tongue, as if it had grown too large for her mouth.

Conversely, she felt shamefully snug and warm. A tentative wriggling of her toes suggested she was inches deep in a thick feather mattress with an equally thick covering of goose down. Other sensations gradually prickled to awareness along her body. She was no longer itchy, no longer belted and buttoned into the strangeness of men's clothing. She was naked, in fact, and it was this last discovery, combined with a memory of the Irishman's scowling face, that prompted her to push herself upright with a small surge of panic.

She did not recognize the room or the bed she was in. But the man sleeping in the chair beside her was breathtakingly familiar. His head was on a precarious tilt, his cheek mashed inward by a supporting fist, the elbow balanced on the arm of the chair. His long legs were fully stretched and crossed at the ankles, and if she filtered out the background noises, she could hear the soft rattle of a snore at the back of his throat.

It wasn't a dream then. It wasn't a nightmare. She had traveled across half of England on a mail coach, had been taken to some squalid tavern on the riverfront where one of Emory's shipmates—a red-haired, green-eyed Irishman—had frightened her into a dead faint.

Looking cautiously around the shadowy room, she identified a table, two chairs, a brick hearth with a fire smoldering in the grate. The small night table next to Emory held the two steel-barreled flintlocks, a bottle of wine, and two partly filled glasses.

There was a window in the far wall, but the shutters were closed and the curtains drawn, giving her no hint if it was day or night.

Gingerly she reached out and took one of the glasses,

then sniffed the inch or so of red liquid in the bottom before taking a small sip. The wine was sweet, a little rusty in flavor, but it cleared the sourness out of her throat. The movement displaced the covers, bringing forth what she thought was a faint hint of rosewater scent. Her skin felt clean, her hair brushed free of its rat's nest of tangles.

She glanced at Emory, but he was sleeping soundly. He was freshly shaved and bathed; his hair gleamed like fine black silk in the lamplight. The shirt he wore was open at the throat, the laces hanging haphazardly over his chest.

"My brother, Arthur, used to do that."

Startled, she saw that his one eye was opened in a lazy slit.

"Used to do what?" she asked.

"He would sneak into my room at night and watch me while I was sleeping. He would perch on the footboard like an owl, and say he was guarding me. Keeping the demons away."

"Did it work?"

He sat straighter on the chair, stretching out the kinks in his spine as he did so. "I had a lot of demons. But it helped me sleep easier, knowing he was there."

Anna drew her knees up beneath the tent of blankets and circled them with her arms. "How long have you been watching over me?"

He turned to glance at the window, cursed at the cramp in his neck, then settled back, a hand to his nape, massaging. "You have slept through most of the day and a good part of the evening."

"And you have been in that chair all that time?"

"Only an hour or so," he said with a frown, "though it surely feels like more."

"The bed is perfectly big enough for two," she pointed out shyly.

"So it is, but I am not a saint, madam, and it posed enough of a challenge just to see you settled without letting my hands wander too far astray. Besides, you looked so comfortable all curled up and purring like a kitten, I did not want to disturb you."

"You undressed me?"

"Both Fysh and Seamus offered, like the gallant louts they are, but I pulled rank."

"And you . . . bathed me?"

"It was not nearly as pleasurable an experience as the last time, I assure you. Not with you waving your hands about, demanding this, demanding that. Rose oil, you claimed I promised, and you would not give me leave to rest until I fetched the damned stuff."

She was surprised. "I was awake?"

"You don't remember cuffing me on the chin when I told you we were lucky just to have soap?"

She shook her head slowly. "No."

"Or draining half a cauldron of beef broth and three unwatered glasses of wine?"

Her breath left her throat in a gust. "No, not at all."

Something flickered in the dark eyes for a moment—the temptation to invent some dreadful sin to accuse her of committing—but in the end he only smiled. "Then you have an idea of how I felt waking up in your aunt's house. You even threatened to call the constabulary down upon me if I dared force you into those breeches again."

"I do not recall saying any such thing, sir, but the sentiment is genuine. How you wear the infernal things, day in and day out, is completely beyond me. They pinch and itch and are downright uncomfortable where . . . where the flesh is particularly sensitive."

His eyes glinted as they roamed across the bare white slope of her shoulders. "And where might that be?"

"You know very well where."

"In truth, I do not," he protested innocently.

Anna stared at his mouth, his smile, and suffered an unexpected tightness in her chest. She was in a smelly tavern in the seedy end of London, hiding from God knew who with a man who, although he was being hunted by every soldier, constable, and magistrate in the country, could not only sit and watch over her while she slept, but could fetch a trifling thing like rose oil, and bathe her, and tease her as if he hadn't a care in the world.

She swallowed hard and steered the conversation to safer ground. "Your friend, Seamus, he seems a very . . . capable man."

"And a hard fellow to forget, you would think, wouldn't you? He was positively crushed to hear I had done so, however, and spent most of the day reminding me of his many heroic feats. Some I was able to remember after some prodding; some were embellished beyond recognition. But to answer your unasked question, we have been sailing together for eight years, during which time he has taught me everything I know—or so he insists."

"Does he know what happened to you in France?"

Emory shook his head. "All he can tell me is that I was present at a midnight meeting with Bonaparte and his advisors the night before he surrendered to the British authorities. I went back on board the *Intrepid* right afterward, but I was followed."

"Cipriani?"

He nodded. "When I went back onshore to speak with him, someone else knocked me on the head and tossed me into a wagon. Seamus took some men and tried to follow, but . . ." He shrugged and stared a moment at the empty glass before tipping more wine into it.

"Does he know about the letter?"

"He thinks I locked some papers away in the strongbox, but he did not see them."

"He was not curious enough to look?"

Emory took a swallow of wine and wiped the back of his hand across his mouth. "He would not have looked unless he was certain I was dead."

"But the papers . . . they might prove your innocence?"

"I won't know that until I retrieve them. In any case, without some insurance to prove I was working for the English government, I cannot think of a thing that would prove I was not working both sides of the fence for profit. It *was* my ship that carried the bastard away from Elba, after all."

She watched him take another harsh swallow of wine, then lean his head against the chair.

"There must be an explanation. Cipriani said your messages were intercepted, that even if they had arrived in London, they would have been stopped before reaching Lord Westford, but surely your Mr. Seamus can testify on your behalf; he must know the truth of what happened."

Emory blew out a soft breath, for he and Seamus had had this discussion already. "No, unfortunately he cannot. He dare not step foot near an English court or he would be tried and hung for murder."

"Murder!"

"It happened a few years ago in Portsmouth—he strangled a man. A rather important gentleman, as it turned out: the elder son of an earl."

"He admits to strangling him?" she whispered.

"He does not have to admit it. I was there. I saw it."

"You watched him strangle a man," she said. "Why did you not stop him?"

"By the time I realized he was *not* going to stop, it was too late." Emory saw the shadow that came into her eyes and guessed that she was remembering the seeming ease with which he'd fired the gun at Cipriani's hand. "He had come upon the young gentleman and another fine chap while they were in the process of kicking a dog to death. It seems the mongrel had lifted his leg on the gentleman's carriage wheel and he'd taken offense at the gesture. While expressing his displeasure, he had such good sport kicking the beast halfway across the road, he made it into a game. When Seamus came upon them, every bone in the poor creature's body was broken, yet the two men were still kicking it back and forth, laughing and making wagers as to how long it would keep whimpering. The second gentleman had the rare good sense to run when he saw Turnbull's face, but the earl's son was arrogant enough to turn and draw his sword. Seamus took him up by the neck and . . . well . . . I imagine he does not know his own strength, especially when he is enraged. I tried to stop him, but for my trouble earned a bullet in my, ah, nether quarters."

"He *shot* you?"

"It was an accident; we were scuffling about in the dirt with about five other men from the *Intrepid* who were trying to help me pull him off the corpse. The gun discharged and I was in the way. He felt terrible afterward, of course." He paused and smiled faintly again. "For shooting me, not for throttling the young nobleman. In that he is steadfastly unrepentant. As a result, he has a charge of murder outstanding against him and a reward of several hundred pounds against his capture. Westford thought it added to my credibility as a rogue mercenary," he added quietly, "to have a murderer as my first officer."

"Where is he now?" she asked, glancing at the door.

"Seamus? I have sent him on ahead to Gravesend. I will meet up with him there at the Bull and Horn Friday night after the Regent's ball."

"You intend to take back your ship?"

"If it is at all possible, yes. Before my men are transferred to a gaol somewhere out of reach."

"But you still intend to see Westford?"

"Cipriani was not in Torquay by accident. He was there for a reason, and if that reason is Bonaparte, then Westford should be alerted. At the very least he should double, treble the guards around him, and move the *Bellerophon* out of Torbay if necessary."

"How can you warn him of an escape plan if you do not know what it is?"

"I can be a pretty persuasive fellow if I put my mind to it," he said, holding her gaze with his. "Ideally, of course, I can convince him to give me back my ship, or to give me enough time to retrieve the letter Cipriani was so anxious to recover. With luck and a fast horse I can be in Gravesend two hours after I speak to Westford. If he sends me with an escort, all the better. If not . . ." He shrugged and left the sentence unfinished.

Annaleah studied his face. "You keep saying 'I.' "

"Do I?"

"You are not planning to take me with you, are you," she said softly.

He stalled for as long as it took him to set his empty glass down, but she did not need to wait for his answer.

"But . . . why?"

"Anna, it's just too damned dangerous."

"More dangerous than being chased and shot at by soldiers? More dangerous than being hunted and very nearly killed by an assassin? Or fleeing halfway across England through the dead of night and having to hide away in some dreadful little inn that smells of slops and . . . and other things I choose not to think about?"

"Anna . . ." He stood and crossed the two steps to the bed, jostling the mattress as he sat beside her. "You have no idea how sorry I am for having put you through all this. I know the toll it has taken, and it is all my fault. All of it. If I had a quarter of the skill I am credited with, I should have just ridden away from Widdicombe House and taken my chances with the patrols and the searches. I should never have turned back, never followed Barrimore's coach, never approached you on the boardwalk—though you have no idea how long I stood there watching you in the sunlight, and how close I came to murdering that young buck with the spyglass for just speaking to you."

She did not lift her head or return his smile, and he sighed again. "It was an unconscionable and selfish act, not to mention a wild and stupid scheme, to use you as a diversion. I should have walked away. I should have run, dammit, and just kept running. And I never, never should have touched you. Not that first afternoon on the cliffs, not that night in your room, not later at the inn."

This did make her tilt her head higher. "Then you regret everything that has happened between us?"

"No," he said and ran a hand up the smoothness of her arm. "*No*, I do not regret one single moment, not since I wakened and thought you an angel. I just . . . never should have touched you, dammit, because it only makes it harder to let you go. And I know I must let you go. I must leave you here. It is the only way I can be sure you are safe."

This last came out as a whisper—a whisper accompanied by a grinding of his teeth, for he wanted to kiss her, but he dared not. Not when he knew she was bare and soft and warm beneath the layer of quilting and he was already struggling with the urge to just drop a bolt across the door and stay in her arms forever.

Anna did not make it easier when she raised her hand and rested it gently on the rock-hard ridge of his jaw.

"I feel safe with you. And the blame for this is not all yours to take. If you had not touched me, I surely would have had to touch you or die from the wanting. If you would call yourself selfish and unconscionable, then I must be the same, for I want nothing more than for you to touch me now; to kiss me and hold me and . . . and make me believe that perhaps you love me even a tenth as much as I love you."

The admission, blurted without thought or conscious effort, caused her voice to catch in her throat and her skin to flush under the sudden, tense scrutiny of his eyes.

"I do," she said again, her voice stronger, firmer. "I do love you. And when I am with you, I am not afraid of anything."

He looked dumbfounded. "Anna—"

"Do you not care for me at all? Not even a little?"

"How the devil can you even ask that? I should think a lack of caring on my part would be more obvious if I let you go ahead and put your neck on the block."

"It is my neck. My choice. Was that not what you told me back on the cliffs? That everyone has the right to make their own choices in life?"

"Not if those choices might get them killed. And this is not the time to be throwing my own words in my face," he said with a husky warning. "If soldiers broke through the door right now, it could still be argued to excellent effect that you were being held against your will. No one would dare suggest otherwise, not with Barrimore and your brother standing behind you. And they *would* stand behind you, regardless if they believed you were kidnapped or not.

"But if you were caught helping me of your own free will, you would be dragged away in iron shackles and tossed into Newgate like a common thief. You would be charged with treason, put on trial, and found to be just as guilty as me, notwithstanding any defense of youthful indiscretion your family could offer. As a mere accomplice, you might avoid the executioner's axe, but you would surely be condemned to the transport ships. Ten years of planting turnips in Australia would be the best you could hope for, assuming you survived the three-month voyage."

Anna paled visibly but did not look away. "Is that a roundabout way of saying you *do* care for me?"

He frowned and released an exasperated little sigh. "This is hardly the time or—"

"This is the *very* time and the *very* place, for if you say no, I will have no *choice* but to believe you. I will have no *choice* but to dress and walk out the door, and you will never have to see me or bathe me or fetch me rose oil again." She paused and, in an attempt not to look desperate, gave a little shrug. "I most definitely could not go home, however, despite your confidence in my brother's sense of honor. For that matter, the mere thought of seeing Mother's face each morning at the breakfast table would make the transport ships look like a holiday. On the other hand, Aunt Florence is convinced Barrimore is quite blind in love with me; perhaps if I prostrate myself at his feet and beg his protection he would take me back in some capacity—as his mistress, or . . . or his doxy, or some such thing."

Emory's frown grew even more ominous, if that was possible. He knew what she was doing and why she was doing it, but jealousy is ever an effective weapon, and it brought forth an immediate image of her naked body in front of the fire, her skin gleaming wet, her hair spilling over her shoulders like dark gold. Only it was not him he saw standing with her, dying slowly of sweet agony as her lips explored his body. It was Barrimore.

"Eventually, I am sure I could convince him of my contrition. Perhaps if he put me with child he would soften even further and—"

Emory made a sound, low in his throat, and raised his hands again, stopping a breath short of touching her. After a minute, when he had gained control of the heat flowing through his veins, he was even able to open his eyes and meet the wide, guileless blue ones waiting for him.

"—and he would see how docile and obedient I had become," she concluded softly.

"Docile *and* obedient?" He scowled. "Which hour of which day of which week would you set aside for such a momentous event?"

"I was fully prepared to accept it as my lot before I met you, sir."

He snorted. "You would never have married Barrimore. He would have stifled you, smothered you, and you would have spent half your life staring out a window, wondering what lay beyond the next valley."

"But now that I know, now that I have been shot at and chased and forced to ride in public conveyances with fat, sour men who reek of garlic and rotten teeth . . . I should consider myself lucky to be so smothered and stifled. Lucky to have a man like Winston Perry willing to forgive me my sins."

"To make you his doxy?"

"If need be, yes."

Seeing the stubborn set to her chin, Emory's lips parted around another soft oath. "Do you even *know* what being a doxy entails?"

A hesitation betrayed her, for it was another one of Anthony's words, used liberally but never precisely defined. "I am sure my Lord Barrimore would instruct me."

"There is a roomful of men belowstairs in the tavern who would happily impart all the instructions you need."

"Then pick one. Or two," she countered smartly. "I expect it takes a considerable amount of practice to become a good doxy."

His eyes narrowed, and Anna's heart rose slowly to lodge at the base of her throat.

"You are not going to let this go, are you?"

She shook her head adamantly.

"Not even if I tie you hand and foot to the bed?"

"Only if you tie yourself alongside me."

"An appealing prospect, I assure you, but . . ." He stopped and stared as Anna lay slowly back against the pillows. She did not take the cover with her, but left it draped over her knees, and when she moved, it slipped off her breasts, baring them to the glow of the lamplight.

"But?" she prompted him.

"But . . ." The word came out a murmur and was followed by an oath as he bowed his head and drove all ten fingers through his hair in frustration.

She waited a moment before running the merest tip of her tongue across her lips to moisten them. Leaning forward again, she pressed a soft kiss onto the back of his hands where they were still locked in his hair, then angled her head down until their brows touched.

"I am sorry to be so much trouble," she whispered.

"No you're not. I believe you are thriving on it."

"I believe I *could* thrive, milord, and become equally as headstrong, obstinate, and willful as you . . . under your expert tutelage, of course."

He grunted. "And now you mock me. A foolish and

pitiable creature who cannot even muster the strength to chase you out the door."

"Only tell me who to thank for this dreadful flaw in your character and I will do so gladly," she whispered, kissing him again on the temple, the cheek, the ridge of his brow.

She folded her knees beneath her and rose enough that she was able to cradle his head against her breast, enough that she could feel the warmth of the sigh he expelled against her skin as his hands surrendered to the soft lure of her flesh.

"Remind me," he murmured, "to thank Barrimore the next time I see him."

"Thank him for what?"

"For being a fool and a prig. For being too damned blind to see what he was throwing away because of his starched manners and unbending presumptions. He is a handsome enough fellow," he said grudgingly. "He likely could have swept you off your feet with a little respect and a lot of good kissing."

She pressed both a smile and a kiss into the soft thickness of his hair. "But I could not even begin to imagine him risking life and limb to fetch me rose oil for my bath."

"It was a trifling thing. I merely had to wrap my head in that ridiculous bandage again and scour half the shops along the waterfront. Fysh thought I was mad, of course, and Seamus, well . . ."

Anna ran her hands along the slope of his shoulders, marveling in the latent power she felt beneath her fingertips. "He probably understood perfectly."

Emory's mouth twitched at the corner as he lifted his head. "He asked me outright if I knew what a damned asinine thing I was doing. And said that I was in danger of throwing away my hard-won freedom for a pretty mouth and a luscious body."

"What did you answer him?"

He studied her mouth a moment. "I fetched the rose oil, did I not?"

"So you did."

"It was not necessarily an admission," he warned.

"I did not ask for any promises, nor do I expect any."

"Fair enough."

"Fair enough," she agreed. "Then can we stop this tiresome arguing and put the time we have to better use?"

His eyes were inky black, gleaming with a combination of admiration and respect and . . . something else. It was the something else that flooded her body with heat and made her realize that everything she was, everything she could be was mirrored in the depths of those eyes.

"What better use?" he asked in a murmur.

Anna smiled through a deep, thrilling breath and sank slowly back down onto the bed. Her breasts were white as ivory, smooth and firm, with the slightest hint of a pink blush at the tips, and she saw the hunger blaze to life on his face as she trailed a long, slender finger from the peak of one ruched nipple to the satiny plane of her belly.

"Take off those wretched breeches," she whispered, "and I will gladly show you."

Chapter 20

I *FETCHED THE ROSE OIL, DID I NOT?*
   Anna let the words play over and over in her mind
as, for the second time that night, she watched Emory
sleep. She was fully aware, then and now, that he had not
used the word "love," yet for all his cool steely nerve, his
ability to mock and measure at a glance, to read her thoughts
with a thoroughness that rendered her naked in more ways
than one, he had not been able to lie to her either. And so
it was enough for now. He cared enough to fetch her rose
oil and that was more than enough.

   He was lying on his back, quite splendidly naked beneath
the coverlet, and she let her gaze idle a moment over the
hillock at the junction of his thighs before continuing on
down to where his feet created tents in the bedding.

   The effects of his lovemaking had left her all warm and
slippery, but try as she might she could not sleep or even
close her eyes. Despite the fact there were plans to be
made and plots to be foiled, in truth all she could think
about was the sensation of his flesh moving inside her,
against her, breast to breast, belly to belly. She now knew
that even the act of kissing—something she had always
regarded as being such an innocent thing—could be as
physical and intimate as the actual act of joining.

   She snuggled closer against the curve of his body and let
her fingers idle in the dark hair on his chest.

   "I refuse to think you have the energy to embark
upon any more lessons," he murmured, keeping his eyes
firmly shut.

   "You have only yourself to blame," she said, kissing his
breast. "You are a very good teacher. In truth, though, I was

thinking about the Regent's ball. We will need costumes, masks. . . ."

"Fysh has already solved that for us."

Her eyebrow arched delicately. "Fysh?"

"He buys his ale from the same stillman who supplies half the theaters in London. They have costumes aplenty, in all sizes and selections."

"But it is not the theater season."

He offered up a sigh of forbearance. "I suspect the seasons along the waterfront may differ somewhat from the ones in Mayfair and Park Lane."

"Oh. Yes, of course. That must have sounded very pretentious."

"Why? Your world has always been in the West End; why should you know or care about what goes on here?"

"I want to know. I want to care about the things you care about."

He opened his eyes and studied her a moment before reaching over and plucking a strand of long chestnut hair off her shoulder. He twined it thoughtfully around his fingers until the pressure drew her lips over to his but stopped her just shy of touching him. "When this is over—"

He was not permitted to finish the thought. A sudden clatter in the outer hallway preceded a loud thumping on the door, and in a series of movements so swift Anna could barely follow them, Emory had leaped out of bed, had snatched up his pistols from the bedside table, and was pressed against the wall, both guns cocked and held tight to his body, the snouts pointed at the ceiling.

He put his ear to the wood and listened a moment, then looked over at her and nodded.

"Y-yes, who is it?"

"Me, miss. It be Fysh. I brung ye breakfast: 'ot biscuit, cheese pie an' mutton bits, some beef toady, an' a nice pot o' groat puddin'."

Emory kept the hammers on his flintlocks cocked until

he verified it was Fysh standing in the hall and that there was not a troop of soldiers crouched in readiness behind him.

"Dropped a plate o' tarts an' one o' the cups on the way up," he said, explaining the noise. "I'll go back an' fotch 'em if ye think ye mout still be peckish wi' this lot an' all."

Unabashedly naked, Emory stalked the scent of the food like a bloodhound, barely waiting for Fysh to set the tray down before he was after a piece of the steaming-hot pie. He set his guns aside and ate with his fingers while the equally naked Annalcah could only watch as she covered herself to her chin with the bedding.

"Any news?" Emory asked, his mouth full.

Fysh puckered his lips and gazed up at the ceiling, trying hard not to look at the hint of Anna's white shoulders and her streaming dark hair. "W-a-all now, there be a stirrin' in the eaves about Old Boney. Word is, they're fixin' to move 'im from Torbay to Plymo't next week, an' from the *Belly-ro-phon* to the *Nort'umberlan'.*"

"The *Northumberland*? She's a seventy-four-gun ship-of-the-line."

"Aye. Figger they need a warship to take 'im where 'ee's goin'."

"And where might that be?"

"Dunno, but it be a two-month sail, I 'ear. Decision were made late last night not to 'ang him, but not to coddle 'im none either. They want 'im well out o' reach o' any Frenchies, an' there'll be 'arf an army goin' along to see 'ee stays put this time."

"He will never honor another exile."

Fysh shrugged and popped a chunk of cheese in his mouth.

"Any reactions from the good citizens of London?"

"Good citizens don't know ow't yet. Won't know 'til he's on board the *Nort'umberlan'* an' she's under sail."

Anna was burning to ask how *he* knew, but the contents of the tray were suddenly far more important than the fate of a defeated French general. The glands under her tongue were flooding her mouth and she could only watch as Emory helped himself again and again to savory chunks of bread and meat, letting crumbs and juices flow freely down his hand.

Emory caught her eye and gave his brow a little crook as if inquiring if he should send down for linens and cutlery. There were two large splatters of butter on his chest and a look of careless disregard in the smile he sent her way, and it was with some trepidation—and not a little annoyance at his mockery—that she stretched out a bare white arm and broke off a piece of pastry. It was delicious, oozing hot cheese, and all traces of annoyance vanished under Emory's approving gaze when she licked every crumb off her fingers. She tried everything, even the groat pudding, which was a complete mystery to her. But following Emory's example, she tore off a round of biscuit and dipped it into the buttery gray mass, and was rewarded with a delectable mouthful of oatmeal and currants sweetened with honey.

"Any word on Le Couteau?" he asked Fysh.

"Yer Corsican friend? Nuthin'."

Emory stopped chewing and set his unfinished biscuit aside. He wiped the back of his hand across his mouth with a thoughtful frown. "Nothing?"

"N'owt. Nary a peep. If 'ee's dead, they ain't found 'is corpse yet. Word o' that would spread faster than the second comin'."

"Then he's not dead," Emory said grimly. "If they found the coachman—and he would have wakened screaming bloody murder in spite of the twenty pounds I stuffed in his pocket—they would have searched the house and found the body."

"Well, why the fuck—ah, beggin' yer pardon, miss—why the sweet good Jaysus wi' daisies up 'is nose didn't ye kill 'im when ye 'ad the chance? 'Ee'll be ripe pissed now."

"I'm sure he will. Did you get the costumes?"

"Aye. Masks an' all. Got wigs an' face paint too. Yer own mithers won't know ye when we're done."

"Just as long as it gets us through the doors, that will be fine."

"Oh, aye. It'll get ye through the doors," Fysh murmured. "Question is whether ye'll get off the street."

A carriage rolled up in front of the tavern door at half past eight o'clock the following evening, a large elegant vehicle with an enclosed box drawn by a fine pair of bay geldings with jaunty sprays of ostrich plumes in their bridles. The locals stopped and gawked openmouthed as two masked, caped figures darted out of the Jolly Tar and climbed quickly into the coach, whereupon the liveried driver wasted no time snapping the horses to a brisk trot. The locals then gawked at each other, wondering if they had just seen what they had just seen.

"I feel like a blithering idiot," Emory grumbled, hearing the whistles and catcalls that followed the coach away from the waterfront.

"I think you look exactly the part," Anna said, smiling behind her mask. " 'A merry wanderer of the night.' "

"I feel like an idiot and I intend to hang Fysh by his ballocks when this is over."

"I thought he did a fine job, considering he barely had two days to arrange everything."

They rode in silence through the London streets, weaving their way toward the West End and Pall Mall. Guests for the fête were invited for nine, but at five minutes to the hour, there was still a queue of carriages lined up at the gates, waiting to enter the forecourt of Carlton House. Anna had not been at the Regent's residence for a year or more and could not help but wonder if the Prince, who was gaining a reputation for renovating the entire premises each time a new architect came into fashion, had changed the interior decor yet again.

Even in the forecourt there was an air of festivity, with lanterns strung from every post and pillar, swagged in the branches of the trees, set into pots in the elaborate formal gardens. The six enormous Corinthian columns that fronted the covered porte cochere were draped in silk bunting and hung with lights. A score or more footmen dressed as harlequins were there to greet the carriages as they drew beneath the arched portico and to assist the masked and bejeweled occupants in alighting.

Anna felt an encouraging squeeze and looked down to where Emory's hand covered hers. She knew her fingers were ice cold. By necessity, they had spent most of the day in the cramped room above the tavern—getting to know one another better, Emory had said. The results of all that knowledge had left her flushed and warm, but she was chilled to the bone now, her heart beating like a wild thing in her breast. What had seemed like a good idea right up until the instant the carriage passed through the gates now felt doomed to fail. They would be stopped at the door, she was certain. There were Beefeaters in their scarlets and gold braid beside the massive entryway and more of the Royal Guard in evidence at the gates, in the court. They would be stopped, challenged, questioned, and dragged away like penny thieves without ever having set foot on the bottom stair.

"Breathe," Emory whispered. "Your own 'mither' would not recognize you behind the mask and the paint."

And there was the crux. They had deliberately delayed, hoping most of the guests would have arrived already and the crush of costumed arrivals in the entrance hall would camouflage their own appearance. Her mother was notoriously prompt at all functions and would have sat in her carriage on St. James's Street until the exact minute the invitation stipulated. She would have presented the gold-embossed invitation upon her arrival, and Anna had to hope her name would be on the list that was being checked at the door. The possibility that it was not, that they would send a footman to fetch her mother or her father to verify her identity, was what terrified her the most. That and the fact she had not yet confessed this tiny flaw in the plan to Emory.

It was their turn beneath the porte cochere. Bright flares of light came through the windows as they rolled forward and the door was being opened. A white-gloved hand was reaching inside and she was grasping it. She was gathering the gossamer silk of her skirts and ducking her head so that the plumes and glittering fairy sprigs woven into her hair would not snag on the frame. She was stepping down onto the wooden coach stair, then onto the paved cobblestones, and she could see the harlequin smiling, extending his arm toward the bottom of the stairs, inviting her to her doom.

Emory cupped his hand beneath her elbow and steered her forward. She felt light-headed, disoriented. Her skin was clammy, and there was sweat beading across her brow. But she took one step, then another, and behind them she could hear the coach door being shut and latched, the driver sent on as another carriage pulled up in its place.

They came to a stony-faced court jester with a leather-bound ledger open before him. Anna vaguely recognized the man as one of the Regent's secretaries.

"Your invitation?"

Anna stared at him, wondering how actors and actresses breathed behind their stifling papier-mâché masks.

"Sir? Madam? Your names please?"

Anna felt Emory's fingers tighten on her elbow. "Fairchilde," she blurted. "Annaleah Marissa Sophia Widdicombe Fairchilde. My father is Percival Fairchilde, Earl of Witham, and my mother"—another pinch, more eloquent this time, halted her before she recited her entire lineage— "my mother arrived earlier. I am certain you will find our names on your list."

The jester was not moved, was probably not in a fair mood at all having had to stuff his rotund figure into a tight-fitting suit of red and green diamond checks topped by a cap with bells tinkling off every point. Moreover, he had probably been hearing similar stories all evening from people without invitations attempting to bluff their way through the doors. "Yes, well, I am afraid, Miss Fairchilde, that I must ask you to—"

"I . . . *we* . . . that is, Lord Barrimore and I were delayed by the need to search—to no avail, I am afraid—for his own invitation. It appears he gave it to his valet, who then gave it to a footman, who then placed it somewhere from which a maid must have mislaid it."

"Lord Barrimore?" The jester looked up with a tinkling of bells. "Yes, of course, milord. I did not recognize you. A fine costume, indeed. You make a very striking . . . er, elf, is it?"

"Puck," Anna supplied. "From Shakespeare's *Midsummer Night's Dream*. And I am Titania, the Queen of the Fairies."

She picked up a fold of the gossamer gown and executed a little half pirouette on her toes, as if she was just *too* excited to be attending such a lavish affair. The silk twinkled with silver dust and was sheer enough to reveal the shape of her legs, something that did not escape the secretary's notice as he stared over the top of his pince-nez and absently waved his pen toward the stairs.

"Thank you. Please do go on straight ahead."

Emory waited until they were out of earshot before he leaned over and rasped in her ear, "Lord Barrimore?"

"You are the same height and general build; I could not think of anyone else on the spur of the moment."

"Suppose he had already arrived?"

"Winston Perry rarely deigns to go anywhere before midnight. It simply would not do."

They passed through the open doors and into the massive, vaulted splendor of the Great Hall. More harlequins were standing in attendance, waiting to whisk away capes and cloaks, and for the first time Anna was able to pull a full breath deep into her lungs. There had to be a hundred people milling about admiring the coffered ceiling, the gilded furnishings, the tall Ionic columns that graced the entrances to the two anterooms. Even Anna was inspired to look up, for the huge bronze lamps had been strung with branches and woven with lengths of silk to form a bower that glittered like some fairy cave in a dream.

"It seems we have come dressed appropriately after all," she murmured, looking over at Emory as he tried in vain to adjust the hem of his abbreviated tunic. His legs were encased in forest green wool woven tight enough to reveal every muscle and sinew in his thighs. Tawny leather boots cross-gartered with rawhide straps reached to his knees, where thin bands of silk were tied, festooned with an assortment of bows, ribbons, and bells. His tunic barely touched the tops of his thighs and boasted short capped sleeves from which more ribbons trailed down over the flared sleeves of his gold silk shirt. A grinning green wood sprite's mask covered his face and his hair was hidden beneath a riot of orange curls.

"Truly," she said, "it could have been worse. You could have played the part of Bottom and worn an ass's head, which in turn would have been better than—"

"Never mind," he growled. "I can see that Fysh is not the only one responsible for the costuming."

"He merely inquired if I had any preferences."

A low rumble in his throat was his only answer as he pointed toward the octagonal vestibule and the magnificent Baroque staircase, where guests were being served iced champagne off silver trays and directed by polite harlequins with ribboned staffs. Anna and Emory did their best to blend in with the crowd of wizards, Romans, and courtly fools as they followed the glittering bower down to the lower level. There were frequent pauses while other guests greeted acquaintances and women squealed over costumes, and, not wanting to appear in any extraordinary hurry, Emory joined some of the men in leaning over the gilded balustrade to comment on the painted glass dome two stories up.

In doing so he allowed the tautness of his buttocks to be regarded by more than a few keen-eyed ladies, several of whom squealed in delight and had to snap open their fans to cool the blush that came to their cheeks.

One young lady, wearing the wide panniers and towering rolled wig similar to those of the dozen other Marie Antoinettes present, was distracted enough to stare openly at the handsome sight. She neither blushed nor squealed, but she did abandon the small group she was with to ease her way through the crush and join the shapely Puck in admiring the gilded patterns in the rail.

Before she could fully raise her vizard and dazzle him with her smile, he excused himself and went back to where Anna was waiting by a plaster bust of Charles James Fox.

"That was rather rude," she observed.

"What?"

"Ignoring the French Queen."

Emory glanced back and had to scan several guests before he found the right one, her face powdered white, her lips bright red, and a heart-shaped patch stuck to her cheek. He began to say, "I pray she does not lose her head over—" but stopped abruptly.

Anna looked up at his sharp intake of breath. "What is it?"

"Move," he said, taking up her arm again. "Just keep walking and do not look back."

The command came a split second too late, for she had already tipped her head to see past his shoulder. She straightened again quickly enough, but she could sense that the woman was staring after them, her gaze narrowed as she followed their progress down the rest of the curving stairs.

"Did you recognize her? Who was she?"

"My esteemed sister-in-law, Lucille Althorpe."

"*What?*" Anna stumbled, missing the bottom step and hanging precariously off Emory's arm for the few seconds it took her to regain her balance. "Are you certain?"

"More than I care to be."

"But how—?"

"She stripped me naked once, in your aunt's parlor, and it is not a sensation one is likely to forget. She did it again just now."

Anna was about to ask what he meant, but then she remembered a comment Florence had made that evening. Something about Lucille staring hard enough to leave scorch marks in his breeches.

"What on earth is she doing here?"

"Stanley said he was sending her to London for a short holiday. Plague take his timing."

Anna thought back to the close call they had had at the posting house in Bath. She had seen Lord Barrimore alight from the berline, then her brother Anthony, then . . .

"Colonel Ramsey," she whispered. "He must have had an invitation to the ball and extended it to Lucille."

"A merry muddle indeed," Emory said, guiding her across the marble rotunda. He paused at the archway to look first left, then right along the crowded corridor. "It would behoove us to find Lord Westford with all due haste, but curse it"— he lifted the green elfin mask and propped it atop his curls as he searched the sea of painted and masked faces—"where do we begin?"

"We could each take a wing," she suggested halfheartedly. "The small dining room, the golden drawing room and library lie one way; the bow room, formal dining room, and conservatory lie the other."

Emory thought a moment, then said, "The music guides us toward the conservatory, but my guess is Westford will not be in too frivolous a mood. The ghostly words of dead philosophers would suit him better."

He dropped the mask back into place and took up her arm again, a sparkling silver queen and her wood sprite escort strolling leisurely through the draped Gothic archway that led toward the library.

Chapter 21

*E*MORY HAD GUESSED right. Geoffrey Peterson, Lord Westford, was in the library, well away from the noise and revelry. He was not in costume, but judging by the haggard caste to his face, he was not overly concerned by the faux pas. A man of medium height and middle age, he carried no extra weight around his girth. He had a plain face that was not much improved by bushy muttonchop whiskers. His hair was gray, thin enough to see the shine of his scalp.

He was standing by the black marble fireplace, his face glowing red in the bright flames, as much from the heat as from the company of the half dozen pirates, clowns, and court knaves who were engaged in a vitriolic debate over the wisdom of exiling Napoleon Bonaparte for a second time.

"What is to say he will stay put this time? We thought Elba a hellish safe place to confine him and look what has come from that. Three, nay, nearly four months of bloodshed, and the deaths of tens of thousands of fine young men. France is in chaos and we show a complete lack of faith in the ability of English justice to punish the man responsible."

"Mercy and honor have their limitations," another man agreed. He was seated in a tall wing chair before the fire and not much could be seen of him other than a sleeve, a cuff, and a snifter of brandy.

"Have you heard what awaits him on St. Helena? It is a bare rock in the middle of the South Atlantic, a thousand miles from the nearest landfall. 'Tis said the devil shit the island out as he flew from one world to the other."

After a short gust of laughter, another voice emerged. "I

heard Napoleon himself had once considered sending a force of fifteen hundred men to capture it, but decided it was not worth the waste of gunpowder. We are sending three thousand, at God knows what cost, just to guard him."

"It would only take one man to wield an axe," said a gruff voice of reason. "And cost us naught but the price of honing a keen edge on the blade."

Westford turned from the fireplace. "Perhaps we should build a guillotine in Piccadilly? Then we could invite the hags to come and knit souvenirs to sell while we showed the rest of the world how civilized we have become after two decades of war."

In the discomfiting silence that met his remark, Westford glanced around the room. Most of the party guests, upon entering the gloom of the library and hearing the topic of discussion, elected not to remain overlong. He saw a tall, broad-shouldered man in a ridiculous elf costume and a quite lovely woman wearing little more than an airy silk veil standing off to one side, and was about to dismiss them when the man lifted his mask.

For all of ten seconds, the significance of the gesture did not register. But then the skin across the back of Westford's neck began to shrink and an arctic chill seemed to settle over the room, freezing out the voices of the men behind him. His every sense, his every instinct was tuned to the dark, bottomless eyes staring at him; a gust of disbelief parted his lips and nearly staggered him back against the marble caryatid.

"I say, Westford." One of the men raised his empty glass. "Will you take another brandy?"

"What? Oh. No, not just yet, thank you. As it happens I, uh, feel the need to, uh, seek out the nearest water closet. If you will excuse me, gentlemen . . ."

He moved clumsily away from the hearth, bumping his hip on a table as he passed. The elf's mask was back in place, but the glitter of dark eyes followed Westford across the library and through the arch to the adjoining drawing room. He hesitated there only long enough to glance back over his shoulder, then continued out of sight.

"Wait here," Emory said, touching Anna's arm.

"Absolutely not," she hissed back, conscious of the men peering around now to have a better look at her wisp of a costume.

She sensed rather than saw his grimace as he took her arm again. "We really must compare our definitions of 'docile' and 'obedient' one day. I am sure they differ."

Anna kept pace with his long strides as he followed Westford through the drawing room and up a small staircase concealed by an elegant swath of gold drapery. At the top, they hastened wordlessly along a narrow servants' corridor into the Regent's private audience room.

This chamber was named, appropriately, the Blue Velvet Room, its walls hung with dark blue panels surrounded by ornate gold moldings. Each panel in turn framed a masterpiece by either Rembrandt, Cuyp, or paintings of British military triumphs. The carpet was blue, woven in a pattern of gold fleur-de-lis to reflect sympathy for the ill-fated monarchy; the furnishings were upholstered in pale blue with heavily gilded arms and legs. Anna had never been in such a grand stateroom before and was unabashedly awestruck. She stared up at the multileveled chandeliers, at the priceless collection of Chinese vases, at the elaborate candelabra featuring female figures holding palm branches, and she again envisioned scarlet-clad Beefeaters bursting through the gilt doors to drag them away in shackles.

Westford merely crossed to the Regent's ornate escritoire and lit a pair of candles to supplement the scant light coming from the wall sconces.

"I hear you have been a busy man," he said, glancing over as Emory removed his mask.

"Better busy than dead."

Westford held his gaze a moment, then looked at

Annaleah. "Perhaps you would prefer to wait back in the anteroom?"

"Perhaps she would prefer to wait right here," Emory said. "I am alive thanks to Miss Fairchilde—not to mention here speaking to you now."

"Yes," Westford drawled. "I will not even ask where you come by your audacity in showing up here tonight, Althorpe. Nor why you, Miss Annaleah Fairchilde"—he turned again to address Anna where she stood in the shadows, the folds of her gown shifting ghostlike in the drafts—"would risk bringing total ruin down upon your family's good name to help him."

Anna felt every drop of blood drain out of her face.

"You appear to be in remarkably high spirits for the victim of a heinous kidnapping," he said sarcastically.

"I wrote my brother a letter explaining—"

"That you lost your senses? Or is it that you have lost something even more valuable to this blackheart and feel you have no choice but to remain in his company?"

"I remain with him because I choose to, milord," she said coldly. "And because I believe him to be innocent of the charges laid against him."

"You do realize what will happen to you if you are caught?" Westford did not wait for an answer before he glared at Emory. "To both of us if we are caught in your company?"

"I was hoping you could call off the hounds, so to speak, and clear up the misconception that I am a traitor and a Bonapartist—even that you might let it be known that in fact I have been in your employ as a spy for the past three years."

Westford looked hard into the dark, probing eyes. "That would be a difficult thing to attest to, sir, since I have not had a single missive from you for several months. Not since you took it upon yourself to sail to Elba and unleash that Corsican plague upon the world again."

"I sent you dispatches," Emory said quietly. "Fully a

score or more. I told you there was a plan afoot to mount a rescue and that I had been approached by Bonaparte's associates to sail the *Intrepid* to Elba."

"I received no such dispatches."

Emory looked startled. "You must have. I sent them through the normal channels, taking all the usual precautions."

"I assure you, I received nothing. Not then, not at any time before or after Napoleon landed at Antibes and began his march to Paris."

"Are you saying none of my subsequent dispatches got through either? None of the messages detailing Bonaparte's movements? The movements of his army?"

"I have received nothing from you, sir. Not for five months or more. Thank God you were not the only coal in the fire or we should have had no prior warning about the positioning or strength of his troops at Waterloo."

Emory, clearly stunned, paced to the far side of the room. "If none of my messages came through," he said hoarsely, "how do you explain the coded replies I received back ordering me to go along with the ruse at Elba? Ordering me to remain in Bonaparte's camp?"

"They did not come from me, sir! I sent no such orders, coded or otherwise! And if you think you can lay any of the blame for your traitorous actions on my shoulders, you have a sadly misguided notion indeed! In the first place, I would never have sanctioned the escape of such a dangerous fugitive—what would be the point? Why in God's name would I unleash that plague upon the earth again?"

Emory blinked. Then blinked again. His right hand went to his temple; his left he held up to Annaleah as she started toward him.

"Cipriani. He said, 'The messages were intercepted.' He also said, 'We knew all about you from the beginning' and implied there was a spy in Lord Casterleagh's offices."

"You are grasping at straws, Althorpe. Is that why you

have come here?" the minister demanded. "Because you expected me to corroborate this outlandish story?"

"I expect you to uphold your word to reveal our relationship should the need arise. You gave it freely enough the day you presented me with the arrest warrant for Seamus Turnbull and used his freedom to blackmail me into signing on as one of your spies."

"You voided that agreement, Althorpe, the day you sailed the *Intrepid* to Elba. And if you think you can barge in here accusing me of collusion and expect me to bow to *your* threat of blackmail, you can damned well think again! Any outlandish accusations you make would amount to your word against mine—and yours, I fear, is not worth the spit required to form the words."

"They are not outlandish accusations, Westford," Emory said in a low voice. "They are the truth, and I will be damned if I am the only one left hanging in the wind."

"If you are hanging in the wind, sir, it is by your own doing, not mine, for as God is my witness I had no foreknowledge of the escape from Elba!"

"Then you have a spy in your cabinet, sir, and he has managed to play us both for fools!"

A violent ache was throbbing in Emory's temple, the pressure so intense against the back of his eyeballs it was almost impossible to think. He had been counting on Westford to support him, to lend credence to his claim of innocence and perhaps even buy him the time necessary to prove it.

He raised a hand to his head, and, finding the stiff orange curls of the wig there to greet him, tore the disguise angrily off, flinging it along with the elf mask halfway across the room. Once freed, his own hair fell in wild black waves around his face, making the green paint and sparkled silver eyebrows Fysh had enjoyed applying seem all the more incongruous.

"I might," Westford said with a calmer, though unconvincing coldness, "be able to argue for leniency if you surrender yourself to the authorities. Do it here, now, to-night, and I promise I will personally guarantee a fair trial."

Emory's hand had risen again to massage the back of his neck. His fingers rubbed across the gold chain and he stopped, narrowing his eyes as he drew the links forward until the iron key dangled free of his shirt. "The dispatches," he murmured, almost to himself. "I did not have time to destroy the last ones you sent." He glanced pointedly at Anna. "I locked them away in the strongbox, dammit, along with—"

"There he is! I knew it was him, I knew it!"

The shrill female cry came from the shadows behind them. All three turned to stare at the doorway, where Lucille Althorpe stood, her arm outstretched, her finger pointing across the room at Emory Althorpe. Standing beside her, his pistol drawn, was Colonel Ramsey, and behind them were four armed Beefeaters fronting a small group of gentlemen who were straining forward to see the cause of the commotion.

One of those gentlemen was Anthony Fairchilde, and the shock of seeing him was enough to keep Anna's feet rooted to the floor, delaying her reaction long enough for Ramsey to push past Lucille's encumbering panniers and aim his pistol across the room.

Anna screamed, and leaped forward. "No!"

She saw the puff of smoke as the hammer struck flint and sparked. There was a split-second delay while the powder in the chamber ignited, followed by the loud explosion of the shot.

Lucille Althorpe clapped her hands to her ears and screeched, falling back against the four Beefeaters as they were about to surge through the door. Two of them went down with her in an upheaval of wire hoops and lace petti-coats; the other two managed to step around the tangle of legs and rush through the doorway. They were armed only with their beribboned pikes, but the latter were ten feet long with viciously hooked steel points at their ends.

Anna had felt the heat of the shot fly past her face, but it had missed her and gouged a deep pit in one of the paneled walls. Emory was shouting something, but before she could turn and run to him, Westford had stepped forward to block her path. In desperation she tried to dart past. He was close enough to grasp her arm and jerk her to a painful halt, and she lashed out with her fist, with the toes of her shoes, and managed to pull free, but she was off balance and spun painfully into the corner of the escritoire.

Across the room, with one hand on the gilded latch, Emory hesitated and started to turn back for her.

"No!" Anna screamed. "Go quickly! Save yourself! Do what you must do—I will be all right!"

The Beefeaters were beside the desk, racing for the opposite door, their pikes raised with deadly intent. Rupert Ramsey was right behind them, shouting and waving his gun; the other two guards were scrambling to their feet, pushing the outraged and still squealing Lucille Althorpe out of the way.

Emory's dark eyes held Anna's for a final helpless moment before he turned and bolted through the door, slamming it shut just as the Beefeaters drove home the points of their pikes, chipping off chunks of the wood and gilt.

Anna had begun to limp painfully after them but was quickly overtaken by her brother, who curled an iron hand around her upper arm.

"Here, here. Not so fast, young woman!"

"For pity's sake, Anthony, let me go!"

"Anna? Anna is that . . . dear God, is that *you*?"

"Anthony, I beg you! Let me go!"

Stunned to discover it was his sister behind the tinseled mask he actually started to loosen his grip. Indeed, she might have been able to twist the rest of the way free had not another ominous figure dressed all in black loomed up beside her and taken a firm hold of her other arm.

She whirled around, fully intending to lash out with the gold letter opener she had picked up off the Regent's desk, but at the last possible moment she recognized the severely cold eyes and squared jaw of Winston Perry, marquess of

Barrimore. Her arm fell limply to her side, concealing the weapon in the folds of her skirt as he reached up and summarily removed the jeweled vizard.

His expression, if it was possible, grew even harder and colder when he confirmed who it was he had unmasked.

"Please," she cried. "Please, you must let me go after him."

Barrimore glared. Her face and throat had been coated with a layer of theatrical oil laced with silver dust, so that it sparkled with a million tiny pinpoints of light. There were tears welling in her eyes and a steady stream of soft pleas on her lips, but he only tightened his grip and pressed his mouth into a grim line. "I'm afraid I cannot do that, Miss Fairchilde."

Westford strode up beside them. "Indeed, madam, you are in nearly as much trouble as the elusive Mr. Althorpe, and you may be sure all the tears in the world will not spare you a moment's sympathy."

Anna was not even aware tears had begun to spill down her cheeks, nor did she hear the questions her brother started hissing in her ear. She was barely able to grasp the fact that between them, Anthony and Barrimore were all but carrying her as they followed Ramsey and the guardsmen through the outer anteroom and into the octagonal vestibule. She was dimly aware of the startled faces that turned to stare, but her fears, her concerns were all for Emory. Carlton House would be a small fortress tonight, with a hundred guards in attendance outside to discourage uninvited guests and a hundred more inside to ensure that the Regent's priceless possessions did not stray into an oversized pocket. An unarmed man dressed in green leggings would not have an easy time of it eluding capture.

At the vestibule, they were directed by a cluster of excited, gawking guests down a narrow servants' access concealed behind a swath of curtains. Anthony was forced to release her arm and hang back, as the width only allowed for two people to descend at once. At the bottom of the stairs he hurried two paces ahead to lead the way down a short corridor toward what could only be—judging by the smell and the three sprawled servants they passed along the way—the kitchens.

As large as would be expected in a house that regularly entertained guests by the scores, the kitchen was teeming with servants, cooks, maids—all of whom were rushing frantically to finalize the preparations for dinner. It was impossible to pass through them, although they could readily see where Emory and the pursuing Beefeaters had done so. More trays lay splattered on the floor; a servant stood nearby wailing, her frock covered in leek soup.

"This way," Barrimore said, pulling Anna along the wall toward yet another door. Anthony held it open while they passed through, and the first thing that hit them was a gust of cool wind from outside. A short flight of stone steps took them up to a rear drive where deliveries were made; beyond that were the buildings that contained the stables, carriage house, and laundry.

Every square inch of empty space in between was taken up with carriages belonging to guests. Shouts and neighing horses pointed out the most likely route Emory had taken, with the guardsmen, who numbered more than a dozen now, and Colonel Ramsey chasing close behind. Anthony plunged into the sea of horseflesh and polished ebony, but Barrimore elected to remain under the flickering light of a coach lamp.

"Please," Anna cried. "You do not understand. They are trying to kill an innocent man."

"Most of the cells in Newgate are filled with innocent men, Miss Fairchilde," he answered dryly. "And most of them die, swearing their innocence with their last breath."

"But Emory *is* innocent. I know he is."

"I am sure you do, else you would not have been so completely blinded to your responsibilities to your family, as well as your loyalties to your King."

"Emory Althorpe's loyalties are as true as your own! All

the time he has been in France he has been working for King and country, spying for our government. Why do you suppose he took such a dreadful risk to come here tonight?"

"I cannot possibly fathom the answer to that, Miss Fairchilde."

"He came to see Lord Westford!"

The stony face remained indifferent, though he gave his signet ring a savage twist.

"Lord Westford! Lord Westford!"

"I assure you my hearing is quite excellent, madam."

"Then why will you not listen to me! Emory Althorpe was hired by Lord Westford—nay, *blackmailed*—into pretending to be a pirate and mercenary in order to spy on the French! He did his job so well, they came to him when they were formulating their plans to rescue Bonaparte off Elba. He sent a dispatch to Westford—a dispatch Lord Westford claims he did not get." She went on, relaying as much as she could remember of the conversation in the Blue Velvet Room; then, in utter desperation, she blurted everything she could remember of the past week, beginning with her walk on the beach that fateful morning when she had found Emory half drowned and unconscious.

She went on to explain that he had awakened with no memory of what had happened to him, that he had kidnapped her off the street in Torquay, yes, but only in order to buy himself some time. After nearly being killed by the Corsican assassin, she had come willingly with him to London because she believed he was telling the truth.

"He has the proof locked in a strongbox on board his ship, and if he is prevented from fetching it, not only will he be unjustly convicted of treason, but Lord Westford—if *he* is telling the truth—will never know the identity of the real traitor in his cabinet, the man who must have intercepted the original messages and replied with forged dispatches of his own. Moreover, they will not be able to stop this new plan to help Napoleon escape—if, indeed, it has not taken place already."

Out of breath, her defiance rapidly losing way to defeat, Anna did not notice the sharp look Barrimore cast her way. "What do you mean? What new plan?"

She wiped the back of her hand across her cheeks, smearing the tears and silvered oil, not hearing Barrimore's question until he asked it a second time.

"I do not know the details, sir; neither does Emory, but he believes there may be a clue somewhere in the papers on board his ship. The assassin—Cipriani—was demanding that Emory return a letter he stole. I don't know—perhaps there is something in it, something that reveals the plan or identifies the spy. I do know Cipriani was prepared to go to great lengths to ensure that Emory did not leave Torbay alive. He would even have killed me, had Emory not overpowered him and shot off his hands. Why would he do so unless he was afraid Emory would discover their plan in time to stop them? Why would Lord Westford swear he neither received nor sent any dispatches unless he truly did not see them, and if so, then there *must* be a traitor in the war cabinet who must be as desperate to capture—or kill— Emory Althorpe as our government is. Who would have had access to the dispatches? Who would have known the proper codes?"

Barrimore was not sharing her enthusiasm for solving the mystery. He was, however, still staring at her in mild astonishment. "Did you say . . . he shot off the assassin's hands?"

She nodded, and, having nothing else to wipe her nose with, used the cuff of her sleeve. "Only one of them. I shot off the other."

"You shot—! No, no, never mind. I do not think I want to hear it."

"His name was Cipriani. Franceschi Cipriani. He had another name . . . Le Couteau, I think Emory said. The Knife."

"Yes, I have heard of him."

"You have?"

"His name is among those listed as Bonaparte's close advisors."

"I am sure it would be if he was helping to plan another escape."

Barrimore glanced out across the sea of carriages, his cold eyes tracking the dozens of lanterns that were moving in and around the rose gardens. "And you say Althorpe has incriminating documents on board his ship?"

She nodded. "The *Intrepid*. She sits in Gravesend with her crew locked in the hold under arrest."

"Then we may assume this is where your Mr. Althorpe will go if he is lucky enough to elude capture tonight," Barrimore said thoughtfully. "It is certainly where I would go in his position, and with all due haste, before Westford arrives at the same conclusion and sends a regiment of dragoons in his wake."

He expelled a gust of breath and, after a moment, took up Annaleah's arm again and led her around the outside of the vast courtyard until they came to the front row of coaches. Without saying a word, he chose one with a brace of stout horses in harness and unlatched the door.

"Get in."

Anna hesitated. It was not the berline, and by the crest on the door, did not even belong to Barrimore. "What are you doing? Where are we going?"

"I am attempting to spirit you away, Miss Fairchilde, unless of course you prefer to remain here and see firsthand the inside of a prison cell?"

Anna felt a wave of faintness wash through her. "Does that mean you believe me? You believe Emory's innocence?"

"It means I am a fool," he said quietly. "And I firmly believe I will regret my rashness before this night is through. Now please, get on board before someone thinks to order the outer gates closed. You there!" He snapped his fingers and called to a group of liveried groomsmen lounging nearby. "The lady is ill. She must be taken home at once and my coach is nowhere to be seen. I am willing to pay ten guineas for the inconvenience, and to provide a letter to the owner explaining the emergency."

The driver separated himself from the group and came forward. "I'd be happy to drive you wherever you wish to go, milord."

Barrimore held out a ten-pound note, which instantly vanished to an inside pocket on the driver's coat, then assisted Annaleah into the coach.

"Where to, milord?"

"Gravesend," he said in a voice only the driver could hear. "And if you get us there before midnight, my good man, there will be another ten guineas in it for your trouble—another twenty if you can provide me with a pistol and shot."

The man squinted one eye and touched the brim of his hat. "Aye, milord. You'll be there in time to hear the clock strike twelve. As it happens, I have both pistol and musket on board. To guard against night riders, of course. Not to mention," he added with a broad wink, "the odd angry husband or two."

Chapter 22

$\mathcal{S}$EVERAL MORE GUINEAS were spent during the perilous ride to Gravesend. Exhausted and foam-flecked horses were changed for fresh teams at two posting houses; a hooded cloak for Annaleah was purchased off a landlord at another. Up to then she sat huddled under a lap robe in the corner of the coach, the occasional beam of moonlight shimmering across her face. She was cold, frightened, confused. She had no idea what Barrimore's intentions might be. She did not know if she had convinced him of Emory's innocence, or if she had foolishly betrayed the man she loved to the man she had humiliated.

"I am sorry," she said at one point, breaking the tense silence that had enveloped the coach since they'd left London. "My actions have been reckless and irresponsible, and . . . and I know I cannot possibly hope to earn your forgiveness. I can also understand how your hatred for me might influence your opinion of Mr. Althorpe, but in truth—and I would swear it to you here and now before God—I did not deliberately embark on a course to either hurt or embarrass you."

"Miss Fairchilde—"

"No, please. Let me finish. Truthfully enough, I was resistant to the notion of . . . of pursuing a more intimate relationship—and please forgive me again if I speak out of turn, but my family was quite convinced you were on the verge of offering a proposal—and I *did* seek to discourage you from putting me in the position of having to refuse you. . . ." She paused to ease some of the dryness in her throat. "But I certainly did not walk out on the cliffs that day with any deliberate intent of insulting you. The embrace you saw just . . . happened. The rashness of my actions startled Mr. Althorpe as much as they must have startled you."

Following the blurted confession, she heard the shifting of wool against wool as he moved an arm. "From what I have learned of Mr. Althorpe, he is a good deal more than a little rash himself."

"He never once acted without complete deference toward me and my aunt," she said in a whisper. "He never once forced me to do anything I did not want to do. Indeed, even when he kidnapped me off the boardwalk in Torquay, part of me was happy enough to burst, for I never thought I would see him again. I never thought he would come back for me. I thought . . ." Her voice trailed off miserably, and he finished the sentence for her.

"You thought you would be required to endure my company all the way back to town. And perhaps even after that."

"No. No, it was not so much that I would have to endure your company, milord. It was knowing that I would rather be somewhere else."

There were thick banks of cloud overhead, with few breaks to allow the moon to shine through. Barrimore had not lit the lamps inside the coach and she had to rely mainly on her senses to know if he moved or looked in her direction.

He was looking at her now; she could feel it. He was studying her with that dark condemnation she had dreaded feeling on the long journey from Torbay to London.

"Do you love him?"

The question came as a surprise, but she answered it without guilt. "Yes. With all my heart."

"All of your heart," he murmured. "I should think that would be a considerable amount, Miss Fairchilde. Something I myself can . . . scarcely imagine or quantify." After another lengthy pause, he asked, "And is the sentiment returned? Has he declared his feelings with an equal lack of reserve?"

"He . . . has said he cares for me, yes."

"Cares for you? Not exactly a resounding commitment from a man who has lived a good deal of his adult life on the whims of the wind and the sea. Do you anticipate he will be content to settle down and raise sheep when this is over?"

Annaleah's hands twisted together. "He has made no mention of his future plans."

"Nor could he have told you much about his past if he has been suffering the effects of amnesia, although I would hazard to guess that the kind of life he has led would be difficult to forget, regardless of the size of the blow to the head. His exploits are quite legendary in certain circles."

"Yes, well, he remembers more and more each day."

"And shares each detail with you when he does? The charges of piracy and smuggling are not without foundation, you know. Avoiding a British court was one of his main incentives when he agreed to work for the foreign office."

The conversation had ended there, and for the rest of the way to Gravesend they traveled in silence. Annaleah's eyes ached and were swollen from crying, her body was drained to the bone with exhaustion, and for a few miles she managed to doze to the churning rhythm of the wheels.

It was the change in the sound that awoke her. They were slowing, rolling over the harder-packed surfaces of a macadamized road sloping down toward a town. When she leaned forward to peer out the window, she could see the lights of the buildings clustered along the shoreline of the harbor. There were more lights sparkling farther out on the water, as lanterns hung from masts reflected off the decks of the small flotilla of merchant ships anchored in the port town of Gravesend.

"You mentioned he was meeting someone here. Do you know where that meeting is supposed to take place?"

"A tavern," she said, rubbing the sleep out of her eyes. "The Bull's Horns, or some such thing, I believe it was."

Barrimore's low laugh startled her into turning around to face him.

"Forgive my ill-timed drollery, Miss Fairchilde, but you yourself would not make for a very good spy. In the span of two short hours, you have confided the gentleman's whereabouts, his intentions, his likely destination. How the devil do you know I am not going to drive straight to the nearest garrison and dispatch a hundred soldiers to surround the tavern and arrest him, or send them aboard the *Intrepid* to lie in wait for him?"

While Anna's heart slowed to a sluggish thumping in her chest, she strained to see Barrimore's face through the shadows. They had left Carlton House in too much of a hurry for him to retrieve his hat or gloves or cape, and it occurred to her that he had probably never traveled in a state of such undress before. His hair was disturbed out of its usual precise waves and curls, softening the high, wide line of his brow. His cravat was loosened, the lower buttons on his satin waistcoat undone.

Thinking of his brow, of his face, made her remember the Regent's secretary. He had apologized for not recognizing "Lord Barrimore" in costume, yet the real Lord Barrimore had attended the party in his usual impeccable tailoring and was not in costume at all.

Another image flashed into her mind: There had been someone sitting in the seat in front of the hearth in the library. The wings of the chair had prevented her from seeing more than an arm and a hand holding a brandy glass. But the sleeve had been black, the cuff white; whoever it was had not been wearing a costume either.

"You were in the library this evening with Lord Westford," she said, amazed she could even hear her own voice through the loud rushing in her ears.

"I was there, yes."

"Yet your name was not marked off the guest list at the main door."

"Main doors can be tedious at times, and the Prince can be rather belligerent with guests who choose not to participate in his little soirees. While I give full credit to your Mr. Althorpe for appearing in green stockings and face paint, I would sooner pound sharp sticks under my fingernails. Moreover, I was returning from a journey that sent me halfway across the country on a fool's errand, as it turns out: the investigation of a rumor concerning a certain gentleman's arrival on our shores. Even more egregious to the sensibilities, I have spent the past two days trapped in a coach with his garrulous sister-in-law. I would happily have forgone the festivities altogether in favor of a full bottle of brandy and ice packs on my brow had there not been a pressing need to speak to Westford and advise him that our former spy extraordinaire had indeed landed in Torbay, but had managed to somehow evade capture."

"*Our* . . . spy?"

"My dear Annaleah, you could not have been expected to know it, I suppose, else we would have been doing a poor job indeed at subterfuge, but I have worked with Westford for the past five years, helping him organize and interpret the information he receives daily from the spies he has placed all over Europe. Further—to what will be your growing horror, I am sure—I know a good deal more than you likely ever will about Emory Althorpe. I know his background, I know his family, I know about the beatings his father gave him, and the name of the first serving girl who took him into a haystack. I know about the brother who believes he has wings and can fly, and believe me, after two *hours* in a coach with that infernal woman, I can even appreciate why he might have preferred to leave all that behind and run away to sea.

"I also know how and when he was recruited, and that he was considered to be our most valuable source of information on the continent until something appeared to turn him around. Half the coded dispatches he received, in fact, were written in my hand and only signed after the fact by Westford."

Anna grew very still. "I'm not s-sure I understand what you are saying."

"I am saying"—he leaned forward, and the leather seat creaked softly—"if there is a traitor working within Westford's very small, very tight-knit group of confidants . . . then he has to be exposed. What is more, if there is proof, and Althorpe has it, then it must be retrieved and taken back to London as soon as possible."

His voice was like a slow curl of mist, low and chilling, and it froze Annaleah to the bone. Barrimore worked with Westford. He knew all about Emory's role in the war. He handled the dispatches. . . .

Had he also intercepted them? Hidden them? Rewritten orders that Westford knew nothing about?

Her hands clenched tightly into fists on her lap and she turned to gaze wildly out the window. What, indeed, had she done? She had led Barrimore straight to Emory Althorpe—but whose interests, exactly, was the marquess looking out for? If Emory did have proof that might expose a traitor inside Westford's cabinet, and if that traitor was the Marquess of Barrimore himself, who better to find it and destroy it before his crimes could be revealed?

She should have suspected something right away. He was always so cold, so aloof, so unapproachable, and suddenly tonight he was warm and talkative, helpful, sympathetic. . . .

Anna almost groaned out loud. She had to do something, of course, but what? She had to warn Emory, but how? There was no way of knowing if he had even managed to get away from Carlton House, if he had ridden for Gravesend right away, if he had arrived there yet, to keep his rendezvous with Seamus Turnbull.

A sharp rapping on the wall of the coach brought Anna's attention snapping back to the Marquess of Barrimore. He had opened the sliding panel and was talking to the driver, instructing him to find the "Bull's Horns" tavern.

The tavern whose name she had simply blurted without thinking.

She unclenched her fists and rubbed the palms on her cloak to dry them. Her fingers brushed over something metallic jutting up from the side of the bench, and she remembered the letter opener she had snatched off the Regent's escritoire. She had hidden it in the folds of her gown, then later tucked it down between the cushion and the coach when they had boarded the diligence in the courtyard. The blade was long and exquisitely sharp, and while she could not for half an instant imagine plunging it into living flesh, it gave her comfort to know she was not as completely defenseless as Barrimore supposed.

Anna was beginning to grow immune to the sights and smells of various waterfront lodgings. Indeed, one could have plucked up the tawdry Bull and Horn tavern and substituted it for the Jolly Tar and no one would have noticed the difference. The air reeked of fish and saltwater, the gutters were clogged with waste. A pair of skinny dogs growling and snapping over a tasty morsel of bone in front of the inn slinked away with their prize when the door of the coach opened and Barrimore stepped down onto the muddy road.

He was clearly not impressed with their surroundings. The driver had wasted time and taken several wrong turns before the proper name of the establishment was determined, and while there were lights and noise blazing on either side of the Bull and Horn, the tavern itself was dark and quiet, the shutters and door closed. The driver was none too pleased, and even before seeing the sharp glance Barrimore cast his way had reached beneath his seat and rested the loaded blunderbuss in plain view across his lap.

"Wait here," the marquess murmured and started to close the coach door.

"If he is here, he might not believe you have come to

help," she said, hoping the tremor she could feel in her throat did not echo in her voice. "And if he is not here, I suspect Mr. Turnbull might shoot you without troubling to ask."

Barrimore saw the logic, though only with the greatest reluctance. "Then stay close behind me and if I tell you to run back to the coach, you will run, is that quite clear?"

Anna's face was partially hidden by the hood of the cloak, but she nodded anyway. She saw him pat the bulge beneath his jacket and knew it was where he had concealed the flintlock pistol the driver had given him earlier.

He approached the door and gave it two brusque raps with his knuckles.

Anna came up behind him, her hand lightly caressing the pocket of the cloak where she had slipped the letter opener. The night was cold enough for her breath to fog, damp enough to add moisture to the tiny beads of sweat already glistening at her temples.

Barrimore knocked again, with sufficient strength to startle the two mongrels away from their bone and set them to barking. The sound of a shout came from one of the second-story windows farther down the street, the ire directed first at the dogs, then at the third spate of heavy-fisted pounding on the tavern door.

"We be closed fer the night," a muffled voice came through the wood slats. "Fever inside. Quench yer thirst elsewhere."

"I am not seeking to quench my thirst," Barrimore said, his voice low and pressed against the crack of the jamb. "I have come from London on a matter of great importance."

"We be closed, I tell ye. Come back in the morning."

"Morning may be too late. The man I have come to see—"

"Ain't here, I tell ye. No one's here but two poxy 'ores an' me."

Barrimore waited a beat, then hissed, "I have come to see Emory Althorpe. Is he here?"

There was a distinct, wary pause on the other side of the

door before the disembodied voice asked, "Who might he be, and who might you be asking after him?"

"My name is hardly important. I—" Barrimore drew a clipped breath as the muzzle of a gun was pressed into the back of his neck, forcing his head roughly against the door.

Behind him, Anna barely had time to react to the shadowy intrusion before an arm was snaking around her waist, dragging her back. Another was clamped firmly over her mouth, muffling her cry of surprise. Out of the corner of her eye she could see where a third man was already climbing up into the carriage beside the driver, a cocked gun aimed squarely between the frightened man's eyes.

"We'll ask again," the first man snarled against Barrimore's ear. "Who might you be?"

"My name is of no immediate consequence, but I must warn you that the young lady you are manhandling is Miss Annaleah Fairchilde. She is here under my protection and should she suffer so much as a bruise, you will pay and pay dearly for the affront."

The man with the gun had no chance to answer the challenge as the sound of an iron bolt scraped beneath Barrimore's ear and the door was yanked open.

As tall as he was, the marquess had to look up into Seamus Turnbull's face. The Irishman stared hard at Annaleah before growling to the men to bring both her and Barrimore inside. The third man nudged the driver with his gun and a moment later, the carriage pulled away.

Annaleah was hustled forward through the darkened portal and left to stand beside Barrimore as the door was shut and bolted again behind them. At a grunt from Seamus Turnbull, a pair of lamps were lit inside the taproom. One of them was brought forward and raised so the light shone on Anna's face.

There was still a residue of silver dust on her skin and in her hair, sparkling softly in the yellow glow, and the effect showed in the startled green eyes.

"What the bejesus are ye doing here, miss? How did ye know where to come, and who might this fancy toff be that ye've brung along with ye?"

"Is Emory here?" she asked anxiously. "Did he manage to get safely away from Carlton House?"

"He managed," said a familiar voice from the opposite side of the room. "No thanks to a wall of thorn bushes that would have tested any man's mettle."

Anna turned and saw a splash of white in the corner, the blur of someone wearing a full-sleeved shirt and black breeches.

"Emory!" She pushed past Barrimore and ran across the room to fling herself into Althorpe's arms. He did not hesitate to catch her or to swing her around, where, shielded from the prying eyes of the other men in the room, he kissed her hard and deep on the mouth. When they broke free, she gasped again and her hand went to his cheek. The skin on his face and throat was scratched in a dozen places where the thorns had cut him; one of his hands was wrapped in a length of cloth, splotched pink. "Dear God," she gasped. "Are you all right?"

"Never mind about me. How did you get here? How did you get away from Barrimore?"

"I did not get away from him," she said, briefly distracted by the stains on his shirt where other cuts, other scratches on his chest and arms had bled through. "He is here. He brought me from London."

"He brought—?" Emory twisted around and stared at the silent figure in the doorway, the shock of recognition tightening his features. "Barrimore?"

The marquess bowed slightly. "Althorpe. You're a difficult man to run to ground."

"He has a gun," Anna cried. "Under his coat. The left-hand side."

Seamus reacted to the urgency in her voice, pushing the marquess back against the wall and brushing his jacket aside to uncover the polished walnut stock of the flintlock tucked into his waist.

"It is him," Anna said. "He is the traitor. He knows you are innocent and he has come to find the proof of his own guilt and destroy it before his treacherous dealings are uncovered!"

Barrimore's mouth slackened. His eyes narrowed and he momentarily forgot to be vexed at the roughness in Seamus's hands as the rest of his clothing was searched for weapons.

"Me? Good God, Annaleah! You think that I—? You think I would—?" He stopped, clearly shocked. "Whatever put such an absurd notion into your head?"

"You all but confessed it to me in the carriage, sir, telling me you knew everything about Emory's activities in France." She turned to Emory. "He admitted to me that he works for Westford and knows all about your spying missions in France. He saw the dispatches you sent. He *wrote* many of the dispatches you received, and could easily have falsified others!"

"I wrote some of them, yes," Barrimore acknowledged. "But not all. Nor was I the only one who would have had access to the codes. In the weeks after Bonaparte's landing at Antibes, there were sometimes two and three hundred dispatches arriving daily. The sheer numbers required us to employ a dozen extra men to cull the important information from the fodder.

"What is more, I have taken a huge leap of faith in *not* driving straight to the nearest garrison and leaving it up to the courts to decide guilt and innocence. Why would I do this, why would I help you and knowingly place myself at risk of being painted with the same tarred brush as Mr. Althorpe, if I were the guilty party?"

Annaleah's lungs deflated slowly. "Then you believe him? You believe Emory is innocent?"

"I can be persuaded to believe he was used as a pawn

by factions on both sides of the Channel. I do not believe he is *totally* innocent of all the charges leveled against him—in particular the most recent events that exposed you to inestimable dangers!"

"But I told you, I went with him willingly. He did not really kidnap me."

"Perhaps not," he said quietly. "But he did a devilish good job of stealing your heart, did he not?"

Anna stared at the shadowy profile, at the starkly handsome features that were always too stern by far. Though the Marquess of Barrimore was very good at keeping his emotions under tight rein, there was no mistaking the rough note of regret in his voice, and she could not help but wonder if her great-aunt Florence hadn't been right after all; Had he, indeed, been in love with her and simply too painfully proud to reveal it?

"You are nothing if not the devil of a man yourself, milord," she countered softly.

"Yes, well, despite the bruising my vanity has just taken, I shall take that as a compliment."

"It was meant as one."

Emory cleared his throat, reminding them they were not alone in the room.

"May I assume we have come to some manner of agreement here? Do I give his lordship to Seamus to drown in a gutter, or do we let him breathe a while longer? And what, in God's name, were you going to do with that?"

Anna followed his gaze down to where she clutched the ornate gold letter opener in her hand. She did not remember taking it out of her pocket, nor was she quite sure what to do with it now, even as the grimness on the faces of the men around her began to give way to crooked smiles.

Emory leaned over and gently plucked the ominous weapon out of her fingers.

"If you believe in my innocence as you say," he said,

looking over at Barrimore, "can you have my ship released and my men set free?"

"To what purpose, sir? That you might run again?"

"No," Emory said quietly. "As it happens, I am getting damned tired of running. If the papers are still there, on board the *Intrepid*, they may not only help clear my name, but might also provide a clue to the identity of the true traitor. Besides which, I have a bad feeling about what is happening in Torbay at the moment."

"Torbay?"

"Napoleon is due to be moved to Plymouth, is he not, where he is to be transferred on board the *Northumberland* and thence taken to St. Helena?"

Barrimore's eyes narrowed. "Your sources are very good, as that is not yet common knowledge, but yes. The captain of the *Bellerophon* is being sent orders to sail to Plymouth at his earliest convenience."

"Then they will have to execute their plan before the ship leaves Torbay."

"What plan? What are you talking about? And who is 'they'?"

" 'They' is your real traitor and whoever else is conspiring to help Bonaparte escape his exile before the sentence is carried out."

"Impossible. He is guarded day and night. He is on board a ship in the middle of a British port surrounded by a dozen brigantines bristling with cannon and men eager to use them."

Emory shook his head grimly. "I have seen the port, the ships, the fairground atmosphere surrounding the *Bellerophon*, and I tell you, sir, I could board her, take a stroll about the deck with Boney and the two of us leave again with no one being any the wiser."

"The hell you say."

"The hell I do say, yes. And to prove my point, I will sail the *Intrepid* there and do exactly that."

"The *Intrepid* is under equally heavy guard."

Emory quirked an eyebrow. "I intend to have her running out in open water before the morning tide comes in."

Barrimore regarded him with a cool, assessing eye. "Do that, sir, and I will gladly stand on the foredeck alongside you."

"We have to get on board first," Seamus growled. "And we weren't exactly planning to stroll down the wharf and whistle for an invitation to dine."

Barrimore studied the big Irishman, whose brow was furrowed like the marquess's as he inspected the marquess's finely tailored evening clothes. With a slight nod to acknowledge the sarcasm, Barrimore reached up and began tugging at his silk cravat to loosen it. "Provide me with more suitable attire, sir, and I would be happy lend my support regardless of what method you use."

Emory studied the noble lines of Barrimore's face a moment, then nodded at Seamus. "Get him something to wear. And give him back his gun; with only seven of us, we may need all the firepower we can muster."

"Eight," Anna said quietly. "You have me."

Every eye in the dingy room turned to stare. Her cloak had fallen open to reveal the veils of sparkly silk she wore beneath. Her slippers glittered with chips of crystal, her face and throat shone with stardust, and her hair, though slightly crushed and displaced from traveling, still held tiny sprigs of flowers woven into the curls. She looked so sorely out of place, not only asking for a gun but doing so while standing in the midst of such grimy surroundings, it took a moment for anyone to react.

"I trust," Barrimore said to Althorpe, "you find the notion as absurd as I do. Beyond absurd, in point of fact, despite her claim of having shot off someone's hand."

Anna arched her eyebrow. "I am actually a very fine shot when not in a runaway carriage or confronted by assassins."

Barrimore bowed. "I am certain you are, Miss Fairchilde. But I would sooner not have you put to the test. The seven of us should be adequate, and there will be no further discussion on the subject. You will remain here until all matters have been resolved, even if we have to lock you in one of the rooms to enforce it."

Whether it was the way Barrimore phrased the pronouncement, or just the fact that he assumed he still had some authority over her, Emory looked at him and said, almost too casually, "Unfortunately, all the doors lock from the inside."

"Are you suggesting she would disobey an order intended to secure her own safety?"

"I may not have had the benefit of your lengthy history with Miss Fairchilde, but I would be willing to speculate that the bolt would *remain* in place only as long as it took us to reach the end of the street."

Anna wanted to smile, to show Emory she was profoundly grateful he was treating her as an equal and not a nuisance to be patted on the head and moved back out of the way, but she could see by the look in his eyes that he was not the least bit happy with the situation himself. Had it been anyone but the Marquess of Barrimore attempting to intervene, she wondered if he might not have agreed out of hand.

"You cannot seriously be thinking of involving Miss Fairchilde any further," Barrimore continued. "To allow her to participate in the smallest part of any plan you may have for the retaking of your ship would place her in a position of utmost peril!"

"Was she recognized at Carleton House?"

"I beg your pardon?"

"Was she recognized?"

Barrimore's thoughts stumbled inward a moment as he remembered removing her mask himself. "I must suppose she was, yes. Her brother was there and Colonel Ramsey addressed her by name, if I am not mistaken."

"Then I suggest she would be no safer here, on her own, than she would be on board the *Intrepid*. I expect there has been a warrant issued, if not for her outright arrest as an accomplice, then at least for detention and questioning."

"A warrant?" Anna whispered in awe. "For my arrest?"

"There is no need to look so pleased with yourself," Emory said dryly. "I doubt it is something to which proper young ladies of society aspire."

She refrained from reminding him aloud that she had done nothing thus far that any proper young lady would have done, but the gleam in her eye was enough to make him clear his throat.

"At any rate," he said, "we will see about amending your ways in the future. For now, we have another intrepid lady to worry about."

Chapter 23

*T*HE MIST HAD thickened considerably by the time they left the tavern. The lights in the harbor were no longer visible and those along the shore looked muffled in tufts of cotton. Somewhere out in the murky soup a cacophony of ships' bells tolled the hour and Emory's head turned, listening for the one that was as distinctive to him as a woman's voice. When he heard it, his footsteps quickened, and Annaleah was hard pressed to keep up with the pace set by his longer strides.

She was dressed in trousers again. Loose-fitting, made of cheap wool, they were held up at her waist with a length of twine. The shirt was equally oversized, but at least it was soft and warm, the hem long enough to tuck down around where the wool could not chafe.

The eight walked quickly, without conversation. The men were all heavily armed, their expressions grim, eyes warily scanning the shadowy alley and doorways as they passed.

When they reached the section of waterfront where the smaller fishing boats were moored, Seamus took two of the crewmen and broke away, whispering orders for the others to wait behind a warehouse until they heard his signal. It was dark and oppressively damp, and they could not see more than a stone's throw in any direction, but when the low trilling whistle came out of the fog, Emory led them unerringly to the edge of the jetty where Seamus and the sailors waited, rocking below them in a small jolly boat.

"Unless the sentries have the power to see through this muck, we should be able to row right up their arses without 'em batting an eye," Seamus said. Then he added with a belligerent snort to British naval efficiency, "If they've bothered to post a watch at all, that is."

Barrimore took his assigned seat in the dinghy, helping Anna in after him. "If I recall correctly from the naval dispatches we received about the *Intrepid*, she was placed under the command of Captain Sir Isaac Landover."

"Landover?" Emory glanced over. "He is one of the navy's most decorated captains. Why the devil would he be sitting guard duty on a prize ship in a godforsaken place like Gravesend?"

"The official story is that he is recovering from a disfiguring wound and requested the solitude."

"And unofficially?"

"Unofficially, the captain had a rather distasteful affair with a young lady—the daughter of a high-ranking member of the admiralty who was not amused to discover that his first grandchild would be the bastard of a married man."

Emory stared through the dark mist a moment longer, having no doubt whatsoever there was a warning meant specifically for him in the marquess's words. He took up an oar, however, and channeled all his energies into rowing, helping the others quickly propel the boat away from the noise and lights of the waterfront.

Soon there were other sounds to take their place: the creak and groan of wooden beams, the soft slap of water against a hull, the chink of metal rings on yardarms. Now and then they heard a bark of laughter from high up in the fog or saw misty lights and knew they were gliding past one of the dozens of ships lying at anchor. Once they heard a splash, followed by good-natured cursing and orders for the sailor not to climb on board again until he had drowned all the lice in his clothing.

Anna's ears perked up at one point, when she heard the tinkle of a woman's laughter, but she knew it was not unusual for wives and loose women to live on board while a ship was in port.

She supposed that was what she was now: a loose woman.

The thought made her grip the side of the bulwark tighter, but she refused to pursue it. She was in a jolly boat with seven desperate men rowing out to steal a ship from His Majesty's naval yards. There was also a steadily increasing pool of water slapping across the bottom of the boat, meaning there was a leak somewhere in the hull, and since she had never learned how to swim, and had no idea how deep the bottom of the harbor was, she had more urgent things to worry about than being snubbed by her peers.

They rowed for nearly fifteen minutes before the level of the water grew deep enough for Barrimore to voice a concern.

"You might have at least stolen a boat that was sound. How the deuce do you know where you are going, anyway? We could be rowing out to open sea."

"We cracked a spar off Cap St. Vincent a few months back and had to replace some of the iron fittings with brass," Seamus grunted. "Ye can hear 'em when she rocks."

Annaleah heard nothing to distinguish a clink from a clank, but she was grateful when Seamus said a few seconds later, "There she be. Dead ahead."

She followed the direction of his finger and saw, like a faintly luminous ghost rising out of the mist, the blurred shape of a huge hull rising above them. A haze of light fanned dully out of the two multipaned windows that slanted outward across the stern, indicating someone was awake in the aftercabin. There were also mottled breaks in the fog on deck where someone had hung lanterns from the rigging. The hull was slick with moisture and the dampness dripped into the water from the miles of rigging that ran between the three towering masts. The mingled odors of fish and pitch and sodden canvas were strong, but there was something else as well. Something Annaleah had smelled once before when the barge she had been on had sailed too close to a prison hulk anchored in the Thames. It was the stink of unwashed bodies, unclean quarters, and despair.

Seamus held up a hand to stop the men from rowing. He

used the drag of his own oar to slow the forward momentum of the jolly boat, and when they were close enough, the two mates on the starboard side reached out with their hands to keep the boat from bumping into the wooden hull. Hand over hand, they pulled and pushed the dinghy in silence until they were beneath the ladder that hung down the ship's side.

When the oars were safely shipped and the boat tied off to the bottom of the ladder, Emory was the first to start climbing, the collar of his jacket pulled high to his chin, his guns tucked at his waist but readily within reach. The four crewmen went up next, nimble as monkeys accustomed to climbing ratlines and rigging. Barrimore was last, not by choice but at the insistence of a freckled paw on his shoulder.

"Ye're to stay close to me, milord," Seamus muttered. "And keep a good grip on the rungs, for we've no time to fish ye out of the drink if ye fall."

Barrimore scowled and would have cut back with a rebuttal, but the big Irishman was already halfway to the top. Higher up, the dark shapes of Emory and the other men were clinging to the deck rails on either side of the gangway.

"You remember what to do?" he asked Anna.

"I am to fire a shot if I see anyone coming," she said through a shiver.

"Are you all right?"

"I am fine. Really."

Barrimore squeezed her arm once for courage, then vanished up into the mist, leaving Anna staring with owlish horror into the gray morass of shifting clouds that surrounded them.

On a signal from Emory, they moved over the rail and jumped quietly down into the waist of the ship, two men running forward on noiseless feet, two running aft. He sent Seamus by way of hand gestures to the forecastle while he took the stern. Not ten paces from the gangway he came across a sentry seated on a keg with his head leaning back against the mast and tipped to the side, his mouth opened around throat-rattling snores. A quick chop across the side of his neck with the pistol butt ensured a deeper sleep, and, after a brief delay to exchange his black pea coat for the scarlet tunic, musket, powder flask, and cartridge belt, Emory moved forward again, fastening the middle two buttons of the jacket as he ran.

At the after hatchway, he stopped and listened to the sounds of his ship breathing. She was in some distress, having been battened down by men unfamiliar with her trim, and he sensed an undercurrent of impatience, as if she had been waiting for him to rescue her from the hands of such clumsy oafs. As if he were placating a woman, Emory caressed the weathered oak of the hatchway and descended the stairs, his first priority the cargo hold, the only area large enough to be transformed into a gaol for the crew. He moved quickly past the silent black shapes of the cast-iron cannon crouched behind closed ports, warmed to the hunt by the familiar smell of gunpowder and metal. He heard a sliding footstep ahead of him and sidestepped into the shadows, but it was only Seamus and Barrimore. Their progress had gone as smoothly as Emory's. The two guards they had encountered were trussed like turkeys and stuffed into a sail locker.

Althorpe lowered the musket and pointed at the shiny new padlock holding the grate in place over the hold. Seamus crossed to one of the long guns and returned with the iron handspike used to adjust the sights. By then there was whispering below them, just a few alert hisses at first that swelled quickly into the sound of an excited beehive. Hands reached through the squares of grating and fingers clutched the bars, muted cheers and cackles of laughter were quickly muffled by a commanding *"Whisht, ye daft bastards!"* from a grinning Seamus Turnbull.

He fed the handspike through the lock and snapped it

with a decisive jerk. None of the men on either side of the grate waited to see if the noise had been detected. Within moments, the dark figures were pouring up the stairs and spreading across the deck, most of them pausing only long enough to tug a forelock in Emory's direction before heading aft to the crew's quarters. Once there, it was a ridiculously simple matter to creep between the hammocks of the sleeping lobsterbacks, arm themselves with confiscated weapons, then kick the startled soldiers awake.

Barrimore did not know whether to be impressed or enraged with the ease of the takeover. The only area not under Emory's complete control now was the aft great-cabin, where it was presumed Captain Sir Isaac Landover would be as easily overcome as the rest of his command. They had seen lights in the cabin when they approached through the mist, and there was a slash of light showing beneath the door as they stood outside it now.

As a courtesy to a fellow captain, Emory knocked.

"Come."

He opened the door, ducking to clear the low lintel as he passed through. He was still in the borrowed scarlet tunic, though it was plain to see by the two straining buttons he had managed to fasten that the garment was not his. Captain Landover's eyes registered this in the same sweeping glance that took in Seamus Turnbull's flaming red hair and the Marquess of Barrimore's intense stare.

Landover was seated at his desk, a writing quill in one hand, a crystal glass of Madeira in the other. He was spare for a seaman, his body thin to the point of emaciation; his face was handsome in an overwrought way, with thick brown muttonchops and hazel eyes.

The pen was slowly set aside, but the glass remained clutched tightly in his hand as he leaned back and coldly studied the faces of the three men opposite him. "Having never had the pleasure of making his acquaintance, I can only assume that one of you gentlemen is the former captain of this vessel?"

Emory stepped forward. "Former and present captain Emory Althorpe at your service, Sir Isaac," he said, bowing slightly. "My men are, at this moment, reacquainting themselves with their duties."

Captain Landover's eyes crinkled at the corners. "I see. I was told you were an enterprising fellow. Of course, I was also told you were dead."

"A premature report, fortunately."

"My men?"

"Apart from the sentries we left sleeping a little deeper than they were before, they are all in good health."

The slow flush that had crept into the captain's cheeks darkened and his hand inched slowly toward the middle drawer of the desk. Emory raised his own cocked pistol and shook his head.

"I would not advise it, Sir Isaac. There is nothing to be gained and a good deal to be lost in any foolish gestures. The ship is mine. You have my word you and your men will be unharmed and set ashore when we are safely out of port."

Sir Isaac's hand relaxed. The fingers tapped lightly on the desktop for a moment, then lifted in a gesture of resignation. "In that case, my compliments on a job well done. Will you gentlemen join me in a glass of wine? I have discovered you keep a rather fine cellar on board, Althorpe."

"I am glad it meets with your approval, Sir Isaac, but I prefer to wait until I have something to celebrate."

He uncocked his pistol and tucked it back into his waist, frowning as he looked around the cabin. It was glaringly apparent that all of his personal belongings had been either removed or destroyed and the cabin stripped of anything of value. A fine oak cabinet in the corner had been smashed open; the glass was gone and only the crisscrossing of lead strips remained. His sea chest was gone, his maps and charts and books had been removed, along with—as he discovered upon opening cupboard after empty cupboard—his logbooks and manifests. A quick search of the desk revealed the same thoroughness. Some enterprising fellow had even found the catch that opened the secret panel in the bottom drawer; it was empty save for a few tufts of dust.

"I am surprised they left the wine stores intact," he mused.

"Only in deference to my command," Landover assured him wanly. "The ship is . . . *was* due to be completely gutted and refitted a week next. But I do agree they were otherwise meticulous in their search and seizures. I daresay not a pannikin was left unturned in their efforts to deprive you of your ill-gotten gains. I'm told even your clothing was sold off in lots, the proceeds naturally going to the crown for the inconvenience."

"Naturally."

"Your charts were most impressive, I must say. I purchased two for my own use. Apart from that"—he waved a hand dismissively—"I confess to being somewhat surprised at the low profits to be made selling out your fellow countrymen."

Emory let the captain savor his barb a moment before crossing over to the small brazier in the corner. He released the metal bolts that locked the splayed iron feet in place and then, using towels to protect his hands from the heat, lifted the stove and set it to one side. He pried up two of the blackened floor planks and reached inside, turning his face away to close his eyes briefly in relief when his fingers brushed against metal. He dragged the heavy strongbox clear and handed it up to Seamus, who carried it to the desk.

Smiling at the fading smirk on Landover's face, Emory pulled the chain over his neck and slotted the key into the lock. The box was crammed with papers, several detailed charts, a second personal logbook, and four large canvas drawstring pouches that were spilling over with gold coins and loose gemstones.

Barrimore leaned forward, his expression mirroring the shock that now overcame the British captain's face. "Have you no faith in banks, sir?"

"Would you trust an English bank that would accept French gold livres without questioning the source?"

"Still and all . . . you must have a small fortune there."

"And another in a less inquisitive institution in Calais." Emory spared a glance for Landover. "I was, in fact, very well paid for my misdeeds."

He plucked the top sheet of some folded, official-looking documents off the pile, scanned it quickly, and set it aside. The second was read and discarded; the third earned a small narrowing of his eyes, but in the end was rejected. There were nine documents bearing admiralty seals, and it was not until he had tossed aside the eighth that he drew and expelled a long breath, handing the last one across to Barrimore.

The marquess took it with a wry twist of his mouth. "My Lord Westford would not be pleased to know you had kept these dispatches. He assumed, as per your original instructions, they would be immediately destroyed."

Emory shrugged. "I was never one for taking instruction well."

Barrimore frowned and tilted the page toward the wash of candlelight, recognizing the code at once. At his polite request, Landover vacated the chair and obliged him with the loan of his quill and a blank sheet of writing paper. It took the marquess several minutes to decipher the code embedded in the seemingly frivolous recounting of events at a summer soiree, and long before he finished, there was no doubt he was extracting a specific set of orders meant for the rogue captain of the *Intrepid.* They acknowledged receipt of the notice he'd sent that he had been approached by Bonaparte's associates with the intent of hiring him and his ship to help the exiled general escape from Elba. Moreover, the instructions were quite specific in ordering Emory to go along with the ruse. He was assured the HMS *Reliant*, a sixty-four-gun ship-of-the-line, would be waiting to intercept and he was instructed that, after offering a token resistance, he was to surrender. His passengers would be removed and transferred onto the warship, after which the *Intrepid* would be allowed to "escape" with all hands.

"Westford did not write these orders," Barrimore murmured, not even bothering to read to the end. "Neither did I."

"Are you certain?"

The marquess held the dispatch up to the light again. "By God's grace, I will grant it is an excellent forgery—the signature is perfect, the code is set down correctly. In fact, if I was not looking for fault, I would not find any. But here—" The edge of the paper was almost touching the flame, and Emory was about to reach out and snatch it away when Barrimore angled it in such a way as to allow both Althorpe and Turnbull to see the sheet illuminated from behind. "The watermark is wrong."

"Watermark?" Seamus frowned. "It looks fair dry to me."

"It is the manufacturer's imprint, left by the roller when the sheet of paper is initially pressed and formed. It can only be seen by holding the page up to the light—thus—and as you can plainly see, there is a stylized R in the center of the sheet."

The two men still looked somewhat baffled—even Landover craned his neck forward to peer over his shoulders while Barrimore traced his finger around the faint shading of the R barely visible beneath the tight lines of script. "It should be a T with a cross through the stem," he explained. "One of Westford's sons-in-law bought a pulp mill and began to supply him with paper a full year before Bonaparte escaped Elba. He used it exclusively for his most private and sensitive dispatches."

"Who else knew that?"

"No one. Only myself and the earl. But there were

probably . . . oh, a half dozen or more who knew the codes we used and could have had access to the old stock of paper."

Emory paced to the row of square-paned windows and stared out at the fog a moment before turning back to Barrimore. "Then that proves I was not acting on my own initiative; that I did not sell out to France; that I was following specific orders that I believed came straight from Westford's pen!"

"I would be inclined to testify on your behalf if it came before the courts," Barrimore agreed slowly, "though I could not, in faith, bear witness to your common sense for not questioning the logic of the orders. What would have been the point of sanctioning such an elaborate—and risky, I might add—scheme when Bonaparte was under lock and key already?"

"We wondered about that ourselves," Emory acknowledged. "And came to the conclusion they had no intentions of taking him back to Elba when they recaptured him. Not alive, anyway."

"I'm not sure I follow you."

Seamus grunted. "We thought ye wanted an excuse to kill the bastard instead of keepin' him like a king on his own wee island."

"You mean murder him?" Landover insinuated himself into the conversation again, puffing up with indignation at the thought of what they were suggesting.

"Ye've never accidently throfted a man overboard in a raging storm?" Seamus asked with a smile.

"Never!"

"Then it's a clear conscience ye'll be having when ye stand before St. Peter."

"If I had refused to accept the commission," Emory added, returning to the topic at hand, "Cipriani would have found someone else. Someone the British navy would have no means of contacting or controlling."

"Or bearing the blame if the scheme failed—which it

did, most miserably," Barrimore mused. He looked down at the forged dispatch again, his brow furrowed in thought as he twisted his ring round and round his finger. "You said there was another letter? One that Cipriani was eager to get back?"

Emory started to reach into the strongbox again, but a sound startled his hand back from the logbook and sent him reaching for his pistol instead. It was the sound of a gunshot, and even though it had been distorted by the fog and the thickness of the hull, he knew it could only have come from the vicinity of the jolly boat.

He tossed Seamus the key to the strongbox and ran for the door. "Stay here, and don't let that box out of your sight."

Annaleah sat in shock, both hands clapped over her mouth, her eyes watering from the cloud of acrid cordite that hung in the mist. The pistol was at her feet, drowned under the two feet of water that had collected in the bottom of the boat. It was the depth of the water, the fact that the boat was close to being swamped, that had prompted her decision to abandon her post and follow the others up the ladder.

She had been sitting in the awful silence for half an eternity, imagining all manner of horrors coming at her through the fog. There were sounds against the hull, and sounds beneath the keel of the dinghy—slippery sliding sounds she had no desire to identify firsthand. She heard voices from other ships echoing off the water, some that sounded a hundred feet away and others ten. There was enough air stirring to create gaps in the shifting mist as well, and there were times it grew thin enough for her to see lights, even to distinguish the shape of another frigate standing several hundred yards off the bow.

She had no idea what was happening on board the *Intrepid*. She was cold, frightened, soaked through to the skin, and she had no idea if Emory was alive or dead, if he had succeeded or failed, if they had forgotten about her down here below the whale's belly, or if the first face she'd see would belong to a scarlet-clad soldier pointing a musket at her breast.

And the water in the jolly boat kept rising.

In all her years, she had never climbed a ladder save for the decorative wrought-iron affair in her father's library. She had never been on board a ship this size before; her knowledge was limited to the barges that ferried partygoers from one bank of the Thames to the other, and small tasseled gondolas that drifted on the lake while ardent suitors read bad poetry.

This was a *ship*. A *fighting* ship that bore the visible scars of beams gouged by cannonballs and scraped by boarding pikes. Although her gun ports were closed, Anna had counted fifteen on the middle deck and twelve on the upper, plus an assortment of smaller guns mounted on her fore and aft rails.

With water lapping over the gunwale, she had no choice but to grab the thick ropes and take her first tentative step up onto a rung. She had checked that the pistol was secure in her belt before she grasped the ladder, but a sudden rocking motion of the jolly boat had sent her swinging crazily against the hull. The gun had caught on the rope and been flipped free, and when it landed on the seat of the boat, the lock had snapped forward. The shot had discharged harmlessly into the side of the boat, but the sound of it had echoed like the booming thunder of a cannonade, startling Anna so badly she lost her footing and slipped into the gap between the boat and the ladder. She managed to stop herself from falling completely into the water, but her arms were jerked nearly out of their sockets and her hands skidded on the ropes, burning the palms. It was all she could do to reach over and clamber back on board the jolly boat, but by then there were voices and shouts on the upper deck, heads poking over the rails, and a sinister picket line of muskets pointing down over the side.

She clung to the ladder and clapped her hands over her

mouth. Someone shouted at her, but she was still listening to the sound of the gunshot reverberating around the bay, bouncing off the hull of every ship in port, amplified by the water, distorted by the mist.

The ladder scraped against the hull as someone climbed down it, and a moment later, Annaleah found herself staring into Emory's worried face.

"Are you all right? What is it? What did you see?"

She shook her head. "It was nothing. It was stupid. It was a stupid mistake. I . . . the b-boat was sinking and . . . I t-tried . . . but the gun fell and . . ."

Standing halfway up to his knees in water, Emory did not have to look down. Nor was there any time to either comfort or chastise her. The immediate silence that had followed the gunshot was now starting to fill with shouts as crews from various ships called out trying to pinpoint the source of the shot. Putting Annaleah before him, he guided her up the ladder, where one of the crew was waiting to lift her up the last few steps and set her down on the deck.

"Quickly and quietly, gentlemen," Emory commanded. "Haul in the anchor and get men into the tops. As soon as she is free of the muck on the bottom, I want all sails loosed and rigged out to catch whatever breeze there is about. Put the men with the sharpest eyes and keenest noses forward to guide us through this soup."

"Aye, Cap'n!"

"I'm sorry," Anna cried softly, pushing a fistful of hair off her face.

"We would have gotten under way with all due haste regardless," Emory said. "Are you certain you are not hurt?"

"Only my pride."

He smiled and kissed her briefly on the crown of her head before beckoning to the ship's cook, a crusty little Spaniard by the name of Juan Diego. "I'm going to take Miss Fairchilde below to my cabin and try to find her some dry clothing. In the meantime, I need to know how we lie for stores and fresh water, if we've enough to make a run down the Channel. Once we are free of the harbor, break out a cask of rum for the men if you can find one; they will no doubt have been deprived of their daily rasher while they've been guests of the King. Biscuits too, enough to tide them over until you can fill their bellies with beef. I plan to be back on deck before the anchor is on board, and I want to be able to smell brisket boiling when I do."

"Aye, *aye*, Señor Captain General! And . . . welcome back aboard."

"It is damned bloody good to *be* back, Mr. Diego."

Chapter 24

SEAMUS WAS WAITING in the aftercabin with Barrimore and Landover. The strongbox had been locked and returned to its hidy-hole in the floor, the stove was bolted back in place and fresh coal added to its belly. After a quick explanation of the gunshot, Emory hung the key around his neck again and sent Seamus topside to take charge of the deck until he returned. Barrimore left to escort the British captain forward with his men.

Emory helped himself to the contents of Landover's sea chest and found a clean dry shirt and breeches. Annaleah took them but was almost afraid to look up into his face, knowing there might be greater repercussions—and at the very least, a look of grave disappointment—now that they were alone.

He only urged her to change quickly out of the wet clothing and to make use of what few amenities there were among Landover's personal possessions. He would have Diego heat water if she wanted to wash—he actually smiled when he commented that her face still bore residue of fairy dust—and he would see that a pot of hot coffee was delivered as soon as the water boiled. He left, promising to return when the *Intrepid* was under way, and it was all Annaleah could do not to burst out in tears the instant the door closed behind him. Why, she was not exactly sure. Possibly because she was once again embroiled in an adventure she had never in her wildest imaginings believed could ever happen to her. Or because he had kissed her in front of all his men. Or because he had *not* kissed her before he went back on deck. . . .

Moving with the wooden limbs of an old woman, she set

the dry clothing on the bed and walked over to the gallery windows. There was not much to see beyond the wall of dirty gray fog, but even as she adjusted her balance she could see threads of mist starting to swirl and spin away like dervishes. The anchor was no longer dragging on the bottom, and the ship was moving. Slowly, to be sure, but she was moving. And one more chance to return to the bosom of her family was creeping away.

Anna supposed she should sit down and compose a letter that might be delivered by Captain Landover when he was set ashore—but what could she possibly say at this point to convince her parents she had not lost all grips on her sanity? She was not only loose, she was fallen. There was now a warrant out for her arrest, and how did one explain that to a family who placed moral righteousness and the appearance of propriety above all else? She could barely justify her actions to herself, let alone others.

Sighing, she leaned her head against the cool pane of glass. Falling in love was hardly an adequate defense, and Emory's gesture of having fetched her rose oil did not exactly ring with conviction. As much as she was loath to admit it, Barrimore was right. She could not see Captain Emory Althorpe living the staid life of a country squire when there was still so much of the horizon to explore. Even less likely was the image of him settling down to a wife and children, content to sit before a blazing fire and read books about other men's adventures. In truth, it was more than likely he would leave England again. Whether he proved himself innocent or not, he had no use for it, and with the war ended, England had no use for him. Spies would be an embarrassment once there was no more spying to be done.

If she was being perfectly honest, she would have to admit that once he was out of the harbor and on the open sea, she would be of little use to him either. She couldn't even swim, for pity's sake. She would be a burden, a nuisance, possibly even a hindrance.

He had made her no promises, of course. Had avoided

making any commitment whatsoever. The presumptions were all hers; she had simply assumed that after everything that had happened, everything they had been through together, once he freed his crew and sailed out of Gravesend he would take her with him, regardless of where he went or what he did.

A faint glitter caught her eye and she stared at the diamond ring her aunt had given her. Had Florence seen ahead to a time when she might need to fend for herself? With the ring, she would not be destitute. She had a fine education, impeccable manners when she was not behaving like a hoyden. There was an inheritance from her grandmother that would come to her on her twenty-first birthday, nine long months away. Just in time . . .

No, she refused to even let her thoughts wander that far into perdition.

She bowed her head and started to twist the ring around her finger but stopped when she realized it was the same habit Barrimore had of toying with the great golden signet ring he wore. She closed her eyes instead, and had no idea how long she stood there, the windowpane cooling her brow, before she heard the door open behind her.

"I brought you some coffee," Emory said after a moment. "You haven't changed yet?"

His remarking upon the obvious did not bolster her confidence any. "No. No, I . . . was watching the ship get under way, wondering how you could see through all this."

Her voice trailed away when she looked at him, his face—even scratched and scabbed—almost too breathtakingly handsome to contemplate against the contrasts of shadow and candlelight. He had taken off the scarlet tunic and wore only a white shirt and black breeches. His hair fell in loose, gleaming waves to his collar. His hands—strong enough to work the rigging lines of a storm-tossed frigate, gentle enough to make her weep with pleasure—were balancing a wooden tray with two cups, a small pot of coffee, and a big bottle of rum.

"Actually, it seems thicker on deck than it is. The men high up in the crow's nest can see fairly well, and as long as we don't steer toward a cliff, we should be fine. Seamus has his fine Irish blood up anyway and would resent having me on deck when he is trying to prove he hasn't lost his touch."

"Lost his touch?"

"Apparently there was fog the night he tried to take her out through the blockade and he sailed straight into the guns of a British frigate."

"I see. And you trust him this time?"

"With my life." His eyes narrowed. "Is something wrong?"

"Wrong? No, nothing is wrong." She attempted a feeble smile. "It just . . . seems odd not to have a dozen coaches chasing after us."

"Well"—he set the tray down on the desk—"with any luck the fog in the harbor will hold and they will not notice we have slipped our mooring until the sun burns it off. By then we should be well into the Channel." He studied her quietly for another moment, then turned and went back to close the door. He blew out most of the lamps that had been blazing such a bright beacon out the gallery windows, leaving only one meager candle flickering in a brass wall sconce.

"We will be stopping before we reach open water to set Captain Landover and his men ashore. I was thinking . . . perhaps you might want to disembark with him."

Her cheeks darkened with a violent flush. "Why would you think that?"

"For one thing, we have just stolen a navy prize out of a British port and they will not take kindly to the insult. For another, I have no idea what manner of welcome might await us in Torbay. The *Bellerophon* is a warship, after all, and I'm sure her captain keeps her guns primed in anticipation of any trouble."

"So you are telling me I will be in the way?"

"No, you are not in the way at all. I am only thinking of

your safety. And no, I have no intentions of arguing with you—I have learned the folly of even hoping to win such an engagement. If you want to stay, I will not mention it again."

"I want to stay," she said softly.

He smiled just long enough to darken the blush in her cheeks, then looked for something to occupy his hands. He took up the pot of coffee and poured some in the mugs, adding a healthy dollop of rum to both.

"Here, this will warm you."

She took the mug, but did not drink. There was something else troubling him; she could see it in his eyes—or rather, in the way his eyes kept avoiding hers.

"You must be relieved to know that Lord Barrimore believes you."

"It is a first step," he agreed.

"And you have your ship back. It is very . . ." She cast around the cabin, searching for the right word, but how did one describe a vessel bristling with guns and swarthy men with no teeth? "Bold. A very bold ship indeed. And I am glad your memories are coming back."

He looked down at his cup a moment, then reached out and spilled the contents through the open gallery window. Walking back to the table, he refilled it with straight rum.

"I recall you telling me once you liked me better when I had no memory."

"I was upset."

"You were damned upset," he corrected her, grinning weakly over a large mouthful of rum. "And accused me of treating you like a common trull."

"We were on a public street and you flung me over your shoulder like a sack of grain."

He looked down at his cup again. "My point is, I haven't exactly been honing my manners these last few years. I haven't done much of anything other than raise hell and play at war."

"I hardly think—"

He held up a hand. "Let me finish. Please. I am trying like the devil to do the right thing here, but if you keep interrupting me, I may never get it out. You see, I *am* remembering. I am remembering that I have done some things I am not too proud of, things I would rather not have to confess at all, and probably wouldn't if it suddenly did not seem so damned important to do so. What I am trying to say, I guess, is that there seems to be more than just a little bit of truth behind some of the charges against me. Enough, in fact, that it gave Westford something to hold over me, to make me agree to 'volunteer' my services to the crown."

"Lord Barrimore told me as much in the coach ride from London."

The dark, bottomless brown eyes gazed at her without wavering. "Did he now? What else did he tell you?"

"Not much. Just that he probably knew more about you than you would ever deign to tell me, and that not all of it was pleasant."

"A polite way of putting it. But then Barrimore is a polite fellow. I may even have to reassess my opinion of him, for he likely could have regaled you with stories that would have made you run screaming back to your family."

It was Annaleah's turn to bow her head. "I am not sure why you are telling me this now."

"Either am I," he conceded in a murmur. "You liked it better when I had no memory. . . . Well, I liked it better when I had no conscience. When everything was just a big blank void and my prime concern was how to get you naked and into my bed."

"And now? What concerns you now?"

"My freedom. My ship. My men. A family I have selfishly ignored these past few years, responsibilities I have neglected or simply refused to acknowledge." He set his empty cup on the table. "Have you no desire to see your family again?"

She gave a little shrug and looked up again. "I was thinking I would like to see Anthony. Of all of them, he is most likely to hear me out and believe, possibly, that I did not set out to deliberately destroy my life."

Her voice faded to a whisper as Emory came and stood in front of her.

For a full minute he did nothing but look at her. Mouth, eyes, the curve of her cheek, the fine reddish-brown wisps of hair at her temples that had coiled tightly in the dampness—all came under such intense scrutiny it was as if he did not trust the recent capriciousness of his memory to recall every detail. In the end, the terrible tautness in his jaw relented and he brushed the pad of his thumb across Anna's lower lip.

"Whereas I have been thinking . . . when this is over, of course . . . I would like to visit your great-aunt Florence again, in the hopes she might see me in a better light, realize I have not become quite the blackhearted scoundrel the naysayers have made of me—or at least see that there is some possibility for redemption. I was also hoping . . ." His thumb stroked from her lip to her cheek, and she was surprised—shocked—to feel that his hand was trembling. ". . . I was hoping if you were not otherwise engaged for the rest of your life, Miss Fairchilde, you might let me court you properly."

Her eyes swam behind a silvery haze for a moment, then cleared. "Court me properly?"

"I am even prepared to promise there will be no touching this time. Not even a chaste kiss to the back of the hand; not until after we are well and truly married."

"Married?" The word was barely a whisper of breath, uttered through a wave of weakness that rippled all the way down to her toes.

"Yes," he said with a hint of a bemused smile. "That is what two people in love usually do—is it not?"

"Well, yes, but . . ."

He sighed and his hand slipped down to cradle her neck. "You asked me once before, and I was reluctant then to give you a proper answer. The timing is hardly better now, but . . . I want you to know that I do love you, Anna-leah Fairchilde. Far more than is sensible for a man of my jaded reputation to admit. I don't know when it happened, or how it happened; I just found myself wanting to be a better person because of you. Because you trusted me. Because you believed me. Because you kept looking at me with those big blue eyes and telling me nothing else mattered. Well . . . I have discovered it does matter. It matters very much."

A small, bewildered gasp was all she could manage as his mouth pressed gently down over hers. It was hardly his best effort, for his lips remained closed and his eyes open. But it was enough. It was more than enough.

When she could speak again—and it was difficult with her heart lodged in her throat, pounding like a jungle drum—she did so with a fat tear sparkling in the corner of her eye.

"If that is what you want, I will certainly hold you to your promise to conduct a chaste and proper courtship. But in the meantime . . ."

"Yes? In the meantime?"

"Could you please," she whispered, "please just kiss me again."

His relief escaped on a sigh as he bent to oblige, his lips parted, his breath warm where it blended with hers. The kiss was slow and wet and deep, a vast improvement over the last. Vast enough she was not even aware he had unfastened the buttons on her jacket and shirt until she felt the heat of his fingers caressing bared flesh.

"I did say all this chasteness would begin *after* we reached Widdicombe House," he pointed out.

"You did?" She smiled with trembling eagerness. "Yes, you did. And until then I shall be most happy to lie in your bed, naked or otherwise."

He kissed her again, the heat of his mouth rivaling the heat that was pouring through her body. She kept her arms by her side while he peeled her jacket and shirt away, then she was reaching up, pulling herself closer, gasping as his hands moved to her waist, her thighs. Her breeches were peeled down her hips, her shoes kicked across the floor, and she could see no point in hiding behind any shy flutters of modesty when he found her wet and wanting.

The bed was narrow, built like a shelf sunk into the wall. The desk was closer, larger, and, with an impatient sweep of his arm, he cleared the surface of paper and writing implements, heedless of the ink that sprayed across the floor. He eased her down, gleaming and soft in her nudity, and his mouth broke roughly away, abandoning her for as long as it took him to fall on his knees before her. His hands skimmed up her thighs, parting them, while his lips, his tongue pushed hungrily into the soft, dark vee.

The shock jolted her like the touch of a spark to powder and the explosion was instantaneous. Each spearing thrust of his tongue caused her body to arch up against him, to tighten with spasms that quaked through to the tips of her toes. And each time she quivered and strained against him, he worked her harder, brought her higher, until she was nearly blinded by the brilliance of her frenzy.

While she was still breathless and orgasmic, he straightened and tore away his own clothes. He lifted her legs and draped them over his shoulders, then thrust himself so deep inside she had to reach out and grip the edges of the desk to keep from flying clean out of her skin. The pleasure was fierce, almost excruciating in its intensity, and he gauged the force of each stroke on the strength of her cries. He watched her face, watched the wildness come and go through a series of clutching shudders, all the while whispering words of encouragement, some in French, some in Spanish, some in a guttural language she had never heard before but that was as rhythmic and primitive as the passion raging through her body.

When his entire body was rock-hard and glistening with sweat, he surrendered with a hoarse, ragged groan. He knew he could not have held back much longer. It was like thrusting into velvet, into silk, and he felt his body stretch and burst, stretch and burst, filling her with the heated rush of his ecstasy. Their cries, their mouths came together and they continued to rock with the waning waves of pleasure. They rocked and strained and arched to chase after every last drop of his strength and when the fury passed and the heat melted away, she collapsed beneath him, her body going limp in his arms, unable to do much more than let him ease her gently back onto the desktop.

"Sweet gracious God," she gasped. "Sweet gracious God."

Emory's body was still rife with tremors, the blood was still reckless in his veins as he lifted his head from the curve of her shoulder. He was about to respond with something equally witty and profound, but a soft click from the shadows behind them made him turn and glance over his shoulder. His lips drew back in a snarl and he was set to soundly curse whoever had dared come into his cabin without permission, but no one was there. The door was closed. Nothing looked disturbed, nor were there any footsteps beating a hasty or embarrassed retreat along the companionway.

A cool, slender hand crept up to his cheek and dragged his head back around. When he saw the luminous look of wonder in her eyes, he forgot about whatever had distracted him and focused all his thoughts and energies on the soft pink mouth that waited for him.

Chapter 25

*T*HE LETTER EMORY had stolen off Napoleon's desk that last night in Aix was from the Emperor's younger brother Jérôme. It had been delivered to Bonaparte earlier that afternoon by a harried courier who had ridden so hard and so relentlessly, his horse had toppled over and died an instant after he dismounted. Emory recalled he had been surprised to see the dispatch later, lying openly on the desk with the other papers, and at the first opportunity he had slipped it into his pocket, assuming it had to be of some monumental importance. He had read it on board the *Intrepid* and nearly tossed it into the fire in disgust, for he had taken an enormous risk in stealing it, only to discover it contained mostly references to family matters. It discussed the health of their mother, Madame Mère, and the stir it had caused in the village after Napoleon had visited Malmaison to say farewell to her and his two illegitimate sons. There was also mention of his four-year-old heir, l'Aiglon— the Little Eagle—and the possibility of his being released from Paris into his grandmother's care. There was some agitated discussion about money and pensions and the fact that while some fools might trust the promises of the allied armies to let Madame Mère live out her days in peace, the sooner they were all on board a ship to America, the better. Arrangements were being made, permissions to leave France were being negotiated. They would naturally look forward to Colonel Duroc joining them in due course. All was well. Duroc had already departed for the coast and would likely arrive in advance of this letter. A great deal of gold had been paid to a "Le Renard" to guarantee his safe passage, not only in Aix, but in England.

All was well. The phrase had been underlined twice for emphasis. To the best of his recollection, Emory did not remember seeing a Colonel Duroc anytime that last day or evening, but there were so many officers coming and going, he could not have hoped to identify them all even if he had not suffered a blow to his head. And who the hell was Le Renard? It was obviously a code name, but although Emory had pored through every dispatch, letter, and document he had locked away in the strongbox, there was no mention of any foxes—no wolves, hawks, or herons either, for that matter.

After leaving the fog-bound harbor of Gravesend he read and reread the letter until his eyes ached. For the two days they were under full sail, he picked it apart word by word until he knew it by heart, hoping that somewhere in the rows of florid script there would be a clue as to how Napoleon Bonaparte planned to escape his captors. That there was a plan in motion, he had no doubt. That the letter provided some sort of key, he was also certain. Why else had Cipriani tortured him? Why had Le Couteau not just killed him, wrapped chains around his ankles, and dumped his body in the Gironde?

Who was Colonel Duroc? And who the bloody hell was the Fox? Was he responsible for the forged dispatches, and was he also involved in this new scheme to save the Emperor from exile?

Trying to detect a hidden code, Emory had studied the letter from every angle, but nothing leaped out and smacked him in the face. The clues were there, he knew they were there; he just could not see them. His French was excellent, but there were always slight nuances that affected the meaning or intent of a phrase, so he had Annaleah read the letter aloud in an effort to jog some elusive memory free. But she proved to be more of a hindrance than a help when he found himself watching the way her mouth moved around the words, the way the wings of her eyebrows drew together in concentration, the way the candlelight shone through the cambric of her shirt and outlined the full shape of her breasts. More than half the time they started out in very serious discussions about codes and translations, then ended up naked in a tangle of damp linens.

Barrimore read the letter, but claimed his French was strictly upper class. He knew of no one in Whitehall who might choose the name Fox or Le Renard or any derivative thereof to conduct secretive missions with the French, but he assured Emory that upon returning to London he would leave no stone unturned to unearth the traitor's identity. For Emory's part, he did not think that would be necessary. He suspected that whoever the traitor was, he would be in Torbay when they arrived.

"Duroc," Emory muttered. "Who the devil is Colonel Duroc and why does the name sound so blasted familiar?"

"Possibly because you have said it a thousand times," Annaleah suggested, "even in your sleep. And this despite my very best efforts to distract you."

She was distracting him now, for she was seated in his lap, a cool white thigh on either side of his own. The ghost watch had been tolling five bells when she had wakened and seen him sitting at his desk, the letter and the papers with his scribblings spread out in front of him. She had padded barefoot across the cabin without his even looking up, though he had certainly noticed when she slipped naked onto his lap and curled herself against the warmth of his body.

He wrapped his arms around her and kissed the top of her head. Her hair smelled faintly of rum from having bathed in the only container available: a sawed-off barrel Diego had improvised from stores. Her skin smelled of woman, soft and warm, and of the two hours he had spent making slow, sweet love to her earlier.

"I feel as though we are still sailing in a fog," he murmured. "We can't see what is ahead of us—we don't even know what to look for."

She sighed again and nestled deeper into the curve of

his shoulder. "Perhaps the plan has been foiled already. I cannot see how any plot to remove him from the *Bellerophon* could possibly succeed. You saw for yourself: The ship is in the middle of the harbor, surrounded by a ring of boats filled with soldiers. No one can sneak aboard without being seen; no one can sneak off. When we left there were a hundred small vessels in the bay day and night. There must be two or three times as many now, and even supposing a man could find a way to slip over the side, someone would be bound to see him in the water."

"Napoleon cannot swim. He is deathly afraid if his bathwater is too deep."

"Well, then, the only other choice is a raid from the sea, but that hardly seems likely. It would take another armada to steal him away from the British navy, and that would be an outright act of war. So, now one has to ask why in heaven's name he surrendered in the first place."

Emory leaned his head back against the padded leather headrest of the chair and absently stroked his hand through her hair. "That is another question I've been asking myself: Why did he seem so unconcerned when he announced his intentions to go peacefully into custody? He acted far too casual for a man facing possible execution."

Anna wriggled a little closer and slipped her hand down between their bodies. "Perhaps he knew Parliament would not condone the use of the axe. Perhaps he assumed the obvious: that they could not cold-bloodedly murder a man who had thrown himself upon their mercy."

"After Elba, he vowed he would never endure prison again. General Montholon even feared he might take his own life after Waterloo."

"It would have saved a good deal of trouble if he had."

Emory shook his head. "He would think it an ignoble, cowardly way to end things."

"I did read once that he considered himself godlike. Maybe he believes he cannot possibly fall victim to mortal complaints, that if they kill him he will just reappear in another guise, resurrected from the dead. Frankly"—she paused and wriggled some more, guiding him to where he was most wanted—"I think he is just mad. They should lock him away in Bedlam where he can be emperor of all the other madmen."

Emory stared at her. "What did you say?"

"About locking him away in Bedlam?"

"No. Before that."

She frowned. "That he thinks himself godlike and indestructible?"

Emory sat forward abruptly, his hands tense where they grasped her around the waist and lifted her off his lap. He snatched up the letter and stared at it for a moment, a look of sheer and utter amazement coming over his face.

"I don't believe it," he murmured. "I don't bloody believe it! Duroc, you bastard! How did you think you would ever get away with it!"

With a surge of energy, he leaped up and went over to the bed, quickly jerking his breeches over his hips, hopping from one foot to the other as he stamped into his boots.

"What is it? What did I say?" Anna asked.

He glanced over at her and his gaze flicked to the gallery windows. The sky was a pearly gray along the horizon, the sea still inky black beneath, but it would be full dawn soon and if his calculations were correct, they were less than forty nautical miles off Torbay.

He came back to where Anna stood and took her face between his hands, kissing her hard enough to leave her lips stinging. "Have I told you that I love you?"

"I'm very pleased to hear it again, but—"

"And that you are brave and beautiful and clever and I plan to fill you full of children so they can all be as brave and beautiful and clever as you?"

"I—"

"Quickly, now"—he kissed her again—"get dressed. I have to go and speak to Barrimore."

"But wait—"

It was too late. He was gone, bare-chested and steely-eyed, leaving only the echo of his boots in his wake.

"Get you on board the *Bellerophon*?" Barrimore knuckled the sleep out of his eyes and hung his legs over the side of the wildly swinging hammock. "You must be mad."

"Perhaps I am, but if I am right, I can clear my name and make a hero out of you at the same time."

"Right about what? What the devil are you on about? And what time is it, for pity's sake?"

"Half gone five bells. The winds are in our favor, the currents are good; we should make port well before noon. My question is, will Captain Maitland honor a white flag?"

Barrimore's eyebrows shot upward. "You plan to sail the *Intrepid* into port? The harbor batteries will blast you out of the water."

"Not if you can convince them it would be in the country's best interest to let us on board the *Bellerophon*."

"Me?"

"Hell, if I'm wrong about this, you will still be the hero, Barrimore. You will have captured the notorious Emory Althorpe single-handedly and brought him in to stand trial."

Both men turned as Annaleah rushed up behind them, her hair in disarray, her shirttails untucked and hanging to her knees.

"Do you know what this is all about?" Barrimore demanded.

"No," she said. "He did not tell me."

"Believe me," Emory said, "you will both think far more highly of my sanity if I keep my thoughts to myself until we are on the *Bellerophon*."

Annaleah had guessed correctly, though her estimate was low. The small boats in the harbor had easily trebled in number and were filled to capacity with curiosity-seekers.

Men in their finery, ladies in frills and parasols sipped wine from crystal glasses and nibbled on tiny cakes during the day, watching for the signs the crew displayed on both sides of the *Bellerophon* indicating their famous prisoner had "gone to breakfast" or "gone back to his cabin." At night, women of a different sort would take to the fishing boats and barges, able to almost walk from boat to boat, where they formed closely packed clusters. From early evening, the sweeping crescent bay would make for a spectacular scene, with every room in every tavern full and lights blazing in windows from the shore to the tops of the cliffs.

It had been Emory's early intention to sail past Torbay and approach from the west, finding anchorage somewhere up the coast, and from there to travel on land to Brixham. But under the bright noon sky, with her sails filling all three masts and curled forward in the wind, the *Intrepid* ran straight in off the Channel, making no secret of either her arrival or her identity. She tacked gracefully to leeward— acknowledging the bristled warning from the dozen armed pinnaces that patrolled the mouth of the harbor—and came to a near stop while she was still three miles out.

Althorpe was not so reckless as to test the range of the garrison batteries, and although he kept the gun ports closed, the crews were crouched at their battle stations, ready to return fire if the pinnaces did not honor the white flag.

Barrimore, his black evening clothes restored and brushed clean, and his cravat knotted in place, was rowed to the nearest gunboat, and from there taken into the harbor. On the deck of the *Bellerophon*, a crowd of men and officers had gathered at the rail, most of them with spyglasses that were trained first on the *Intrepid*, then on one of the pinnaces as it maneuvered its way through the sea of fishing boats. It was in turn met by four longboats crammed with scarlet-clad soldiers, whereupon Barrimore transferred vessels again and was escorted through the inner ring to the hull of the warship.

Annaleah, watching anxiously from the deck of the *Intrepid*, saw the speck that was Barrimore winched aboard on the bully chair. She glanced sidelong at Emory, but he had his eye fixed to the spyglass. His jaw was squared, his mouth pressed into a grim line, and during the brief moments he relaxed his vigil, his knuckles were white where they gripped the rail.

An hour later, the pinnace was on its way back, a white flag fluttering officiously on its mainmast.

"What does it mean?" she asked in a whisper.

"They have not run out their guns yet; I would say that was a good sign."

When the pinnace was within hailing distance, the lieutenant in command identified himself and his vessel. He conveyed the compliments of Captain Frederick Maitland of HMS *Bellerophon* and a request for the captain of the *Intrepid* to join him on board the British frigate.

"He's giving no guarantee of safe passage, lad," Seamus noted dryly.

"Did you really expect one?"

The Irishman hawked and spat over the side of the ship by way of an answer.

"Once I am away, keep a close eye on the gunboats. If they start to close, or make any attempt to maneuver behind us, run up the sails and catch the wind. If I don't come back"—he looked solemnly at his companion—"get the *Intrepid* clear by any means necessary. They will not be so careless with you the next time, my friend."

Seamus would have spat again, but his mouth was too dry.

Emory turned to Annaleah. "Before you puff up and start giving me twenty different reasons why you should be allowed to come with me, let me save you the bother. If there is trouble, the last place I want you to be is on board the *Intrepid*. Barrimore has offered his protection and I have accepted it on your behalf. Regardless of what happens"—

he hesitated, and it was obvious he had to steel himself before he could continue—"I have given Barrimore the name of my banker in Calais and instructions that he is to release everything I have to you. It should be more than enough to thumb your nose at whomever you please for as long as you please."

"I don't want your money," she cried, aghast. "I want you."

He tucked a finger under her chin. " 'Would she could make of me a saint, or I of her a sinner,' " he quoted, smiling as he touched his lips to hers. "Do not count me lost yet, madam, for I intend to do my damnedest to see that you have me for a very long time. I have not grown *that* fond of Barrimore."

He lowered his hand and swept it by way of an invitation toward the gangway.

"Wait," Seamus grunted. "I'll not be seeing ye away with only the brass of your ballocks to threaten them with if they corner ye. They will be sure to search ye before you go on board, but I've something here small enough to fit where no real man would dare put a hand."

Emory looked at the pistol Seamus laid in his palm. It was a pocket pistol with a box-lock built to hold the firing mechanism inside the round, stubby barrel.

"Wear your saber and a brace of guns in plain sight and I warrant they'll look no further. She's only good for one shot, but she makes enough noise for twenty. The trigger is made a bit stiff to keep ye from blowing off your own parts, so give it a good snap and mean business. As for you, miss"—he looked to Annaleah with a steady eye—"they'd be fair proper sods to give ye a brushing, so if ye think ye can handle it—"

"No," Emory said, glaring at the second weapon that appeared in Seamus's hand. "No gun. Barrimore's protection would not be worth spit if she went on board armed."

He strode toward the gangway, turning his back for the

split second it took for Anna to snatch the gun out of Seamus's hand and slide it into her waistband. She tucked the loose folds of the shirt around the barrel and buttoned her pea coat to conceal it, then followed after Emory, trusting him to guide her feet to each rung of the ladder as they climbed down to the boatful of soldiers waiting below.

Chapter 26

THE HMS *BELLEROPHON* was a heavy frigate carrying seventy-four guns and a crew of three hundred and forty. The latter number had swelled by nearly a hundred to include the officers, advisors, friends, and emissaries who had accompanied Napoleon from France. The decks were crowded with guards in scarlet tunics, sailors in striped shirts and canvas trousers, naval officers in blue and gold, civilians in somber black coats and severe white collars. To a man they stared at Emory Althorpe as he stepped through the gangway, and, as if they were following a ball at a tennis court, their heads swiveled to watch the bully chair swing Annaleah on board.

Captain Frederick Maitland was a twenty-year man, having enlisted as a midshipman shortly after the citizens of France had stormed the Bastille. He had won honors during the campaign for control of the Nile, and later fought with Nelson at Trafalgar. One of the most respected captains in the English fleet, he was known for being fair, and while he had assumed the task of bringing Bonaparte to England, he was not the least amused by the fairground atmosphere that had developed both on board and off.

Flanked by four lieutenants and half a dozen midshipmen, he stood on the forecastle and glowered down over his quarterdeck. He was, on the one hand, clearly not impressed with the rogue captain's audacity in demanding an audience. On the other, he could not completely conceal his admiration for Emory Althorpe's impudence in coming on board a fully manned ship-of-the-line with only a slender rapier and two single-shot pistols—both of which were peremptorily removed at the gangway.

Annaleah Fairchilde earned only a slightly more penetrating stare. He had heard the story of her abduction shortly
after it happened, then a much different version an hour
ago from the Marquess of Barrimore. Watching the way she
alighted from the bully chair and instantly moved to stand
by Althorpe's side, he knew which version to be the truth,
and wondered what her father would make of it to see the
elegant young gazelle dressed in sailor's garb, her hair
flown loose around her shoulders, her skin a healthy blush
from the wind and the sea—and likely from other things
that did not warrant speculation. Maitland, a married man
with four silly daughters, did not know quite what to make
of it himself, and so turned his eye to Althorpe again.

"You do realize, sir, you are now on British soil and as
such are subject to immediate arrest."

"If you feel inclined to arrest me after you have heard
what I have to say, then by all means feel free to disregard
the white flag."

Maitland's skin prickled, but his expression remained
calm. "I assure you, sir, you have my full attention."

Emory glanced around the crowded deck. "What I have
to say might be better said in private, Captain."

Eyes icier than frost narrowed. "Mr. Witherspoon," he
said to his first lieutenant, "you will kindly escort our guests
to my day cabin. I also want men in the tops, and I want to
know if anything on that pirate ship moves. Have the crews
remain at battle stations and, for heaven's sake, clear my
decks of this French rabble."

The captain's day cabin spread across the width of the ship
and was furnished with, among other things, a long table
and twelve chairs. Beneath them, the floor had been covered with stretched canvas painted in black and white
squares to resemble tiles. A parrot sat in a gilded cage in one
corner, a manservant stood attendance in the other, neither
reacting to the sudden influx of men other than to tilt their
heads a little higher.

Maitland strode directly to the head of the table and handed his bicorn to his servant.

"Miss Fairchilde, Mr. Althorpe, Lord Barrimore . . ." He waved a hand to indicate the empty seats. "Please. Ogilvie, I believe brandy would be in order."

When the servant had carried a bottle and glasses to the table, he was dismissed. Barrimore declined a chair and elected to stand by the gallery windows; Witherspoon, the only other ship's officer present, remained by the door.

"We will dispense with formalities within these four walls, shall we?" Maitland suggested. "Naturally, that comes with a small caution, Mr. Althorpe, allowing that we are none of us fools who tolerate the wasting of time. I have already given you more leeway than my better judgment advises, due in no small part to Barrimore's intervention. He says you have proof that clears your name of some of the charges outstanding against you, namely those of treason and sedition. This is not a court of law, so I can neither accept nor reject this proof at face value; your ultimate innocence or guilt will still have to be adjudicated by a higher authority."

"I am well aware of that, Captain," Emory said. "I have taken the liberty of bringing certain documents with me, however, and would request you take them into your care to be delivered safely into the hands of the foreign office."

Annaleah, trying to remain as invisible as possible, glanced over at Barrimore and saw the muscles in his jaw tighten. He had offered earlier to take charge of the forged dispatches, but Emory had said he was taking no further chances of their falling into the wrong hands. However, if the admiralty trusted Maitland to safeguard England's most powerful enemy, Emory reasoned, he could in turn be trusted with a packet of documents.

The dispatches were produced from an oilskin pouch and set on the table for Maitland to examine. For the next twenty minutes Emory explained the role he had been playing for the past three years, that of spy and mercenary privateer, with his ship and guns for hire. His remarkable success in running the naval blockades had been due mainly to orders from Whitehall instructing the fleet captains to turn a blind eye to his vessel when it was slipping past. All of this Barrimore verified, up to and including the forged documents acknowledging that the *Intrepid*'s captain had been hired to sail to Elba.

Maitland, to his credit, rarely interrupted. Whether he was convinced or not was another matter, but to all outward appearances he seemed to accept the possibility that Althorpe was not a complete madman and that he had not come on board the *Bellerophon* seeking absolution.

This last suspicion was confirmed when Emory broached the subject of the Emperor's plans for the immediate future.

"They do not concur with either yours or the government's," he said flatly. "He has no intentions of returning to exile, sir."

"Whereas I put it to you, Althorpe, that he has no choice in the matter. He is due to be transferred to the *Northumberland*—"

"Yes, and from there transported to St. Helena, a tiny knoll of rock and seagull guano in the South Atlantic. But I assure you he will not go quietly."

Maitland's face darkened. "He will go in chains, if need be—allow *me* to assure *you* of that."

Emory drew a breath and spoke his next words slowly and carefully. "The man you currently have on board the *Bellerophon* may indeed be bound for St. Helena, chains or no chains, but he is not Napoleon Bonaparte."

Maitland, Barrimore, even Annaleah stared at Emory. The silence in the cabin was all the more pronounced due to the sounds that emanated from the boats outside in the harbor, and it lasted long enough for one dominant voice among them to conduct a good-natured auction for a crate of fresh chickens.

Maitland reached for his glass and took a deep swallow of brandy. "I presume you have your reasons for making such an astounding statement, although I am not completely certain I wish to hear them."

"If you will read the letter from Jérôme Bonaparte, you will notice a reference to Colonel Duroc. The name eluded me until I remembered overhearing one of Napoleon's aides mention a soldier named Duroc who had thrown himself in front of a saber intended for Bonaparte. It happened very early on in the general's career, but he never forgot that act of bravery and sacrifice."

Maitland scoffed. "Are you suggesting this Duroc has come back from the dead in order to sacrifice himself again? And come back, no less, in the perfect guise of Napoleon Bonaparte?"

Annaleah was hardly able to breathe. She glanced at Barrimore, who in turn looked straight ahead, clearly shaken by the thought that he might have erred in his judgment after all. He stared unblinkingly at Emory as if he wished he could have forced this revelation from him on board the *Intrepid* and not risked what was sure to happen to his career at Whitehall if it was thought he had given an ounce of credence to such a wild notion.

Emory merely leaned back and folded his arms across his chest. "As outlandish as the idea sounds, Captain, might I nevertheless suggest you extend an invitation to the general to join us? If I am wrong, I will offer my wrists for the shackles. But if I am right, you will be saving the British government an embarrassment of such magnitude it might never be overcome."

"Invite him here to verify his identity? Damn me, sir, but you are mad, not to mention insolent in thinking he would even deign to leave his quarters to acknowledge such lunacy firsthand."

"Invite him here to share a glass of brandy with an old friend. Tell him a lady by the name of Madame Muiron has come to pay her respects and you will be surprised how quickly he accepts."

"Who the devil is Madame Muiron?" Maitland demanded, glancing instinctively at Witherspoon and Barrimore, both of whom responded with imperceptible shakes of their heads.

"Muiron is the name he used during his six-year affair with the actress Mademoiselle Georges. He has no doubt heard by now that a young lady has come on board under strange circumstances, and since Miss Fairchilde matches the general description . . ."

"He would believe the British admiralty has allowed his courtesan on board? Really, Althorpe, this is too much!"

"I doubt the real Bonaparte would believe it, but the man posing as him might be nervous enough to show some curiosity. And his advisors, if they are intent upon keeping up the masquerade, would not wish to have Mademoiselle Georges cause too much of a stir if her request for an audience is denied."

Maitland's complexion was fairly ruddy by now. He refilled his empty glass but left the brandy untouched while his free hand tapped out a muted drumbeat on the table. "Barrimore tells me you recently took a severe blow to the head, sir. One that caused you to lose your memory along with most of your faculties."

"I assure you, sir—apart from an occasional headache, my senses are fully restored."

Maitland only tapped and contemplated. "I am also told of the recent apprehension and arrest of a certain Franceschi Cipriani, a Corisican patriot known for his affinity for slitting throats in the dark. He was found bound and gagged in a house in Torquay, beaten and severely mutilated, which nearly caused him to bleed to death before he was transported to the hospital. Since then, he has lapsed into fever and delirium, claiming he was shot by a woman. I'll not repeat the precise adjectives he used to describe her, though the general attributes appear to match those of Miss Fairchilde." He focused once again on Annaleah and his hand stilled. "Is any of this true?"

"He was trying to kill us," she said evenly. "He had been sent to kill Mr. Althorpe and he made no secret of his intentions to kill me as well."

Maitland's frown deepened. "I hold a passing acquaintance with your father, young lady. Is he aware of your recent activities?"

Anna clasped her hands more tightly in her lap. "I have not had an opportunity to see or speak to my father in several days, sir."

"Your brother is here in Torbay, were you aware of that?"

"Anthony? Here? But how—?"

"Out of necessity, I am informed almost hourly of the comings and goings in the vicinity. Viscount Ormont arrived from London early this morning with Lord Westford and Colonel Rupert Ramsey."

"They must have ridden straight through," Barrimore murmured.

"There was a certain air of urgency in the communication I received. Ramsey, in particular, informs me the garrison at Berry Head is on full alert and vows to me that neither Althorpe nor his ship will get within a hundred yards of the harbor. No doubt he has seen the *Intrepid* by now and is likely being rowed from shore as we speak."

"I have never met the fellow personally, but he sounds enthusiastic about his work," Emory mused.

"Westford was equally flattering with regards to your ingenuity, sir. He says"—the captain fixed Emory with a cold stare—"you had the brass to intrude upon a masquerade at Carlton House uninvited, to cause bullet holes to be made in the Regent's offices, and to walk out again as if a Royal Guard of two hundred marksmen was an inconvenience, nothing more."

Emory brushed his fingertips across the scabbed scratches

on his cheek. "I assure you it was not the trifling matter he may have implied."

"And stealing your ship out of Gravesend? Another exaggeration of your talents?"

Emory's expression mirrored the captain's earlier one of grudging admiration, for the naval officer was indeed well-informed. "I am not here to steal your prisoner. As for the *Intrepid*, my lieutenant has orders to take her out full-and-by at the first sign of trouble and to keep her running before the wind until she is well away from England."

Maitland stared and resumed tapping out a silent litany of reasons why he should not believe any of this. Forged documents, assassins, impostors . . . proper young ladies dressed like common tars, rogue captains who squandered their God-given gifts on subterfuge and intrigue . . .

"Damn and blast," he muttered. "I find myself believing that the hoax being played out here today is the one on me. Lieutenant Witherspoon, fetch me the stoutest pair of leg irons we have on board."

"Yes sir!"

"Then convey my compliments to General Bonaparte and ask if he might spare us a few moments of his time."

"Sir?" The young officer looked astonished.

"Just do it, Mr. Witherspoon!"

"Yes sir. Right away, sir. And, ah, if he refuses?"

"Then use the leg irons on him, dammit to hell. He is still a prisoner on this ship, not a prima donna."

"Yes sir."

The lieutenant hurried out of the cabin and the captain's gaze relented long enough to drain his glass and set it with exaggerated care on the table. "You had best hope I do not regret this, sir," he said with quiet vehemence, "or the few scratches on your face will indeed seem a trifling matter."

He would have elaborated on the threat, but the shrill sound of a whistle topside announced the arrival of new visitors on deck.

When the captain excused himself, the two lieutenants who had been stationed outside the door were invited inside to maintain their guard. Annaleah tried very hard to take strength from the reassuring smile Emory sent her way, but it was poor solace at best. All she could think about was the utter improbability of his belief that the prisoner on board the *Bellerophon* was not Napoleon Bonaparte. No wonder he had not told either Barrimore or herself his suspicions! She seriously doubted they would be here now if he had.

Emory stood and walked behind her, electing to lean against the wall next to where the two midshipmen watched him with wary eyes. Wondering if he had sensed her betrayal in faith, Anna looked down at her hands. The palms were clammy and damp. Her stomach was turning somersaults and she wished there were some socially acceptable way to ask the two stone-faced naval officers where she could go on a ship of war to throw up in private.

Barrimore was standing against the window, his hands clasped behind him, his face as remote as she had ever seen it. From her angle she could see where he clenched and unclenched his fists, but outwardly he appeared as aloof and unmoving as a statue. She looked down at his hands again and frowned, wondering what was different, and after a moment realized his fingers were bare. The heavy gold ring he habitually twisted to vent his disapproval was not there, leaving him nothing to do but flex his fingers. She dearly hoped he had not lost the ancestral ring in the harbor at Gravesend; it would just be something else to hold against Emory when the final tally of his sins was compiled.

A faint commotion sounded outside in the companionway and a moment later the captain ducked his head beneath the lintel, followed by Lord Westford, Colonel Ramsey, and a very distraught-looking Anthony Fairchilde.

"Sweet bleeding Jesus," her brother exclaimed, hastening over to Annaleah's side. She had half risen to her feet already, but he lifted her the rest of the way, hugging her so tightly he nearly throttled her. "You foolish, foolish girl, have you any idea what we have been going through these past few days? I tried my damnedest to keep the worst of it from Mother, truly I did. I lied through my britches by telling her you were ill and had to remain with Aunt Florence another week, but nothing, *nothing* could spare her from hearing about your escapades at Carlton House! The gossips and wags were lined up fifty deep, drooling in their eagerness to offer their commiserations, and within the half hour she had to be carried home on a litter. By morning the news had spread through all of London like another great bloody fire and Father had to put her in restraints to keep her from hurling herself out a window."

"I am so sorry, Anthony. I—"

"And what is this? What is this?" he demanded, pushing aside the folds of her jacket. "A gun! You have a gun!"

"I can explain—"

"A gun, by Christ! My sister is carrying a gun!" He jerked it out of her waistband and waved it wildly about for a moment before his outraged gaze found Barrimore. "Did you know about this, sir? Did you know about this?"

The marquess spread his hands, but there was nothing he could say to placate the enraged viscount.

"Since you were directly responsible for removing her from Carlton House, you leave me no choice," Anthony declared, his voice shaking, "but to demand a settling of accounts!"

Lord Westford reached up quickly to pry the gun from Anthony's hand and set it on the table, pushing it out of reach. "I am certain there must be a very good explanation for all of this, if you will only wait to hear it."

"Oh yes, Anthony, please," Anna cried, "just listen to what Emory has to say—"

"Emory, is it?" He rounded on her again, cutting the protest short. "Rest assured I shall deal with him too, and long before the courts ever get a chance. Where is the bastard? Indeed, where is he?"

He whirled around, his eyes wild with fury, and before anyone could stop him, he launched himself across the room, swinging out with his fist and catching Emory high and hard on the cheekbone. There was enough force behind the blow to send Althorpe staggering back a step, and in spite of a sharp command from the captain, two more punches followed in swift succession, one of which split Emory's lip and sent a spurt of blood down his chin. Emory did not even try to block the punches, nor did he show any reaction when the hard-pressed Westford finally managed to drag the enraged young lord away, other than to blot the back of his hand across his mouth and stare down at the smear of blood.

"Enough!" Maitland was incensed. "There will be none of this on board my ship! If you wish to avenge the insult to your sister's reputation, you have every right to do so, Ormont, but you will not do it here and you will not do it now."

"Nor will you do it until a judge and jury have taken their pound of flesh," Colonel Ramsey declared, waving a folded document in his hand. "I have here a warrant for the arrest of Emory Althorpe on charges of treason, sedition, piracy, and murder! What is more, I have arrests for every man jack on board his ship and I insist, Captain, that after you have clapped him in chains and transferred him into my custody, you train your guns on the *Intrepid* and demand her surrender!"

"Whereas I insist he be transferred into my care," Lord Westford interjected, producing yet another folded sheet of official-looking parchment. "And since my warrants come straight from Whitehall, they most certainly take precedence over all others that may be outstanding."

"I am transferring him nowhere for the moment," Maitland said harshly. "Nor do I have any intentions of training my guns anywhere other than where they might cause the occupants of this room the greatest discomfort. Mr. Witherspoon! Where the devil have you been?"

The lieutenant was standing ashen-faced in the doorway. "I . . . ah . . . that is, the general wishes to pay his compliments, sir."

Behind him was Napoleon Bonaparte and two of his aides, the former grand marshal Henri-Gratien Bertrand and Colonel Charles-Tristan de Montholon.

"Have we come at a bad time, Captain?" Bertrand inquired, clearly amused by all the shouting and waving of documents. "I expect we can return when you have a quieter moment."

"It will be absolutely quiet from this moment on," Maitland said, glaring around the room. "Please, do come in."

The marshal waited until Anthony had stalked back to stand beside his sister, then stepped aside and bowed to the shadow behind him. General Napoleon Bonaparte, the erstwhile Emperor of France and Master of the Continent, strode imperiously into the cabin, his hands clasped behind his back, the buttons of his dark green uniform stretched over the protruding expanse of his belly.

Annaleah's first reaction was surprise, for in spite of the frequent cartoons that depicted him needing a ladder to climb up onto his horse, he was much shorter than she had imagined—barely five feet tall. Moreover, he had bloated cheeks and double chins that did little to complement the natural pout of his lips. His hair was more red than brown, combed forward in front so that a single silky curl fell over his brow.

The piercing slate eyes, known to cause grown men to melt in their boots, circled the room once before seeking out Annaleah. She had moved to stand by Barrimore when the fisticuffs had broken out, and with the glare from the windows behind her, the darkness of her hair glowed with fiery red and gold highlights.

Marshal Bertrand leaned forward to whisper something

in Bonaparte's ear, but the general raised a hand, cutting him off.

"I was told I had a visitor, a Madame Muiron—a very old and dear friend—but I see only this . . . this woman of questionable origin before me. Is this your idea of a poor jest, Captain?"

"Unfortunately, the situation is far from amusing, General. I invited you here in the hopes you could clear up some questions pertaining to your arrest."

"My *surrender*, Captain, was conducted with strict adherence to the codes of war. What is more, not only do I find this an odd time to be questioning such a thing, but I hardly expect you have the authority to be doing so on your own. When you have finished playing your games, feel free to address me again. In the meantime, I left an extremely tasty leg of mutton chilling on my table."

He turned to leave, and his gaze skimmed past the lone figure standing by the door. It stopped . . . skipped back again, and settled with a shocked jolt of recognition on Emory Althorpe. Emory's lip was still leaking blood down his chin and drops had stained the front of his shirt. In a remarkable display of recovering his wits, the general offered up a weak smile.

"You should try to remember to duck the next time, m'sieur."

"Excellent advice, *Colonel Duroc*," Emory said quietly. "I shall endeavor to take it to heart the next time I am ambushed."

There was a second flicker of surprise—or was it panic?—in the gray eyes before Marshal Bertrand stepped between the two men. "You are plainly and stupidly unaware to whom you are speaking, m'sieur."

"Ah, yes. Forgive me my mistake. After you abdicated the Spanish throne, you were still permitted to retain the rank of general, despite your brother's displeasure at the way you allowed Wellington to chase you out of the peninsula."

Bertrand stared a moment, then swelled his chest with

indignation. "We shall not even dignify such an outrageous insult with a response, m'sieur. Kindly step out of the way that His Excellency might pass."

"If it was His Excellency, I might be inclined to do so," Emory said, moving parallel with the marshal to firmly establish himself as an obstacle in the doorway. "Granted, he is a little heavier than he should be to play the part, but his brother's girth has been expanding steadily since he crowned himself Emperor of France. The hair is a shade lighter, the chin rounder, but if your only exposure to the man was across a battlefield and through a spyglass, you would not know you were in the company of the wrong Bonaparte."

"The wrong Bonaparte?" Maitland gasped.

"Indeed, Captain. Allow me to introduce General *Joseph* Bonaparte," Emory said evenly. "Older by a year than Napoleon, but sharing enough of a likeness to have generated more than one mistaken report concerning the Emperor's whereabouts."

The blood had drained from Bertrand's face with the swiftness of an avalanche. "You are mistaken, sir," he rasped.

"And you are a fool, Bertrand, to think you could get away with such an outlandish deception."

"Captain—" The French officer whirled around. "I insist you remove this madman at once."

"What were you planning to do?" Emory asked. "Wait until you had word your brother was safely in America before you threw off the pretense and revealed the hoax to the world? How much did you pay Le Renard to guarantee you would be kept on board a ship in the middle of a harbor where access to visitors would be severely limited and the chances of being discovered dramatically reduced?"

Barrimore, standing quiet until now, as stunned as the others in the room, looked hard at Lord Westford. "That was your idea," he said tersely. "You were quite vehement, in fact, in insisting he remain isolated."

"Isolated, yes, and his movements restricted," Westford replied, startled by the implied accusation. "But only because we dared not risk another escape! Not with"—he glanced at Emory—"not with Althorpe's whereabouts unaccounted for. Good God, man, you are not suggesting . . . !"

"He is suggesting there is a fox in the henhouse, sir, and he must be flushed out," Emory said quietly. "Thanks to the documents now in Captain Maitland's hands, we have established that Le Renard is someone who has access to the foreign office and is more than passingly familiar with the codes used in secret dispatches."

Westford looked genuinely desperate for a moment before he turned suddenly and stared at Colonel Ramsey. "Renard. By Christ . . . we went to Oxford together," he whispered. "You were nicknamed the Fox because of your ability to sneak women in and out of your rooms at any hour of the day or night. And right up to a month ago, you were in London, working out of the foreign office."

Ramsey backed up, and his hand went instantly to the pistol he wore strapped around his waist. It was drawn and cocked before anyone had a chance to react.

"No," he said. "No, sir. I will not be set up as the scapegoat, not for this."

"You have been clearly obsessed with Althorpe's capture these past few weeks," Barrimore remarked. "I would suggest that makes *you* look like the one who was desperate to find a scapegoat."

"Of course I wanted to capture the whoreson bastard," Ramsey hissed. "He is a traitor and a cold-blooded murderer!"

Emory frowned. "That is the second time you have accused me of murder, sir. I grant you I may be guilty of some of the crimes which have been attributed to me, but I have never *murdered* anyone. Killed, yes, in honest battle when my own life or the lives of my men were at risk, but never for the sheer pleasure of it."

"Never?"

"No." Emory glanced briefly at Annaleah. "Never, dammit."

"Then we may add 'liar' to your charges, for there were witnesses to your crime. All three identified you as the man who coldly and deliberately choked an unarmed man to death in the streets of Portsmouth. They subsequently followed you back to your ship, whereupon the authorities were later met with a hail of gunfire. You cast off and sailed away without so much as a by-your-leave." He gripped the butt of the pistol tighter and curled his finger close around the trigger. "That man, the one you left broken and bleeding in a filthy laneway, was my brother, sir, and the day I shoveled the earth over his grave, I took a solemn vow to do the same to you."

Emory's complexion darkened and, watching him, Annaleah felt her stomach give another wrenching twist. She recalled the incident he had told her about Seamus Turnbull's coming upon a young, drunken lord who had kicked a small dog to death for sport. It was Seamus who had throttled Ramsey's brother, not Emory, though the blame had clearly been transferred to his shoulders.

"Put the gun down, Colonel," Westford advised. "You do nothing to help your cause, and if Althorpe is guilty of murdering your brother, I promise you he will be held to account."

"There is nothing to be held accountable for," Annaleah cried, stepping forward. "He did not do it!"

"And who the devil are you to bear witness to his character!" Ramsey demanded, a small dribble of saliva forming at the side of his mouth. "A woman who bases her judgment on the strength of what he puts between her thighs!"

Anthony was only a split second slower than the others to react, but he was closest and thus the first to plow his weight into Ramsey's shoulder, lifting him half off his feet before driving him furiously back into the wall. The gun went off with a puff of smoke, the bullet smashing through the gallery windows, chipping the frame and shattering the glass in two panes. A second shot was fired almost instantaneously, the bullet catching Ramsey squarely in the center of the forehead, leaving a remarkably neat, round, red hole in its wake. Colonel Ramsey's startled eyes focused a moment on the smoking pistol held in Barrimore's outstretched hand, then drifted half closed as his body slid into a dead heap on the floor.

"Good God!" Maitland looked from the marquess to the slumping corpse, and back to the marquess. "Good God, sir, you have killed him!"

"Would you have preferred me to wait to see if he had another weapon concealed on his person?" Barrimore lowered the gun—the one Anthony had taken from Annaleah. The marquess waited for the smoke to funnel out of the barrel before he set it carefully back on the table. "I expect he knew his story of woe and revenge would not hold up against the greater charge of treason."

"You are all mad," declared Bonaparte from behind the shield formed by his marshals, Bertrand and Montholon. "I insist on being allowed to return to my quarters at once!"

"Not until we have the truth from you," Emory said, producing the small pocket pistol and pressing it against the Corsican's cheek. "And believe me, General, I am in a fit mood to use this if you do not admit here and now the rightful name given you at birth."

The familial gray eyes met his over the barrel of the gun and his lips drew back in a snarl. He looked for a moment as if he would still deny the charge, but then his face cracked into a smile and he gave a short bark of laughter.

"For all the good it will do you, m'sieur, my name is Joseph Louis Bonaparte, and I have no qualms in admitting I have played my part well. By now my brother is indeed halfway to America, where he will be welcomed like royalty, and once again take his place at the head of an army—an army he will lead to ultimate victory over his English enemies!"

Maitland stared, then walked slowly over to where they stood at the door. His eyes were themselves formidable weapons, glowering as they did from beneath the weathered brow. While Bonaparte displayed the good sense to shrink back against his two officers, Emory was slightly reluctant to allow the captain to take the gun out of his hand.

His eyes never leaving the general's face, Maitland carefully uncocked the hammer and addressed Witherspoon. "Get them out of here. Get them out before I forget my duty and shoot them myself. Take them below and lock them in their quarters. Put guards on the doors twenty-four hours a day and let no one in or out without my express permission. And Mr. Witherspoon . . . send a man over the side to seal the ports. I want no more bits of paper tossed out in the night. We cannot allow a whisper of this to escape the ship until it has been decided what course to take. Clap them in irons and throw them in the bilges if you have to."

"Yes sir. My pleasure, sir."

The general tossed a final blazing look of triumph over his shoulder before Witherspoon ushered them out the door. When they were gone, Maitland turned equally blazing eyes to Emory and held up the gun. "Have you or Miss Fairchilde any more little surprises to share with us, Mr. Althorpe?"

Emory glanced at Annaleah and arched his eyebrows. "No. No, I think that about uses up our quota for the day."

Maitland made a growling sound in his throat and walked back to the table, barely acknowledging Rupert Ramsey's body where it sprawled on the floor. He set the gun down, careful to keep it squarely in front of him, then leaned his hands on the table and bowed his head.

"What in the name of all the holy saints am I to do now? The world believes we have Napoleon Bonaparte imprisoned on board this ship. When it comes to light he has escaped again . . . that we never had him . . . that he was able to dupe us with such a childish ruse . . ."

He turned his head toward the window, staring at nothing, undoubtedly seeing his entire career go up in flames before his eyes. The battles he had fought would count for nothing, the honors he had won would be forgotten. He would go down in history as the fool who had accepted the surrender of Joseph Bonaparte and let his brother sail away to build another empire across the ocean.

Westford joined him in short order, taking a seat at the table, his forehead cupped in his hands, the heels pressing against his eyes as if to contain the pressure in his skull before it exploded. Anthony helped himself to a full glass of brandy, draining it in several loud gulps before he set the glass down with a bang and went to stand at the windows.

Annaleah tried to catch his eye, but his face remained turned away and his hands stayed laced together behind his back. Emory, on the other hand, was only too willing to meet her gaze, though the message he conveyed was distinctly mixed. The ruse had been uncovered, but she had disobeyed him again by bringing the gun on board, and a man was dead because of it. To make matters worse, they might never know for sure now if Rupert Ramsey had indeed been the Fox.

"You are more familiar with the Corsican's habits than anyone else in this room, Althorpe," Westford said, working his hands around to his temples. "Where would he go? Where would he feel safe? Is it *possible* he has slipped through our hands and is on his way to America?"

"His younger brother Lucien spent four years there. He has undoubtedly established a loyalist base."

The earl sighed. "And the bastard was right. The Americans would welcome a soldier of his caliber with open arms. They would press north into Canada and join forces with the French in Quebec. He would have a vast, rich empire to rule again."

Emory moved away from the door. His lip had stopped

bleeding and he dampened a linen napkin in water he found on a side table, then used it to swab away the stains on his chin and throat.

"Empires," he said thoughtfully, "need heirs."

"What?"

"His son is still in Paris. He would not leave France without his Little Eagle."

"It has been more than six weeks since his 'surrender.' He would be a fool to have remained in France this long."

"How long did Bonny Prince Charles remain in the Highlands of Scotland after the rout of '45?" Emory asked.

Maitland straightened and turned his head toward Emory; even Anthony looked back over his shoulder at him.

"At the time, the Prince had a reward of thirty thousand pounds on his head, but not one of his loyal Highlanders betrayed his wherabouts. They kept him hidden for three months until it was safe for a ship to transport him back across the Channel. In this instance, there is no bounty; no one is even looking for Napoleon, because they believe him to be here, on board the *Bellerophon*. For that matter, if the masquerade has worked in the one direction, it could easily work in the other. A wig, a sprout of whiskers, and he could conceivably assume the guise of Joseph. And do not forget, he would be confident of receiving ample warning from our elusive friend Le Renard should anyone's suspicions be roused."

"Yes, well," Anthony said, looking down at Ramsey, "that appears to be one problem we have resolved, anyway."

Emory shook his head. "I am not so sure we have."

"Why ever not?" Anthony demanded. "You heard yourself he was in London, in Whitehall, during the time your so-called forged orders were dispatched. He moved about as freely as Westford or Barrimore or . . . or me, for that matter. My French is nearly as excellent as Barrimore's and I was called upon more than once to help in translations when there were so many dispatches pouring in daily."

"Did you know the codes?" Emory asked.

"Would I confess to it in this roomful of excitable individuals if I did?" the viscount snorted.

It was a fair point Anthony had made, and Annaleah glanced at Barrimore to see how he was reacting to being called excitable. His face was granite, his body rigid. Only the thumb of his left hand moved, rubbing the empty place on his middle finger where his ring should have been.

She looked down at his hand again and felt a small shiver run across the back of her neck.

How many times had she stared at that ring, watching it wink in the sunlight or gleam by candlelight as he turned it round and round his finger? It had been an inheritance from his maternal grandfather, along with minor estates and titles belonging to the Ashworth heir—knowledge she was certain only a handful of people would be able to include in a recitation of his lineage. But her mother, a scavenger for the smallest piece of information that might be of benefit in a prospective marriage, had gone through an endless litany of insignificant details a hundred times.

The shiver turned into a slow, cold flush that began at the nape of her neck and spread downward, leaving everything frozen in its wake.

Annaleah had commented on the ring once—most likely out of annoyance—and had been corrected in her misinterpretation of what she'd thought was a wolf sejant in the crest. It had been a fox sitting back on its haunches—a rarely used element in family arms.

Barrimore had not lost the ring at all. He had deliberately removed it on the off chance someone might notice it again.

On board the *Intrepid*, he had claimed his French was strictly formal, yet Anthony had just said it was excellent—as it would have to be, logically, if he worked with coded dispatches going to and from enemy territory. Earlier, on the coach to Gravesend, she'd harbored suspicions about all his questions, but he had managed to neatly defuse them. Only minutes ago, he'd tried to focus attention on Westford, and then he had simply, coldly shot Ramsey . . . hoping what? That the dead colonel would indeed be made the scapegoat?

She looked up and found his eyes waiting for her. He knew what she was thinking, and so did she. It was him. He was the Fox. He was Le Renard.

Chapter 27

ANNA GLANCED OVER at Emory, but he was talking to Westford. Anthony was bent over the table pouring another glass of brandy, blocking her view of the captain and consequently impeding his view as Barrimore swiftly closed the gap between them. He wrapped the fingers of one hand around her arm and something painfully sharp gouged into the small of her back, piercing through her pea coat as if it were butter.

"Say one word," he murmured, "and I will sever your spine. You will spend the rest of your days in a chair with wheels on it."

She closed her mouth and swallowed her cry. His face was only inches from hers, his eyes like two shards of green ice.

"W-why?" she gasped. "*Why?*"

Instead of answering, he dug the point of the blade deeper into her skin. "Ask if you might excuse yourself. Claim faintness—whatever—so long as it gets us out of this cabin. And if you try anything, anything at all, I will kill you, and then I will kill your lover. From this moment on, I have absolutely nothing to lose, Miss Fairchilde, so you had best believe me."

She did. She had no reason not to. His eyes, his voice were dead calm, his fingers like iron pincers around her arm.

"Now, if you please," he said calmly. "Do it."

She shifted her gaze back to the four men huddled at the end of the table. Why did they suddenly seem so far away? Why were none of them aware of the little drama taking place less than a dozen paces away?

"E-excuse me," she whispered.

No one turned. No one looked in her direction.

She felt the blade dig deeper and realized her throat was so dry, no one had heard her.

"Excuse me," she managed with more force. "I hate to trouble you, Captain, but would it be possible for me to go out on deck for some fresh air? It . . . it is suddenly so close in here, I . . . I find myself feeling unwell."

Maitland scraped to his feet at once with an apology. "Forgive my lack of sensitivity, Miss Fairchilde. I will have someone escort you immediately."

"I confess to feeling a little warm myself," Barrimore said from behind her. "I would gladly volunteer my company . . . if no one has an objection, that is."

Annaleah imagined this last bit was added with a concessionary smile in Emory's direction, for he looked over and the quick flash of concern that had wrinkled his brow gave way to a crooked grin.

"If Anna has no objections, I can think of none."

"It is hardly your place to object or not, young man," Maitland reminded him dryly. "Since I have not yet decided what is to be done with you."

Emory acknowledged the captain's dilemma by offering a faintly mocking bow, then moved toward the door to open it as Anna and Barrimore came around the end of the table.

Annaleah's legs felt like two stumps of wood and her heart was beating so loudly in her breast she felt sure he had to hear it when they drew near. But his attention was not entirely focused on her, for he was still trying to hear what Westford and Maitland were saying as they resumed their conversation.

She stepped out into the bright burst of sunlight and, at the urging of the hand Barrimore kept gripped tightly around her upper arm, headed across the quarterdeck to the narrow flight of stairs that led down to the main gun deck. The stairs were more of a ladder than steps, and she knew Barrimore would have difficulty keeping close to her, and that he could hardly show the knife in plain view of the sailors and soldiers working all around them. There were members of the crew standing by the cannon, more balancing up in the rigging, flashes of red and white in the uniformed infantrymen on all decks. If she stumbled, pretended to lose her balance, screamed . . .

"Don't even think about it," he warned. "You will only cost another innocent man his life."

"You are quite despicable, sir," she said.

"Whereas you are every bit the whore Ramsey accused you of being. And a surprisingly enthusiastic one too, I might add. You succeeded in shocking me rather profoundly the other night when I went back to the cabin and saw you spread out on his desk, clawing at him, bleating his name each time he pounded into you."

She stopped and turned her head. "You saw us?"

"Briefly. I had expected that your lover would be occupied on deck steering his ship out of the fog and that you would be standing alongside him."

"You went back to steal the papers."

"He does not take to following orders very well. He was supposed to destroy all communications between himself and Westford's office."

They had nearly reached the ladder. The sun was in the westerly sky shining through the shrouds, making a checkerboard pattern on the deck. The air smelled of salt and fish and the heat radiating off the oak planking. Her foot truly did stumble on the way down the narrow rungs, but Barrimore had hold of her jacket and kept her upright. At the bottom, he forced the turn toward the open gangway in the rail. There were twenty feet of deck between him and freedom, and while Annaleah had never really pondered a situation in which she might be called upon to make a noble sacrifice for King and country, she knew she could not let him reach that opening. Good men—fathers, sons, brothers, lovers—had died in the hundred days of renewed fighting that followed Napoleon's escape from Elba, and Barrimore had been instrumental in making that escape possible. He had used Emory Althorpe, then thrown him callously to the wolves, and if not for the sheer luck of her having taken a walk on a hazy morning in her aunt's cove, the true magnitude of this most recent deception might not have been discovered until it was too late.

She looked up at the tall mizzenmast that stood before her, at the fat rolls of sail furled to the spars, and remembered a quote she'd once heard about it being a good day to die.

"Move," he said in her ear.

"First tell me why. Why did you do it? You are a rich man, an important man. You belong to the nobility, for pity's sake—how could you do something so contemptible, so disgraceful, so . . . so *dishonorable*?"

"If we had a month together, madame, I could possibly explain my motives, but since we are reduced to minutes, suffice it to say the vast reserves of wealth attributed to the Perry name were illusionary. My father squandered nearly every penny he inherited on gambling and bad investments. There was not one estate that did not come to me burdened under staggering debts, so much so, they were in danger of being sold at a creditor's auction."

"Money?" She stopped again, and this time turned fully around to gape at him. "You sold out your country for money?"

"Do without it for few years, and you would be surprised how very important it becomes. And it was not my intent in the beginning to 'sell out my country.' It began innocently enough, with a few hundred pounds here, a few hundred there for information that could have been obtained a dozen different ways. No one tells you, however, when you are young and stupid and blaming all the world for your woes, that once you sell your soul to the devil, he is an unforgiving bastard. He grabs you by the guts and holds on fast and even if you want to break away, he has the power to eviscerate you before your peers. By the time I realized this, it was too late to back away, so the object then became to push forward. This"—he waved a hand to encompass the *Bellerophon*—"was to be my last foray into the darker side of intrigue and afterward . . . well . . . America is the land of opportunity, they say. I was truly hoping you would come with me." His gaze raked appreciatively over the high bloom of color in her cheeks, the glossy tangle of her hair. "You would have made a magnificent duchess. You still could, you know, for Althorpe will never clear his name. Neither will Westford, I'm afraid."

"He has the dispatches. He can prove they are forgeries."

"How? By the watermark?"

Annaleah did not think she was capable of feeling a deeper sense of horror, but when she saw the coldness of his smile, she knew she was wrong. "There was no change in the mark?"

"A rather creative piece of impromptu gibberish, I thought."

"Oddly enough," a familiar voice said from behind them, "we were just discussing that."

Barrimore spun around. Emory was standing in the sunlight, his long legs braced apart to counter the gentle roll of the deck. Westford, Anthony, and Maitland were formed up beside him, presenting a formidable phalanx of grim faces, though none as grim as Emory's as he stared along the steel barrel of the gun he held aimed at Barrimore's head.

The marquess's knife flashed upward and sank into the tender flesh beneath Anna's ear.

"Back away, gentlemen. Back away or Miss Fairchilde will pay a dear price for your bravado."

"Look around you, Barrimore," Emory said. "Where do you think you can go?"

As hushed as the crowded deck had been when they had initially come on board, it was twice as silent now as men stopped what they were doing to watch the facing-off of the nobleman and the notorious privateer. On a signal from Maitland, a line of scarlet-clad infantrymen formed up across the quarterdeck rail and another mustered forward, the click of hammers being cocked on their muskets the only sound on the still air.

The blade forced Anna's head back against Barrimore's shoulder. She closed her eyes against the sharp sting of the edge slivering through her skin. She did not have to see the look on Emory's face, or on the faces of the other men, to know that the warmth she felt trickling down her neck was blood.

"I think I have more than enough leverage to reach shore," Barrimore said, his voice silky in her ear.

"Even if you do. Even if you manage to get off this ship, where can you go? How long can you hold a knife to her throat before your arm tires, or you take a false step"—Emory was hissing the words through his teeth now—"or turn your back, knowing that I will be right behind you."

"You have an alternative to suggest?"

"You and I can settle it right here, right now. You win, you leave the ship unmolested with a guarantee of safe passage as far as the shore."

"Now see here, Althorpe—" Maitland began.

"Agreed," Barrimore said, cutting off the protest. "You and I, here and now; the victor goes free—assuming, of course, we have the captain's word as an officer and a gentleman that the terms will be honored."

Anna held her breath. The ship, it seemed, held her breath as well, for what little breeze there was died and the pennants flying high on the masts wilted and fluttered down around the oak. Anna was aware of Barrimore's heartbeat against her back and the tension in the fingers that gripped her arm. She could not judge how deeply the knife had cut her, but it felt as though there was a veritable torrent of blood pouring down to soak her shirtfront.

All eyes, however, were on the gruff face of Frederick Maitland. "Damn you, Althorpe," he muttered, "this should be left to a higher authority."

"On board this ship, sir, you are the highest authority. You are both judge and jury. And if you are willing to let this thing be settled here and now, I am more than willing to oblige the man."

Maitland's gaze held Emory's for a long, long moment before he looked at Westford. The earl, in turn, gave a small, less than resoundingly supportive nod.

Barrimore eased the knife from Annaleah's throat and an instant later she was running across the deck, throwing herself into Emory's waiting arms.

A fresh ripple of excitement spread across the deck, and even before the choice of weapons was decided, the men began to back up and form a clear ring of open space.

"It should be me who fights him," Anthony insisted, "I have already made my challenge."

"Yes, well"—Emory lifted his face out of the crush of Anna's hair long enough to grace the viscount with a wry smile—"if I fail, you can take my place."

"He is an expert marksman and a master of the sword—a member of *le cadré noir*! I have practiced with him on occasion and know the way he plies the rapier. And besides which, Anna is my sister! I should be the one to avenge the insult!"

"I am Emory's wife," Annaleah stated flatly, "in every sense but the final prayer. To that end, Captain, may we beg another small favor of you when this business is done?"

To Anthony's spluttered shock, and Emory's bemused smile, Maitland swelled his chest and gave a brusque nod. "It would be both my honor and my pleasure, young lady."

Emory was stripped to his shirt and breeches. The marquess had removed his coat and vest, and was engaged in the process of testing the weight and balance of the dozen swords that had been offered for his approval.

"Can you not just shoot him where he stands and be done with it?" Anna asked, her fear for Emory beginning to dampen her earlier enthusiasm regarding loyalty to King and country.

He turned and looked at her a moment, the telltale shiver

in his cheek belying his outward calm. He took her face tenderly between his hands and kissed her long and deep, and without a care as to who was watching. When she had been duly subdued into a blushing silence, he steered her gently into her brother's custody, then took up the sword he had selected, running the pad of his thumb lightly along the keen edge. He held the tip and tested the strength of the steel, sliced the air in several blurred flashes, and nodded his final approval.

Across the deck, Barrimore finished his own series of brisk preparatory strokes. He had glanced over during the kiss and his mouth was pinched with disdain.

"If you are quite ready . . . ?"

Both men had waived the formal rules governing a duel, each knowing from the outset that it would be a fight to the death. They moved forward into the cleared ring, taking casual, normal strides at first, then slowly easing into the precise beauty of slow, lethal steps that moved them in a tense, watchful circle facing each other. As they prowled, each assessed the other's stance, his grip, the position he held his blade, and each made minor adjustments in his own attitude.

"Anthony informs me you are a master," Emory mused. "A member of *le cadré noir*."

Barrimore tipped his head to acknowledge the remark. "I had occasion to study under Riveaux, in Brussels, but I found his theory on defenses lacking. I preferred the Italian school of Strecci, though I must say I have some appreciation for the subtle strategies put forward by the Spaniard Leopoldi."

Emory circled, teeth and sword flashing in the sunlight. "I studied under the Celt, Turnbull. He taught me to kill or be killed."

"Difficult to argue with that logic," Barrimore agreed. "But it does make for some gaps in technique."

Quicker than the eye could follow, he lunged forward, thrusting with the point of his blade, cutting with the edge as he flew back. The speed of the attack and the resultant stripe of blood on Emory's thigh had barely registered before Barrimore was coming in again, striking and thrusting in a series of parries and ripostes that forced Emory to guard and block during every step of a harried retreat.

As swiftly as it had erupted, the clash ended, with Barrimore falling away and circling again, smiling as he admired the damage he had wrought. Aside from the cut on his thigh, there was a crimson stripe high on Emory's arm, another on the wrist of his left hand, and a fourth on a knuckle that dripped blood through the scrolled figure eight of his guard. He had also lost the scrap of ribbon that held his hair tied at his nape, and the thick black waves fell forward onto his cheeks and neck, curling over the stark whiteness of his collar.

Behind them, the whispers swelled to a buzz as wagers were made on the outcome. The soldiers crowded the rails along the upper decks. Not a spar or shroud was empty of sailors; they even stood on the barrels of the cannons to gain extra height.

Barrimore came in once more, lunging, thrusting. Steel clashed again and again as Emory blocked and parried and this time held his ground, ending the assault with an expert twist of his wrist that crossed their blades and locked the points downward in a *bastard guardant*, a threat to nothing but the deck at their feet.

"Very good," Barrimore said, genuinely surprised at the deftness of the move.

"I am a quick study," Emory countered, twisting his wrist again to break the guard. He took a small circular step to the side, feinting left, and when Barrimore rose to block the phantom thrust, he struck on the right instead, slicing through the silk of the marquess's shirt and leaving a bright scarlet ribbon across his upper torso. He spun again and slashed down in a forehand ward, coming close enough to Barrimore's ear to nick a lock of hair. The marquess counter-thrusted, advancing fast and hard, forcing Emory to leap sideways in order to avoid slamming into the trunk of the mainmast.

The ring of sailors pressed back to clear a wider space. There were open shouts of encouragement now, and hotter wagering. Word of what was happening on board had been conveyed to the boats in the water below and although their occupants could not see either the action or the participants, they were given odds, and bets were taken on the outcome, each touch and slash duly relayed.

Althorpe went in on the attack, retaliating for a stinging cut on his ribs. Barrimore was good—too good to give away the smallest advantage, and Emory found himself turned into the sun, his back to the stairs with nowhere to retreat. His shirt was starting to stick to his back in patches and his face was bathed in sweat. He had a very real sense the marquess was merely playing with him, leading him here and there, wearing him down with a series of feints and thrusts that nicked at bits of flesh and did no real damage except to his pride. He tried to execute a *demi volte*, a clever, classical move that failed miserably and earned another mocking slap from Barrimore's blade. And instead of finding himself clear, he was trapped on the bottom rung of the companionway, sandwiched between the two wooden rails.

Barrimore grinned and lunged, the point driving straight and true for the middle of Emory's chest. Deflecting the blade at the last possible instant, Emory grasped the rail and elected this time to use a classic Turnbull move, swinging himself up and over, using the heels of his boots to kick the marquess full in the belly, startling him back and buying himself a precious few seconds of breathing space.

The unconventional brawler's move wiped the amusement from Barrimore's face and he came in hard and furious, his blade moving almost faster than the eye could follow. Emory was forced to retreat to the side of the ship, parrying stroke after powerful stroke with jarring blows that tore at the strength in his arm and shoulder. The open gap of the gangway was directly behind him and he veered toward it, warding off the snarled curses and beads of sweat that told him Barrimore was finished playing. He was driving with purpose now, cutting, slashing, thrusting with a master's skill and brute power.

Emory was at the rail. He was out of room and rapidly running out of defensive moves.

He saw the glint of Barrimore's steel coming toward him and met the thrust with his left hand. He grabbed Barrimore's forearm near the wrist and used the marquess's own forward momentum to drag him close enough to trap his hand and sword under his arm. Holding fast, Emory made a sharp outward turn with his body, bending the captured arm fully back until it snapped at the elbow. At the same time, he pressed up behind Barrimore and with one clean slash of his sword drew it across the front of the marquess's neck, cutting his scream of agony short in a spray of bright red foam.

Barrimore staggered two steps forward, his broken arm hanging, his sword still hooked through useless fingers and trailing on the deck. With his left hand he groped at the severed skin and cartilage on his throat, but the life was pumping out of him faster than he could stanch it. He teetered a moment in the opening of the gangway, then seemed to twist outward in a graceful pirouette, falling over the side and landing with a heavy splash in the water below.

There was perhaps of beat of silence before the ship's crew erupted with a roar. Emory let his own sword drop and doubled over at the waist, his hands braced on his thighs as he sucked at lungfuls of air. Annaleah broke free of her brother's grasp and skidded down the ladderway and across the deck, flinging herself at Emory a scant moment before he would have toppled forward onto his face.

"I am fine," he gasped. "I am fine. I just . . . need to catch my breath."

"You were bloody magnificent, Captain Althorpe," Maitland declared, striding up beside them.

"Indeed," Westford agreed, frowning despite the raucous cheering and shouting going on all around them. "But unfortunately, that only solves one of our problems."

Emory gulped a few more deep breaths, then straightened, his arm tight around Anna's shoulders. "If you gentlemen will take one more leap of faith and allow me the time it takes to travel to Paris and back, I think I can resolve our other 'problem' to everyone's satisfaction."

"What are you suggesting?" Westford asked.

"I'm suggesting I know where our elusive friend is and can have him back here before anyone in the admiralty is any the wiser."

Chapter 28

ANNALEAH SAT CLOSE to the coach window and looked out at the streets passing by. She had never been in Paris before and wished they had time to take a long, leisurely ride around the city. She had to settle for Emory's promise to bring her back one day to see all the beautiful castles and estates and palaces that had been built by generations of the French aristocracy and that were now, for the most part, owned by complete strangers whose only claim to nobility was the fact they still had their heads.

She was not half so nervous as she had expected to be. The *Intrepid* had sailed from Torbay within two hours of Lord Barrimore's death—barely enough time for Captain Maitland to assemble his officers, fetch his Bible, and perform a hasty wedding ceremony. She had been married in a short naval pea coat and canvas breeches, with a bandage wrapped around her neck, and a smile as bright as the sun on her face. Emory had insisted they would repeat their vows in a proper church with all the pomp and ceremony the occasion deserved, but she was just happy to be Mrs. Emory St. James Althorpe. So happy she smiled every time she looked down at her hand and saw the glitter of her aunt's diamond ring sitting next to the flattened iron nail he had insisted upon hammering into a wedding band.

She drew a deep breath to settle herself and adjusted the delicate folds of silk in her gown. The lace fichu she wore high around her neck required a minor alteration as well to cover the angry red scab, and an impatient finger jabbed beneath the heavy crown of mahogany curls to reach an elusive itch. Had it only been a little over a fortnight ago, before her banishment to Widdicombe House, that stiff curls and scratchy lace had been the order of the day? Two weeks of undressed hair and windblown walks on the cliffs and beach, combined with the introduction to soft cambric shirts and an increasing comfort with wearing little else while in her husband's company, had definitely soured her to confining bodices and steel hairpins.

It had plainly caught Emory off guard too, after the maid and hairdresser and clothier had departed the hotel earlier that day. She had walked out of the bedroom in her filmy silken finery, her hair an elegant upsweep of glossy curls, and he had just stared. Seamus's jaw had dropped as well. Both men had shot awkwardly to their feet and Anna had been hard pressed not to laugh out loud.

She had suffered a minor spate of the giggles an hour or so later when Emory had been similarly transformed—not into an elegant, well-bred gentleman, but rather a liveried footman in a pink satin frock coat, tight white knee breeches, and high-buckled shoes. His hair had been confined beneath a powdered wig but his scowl managed to crack through the layer of cosmetics required to tone down the incongruous bronze shade of his skin. Seamus looked only slightly less amusing, his barrel chest straining the buttons of the black jacket he wore, his own carrot red hair tamed and crushed beneath a brimmed stovepipe hat.

Two men and a nervous bride. Not exactly the force one would choose to dispatch to recapture the world's most notorious prisoner, but they had been to Château de Malmaison and seen the spiked iron gates, the small, personal army of "gardeners" and "servants" who pretended to work about the sprawling grounds. Nothing less than a full-scale assault would have pried him loose, and so they had decided to attack with audacity.

"The ruse worked once, and it will work again," Emory had assured her. "He will have no way of knowing his brother has been compromised, and because his mother, Madame Mère, was completely devoted to Josephine and would never tolerate any other woman setting foot on the empress's grounds, any liaison, carnal or otherwise, would have to be arranged in utmost secrecy, with only one or two trusted bodyguards in attendance."

"Are you so certain he would risk leaving Malmaison for a tryst with an old lover?"

"In the first place, Mademoiselle Georges is hardly old at eight and twenty, and he was as besotted with her as I am with you. Secondly, he has not seen her since he was exiled to Elba. He sent repeated pleas to her after his landing at Antibes, but none of his couriers could find her, or if they did, they were too terrified to relay the message that she refused to see him. If it was me, and if I had been trapped in a palace with my mother for six weeks, and I received a note from a woman who could . . . well, who could send my eyes rolling back into my skull, I would be running on three legs, not two, to meet her."

Since his hands had been on her naked breasts when he'd said this, and she had been sitting astride him on the hotel bed, demonstrating her willingness to master the art of behaving like a doxy, it had taken several minutes for her thoughts to process his words.

"You seem to know a great deal about this Mademoiselle Georges," she remarked, halting her movements just as his body was straining helplessly up inside her.

He let the air hiss out from between his teeth and clutched his hands around her waist as he lowered his hips carefully back onto the bed. "She is quite a famous actress."

"Beautiful?"

"Yes, very."

"You know her?"

He swallowed and opened his eyes. "I have made her acquaintance."

Anna leaned forward, her hands pushing firmly against the bedboard as she started to move over him again. "How *well* did you know her?"

"What kind of question is that to ask?"

"The kind that wants an answer," she warned, halting

again. He was big and thick and harder than he had been through several previous "lessons," and she just smiled, confident she could outlast him . . . this time. A few moments earlier, she would not have been so positive, but he was ever the generous lover, and now their positions were reversed. She was enjoying the tightness that came and went on his face, the powerful tremors that were shaking his body, the moisture on his brow and the little gasps and grunts that came through his lips on each rolling thrust of her hips. Conversely, he was discovering just how apt a pupil she was, and how inventive. Fool that he was, he had shown her how to ply his flesh with the skills of a medieval torturer armed with velvet gloves.

"How well did you know her? How do you know she could make your eyes roll back in your skull?"

"Rumors," he gasped. "Men gossip too, you know. Christ, Anna, don't stop again—! I swear it was just rumors. Rumors, dammit."

The carriage rolled down a tree-lined avenue, the clatter of the wheels pulling Annaleah's thoughts back to the present. She squirmed in her seat and required a moment to settle the blush in her cheeks, and when she looked out the window again, they were slowing, turning into a graveled drive.

The house chosen for the tryst was small and clean, set back from the road on a quiet avenue of private residences that followed the lazy course of the River Seine. It was less than two miles from Malmaison and as the diligence rolled past, Anna saw shadows here and there step out from behind the thick trunks of the oaks and exchange prearranged signals with Seamus. There were more men waiting down by the river with two boats to ferry their captive across the Seine, from whence they would fly by coach to Calais and take him on board the *Intrepid*.

The carriage halted, and a moment later Emory was opening the door. He handed her out and the two stood in the late afternoon sunlight looking up at the classic Baroque design of the house, with its long windows and pale stone exterior.

"We are an hour earlier than the note specified. Seamus managed to get the doors open, but it would have taken more time than we had to tidy the interior enough to make it look like someone has been living here." He pointed to a sunny spot in the gardens where a wrought-iron gazebo had been built in the midst of a small sea of roses. "It should be far enough away to deceive him. He is a vain little wretch when it comes to wearing his spectacles, so until he is about ten feet away from you, all he will see is a pale blur. A glowing, dark-haired angel, much like I saw when I woke up at your aunt's house."

She looked up and suppressed a shiver. "You will be closer than ten feet; are you not worried he will recognize you?"

"He will see this pink buffoon's costume and dismiss me as nothing more important than a servant."

"But you will be careful," she whispered. "For you are very important to me."

He bowed his head and kissed her, then nodded once at Seamus before escorting her toward the rose garden.

Anna could have sworn a hundred hours passed before she heard a landau turn into the drive. Emory had seated her carefully so that she was turned away from the house and he had positioned their own coach in such a way as to force a second vehicle to park in clear view of the gazebo.

The landau was small and nondescript. No crests were scrolled on the doors, no gilt covered the wheels or rimmed the windows. The horse looked lively enough, but a far cry from the teams of six and eight matched blacks that had been the custom in the past when transporting the former Emperor from one place to another.

One of three brutish-looking servants in plain black coats and trousers stepped quickly off the backboards and stood to one side, his eyes scanning the trees, the house, the lane they had just ridden along. He did not look pleased when he saw Seamus hunched over the carriage ahead working diligently with his polishing cloth, and he nodded to one of the other brutes to go forward. The third man opened the coach door and dropped the step into place.

A head appeared in the doorway and some words were exchanged. The first brute—who was as much a footman as Emory or Seamus—shook his head and appeared to be reiterating his discomfort with the entire situation, but then Napoleon Bonaparte caught sight of the gazebo, of the woman sitting in the dappled sunlight, and an impatient hand waved the man to silence.

Displaying the eagerness of someone who cared less about his safety than hurrying to his lover's arms, he disembarked and hastened across the lawn, following the narrow path into the gardens. Emory executed a formal bow as he hurried past, then fell casually into step behind him as if he had just emerged from the servants' entrance. In his gloved hand, he carried a tray with a bottle of champagne and two crystal glasses.

"My dearest Marie," Bonaparte cried in French. "My very dearest Marie! You have no idea how worried I have been over these past few months!"

Huffing, his belly rolling a bit with the haste of his footsteps, the general rounded the last curve in the path and stopped just shy of the arched entrance to the gazebo. The sun was low in the sky and already the few puffs of cloud overhead were turning rosy in anticipation of a glorious sunset. Anna had waited until the last possible moment before she slowly stood and turned to face him.

At a quick glance, she might have thought it was the same man she had seen two days ago on board the *Bellerophon*. The differences were there, to be sure, but unless the two men stood side by side, she could see how a mistake could easily be made—or encouraged. This Napoleon was distinctly heavier around the middle. His hair was thinner, his nose sharper, and his eyes . . .

The sheer penetrating power of his eyes would have distinguished him as an emperor of common men. They held all the cunning, the triumph and horror of war. There was arrogance and conceit, smugness and surety—yet when his gaze searched Anna's face and did not see the familiarity he was expecting, they clouded with the wounded confusion of a man who had already been betrayed too many times by fate.

"Who are you? Where is Marie?"

"I am afraid she could not be here today, Excellency," Emory said, coming up behind him. He still balanced the tray in one hand, but he had moved aside a linen napkin to expose one of the steel-barreled flintlocks.

Bonaparte whirled around. He saw the gun, saw the lop-sided grin on the powdered white face, and, in the distance, saw his driver and three bodyguards being disarmed and scuffed against the side of the house by half a dozen men led by a red-haired giant.

"Who are you?" he asked coldly. "What the devil is going on here? If it is a robbery, you have wasted your efforts, for I have nothing."

"You don't recognize me?" Emory set the tray aside and pulled off the horsehair wig. "I am crushed, Excellency. Your brother Joseph knew me right away."

As soon as the jet black hair was freed, Bonaparte's eyes widened. "You! Franceschi assured me you were dead."

"Your wolfhound should have looked to his own health first—which is not too good at the moment, I am not sad to say. At the very least he will be needing someone to carve his dinners for him the rest of his life. As for Joseph . . . Well . . . he is not much happier. He sends his felicitations, by the way, and his apologies. It seems as though he will not be able to keep your appointment with Admiral Cockburn after all."

"What appointment?" The question came out on a disbelieving rasp of breath. "Who is Cockburn?"

"Rear Admiral Sir George Cockburn, of the HMS

Northumberland. Both he and his ship are waiting in Plymouth to take you to your new home. It is an idyllic little island in the South Atlantic—St. Helena. Perhaps you have heard of it?"

Bonaparte took one, two steps backward, almost staggering into a bank of rosebushes. He turned, but the gazebo had only one entrance and Annaleah was standing under the arch of wrought-iron ivy, holding a second gun that was aimed steadily at his chest.

The general turned slowly back to face Emory. If he felt any fear or panic, it did not show, for his eyes blazed and his mouth flattened into a thin, grim smile. "And so they have sent their bold seahawk to capture the eagle? How fitting." His smile faded and the gleam in his eyes hardened. "I should have let Cipi kill you months ago."

"In hindsight, we are all wise beyond our years."

Seamus came hurrying up the path then, rubbing a set of scraped knuckles. "Bastard's jaw was as hard as an anvil, but they're all quiet now. Trussed up like Christmas geese, they won't be sounding any alarms until they've chewed through their bindings. Excellency . . ." He touched a red forelock from force of habit but continued to address his remarks to Emory. "The men are making for the boats and we've about lost the light."

"I have millions set aside," Bonaparte said quietly. "Half the wealth of a dead aristocracy, which I am prepared to share with you, Althorpe. More gold, more jewels than you could fit into the hold of your ship."

"I already have gold and jewels, Excellency. Far more than I can expect to spend in this lifetime or the next. And besides, I have promised my wife I will do my best to mend my scurrilous ways, and I would not want to disappoint her."

Bonaparte glanced at Annaleah, at the gun she held so unwaveringly in her hand. He pursed his lips and clasped his hands behind his back, and Anna could have sworn he gave a small nod to acknowledge the beauty and courage it took to hold sway over such a man.

"I would like to say farewell to my family."

Emory shook his head. "I'm afraid that will not be possible."

"My son is expected at Malmaison before the week's end. . . ." He turned his face to the setting sun, and for the briefest moment, his eyes glistened as he stared at the western sky, thinking perhaps of lost opportunities, of the glory that might have been his once again but for this newest cruel twist of fate. "Five days," he whispered. "Just five more days. Ah well . . ." He looked at Emory and smiled. "St. Helena, you say? I am not familiar with the place, but I expect that your English hospitality will be adequate for the time being."

He unclasped his hands and tucked one into the front of his jacket as he started walking across the lawns toward the riverbank. Seamus and two other men followed, keeping a respectful few paces behind.

Anna released the breath she had been holding and the gun wavered down to her side. "Is that it? Just like that? And what did he mean . . . 'for the time being'?"

Emory had used the napkin to wipe the powder off his face. He moved closer and took the gun from her hand, easing the hammer down to uncock it. "I imagine he means he does not expect to remain in captivity any longer than he did the last time. In fact"—he glanced over his shoulder—"he is probably discussing the matter with Seamus right now."

She arched her eyebrows in surprise. "And what will Seamus do?"

Emory looked down at the gun. "Half the treasures of a continent . . . It is a powerful temptation."

"You resisted," she pointed out.

"I have you," he said, bending his lips to hers. "That is treasure enough for ten lifetimes."

Epilogue

*A*NNALEAH STOOD IN the center of the conservatory, her arms outstretched, her head back, her skirts settling into a swirl around her ankles. Slightly breathless from spinning, she was still smiling when a movement drew her eye to the door. Florence Widdicombe was standing there, her hands crossed over the silver head of her cane, a snow white eyebrow raised in amusement.

"It was the sunlight," Anna explained shyly, letting her hands fall to her sides. "All the colors."

She looked down by way of explanation and spread the soft white muslin folds of her skirt. The sunbeams breaking through the tall stained-glass windows had painted her in shades of blue and gold and pink, like a rainbow.

"May I assume, then, that Willerkins's efforts have not been in vain?"

Anna looked around. An army of household servants had been brought from the village to clean the conservatory, the ballroom, the parlors, and the dozen bedrooms that would be filled through the next two days by guests invited to attend and celebrate the second wedding ceremony that Emory had promised her. His brother Stanley would be presiding, and Lord Westford was coming all the way from London. There was even a rumor the Regent had announced a desire to take in the sea air and would be stopping in Torquay for a few days. Though it would never be made common knowledge how closely the empire had come to complete disaster, the Regent had expressed his gratitude to Emory and the crew of the *Intrepid*. They had all been granted full pardons, and, according to papers carefully leaked to the London *Gazette*, Captain Emory St. James

Althorpe was nothing short of a hero for risking his life many times over in spying for England all those long, perilous years.

Florence came fully into the room, scowling as a servant hurried past on his way to the tall french doors. There was another army of servants working outside with rakes and paintbrushes to restore the terraces and gardens to a degree of their former elegance.

"I have just received a note advising me that I might expect the arrival of your father and mother by suppertime. I do so with bated breath, as does Mildred, who is burning some of Ethel's feathers and consulting with her ghostly advisor to plan the perfect meal."

"Ghostly advisor?"

"Did you not know she refuses to cook anything that is not approved by her late husband? I have come to include the man in my prayers of an evening hoping to discourage him from suggesting too much fennel in the tripe."

"Mother hates tripe whether it is seasoned or not."

"I know. I have ordered Mildred to prepare mounds of it. With luck it should send your mother swanning off to her bed before I am forced to do violence. Thank the good Lord above that Lucille Althorpe has exhibited the fine sense to remain in seclusion at the rectory since her return from London, or I should have thrashed her silly, and delighted in counting the strokes while I did so. Your husband has showed remarkable restraint in not throttling her. Where is he, by the way?"

"He was with Arthur all morning," Anna said. "I believe I saw them up in an apple tree not too long ago."

"I hear he has promised to take him on board the *Intrepid* when she is cleaned and refitted."

Anna nodded. "He wants to take him up into the crow's nest, where he can feel as if he is truly flying. I know. I was up there myself and could barely catch my breath for the beauty of it."

"I expect he kissed you again while you were up there,"

Florence said dryly. When Anna's blush betrayed the fact he had done much more, her aunt chuckled. "Well, no wonder you were short of breath, child. I recall doing it on the roof of the stable one fine summer day and it felt as if the earth was moving to and fro."

"On the roof?" Anna's brows edged upward, for she had thought it strange enough to count floors and walls, desktops and crow's nests among the more impulsive locales for lovemaking.

"Indeed. We damn near broke our necks in the process, but it was a hot day, he had his shirt off, and his muscles were deliciously bathed in sweat. I had taken him a cool drink, you see, and, well, one thing led to another and the next thing I knew, my skirts were over my head and . . ." She gave a little shrug and half turned as Willerkins entered the conservatory carrying an enormous bouquet of red roses. Her cane came out with the swiftness of a cobra, catching him on the shin with a solid *thwack*. "Where the devil do you think you are going with that?"

He looked pained in more ways than one. "You told me to fill the alcoves with flowers, madam."

"Not *those* flowers, dolt. I specifically ordered the red roses for my bedroom. There are enough roses and other blooming creations of every description and color to turn this entire house into a bordello, but I want *these* roses for my room."

"Yes, madam." He bowed and turned away. "I live for your forgiveness."

Florence waited until he was gone before she gave her head an annoyed little shake. "His memory, I vow, must be fraying at the edges, for he knows how I adore the color red. There are times I am convinced I should have left him in the stable with his horses."

The significance of what she said did not register at first, but when it did, Anna regarded her aunt through greatly rounded eyes. "Willerkins was the groomsman you fell in love with?"

"He may not be much to look at beneath all those wrinkles, I grant you, but when he was young, dear Lord." She sighed. "When he was young he could put me on my knees with just a glance. I vow there is not a chair, a carpet, a cranny in this house we have not put to good use over the years. Even now, I frequently have occasion to call him Old Tremble Legs—which is another reason why he should be prudent with red roses. He knows how they inspire me when the petals are sprinkled between the sheets."

With Anna still staring in amazement, Florence glanced at the door and murmured, "Perhaps I should go and see that he places them properly." She turned back to Anna and gave a broad wink. "If we are gone missing for a few hours, do not send anyone to look for us. Any questions that want answers, I am sure you can provide them."

It was not until she was well gone, and the sound of her cane thumping rhythmically on the floor only a fading echo, that Anna managed to pull her gaze away from the door. She did so with a wistful smile, and with another echo whispering in her ear—that of her aunt's advice the morning they were in her bedroom and she was looking for the sapphire ring.

I would not have traded his love for all the princely titles in the world. You deserve nothing less, Annaleah Fairchilde. And you should not settle for anything less either.

She had not settled. Despite every obstacle fate could throw against them, she had not settled, and her reward was a man who loved her for all the right reasons. Florence had been ecstatic when she had seen them alight from the carriage, and she had gazed at them through watery eyes when they told her they had married on board the *Bellerophon*. That had not stopped the cane from lashing out and bruising Emory's shin for not having had the courtesy of inviting her, but all had been forgiven when they asked if they might have a more formal ceremony here, at Widdicombe House.

Anna walked out the french doors and held a hand above

her eyes to shield them from the bright sunlight. She saw Arthur right away, his arms outstretched, stalking a stray cat as if he were a hawk circling above his prey. Stanley and Seamus Turnbull were with him, but there was no sign of Emory.

The big Irishman saw her first and pointed toward the cliffs, and ten minutes of brisk walking later, that was where she found him. He was on the beach, standing almost in the exact place where he had been washed ashore almost two months earlier. In anticipation of the upcoming ceremony, he had cut his hair and taken to dressing in fine jackets with proper shirts and tightly wound cravats, but his sleeve was stained from climbing trees with his brother and he had removed his boots and stockings to walk barefoot in the surf.

You deserve nothing less, Annaleah Fairchilde.

Laughing to herself, she picked her way carefully down the path, but he did not look around until the soft crunch of sand marked her approach. He held out both arms and when she came into them, she was happy to let him kiss her a long, leisurely time.

"My dark-haired angel," he murmured. "I have been standing here wondering what would have become of me had you not come walking that day."

"It does not even bear thinking about," she said, nestling close against his chest.

"No," he said, tipping her mouth up to his again. "It does not."

Author's Note:

Often I am asked where I get my ideas for a book, and most times I reply with a blank look and a shrug and say: It just happens. In this instance, the idea came from a small notation in a history book stating that Napoleon and Joseph Bonaparte did indeed look enough alike that they attempted to switch places after the defeat at Waterloo. It started me thinking, wondering what might have happened if they had succeeded in pulling off the charade and Napoleon had escaped to America. . . .

What really happened, however, was that Napoleon was sent to the barren island of St. Helena in the South Atlantic, where he remained until his death in 1821. There has been some speculation over the past century and a half over the exact *cause* of that death. Reports at the time listed it as a malignant tumor in his stomach that perforated. Modern DNA testing on strands of his hair, however, have revealed an inordinately high concentration of arsenic, suggesting he most likely had been slowly poisoned to death.

Romance Readers Never Go to Bed Alone!

SWEEPSTAKES

GREAT READING MEANS YOU NEVER GO TO BED ALONE AGAIN!

**You could be one of 100 lucky readers
to win this limited-edition "Romance Readers
Never Go To Bed Alone!" nightshirt
<u>ABSOLUTELY FREE</u> from Bantam Books!**

To be eligible for a free nightshirt, submit your entry to:
**ROMANCE READERS NEVER GO TO BED ALONE! Sweepstakes,
2 Accradata Drive, P.O. Box 5812, Dept. GJ, Unionville, CT 06085-5812**

100 winners will be chosen in a random drawing from all eligible and completed entries.
Your entry must be received by December 1, 1999.

Have you read this author before?
- ☐ Yes   ☐ No

What format books do you buy?
- ☐ Paperback   ☐ Hardcover
- ☐ Trade Paperback

What other kinds of books do you buy?
- ☐ Mystery   ☐ New Age
- ☐ Scifi/Fantasy   ☐ Nonfiction
- ☐ Thrillers/Suspense

How did you choose this book?
- ☐ Author ☐ Title ☐ Cover
- ☐ Advertisement ☐ Recommendation

How many books do you read a month?
- ☐ Less than one   ☐ 1-2
- ☐ 3-5   ☐ More than 5

How many of the books you read are romances?
- ☐ Less than one   ☐ 1-2
- ☐ 3-5   ☐ more than 5

Where did you buy this book?_____

NAME _____AGE _____

ADDRESS _____

CITY _____STATE _____ZIP _____

E-MAIL ADDRESS _____

NO PURCHASE NECESSARY.
Be sure to get your entry in by December 1, 1999!
See reverse for Official Entry Rules.

Bantam

Romance Readers Never Go to Bed Alone!

Official Entry Rules:

1. NO PURCHASE NECESSARY.

2. Enter by completing the official entry coupon, or by printing your name, address, age, and answers to the questions on the previous page on a 3"x 5" card and mail the coupon or card to:

ROMANCE READERS NEVER GO TO BED ALONE! Sweepstakes,
2 Accradata Drive
P.O. Box 5812, Dept. GJ
Unionville, CT 06085-5812

Entries must be received by December 1, 1999. No mechanically reproduced entries allowed. Entries are limited to one per person. Not responsible for late, lost, stolen, illegible, incomplete, postage due or misdirected entries or mail.

3. One Hundred (100) Prizes will be awarded: The Prize is a free "Romance Readers Never Go To Bed Alone" nightshirt (100% cotton; one size only). Estimated value of prize: Approximately $18.00. No transfer or substitution of the prize will be permitted, except by Bantam Books, a division of Random House, Inc. ("Sponsor") in its sole discretion, in which case a prize of equal or greater value will be awarded.

4. On or about December 15, 1999, the winners will be chosen in a random drawing conducted by Sponsor's marketing department from all eligible and completed entries received by the entry deadline, and the winners will receive their prizes by mail. Odds of winning depend upon the number of eligible entries received, which is anticipated to be approximately 10,000.

5. Entrants must be residents of the United States and Canada (excluding Quebec). Limit one entry per person. Void in Puerto Rico, Quebec and where otherwise prohibited or restricted by law. All federal, state and local regulations apply. Employees of Bantam Books, Random House, Inc., its parent, subsidiaries, affiliates, suppliers and agencies and their immediate family members and persons living in their household are not eligible to enter this sweepstakes. All federal and local taxes, if any, are the sole responsibility of the prize winner. By accepting the prize, winner releases Bantam Books, Random House, Inc., and their parent companies, subsidiaries, affiliates, suppliers and agents from any and all liability for any loss, harm, damages, cost or expense, including without limitation, property damages, personal injury and/or deaths arising out of participation in this sweepstakes or the acceptance and use of the prize.

6. By entering, entrants agree to abide by these Official Rules and the decision of the judges, which shall be final.

7. For the names of the prize winners, available after December 31, 1999, send a stamped, self-addressed envelope, separate from your entry, to Romance Readers Never Go To Bed Alone! Sweepstakes Winners, Bantam Books, Dept. DS2, 1540 Broadway, New York, New York, 10036 by December 31, 1999.

8. Sponsor: Bantam Books, a division of Random House, Inc., 1540 Broadway, New York, New York, 10036.